Praise for Val McDermid's Kate Brannigan Series

"McDermid combines her wit and exuberant writing with a careful and clever plot and oodles of perceptive social observation."
—*Times* (UK), on *Star Struck*

"Fresh and funny, with a spanking sense of time and place."
—*Literary Review*, on *Dead Beat*

"Fast moving and entertaining."
—*Crime Writers' Association: Chairmen's Choice*, on *Kick Back*

"Val McDermid's Kate Brannigan should remain firmly at the top of the private investigator's league."
—*Sunday Telegraph* (UK), on *Blue Genes*

"McDermid's heroine is as likeable as they come—she's tough and tender in equal measures and has a lovely way with witty one liners." —*Liverpool Daily Post* (UK), on *Crack Down*

"McDermid's snappy, often comic prose keeps the story humming as Kate is drawn deeper and deeper into the twisted plot of her murder investigation."
—*Publishers Weekly*, on *Dead Beat*

"Clever plot twists—and Kate's wit has the bite of Fran Leibowitz's." —*Kirkus Reviews*, on *Kick Back*

"Kate Brannigan is truly welcome. Hot on one-liners, Chinese food, tabloid papers and Thai boxing, she is refreshingly funny."
—*Daily Mail* (UK), on *Kick Back*

"Kate is a worthy protagonist. Long may she thrive."
—*Books Magazine*, on *Crack Down*

"This Manchester-set series is among the best with a slangy, wise-cracking heroine; good plots and a great cast of characters. A sure winner." —*MLB News*, on *Clean Break*

DEAD BEAT

AND

KICK BACK

Also by Val McDermid

A Place of Execution
Killing the Shadows
The Grave Tattoo
A Darker Domain
Trick of the Dark
The Vanishing Point
Northanger Abbey

TONY HILL/CAROL JORDAN NOVELS

The Mermaids Singing
The Wire in the Blood
The Last Temptation
The Torment of Others
Beneath the Bleeding
Fever of the Bone
The Retribution
Cross and Burn
Insidious Intent

KAREN PIRIE NOVELS

The Distant Echo
A Darker Domain
The Skeleton Road
Out of Bounds

KATE BRANNIGAN NOVELS

Crack Down
Clean Break
Blue Genes
Star Struck

LINDSAY GORDON NOVELS

Report for Murder
Common Murder
Final Edition
Union Jack
Booked for Murder
Hostage to Murder

SHORT STORY COLLECTIONS

The Writing on the Wall and Other Stories
Stranded
Christmas is Murder (ebook only)
Gunpowder Plots (ebook only)

NON FICTION

A Suitable Job for a Woman
Forensics

VAL McDERMID

DEAD BEAT

AND

KICK BACK

Grove Press
New York

Dead Beat first published in Great Britain in 1992 by Victor Gollancz.
Paperback edition in 1999 by Orion Books Ltd. Paperback edition in 2002
by HarperCollins Publishers. First published in the United States in 1993 by
St. Martin's Press.

Kick Back first published in Great Britain in 1993 by Victor Gollancz.
Paperback edition in 1999 by Orion Books Ltd. Paperback edition in 2002
by HarperCollins Publishers. First published in the United States in 1993 by
St. Martin's Press.

Printed in the United States of America
Simultaneously published in Canada

First Grove Atlantic edition: July 2018

This book was designed by Norman Tuttle at Alpha Design & Composition

This book was set in 11.5 point Bembo by Alpha Design & Composition of
Pittsfield, NH

Library of Congress Cataloging-in-Publication data is available for this title.

ISBN 978-0-8021-2829-4
eISBN 978-0-8021-4618-2

Grove Press
an imprint of Grove Atlantic
154 West 14th Street
New York, NY 10011

Distributed by Publishers Group West

groveatlantic.com

18 19 20 21   10 9 8 7 6 5 4 3 2 1

INTRODUCTION
TO THE GROVE EDITION

When I started writing crime fiction, I planned to write a trilogy because the book I really wanted to write was the third one, but I couldn't figure out how to get there without writing the first two. And so my first series character, Lindsay Gordon, was born.

I'd always known that I'd move on to something different after those first three books. And what really tempted me was the private eye novel. Sara Paretsky, Sue Grafton, Barbara Wilson and their American feminist sisters had taken that genre by the scruff of the neck and remade it in our image. And I was desperate to see whether I could make that work in the UK, with our different laws and social mores.

Kate Brannigan was the result of that desire. I had three main aims with the Brannigan books. The first—and probably the most important—was that I wanted to stretch myself as a writer. Fledgling writers are often told to write what they know. I took that injunction literally and started my career with a protagonist whose life mirrored my own in many respects. Our personalities were very different, but the superficialities were broadly similar. Ethnicity, gender, occupation, politics.

The question I asked of myself was whether I could create a credible character whose experience of the world was very different from my own. An imaginary best friend rather than an alter ego, I suppose. Because it was important to me that I liked her. If she was going to be a series character, I had to be sure I'd want to come back to her again and again.

So I considered my friends. What was it about them I liked and respected? But equally, what was it about them that drove me nuts? Because Brannigan had to be human, not some goody two-shoes who would make me feel perpetually inadequate.

The Kate Brannigan I ended up with grew up in Oxford. Not the dreaming spires of academe—the working class row houses where the workers at the car plant lived. Unlike Lindsay, we know what she looks like—petite, red-headed, a fit kickboxer with an Irish granny. She has a boyfriend, Richard, a rock journalist. Kate knows them both well enough not to live directly with him. They're next-door neighbours whose adjoining houses are linked by a conservatory that runs along the back of both homes.

She's a law school dropout who became an accidental PI. She starts out as the junior partner in Mortensen and Brannigan but eventually becomes her own boss. She has a social conscience but what really drives her is the desire to figure out what is going on. As with most PI novels, we hear the story in the first person. We see things through Kate's eyes and hear her whip-smart wisecracks in real time. Because she always gets to come up with the smart retort that most of us only think of two days later in real life.

There were some tropes of the PI novel I was less comfortable with. For a start, civilians absolutely don't have access to guns in the UK. So I did not have available to me Raymond Chandler's solution to the problem of what to do next: 'Have a man walk through the door with a gun in his hand.' I had to get my kicks in other ways. Literally. With the Thai kickboxing.

More importantly, I felt the new wave feminist crime writers from the US had missed a trick. Most of their protagonists were loners. They maybe let one or two people close but that was the limit. To me, this seemed at odds with my experience of the way women connected. I myself had a nexus of close friends with different backgrounds and skills; we all weighed in and provided help and support both practically and emotionally when needed. This was a pattern I saw all around me. I was determined to reflect that in my work so I gave Kate a network and a significant other. It made the storytelling a damn sight easier too!

The Lindsay Gordon novels had been published originally by a small feminist publishing house, The Women's Press. The advances were small and so were the sales. My second aim was to become a full-time writer of fiction and I knew that to achieve that I had to find a home with a more commercial publisher. So while I didn't tailor my writing to the market place, I knew that the decisions I'd made in giving Kate her personal attributes would mean she'd appeal to a wider audience. I also felt very strongly that I didn't want to live in a ghetto or write in a ghetto. I wanted to embrace the wider world that I inhabited. Kate allowed me to do that, and by giving her a lesbian best friend, I could be inclusive too.

My third goal was political subversion. I've been addicted to crime fiction since childhood. I know how crime lovers read. When we find a new author we like, we search out their backlist and devour that too. What better way to persuade people to read Lindsay Gordon than to give her a seductive sister under the skin? It worked—every time a new Brannigan appeared, there would be a spike in those Lindsay Gordon sales.

The one thing I didn't foresee when I started writing the Brannigan novels was how important their setting would become. The six Brannigan novels are as much a social history of Manchester and the North of England in the 1990s as they are mystery novels. This decade was a fascinating time to live and work there. A former industrial city known in the nineteenth century as Cottonopolis, it had been hollowed out and brought to its knees by the economic policies of Margaret Thatcher's government. But Mancunians don't give up easily. They gritted their teeth and set about reinventing the city throughout the decade. Football, music, financial services and sheer bloody-mindedness produced a reinvigoration and reinvention of the city. Watching that and writing about it was one of the greatest pleasures of writing this series.

I hope reading them gives you as much pleasure.

Val McDermid, 2018

DEAD BEAT

*For Lisanne and Jane; can we just
tell them that, then, darlings?*

ACKNOWLEDGEMENTS

I picked a lot of people's brains and stole a few jokes during the writing of this book. I'd like to thank Diana Cooper, Lee D'Courcy, Brother Brian, everyone at Gregory & Radice . . . Most of all, I owe an enormous debt to Linzi Day, who convinced me that I ought to believe in myself as much as she does.

PART I

1

I swear one day I'll kill him. Kill who? The man next door, Richard Barclay, rock journalist and overgrown schoolboy, is who. I had stumbled wearily across the threshold of my bungalow, craving nothing more exotic than a few hours' sleep when I found Richard's message. When I say found, I use the term loosely. I could hardly have missed it. He'd sellotaped it to the inside of my glass inner door so that it would be the first thing I saw when I entered the storm porch. It glared luridly at me, looking like a child's note to Santa, written in sprawling capitals with magic marker on the back of a record company press release. "Don't forget Jett's gig and party afterwards tonight. Vital you're there. See you at eight." Vital was underlined three times, but it was that "Don't forget" that made my hands twitch into a stranglehold.

Richard and I have been lovers for only nine months, but I've already learned to speak his language. I could write the Berlitz phrasebook. The official translation of "don't forget" is, "I omitted to mention to you that I had committed us to going somewhere/doing something (that you will almost certainly hate the idea of) and if you don't come it will cause me major social embarrassment."

I pulled the note off the door, sighing deeply when I saw the sellotape marks on the glass. I'd weaned him off drawing pins, but unfortunately I hadn't yet got him on to Blu-Tack. I walked up the narrow hall to the telephone table. The house diary where Richard and I are both supposed to record details of anything mutually relevant lay open. In today's space, Richard had written, in black felt-tip pen, "Jett: Apollo then Holiday Inn." Even though he'd used a different pen from his note, it didn't fool the carefully cultivated memory skills of Kate Brannigan, Private Investigator. I knew that message hadn't been there when I'd staggered out an hour before dawn to continue my surveillance of a pair of counterfeiters.

I muttered childish curses under my breath as I made my way through to my bedroom and quickly peeled off my nondescript duvet jacket and jogging suit. "I hope his rabbits die and all his matches get wet. And I hope he can't get the lid off the mayo *after* he's made the chicken sandwich," I swore as I headed for the bathroom and stepped gratefully under a hot shower.

That's when the self-pitying tears slowly squeezed themselves under my defences and down my cheeks. In the shower no one can see you weep. I offer that up as one of the great twentieth-century aphorisms, right up there alongside "Love means never having to say you're sorry." Mostly, my tears were sheer exhaustion. For the last two weeks I'd been working on a case that had involved driving from one end of the country to the other on an almost daily basis, staking out houses and warehouses from the hours before dawn till past midnight, and living on snatched sandwiches from motorway service stations and greasy spoons my mother would have phoned the environmental health inspectors about.

If that sort of routine had been the normal stock in trade of Mortensen and Brannigan it might not have seemed so bloody awful. But our cases usually involve nothing more taxing than sitting in front of a computer screen drinking coffee and making phone calls. This time, though, my senior partner Bill Mortensen and I had been hired by a consortium of prestigious watch manufacturers to track down the source of high-quality copies of their merchandise which had been flooding the market from somewhere in the Greater Manchester area. Surprise, surprise, I'd ended up with the sticky end while Bill sat in the office moodily staring into his computer screens.

Matters had come to a head when Garnetts, the city's biggest independent jeweller, had been broken into. The thieves had ignored the safe and the alarmed display cases, and had simply stolen the contents of a cupboard in the manager's office. What they had walked away with were the green leather wallets that are presented free to purchasers of genuine Rolex watches, the luxury market's equivalent of a free plastic daffodil with every packet of soap powder. They'd also taken the credit card wallets that Gucci gives to their customers, as well as dozens of empty boxes for Cartier and Raymond Weil watches.

This theft told the manufacturers that the counterfeit business—known in the trade as schneids—was moving up a gear. Till now, the villains had been content to sell their wares as copies, via a complicated network of small traders. While that had infuriated the companies, it hadn't kept them awake at night because the sort of people who part with forty pounds in a pub or at a market stall for a fake Rolex aren't the sort who've got a few grand tucked away in their back pockets for the real thing. But now it looked as if the schneid merchants were planning to pass their clever copies off as the genuine article. Not only might that take business away from straight outlets, it could also affect the luxury watchmakers' reputation for quality. Suddenly it was worth spending money to knock the racket on the head.

Mortensen and Brannigan might not be up there in the top ten of Britain's major private investigation companies, but we'd landed this job for two good reasons. Although our main area of work is in computer fraud and security systems, we were the first people who sprang to Garnetts' minds, since Bill had designed their computerized security system and they had ignored his suggestion that the cupboard in question be linked into the overall system. After all, they'd argued, there was nothing in there worth stealing . . . The second reason was that we were one of the few firms of specialist private investigators operating out of Manchester. We knew the territory.

When we took the job on, we anticipated clearing it up in a matter of days. What we hadn't grasped was the scale of the operation. Getting to grips with it had worn me into the ground. However, in the last couple of days, I'd started to feel that warm glow of excitement in the pit of my stomach that always tells me I'm getting close. I had found the factory where the schneid watches were being produced, I knew the names of the two men who were wholesaling the merchandise, and who their main middle men were. All I had to do was establish the pattern of their movements and then we could hand over to our clients. I suspected that some time in the next couple of weeks, the men I had been following would be on the receiving end of a very unwelcome visit from the cops and Trading Standards officials. Which would ultimately mean a substantial reward for Mortensen and Brannigan, on top of our already substantial fee.

Because it was all going so well, I had promised myself a well-deserved and much-needed early night after I had followed Jack "Billy" Smart, my number one suspect, back to his Gothic three-storey house in a quiet, tree-lined suburban street that evening at six. He'd walked in with a couple of bottles of Moët and an armful of videos from the shop round the corner, and I figured he was all set for a kiss and a cuddle in front of the television with his girlfriend. Come to that, I could have kissed him myself. Now I could go home, have a quick shower, send a cab out for a takeaway from nearby Chinatown and watch the soaps. Then I'd have a face pack and luxuriate in a long, slow bath and beauty routine. It's not that I'm obsessive about personal hygiene, by the way, just that I've always felt that showers are for getting rid of the dirt, while baths are for serious pleasures like reading the adventure game reviews in computer magazines and fantasizing about the computer I'll upgrade to when Mortensen and Brannigan's ship comes in. With luck, Richard would be out on the town so I could perform my ablutions in total peace, accompanied only by a long cool drink.

Well, I'd been right about one thing at least. Richard was certainly going out on the town. What I hadn't bargained for was being there with him. So much for my plans. I knew I was no match for Richard tonight. I was just too tired to win the argument. Besides, deep down, I knew I didn't have a leg to stand on. He'd bitten the bullet and got suited up to escort me to an obligatory dinner party the week before. After subjecting him to an evening with a bunch of insurance executives and their wives, spinach pancakes and all, I owed him. And I suspected he knew it. But just because it was my turn to suffer didn't mean I had to cave in without a whinge.

As I vigorously rubbed shampoo into my unruly auburn hair, a blast of cold air hit my spine. I turned, knowing exactly what I'd see. Richard's face smiled nervously at me through the open door of the shower cubicle. "Hi, Brannigan," he greeted me. "Getting ready for a big night out? I knew you wouldn't forget." He must have registered the snarl on my face, for he quickly added, "I'll see you in the living room when you're finished," and hastily shut the door.

"Get back in here," I yelled after him, but he sensibly ignored me. It's at moments like this I just don't understand why I broke all the rules of a lifetime and allowed this man to invade my personal space.

I should have known better. It had all started so inauspiciously. I'd been tailing a young systems engineer whose employer suspected him of selling information to a rival. I'd followed him to the Hacienda Club, breeding ground for so many of the bands that have turned Manchester into the creative centre of the nineties music industry. I'd only been there a couple of times previously because being jammed shoulder to shoulder with a sweating mass of bodies in a room where conversation is impossible and the simple act of breathing gets you stoned isn't my idea of the perfect way to spend what little free time I get. I have to confess I'm much happier playing interactive adventure games with my computer.

Anyway, I was trying to look unobtrusive in the Hassy—not an easy task when you're that crucial five years older than most of the clientele—when this guy appeared at my shoulder and tried to buy me a drink. I liked the look of him. For a start, he was old enough to have started shaving. He had twinkling hazel eyes behind a pair of large tortoiseshell-framed glasses and a very cute smile, but I was working and I couldn't afford to take my eyes off my little systems man in case he made his contact right before my eyes. But The Cute Smile didn't want to take no for an answer, so it was something of a relief when my target headed for the exit.

I had no time for goodbyes. I shot off after him, squeezing through the press of bodies like a sweaty eel. By the time I made it on to the street, I could see his tail lights glowing red as he started his car. I cursed aloud as I ran round the corner to where I'd parked and leapt behind the wheel. I slammed the car into gear and shot out of my parking place. As I tore round the corner, a customized Volkswagen Beetle convertible reversed out of a side alley. I had nowhere to go except into the nearside door. There was a crunching of metal as I wrestled my wheel round in a bid to save my Nova from complete disaster.

It was all over in seconds. I climbed out of the car, furious with this dickhead who hadn't bothered to check before he reversed out into a main street. Whoever he was, he'd not only lost me my surveillance target but had also wrecked my car. I strode round to the driver's door of the Beetle in a towering rage, ready to drag the pillock out on to the street and send him home with his nuts in a paper bag. I mean, driving like that, it had to be a man, didn't it?

Peering out at me like a very shaken little boy was The Cute Smile. Before I could find the words to tell him what I thought of his brainless driving, he smiled disarmingly up at me. "If you wanted my name and phone number that badly, all you had to do was ask," he said innocently.

For some strange reason, I didn't kill him. I laughed. That was my first mistake. Now, nine months later, Richard was my lover next door, a funny, gentle divorcé with a five-year-old son in London. I'd at least managed to hang on to enough of my common sense not to let him move in with me. By chance, the bungalow next to mine had come on the market, and I'd explained to Richard that that was as close as he was going to get to living with me, so he snapped it up.

He'd wanted to knock a connecting door between the two, but I'd informed him that it was a load-bearing wall and besides, we'd never manage to sell either house like that. Because I'm the practical one in this relationship, he believed me. Instead, I came up with the idea of linking the houses via a huge conservatory built on the back of our living rooms, with access to both houses through patio doors. Erecting a partition wall to separate the two halves would be a simple matter if we ever move. And we both reserve the right to lock our doors. Well, I do. Apart from anything else, it gives me time to clear up after Richard has been reducing the neat order of my home to chaos. And it means he can sit carousing with his rock buddies till dawn without me stomping through to the living room in the small hours looking like a refugee from the Addams family, chuddering sourly about some of us having to go to work in the morning.

Right now, as I savagely towelled my hair and smoothed moisturizer into my tired skin, I cursed my susceptibility. Somehow he always manages to dig himself out of his latest pit with the same cute smile, a bunch of roses and a joke. It shouldn't work, not on a bright, streetwise hard case like me, but to my infinite shame, it does. At least I've managed to impress upon him that there are house rules in any relationship. To break the rules knowingly once is forgivable. Twice means me changing the locks at three in the morning and Richard finding his favourite records thrown out of my living room window on to the lawn once I've made sure it's raining. It usually is in Manchester.

At first, he reacted as if my behaviour were certifiable. Now, he's come to accept that life is much sweeter if he sticks to the rules. He's still a long way from perfect. For example, being colour-blind, he's got a tendency to bring home little gifts like a scarlet vase that clashes hideously with my sage green, peach and magnolia decor. Or black sweatshirts promoting bands I've never heard of because black's fashionable, in spite of the fact that I've told him a dozen times that black makes me look like a candidate for the terminal ward. Now, I simply banish them to his home and thank him sweetly for his thoughtfulness. But he's getting better, I swear he's getting better. Or so I told myself as the desire to strangle him rose at the thought of the evening ahead.

Reluctantly abandoning the idea of murder, I returned to my bedroom and thought about an outfit for the evening. I weighed up what would be expected of me. It didn't matter a damn what I wore to the concert. I'd be lost in the thousands of yelling fans desperate to welcome Jett back in triumph to his home town. The party afterwards was more of a problem. Much as I hated having to ask, I called through to Richard, "What's the party going to be like, clothes-wise?"

He appeared in the doorway, looking like a puppy that's astonished to have been forgiven so easily for the mess on the kitchen floor. His own outfit was hardly a clue. He was wearing a wide-shouldered baggy electric blue double breasted suit, a black shirt and a silk tie with a swirled pattern of neon colours that looked like a sixties psychedelic album cover. He shrugged and gave that smile that still made my stomach turn over. "You know Jett," he said.

That was the problem. I didn't. I'd met the man once, about three months before. He'd turned up on our table for ten at a charity dinner and had sat very quiet, almost morose, except when discussing football with Richard. Manchester United,

those two words that are recognized in any language from San-
tiago to Stockholm, had unlocked Jett as if with a magic key.
He'd sprung to the defence of his beloved Manchester City
with the ardour of an Italian whose mother's honour has been
impugned. The only fashion hint I'd had from that encounter
was that I should wear a City strip. "No, Richard, I don't know
Jett," I explained patiently. "What kind of party will it be?"

"Not many Traceys, lots of Fionas," he announced in our
own private code. Traceys are bimbos, the natural successors
to groupies. Blonde, busty and fashion-obsessed, if they had a
brain they'd be dangerous. Fionas share the same characteristics
but they are the rich little upper-crust girls who would have
been debutantes if coming out had not become so hopelessly
unfashionable with everyone except gays. They like rock stars
because they enjoy being with men who lavish them with gifts
and a good time, while at the same time shocking their families to the core. So Jett liked Fionas, did he? And Fionas meant
designer outfits, an item singularly lacking in my wardrobe.

I flicked moodily through the hangers and ended up with
a baggy long cotton shirt splashed with shades of olive, khaki,
cream and terracotta that I'd bought on holiday in the Canaries
the year before. I pulled on a pair of tight terracotta leggings.
That was when I knew the motorway sandwiches had to go.
Luckily, the shirt covered the worst of the bulges, so I cinched
it in at the waist with a broad brown belt. I finished the outfit
off with a pair of high-heeled brown sandals. When you're only
5'3", you need all the help you can get. I chose a pair of outrageous earrings and a couple of gold bangles, and eyed myself in
the mirror. It wasn't wonderful, but it was better than Richard
deserved. Right on cue, he said, "You look great. You'll knock
them dead, Brannigan."

I hoped not. I hate mixing business with pleasure.

2

We didn't have to scramble for a parking place near the Apollo Theatre, since we live less than five minutes' walk away. I couldn't believe my luck when I discovered this development halfway through my first year as a law student at Manchester University. It's surrounded on three sides by council housing estates and on the fourth by Ardwick Common. It's five minutes by bike to the university, the central reference library, Chinatown, and the office. It's ten minutes by bike to the heart of the city centre. And by car, it's only moments away from the motorway network. When I discovered it, they were still building the little close of forty houses, and the prices were ridiculously low, probably because of the surrounding area's less than salubrious reputation. I worked out that if I pitched my father into standing guarantor for a hundred per cent mortgage and moved another student into the spare room as a lodger, I'd be paying almost the same as I was for my shitty little room in a student residence. So I went for it and moved in that Easter. I've never regretted it. It's a great place to live as long as you remember to switch on the burglar alarm.

We arrived at the Apollo just as the support band were finishing their first number. We'd have caught the opener if they hadn't left the guest list in the hands of an illiterate. One of the major drawbacks to having a relationship with a rock writer is that you can't put support bands to their traditional use of providing a background beat while you have a few drinks before the act you came to hear gets on stage. Rock writers actually listen to the support band, just so they can indulge in their professional one-upmanship with lines like, "Oh yes, I remember Dire Straits when they were playing support at the Newcastle City Hall," invariably to some band that everyone has now forgotten. After two numbers, I couldn't take any more and I abandoned Richard in his seat while I headed for the bar.

The bar at the Apollo reminds me of a vision of hell. It's decorated in a mosaic of bright red glitter, it's hot and it reeks of cigarette smoke and stale alcohol. I elbowed my way through the crowd and waved a fiver in the air till one of the nonchalant bar staff eventually deigned to notice me. At the Apollo, they specialize in a minuscule selection of drinks, all served at blood heat in plastic tumblers. It doesn't matter much what you order, it all seems to taste much the same. Only the colours vary. I asked for a lager, which arrived flat and looking like a urine sample. I sipped tentatively and decided that seeing is believing. As I pushed my way back towards the door, I saw someone who made me stop so suddenly that the man behind me cannoned into me, spilling half my drink down the trousers of the man next to me.

In the chaos of my apologies and my pathetic attempts to wipe up the spilled beer with a tissue from my handbag, I took my eyes off the source of my surprise. When I managed to make my embarrassed escape, I looked over to the corner where he'd been standing. But it was now occupied by a threesome I'd never seen before. Gary Smart, brother and partner of Billy, had vanished.

I stared round the crowded bar, but there was no trace of him. He'd been standing with a tall, skinny man who'd had his back to me. I didn't hear a word of their conversation, but their body language suggested a business deal. Gary had been putting some kind of pressure on the other man. It certainly hadn't looked like a pleasant, concertgoers' chat about which of Jett's albums they liked best. I cursed silently. I'd missed a great chance to pick up some interesting info.

With a shrug, I drank the few remaining mouthfuls of my drink and went back down to the foyer. I checked out the tour merchandise just to see if there was anything among the t-shirts, sweatshirts, badges, programmes and albums that I fancied. Richard can always get freebies, so I usually have a quick look. But the sweatshirts were black, and the t-shirts hideous, so I walked back through the half-empty auditorium and slumped in my seat next to Richard while the support band ground out their last two numbers. They left the stage to muted applause, the lights went up and a tape of current chart hits filled the air. "Bag of crap," Richard remarked.

"That their name or a critical judgement?" I asked.

He laughed and said, "Well, they ain't honest enough to call themselves that, but they might as well have done. Now, while we've got a minute to ourselves, tell me about your day."

As he lit a joint, I did just that. I always find that talking things over with Richard helps. He has an instinctive understanding of people and how their minds work that I have come to rely on. It's the perfect foil to my more analytical approach.

Unfortunately, before he could deliver his considered verdict on the Smart brothers, the lights went down. The auditorium, now full to capacity, rang with cries of "Jett, Jett, Jett . . ." After a few minutes of chanting, wavering torch beams lit up pathways on the stage as members of Jett's backing band took the stage. Then, a pale blue spot picked out the drummer, high on his platform at the rear of the stage, brushing a snare drum softly. The lighting man focused on the bass player in pale purple as he picked up the slow beat. Then came the keyboards player, adding a shimmering chord from the synthesizer. The sax player joined in, laying down a line as smooth as chocolate.

Then, suddenly, a stark white spotlight picked out Jett as he strode out of the wings, looking as frail and vulnerable as ever.

His black skin gleamed under the lights. He wore his trademark brown leather trousers and cream silk shirt. An acoustic guitar was slung round his neck. The audience went wild, almost drowning out the musicians in their frenzy. But as soon as he opened his mouth to sing, they stilled.

His voice was better than ever. I've been a fan of Jett since his first single hit the charts when I was fifteen, but I find it as hard now to categorize his music as I did then. His first album had been a collection of twelve tracks, mainly acoustic but with some subtle backings ranging from a plangent sax to a string quartet. The songs had ranged from simple, plaintive love songs to the anthemlike "To Be With You Tonight" which had been the surprise hit of the year, hitting the top of the charts the week after its release and staying there for eight weeks. He had one of those voices that has the quality of a musical instrument, blending perfectly with whatever arrangement flows beneath it. As a lovesick teenager, I could lose myself completely in his yearning songs with their poignant lyrics.

Eight other albums had followed, but I'd increasingly found less delight in them. I wasn't sure if it was the changes in me that were responsible for that. Maybe what strikes a teenager as profound and moving just doesn't work once you're halfway through your twenties. But it seemed to me that while the music was still strong, the lyrics had become trite and predictable. Maybe that was a reflection of his reported views about the role of women. It's hard to write enlightened love songs about the half of the population you believe should be barefoot and pregnant. However, the packed crowd in the Apollo didn't seem to share my views. They roared out their appreciation for every number, whether from the last album or the first. After all, he was on home ground. He was their own native son. He'd made the northern dream a reality, moving up from a council flat in the Moss-side ghetto to a mansion in the Cheshire countryside.

With consummate showmanship, he closed the ninety-minute set with a third encore, that first, huge hit, the one we'd all been waiting for. A classic case of leaving them wanting more. Before the last chords had died away, Richard was on his feet and heading for the exit. I followed quickly before the crowds built up, and caught up with him on the pavement outside as he flagged down a cab.

As we settled back in our seats and the cabbie set off for the hotel, Richard said, "Not bad. Not bad at all. He puts on a good show. But he'd better have some new ideas for the next album. Last three all sounded the same and they didn't sell nearly enough. You watch, there'll be a few twitchy faces around tonight, and I don't just mean the coke-heads."

He paused to light a cigarette and I snatched the chance to ask him why it was so important that I be at the party. I was still nursing the forlorn hope of an early night.

"Now that would be telling," he said mysteriously.

"So tell. It's only a five-minute cab ride. I haven't got time to pull your fingernails out one by one."

"You're a hard woman, Brannigan," he complained. "Never off duty, are you? OK, I'll tell you. You know me and Jett go way back?" I nodded. I remembered Richard telling me the story of how he'd landed his first job on a music paper with an exclusive interview of the normally reclusive Jett. Richard had been working for a local paper in Watford and he'd been covering their cup tie with Manchester City. At the time, Elton John had owned Watford, and Jett had been his personal guest for the afternoon. After City won, Richard had sneaked into the boardroom and had persuaded an elated Jett to give him an interview. That interview had been Richard's escape ticket. As a bonus, Jett had liked what Richard wrote, and they'd stayed friends ever since.

"Well," Richard continued, interrupting my reference to my mental card index of his past, "he's decided that he wants his autobiography written."

"Don't you mean biography?" Always the nitpicker, that's me.

"No, I mean *auto*. He wants it ghosted, written in the first person. When we saw him at that dinner, he mentioned it to me. Sort of sounded me out. Of course, I said I'd be interested. It wouldn't be a mega-seller like Jagger or Bowie, but it could be a nice little earner. So, when he rang me up to invite us tonight and he was so insistent that you come along too, I thought I could read between the lines."

Although he was trying to sound nonchalant, I could tell that Richard was bursting with pride and excitement at the idea. I pulled his head down to mine and planted a kiss on his warm mouth. "That's great news," I said, meaning it. "Will it mean a lot of work?"

He shrugged. "I shouldn't think so. It's just a case of getting him talking into the old tape recorder then knocking it into shape afterwards. And he's going to be at home for the next three months or so working on the new album, so he'll be around and about."

Before we could discuss the matter further, the taxi pulled up outside the ornate facade of the grandiosely named Holiday Inn Midland Crowne Plaza. It's one of those extraordinary Manchester monuments to the city's first era of prosperity. One of the more palatable byproducts of the cotton mills of the industrial revolution. I can remember when it used to be simply the Midland, one of those huge railway hotels that moulder on as relics of an age when the rich felt no guilt and the poor were kept well away from the doors. Then Holiday Inn bought the dinosaur and turned it into a fun palace for the city's new rich—the sportsmen, businessmen and musicians who gave Manchester a new lease of life in the late eighties.

Suddenly, in the nineties, London was no longer the place to be. If you wanted a decent lifestyle with lots of buzz and excitement packed into compact city centres, you had to be in one of the so-called provincial cities. Manchester for rock, Glasgow for culture, Newcastle for shopping. It was this shift that had brought Richard to Manchester two years before. He'd come up to try to get an interview with cult hero Morrissey and two days in the city had convinced him that it was going to be to the nineties what Liverpool was to the sixties. He had nothing to keep him in London; his divorce had just come through, and a freelance makes his best living if he's where the most interesting stories are. So he stayed, like a lot of others.

I followed him out of the taxi, feeling like partying for the first time since I'd come home. Richard's news had given me a real adrenaline rush, and I couldn't wait for the official confirmation of what he already suspected. We headed straight to the bar for a drink to give Jett and his entourage time to get over to the hotel.

I sipped my vodka and grapefruit juice gratefully. When I became a private eye, I tried to match the image and drink whisky. After two glasses, I had to revert to my usual to take the taste away. I guess I'm not cut out for the "bottle of whisky and a new set of lies" Mark Knopfler image. As I drank, I listened with half an ear while Richard told me how he saw Jett's autobiography taking shape. "It's a great rags to riches story, a classic. A poor childhood in the Manchester slums, the struggle to make the music he knew he had in him. First discovering music when his strict Baptist mother pushed him into the gospel choir. How he got his first break. And at last, the inside story on why his songwriting partnership with Moira broke up. It's got all the makings," he rambled on. "I could probably sell the serial rights to one of the Sunday tabloids. Oh, Kate, it's a great night for us!"

After twenty minutes of bubbling enthusiasm, I managed to cut in and suggest that we made our way to the party. As soon as we emerged from the lift, it was clear which suite Jett had hired for the night. Already a loud babble of conversation spilled into the hall, overlaying the mellow sounds of Jett's last album. I squeezed Richard's hand and said, "I'm really proud of you," as we entered the main room and the party engulfed us.

Jett himself was holding court at the far end of the room, looking as fresh as if he'd just got out of the shower. His arm was draped casually round the shoulders of a classic Fiona. Her blonde hair hung over her shoulders in a loosely permed mane, her blue eyes, like the rest of her face, were perfectly made up, and the shiny violet sheath that encased her curves looked to me like a Bill Blass.

"Come on, let's go and talk to Jett," Richard said eagerly, steering me towards the far side of the room. As we passed the table where the drinks were laid out, a shirtsleeved arm sneaked out from a group of women and grabbed Richard's shoulder.

"Barclay!" a deep voice bellowed. "What the hell are you doing here?" The group parted to reveal the speaker, a man of medium height and build, running slightly to paunch round the middle.

Richard looked astonished. "Neil Webster!" he exclaimed with less than his usual warmth. "I could ask you the same thing. At least I'm a bloody rock writer, not an ambulance chaser. What are you doing back in Manchester? I thought you were in Spain."

"A bit too hot for me down there, if you catch my drift," Neil Webster replied. "Besides, all the news these days seems to happen in this city. I thought I was about due to revisit my old haunts."

Their exchange gave me a few minutes to study this latest addition to my collection of Journalists of the World. Neil Webster had that slightly disreputable air that a lot of women seem to find irresistible. I'm not one of them. He looked to be in his late thirties, though a journalist's life does seem to accelerate ageing in everyone except my own Peter Pan Barclay. Neil's brown hair, greying at the temples, looked slightly rumpled, as did the cream chinos and chambray shirt he was wearing. His brown eyes were hooded, with a nest of laughter lines etched white in his tanned skin. He had a hawk nose over a full pepper and salt moustache and his jawline was starting to show signs of jowls.

My scrutiny was interrupted by his own matching appraisal. "So who's the lovely lady? I'm sorry, my love, that oaf you came with seems to have forgotten his manners. I'm Neil Webster, real journalist. Not like Richard with his comic books. And you're . . . ?"

"Kate Brannigan." I coolly shook his proffered hand.

"Well, Kate, let me get you a drink. What's it to be?"

I asked him for my usual vodka and grapefruit juice, and he turned to the bar to pour it. Richard leaned past him and helped himself to a can of Schlitz. "You didn't say what exactly you were doing back here," Richard pressed Neil as he handed me my drink. I tasted it and nearly choked, both at the strength of the drink and the impact of Neil's reply.

"Didn't I? Oh, sorry. Fact of the matter is, I've been commissioned to write Jett's official biography."

3

Richard's face turned bright scarlet and then chalky white as Neil's words hit him. I felt a cold stab of shock in my own stomach as I shared his moment of bitter disappointment. "You've got to be joking," Richard said in an icy voice.

Neil laughed. "Quite a surprise, isn't it? I'd have thought he'd have gone for a specialist. Someone like you," he added, twisting the knife. "But Kevin wanted me. He insisted." He shrugged disarmingly. "So what could I say? After all, Kevin's an old friend. And he's the boss. I mean, nobody manages a top act like Jett a dozen years without knowing what's right for the boy, do they?"

Richard said nothing. He turned on his heel and pushed his way through the growing crowd round the bar. I tried to follow, but Neil stood in my way. "I don't know what's rattled his cage, but why don't you just let him cool down," he said smoothly. "Stay and tell me all about yourself."

Ignoring him, I moved away and headed towards Jett. I could no longer see Richard's dark head, but I guessed that's where he'd be. I reached Jett's couch in time to hear Richard's angry voice saying, "You as good as promised me. The guy's a wasted space. What the hell were you thinking?"

The adulatory crowd that had been eagerly congratulating Jett and trying to touch the hem of his garment had fallen back under the force of Richard's onslaught. He was towering threateningly above Jett, whose Fiona looked thrilled to bits by the encounter.

Jett himself looked upset. His honey-sweet voice sounded strained. "Richard, Richard. Listen to me. I wanted you to do the book. I said that all along. Then out of the blue, Kevin dumps this guy on me and tells me I have to play ball, that he knows who's the best man for the job. And it's too late for me to do anything about it. Kevin's already signed the man up on a contract. If I don't play, we still have to pay. So I have to play."

Richard had listened in silence, his face a tight mask of anger. I'd never seen him so upset before, not even when his ex-wife was being difficult about his access to Davy. I reached his side and gripped his right arm. I know what he's like when he's angry. The holes in the plasterboard walls of his hall bear eloquent testimony to his frustrations. I didn't think he'd hit Jett, but I didn't want to risk it.

He stood and stared at Jett for what seemed like an eternity. Then he spoke slowly and bitterly. "And I thought you were a man," was all he said. He tore his arm out of my grip and plunged into the crowd towards the door. Only then was I aware that the room had fallen silent, every ear in the place tuned in to their conversation. I glared around, and slowly the buzz of conversation built again, even louder than before.

I desperately wanted to chase after Richard, to hold him and make useless offers of comfort. But more pressingly, I needed to know what my part in this whole charade was. I turned back to Jett and said, "He feels very let down. He thought you asked me here tonight to celebrate a book deal with us."

Jett had the grace to look sheepish. "I'm sorry, Kate, I really am sorry. I feel like a piece of shit over this, believe me. I wanted to tell Richard myself, not let him hear it from someone else. I know he'd have done a good job, but my hands are tied. People don't realize how little power guys like me actually have."

"So why did you want me here tonight?" I demanded. "To keep Richard under control?"

Jett shook his head. He half-turned his handsome head to the Fiona. "Tamar," he said, "why don't you get yourself another drink?"

The blonde smiled cattily at me and poured herself off the couch. When we were reasonably private, Jett said, "I've got a job for you. It's something that's very important to me, and I need to be able to trust the person I give it to. Richard's told me a lot about you, and I think you're the right one. I don't want to tell you about it tonight, but I want you to come and see me tomorrow so we can discuss it."

"Are you kidding?" I flashed back. "After the way you've just humiliated Richard?"

"I didn't think you were the kind of lady who let personal stuff get in the way of her work." His voice was velvet. To an old fan, irresistible. "I heard you were too good for that."

Flattery. It never fails. I was intrigued, in spite of my anger. "There's a lot of stuff Mortensen and Brannigan don't handle," I hedged.

He looked around him, trying to appear casual. He seemed satisfied that no one was in earshot. "I want you to find someone for me," he said softly. "But not a word to Richard, please."

That reminded me how angry I was on Richard's behalf. "Mortensen and Brannigan always respect client confidentiality," I said, sounding stuffy even to my ears. God knows what the king of thirty-something rock was making of it all.

He grinned, flashing a display of brilliant white teeth at me. "Come to the manor tomorrow about three," he said, not expecting any more problems.

I shook my head. "I don't know, Jett. We don't usually touch missing persons."

"For me? As a personal favour?"

"Like the one you've just done Richard?"

He winced. "OK, OK. Point taken. Look, Kate, I'm truly sorry about that. I shouldn't have mentioned it to Richard and raised his hopes without clearing it with Kevin. When it comes to things like contracts, he's the man who makes the decisions. He keeps me right. In the business side of things, he's the boss. But this other thing, it's personal. This is really important to me, Kate. Listening to what I want won't cost you anything. Please." He added. I had the feeling it was a word he'd lost familiarity with.

Wearily, I nodded. "OK. Three o'clock. If I can't make it, I'll ring and rearrange it. But no promises."

He looked as if I'd taken the weight of the world off his shoulders. "I appreciate it, Kate. Look, tell Richard what I said. Tell him I'm really sorry, would you? I've not got so many friends among the press that I can afford to lose my best one."

I nodded and pushed my way through the crowds. By the time I'd reached the door, Jett and his problems were at the back of my mind. What was important to me now was helping Richard through the night.

When the alarm went off the following morning, Richard didn't even stir. I slid out of bed, trying not to disturb him. If how I felt was any guide, he'd need at least another six hours' sleep before he returned from Planet Hangover. I headed for the kitchen and washed down my personal pick-me-up. Paracetamol, vitamins C and B complex and a couple of zinc tablets with a mixture of orange juice and protein supplement. With luck, I'd rejoin the human race somewhere around Billy Smart's house.

I had a quick shower, found a clean jogging suit and picked up a bottle of mineral water on the way out of the front door. Poor Richard, I thought as I slipped behind the wheel of the car and drove off. I'd caught up with him in the foyer, kicking his heels for want of a better target while he waited for a taxi. He'd been grimly silent all the way home, but as soon as he'd had half a pint of Southern Comfort and soda, he'd started ranting. I'd joined him in drink because I couldn't think of anything else to do or say that would make it better. He'd been shat on from a great height, and that was an end to it. It didn't make me feel any better about having agreed to Jett's request for a meeting, but luckily Richard was too wrapped up in his own disappointment to wonder why it had taken me so long to catch up with him.

I drove through the pre-dawn deserted streets and took up my familiar station a few doors down from Billy's house. It always amazes me that people don't pick up on it when I'm staking them out. I suppose it's partly that a Vauxhall Nova is the last car anyone would expect to be tailed by. The 1.4 SR model I drive looks completely innocuous—the sort of little hatchback men buy for their wives to go shopping in. But when I put my foot down, it goes like the proverbial shit off a shovel. I've followed Billy Smart to the garage where he swaps his hired cars every three days, I've tailed him in his Mercs and BMWs all over the country, and my confidence in my relative invisibility hasn't been dented yet. The only worry I have on stakeouts is a uniquely female one. Men can pee in a bottle. Women can't.

Luckily, I didn't have long to hang around before Billy appeared. I sat tight while he did his routine once-round-the-block drive to check he had no one on his tail, then I set off a reasonable distance behind him. To my intense satisfaction, he followed the same routine he'd used on the previous Wednesday. He picked up brother Gary from his flat in the high-rise block above the Arndale shopping centre, then they went together to the little back-street factory in the mean area dominated by the tall red-brick water tower of Strangeways Prison. They stayed in there for about half an hour. When they emerged they were carrying several bulky bundles wrapped in black velveteen, which I knew contained hundreds of schneid watches.

I had to stay close to their hired Mercedes as we wove through the increasing traffic, but by now I knew their routine and could afford to keep a few cars between us. True to the form of the last two weeks, they headed over the M62 towards Leeds and Bradford. I followed them as far as their first contact in a lock-up garage in Bradford, then I decided to call it a day. They were simply repeating themselves, and I already had photographs of the Wednesday routine from my previous surveillance. It was time for a chat with Bill. I also wanted to talk to him about Jett's proposition.

I got back to the office towards the end of the morning. We have three small rooms on the sixth floor of an old insurance company building just down the road from the BBC Oxford Road studios. The best thing I can find to say about the location is that it's handy for the local art cinema, the Cornerhouse, which has an excellent cafeteria. Our secretary, Shelley, looked up from her word processor and greeted me with, "Wish I could start work at lunchtime."

I was halfway through a self-righteous account of my morning's work when I realized, too late as usual, that she was winding me up. I stuck my tongue out at her and dropped a micro-cassette on her desk. It contained my verbal report of the last couple of days. "Here's a little something to keep you from getting too bored," I said. "Anything I should know about?"

Shelley shook her head, and the beads she has plaited into her hair rattled. I wondered, not for the first time, how she could bear the noise first thing in the morning. But then, since Shelley's mission in life is keeping her two teenage kids out of trouble, I don't think there are too many mornings when she wakes with a hangover. There are times when I could hate Shelley.

Mostly I find myself in her debt. She is the most efficient secretary I have ever encountered. She's a 35-year-old divorcée who somehow manages to look like a fashion plate in spite of the pittance we pay her. She's just under five feet tall, and so slim and fragile-looking that she makes even me feel like the Incredible Hulk. I've been to her cramped little two-up, two-down and in spite of living with a pair of teenagers, the house is spotlessly clean and almost unnaturally tidy. However, Richard has pointed out to me more than once that I am a subscriber to the irregular verb theory of language—"I have high standards, you are fussy, she is obsessive."

She picked up the cassette and slotted it into her own player. "I'll have it for you later this afternoon," she said.

"Thanks. Copy in Bill's system as well as mine, please. Is he free?"

She glanced at the lights on her PBX. "Looks like it."

I crossed the office in four strides and knocked on Bill's door. His deep voice growled, "Come in." As I shut the door behind me, he looked up from the screen of his turbo-charged IBM compatible and grunted, "Give me a minute, Kate." Bill likes things turbo-charged. Everything from his Saab 9000 convertible to his sex life.

There was a fierce frown of concentration on his face as he scanned the screen, tapping the occasional key. No matter how often I watch Bill at his computers, I still feel a sense of incongruity. He really doesn't look like a computer boffin or a private investigator. He's six foot three inches tall and resembles a shaggy blond bear. His hair and beard are shaggy, his eyebrows are shaggy over his ice-blue eyes, and when he smiles his white teeth look alarmingly like the ones that are all the better to eat you with. He's a one-man EC. I still haven't got the hang of his ancestry, except that I know his grandparents were, severally, Danish, Dutch, German and Belgian. His parents settled over here after the war and have a substantial cattle farm in Cheshire. Bill shook them to the core when he announced he was more interested in megabytes than megaburgers.

He went on to take a first in computer sciences at UMIST. While he was working on his Ph.D., he was headhunted by a computer software house as a troubleshooter. After a couple of years, he went freelance and became increasingly interested in the crooked side of computers. Soon, his business grew to include surveillance and security systems and all aspects of computer fraud and hacking. I met him towards the end of the first year of my law degree. He had a brief fling with my lodger, and we stayed friends long after the romance was over. He asked me to do a couple of legal jobs for him—process serving, researching particular Acts of Parliament, that sort of thing. I ended up working for him in my vacations. My role quickly grew, for Bill soon discovered it was easier for me to go undercover in a firm with problems than it was for him. After all, no one ever looks twice at the temporary secretary or data processor, do they? I found it all infinitely more interesting than my law degree. So when he offered me a full-time job after I'd passed my second year exams, I jumped at the chance. My father nearly had a coronary, but I appeased him by saying I could always go back to university and complete my degree if it didn't work out.

Two years later, Bill offered me a junior partnership in the firm, and so Mortensen and Brannigan was born. I'd never regretted my decision, and once my father realized that I was earning a helluva lot more than any junior solicitor, or even a car worker like him, neither did he.

Bill looked up from his screen with a satisfied smile and leaned back in his chair. "Sorry about that, Kate. And how is Billy Smart's circus today?"

"Sticking to the pattern," I replied. I brought him quickly up to date and his look of happiness increased.

"How long till we wrap it up?" he asked. "And do you need anything more from me?"

"I'll be ready to hand over to the clients in a week or so. And no, I don't need anything right now, unless you want to get a numb bum watching Billy for a day or two. What I did want to discuss with you is an approach I had last night." I filled him in.

Bill got up from his chair and stretched. "It's not our usual field," he said eventually. "I don't like missing persons. It's time-consuming, and not everyone wants to be found. Still, it might be straightforward enough, and it could lead us into a whole new range of potential clients. Plenty of schneid merchants around in the record business. Go and see what he wants, Kate, but make him no promises. We'll talk about it tomorrow when you've had a chance to sleep on it. You look as if you could do with a good night's sleep. These all-night rock parties are obviously too much for you these days."

I scowled. "It's nothing to do with partying. It's more to do with mounting surveillance on a hyperactive insomniac." I left Bill booting up his AppleMac and headed for my own office. It's really only a glorified cupboard containing a desk with my PC, a second desk for writing at, a row of filing cabinets and three chairs. Off it is an even smaller cupboard that doubles as my darkroom and the ladies' toilet. For decoration, I've got a shelf of legal textbooks and a plant that has to be replaced every six weeks. Currently, it's a three-week-old lemon geranium that's already showing signs of unhappiness. I have the opposite of green fingers. Every growing thing I touch turns to brown. If I ever visit the Amazonian rainforests, there'll be an ecological disaster on a scale that even Sting couldn't prevent.

I sat down at my computer and logged on to one of several databases that we subscribe to. I chose the one that keeps extensive newspaper cuttings files on current celebrities, and I downloaded everything they had on Jett into my own computer. I saved the material to disc, then printed it out. Even if we decided not to go ahead with Jett's assignment, I was determined to be fully briefed when we met. And since Jett himself had deprived me of my best source, I would have to do the best I could without Richard's help.

It didn't take me long to go through the printout, which ironically included a couple of Richard's own articles. I now knew more than I had ever wanted to about any pop star, including Bjorn from Abba, focus of my own pre-teen crush. I knew all about Jett's poverty-ridden childhood, about his discovery of the power of music when his deeply religious mother enrolled him in the local church's gospel choir. I knew about his views on racial integration (a good thing), drugs (a very bad thing),

abortion (a crime against humanity), the meaning of life (funda-
mentalist Christianity heavily revised by a liberal dollop of New
Age codswallop), music (the very best thing of all as long as it
had a good tune and a lyric that made sense—just like my dad)
and women (the object of his respect, ho, ho). But among all the
gossipy pieces of froth were a couple of nuggets of pure gold.
If I were a gambling woman, I'd have felt very confident about
putting money on the identity of the person Jett wanted found.

4

Jett's new home couldn't have been more of a contrast to the area where he'd grown up, I reflected as I pulled up before a pair of tall wrought-iron gates. To get to this part of Cheshire from the centre of Manchester, you have to drive through the twitching heart of Moss-side, its pavements piled with the wares of the secondhand furniture dealers. Not the only kind of dealer you spot as you drive through the Moss. I'd been glad to get on to the motorway and even more glad to turn off into the maze of country lanes with their dazzling patches of spring bulbs.

I wound down the window and pressed the entryphone buzzer that controlled the security system on the gates. At the far end of the drive, I could just make out the honey-coloured stone of Colcutt Manor. It looked impressive enough from here. The entryphone quacked an inquiry at me. "Kate Brannigan," I announced. "Of Mortensen and Brannigan. I have an appointment with Jett."

There was a pause. Then a distorted voice squawked, "Sorry. I have no record of that."

"Could you check with Jett, please. I do have an appointment."

"Sorry. That won't be possible."

I wasn't exactly surprised. Rock stars are not widely renowned for their efficiency. I sighed and tried again. This time the voice said, "I will have to ask you to leave now."

I tried for a third time. This time there was no response at all. I shouted a very rude word at the entryphone. I could always turn round and go home. But that would have hurt my professional pride. "Call yourself a private eye, and you can't even keep an appointment?" I snarled.

I reversed away from the gates and slowly drove along the perimeter wall. It was over seven feet high, but I wasn't going to let a little thing like that put me off. About half a mile down the lane, I found what I was looking for. Some kind of sturdy looking tree grew beside the wall with a branch that crossed it about a foot above. With a sigh, I parked the car on the verge and slipped off my high-heeled shoes, swapping them for the Reeboks I always keep in the boot. I stuffed the heels in my capacious handbag. I'd need them at the other end, since I was trying to impress a new client with my professionalism, not my ability to run the London marathon. Incidentally, it's one of life's great mysteries to me how men survive without handbags. Mine's like a survival kit, with everything from eye pencil to Swiss Army knife via pocket camera and tape recorder.

I slung my bag across my body and slowly made my way up the tree and along the branch. I dropped on to the top of the wall then let myself down by my arms. I only had about a foot to drop, and I managed it without any major injury. I dusted myself down and headed across the tussocky grass towards the house, avoiding too close an encounter with the browsing cattle. Thank God there wasn't a bull about. When I got to the drive, I swapped shoes again, wrapping my Reeboks in the plastic bag I always keep in the handbag.

I marched up to the front door and toyed with the idea of ringing. To hell with that. Whoever had refused me entry previously wouldn't be any better disposed now. On the off chance, I tried the handle of the massive double doors. To my surprise, it turned under my hand and the door swung open. I didn't hang about thanking whoever is the patron saint of gum-shoes, I just walked straight in. It was an awesome sight. The floor was paved with Italian terrazzo tiles, and ahead of me was an enormous staircase that split halfway up and headed in two different directions. Just like a Fred Astaire movie.

As I started to cross the hall, an outraged voice called from an open doorway near the entrance, "What do you think you're playing at?" The voice was followed in short order by a blonde woman in her mid-twenties. She was strictly average in looks and figure, but she'd made the most of what she'd got. I took in the eyelash tint, the make-up so subtle you had to look twice to make sure it was there, and the tan leather jumpsuit.

"I'm here to see Jett," I said.

"How did you get in? You've no right to be here. Are you the woman at the gate a few minutes ago?" she demanded crossly.

"That's me. You really should get someone to look at your security. We'd be happy to oblige."

"If you're trying to drum up business, you've come to the wrong place. I'm sorry, Jett can't see anyone without an appoint-ment," she insisted with an air of finality. The smile she laced her reply with had enough malice to keep a gossip columnist going for a year.

For the third time, I said, "I *have* an appointment. Kate Brannigan of Mortensen and Brannigan."

She tossed her long plait over her shoulder and her corn-flower blue eyes narrowed. "You could be the Princess of Wales and you still wouldn't get past me without an appointment. Look for yourself," she added, thrusting an open desk diary at me.

She couldn't have been more than twenty-three or-four, but she had all the steely intransigence of the Brigade of Guards. I glanced at the page she was showing me. As she'd said, there was no appointment marked down for me. Either Jett had forgot-ten to mention it to her, or she was deliberately trying to keep me away from him. I sighed and tried again. "Look, Miss . . ."

"Seward. Gloria Seward. I'm Jett's personal assistant. I'm here to protect him from being troubled by people he doesn't want to see. All his appointments go through me."

"Well, I can only assume he forgot to mention this to you. The arrangement was only made last night after the concert. Perhaps it slipped his mind. Now, can I suggest that you pop off and find Jett and confirm our arrangement with him?" I was still managing to be sweet reason personified, but the veneer was beginning to wear thin.

"I'm afraid that won't be possible. Jett's working and can't be disturbed," she smirked.

It was the smirk that did it. Beyond her, I could see the cool marble hall beckoning me. I pushed past her and I was halfway to the nearest door before she'd even realized what was going on. As I strode down the hall, not pausing to admire the paintings or the sculptures dotted around, I could hear her shrieking, "Come back here. You've got no right . . ."

I opened the first door I came to. It was a square drawing room done out in watered blue silk and gilt. Very country house and garden. A stereo system heavily disguised as a Queen Anne cabinet was blasting out Chris Rea's *Road To Hell* album. The only sign of life was reclining on a blue silk sofa that looked too delicate for anything heftier than Elizabeth Barrett Browning in her last days. There was nothing tubercular about Tamar, however. She looked like she'd had more than the three hours' sleep I'd managed, that was for sure. She glanced up at me from the magazine she was reading and said, "Oh, it's you again."

She was wearing a cobalt blue shell suit that clashed so violently with the furnishings it hurt my head to look at her. "Hi," I said. "Where's Jett?"

"The rehearsal room. Straight down the hall, down the passage at the back and first right." Before she'd even finished talking, she'd returned to her magazine, her foot tapping in time to the music.

I emerged in the hall to find a furious Gloria standing guard outside the door. "How dare you!" she exploded.

I ignored her and set off to follow Tamar's directions. Gloria chased after me, plucking ineffectually at my jacket sleeve. When I got to the door of the rehearsal room, I shook off her arm and said, "Now you'll see whether or not I've got an appointment."

5

I opened the door and walked in to hear a man shouting, "How many times do I have to tell you? You just don't need anyone else to . . ."

At the sound of the door, he whirled round and fell silent. There were two other men in the room. Neil Webster was sitting in a canvas director's chair with an air of fascinated satisfaction. Jett was leaning against a white grand piano with a sulky expression on his face. The third man, the shouter, I recognized at once. I'd seen him talking to Jett at the dinner where we'd met. Richard had told me he was Kevin Kleinman, Jett's manager.

Before any of us could say anything, Gloria erupted into the room and shoved past me. I couldn't believe the transformation in her. She'd altered from the dragon at the gates to a sweet little kitten. "I'm so sorry, Jett," she purred. "But this woman just forced her way in. I tried to stop her, but she just pushed past me."

Jett shrugged away from the piano with an exasperated sigh. "Gloria, I told you I was expecting Kate. Christ, how could you have forgotten?"

The effect of Jett's words on Gloria was out of all proportion to their sting. She blushed scarlet and almost seemed to cringe out of the room, muttering apologies. To Jett, not to me.

Her exit did nothing to diminish the air of awkwardness in the room. With an almost palpable effort, Jett turned the full force of his charm on me and smiled. "Kate," he said. "I'm really glad you could make it."

My reply was drowned by Neil, who called across, "You're really going to be doing all of us a big favour, Kate. I can't tell you how pleased I am for Jett that you're going to sort this business out."

I caught Kevin's scowl at Neil before he too turned to me and gave a forced smile. "Kate hasn't made any decision yet, if I understand it correctly," he said. "Maybe we should wait and see what she decides before we start dishing out the congratulations."

I hadn't been too impressed by Kevin when I'd first seen him, and the second meeting wasn't improving my opinion. His average height and build were diminished by his lousy posture and rounded shoulders, and when he walked his feet seemed to slide over the floor. His thin brown hair was receding fast, emphasizing the sharpness of his features. Richard had told me he'd had a nose job, but looking at the finished product I found that hard to believe. Judging by his outfit—a soft brown leather blouson over a toffee-coloured cashmere crew neck and a pair of Levi 501s, he was doing his damnedest to ignore the fast approaching fortieth birthday. Aware of my scrutiny, he moved over to me and extended his hand. "You must be the lovely Kate. I've heard so much about you from Richard. I'm Kevin, I take care of business for Jett."

"Pleased to meet you," I lied.

"I want to make it perfectly clear that whether or not you take on this job for Jett, it's vital that you do not mention outside this room what we discuss today. In the wrong hands, that information could do Jett a great deal of damage," Kevin smarmed, holding on to my hand for fractionally too long. I had to fight the impulse to wipe it on my trouser leg.

"I've already told Jett that our confidentiality is guaran-teed. We wouldn't have so many corporate clients if we had loose mouths." My reply came out sharper than I intended and I noticed Neil smiling wryly.

"Fine, fine, I just wanted to be sure we understood each other," Kevin oozed.

I deliberately walked away from him and crossed the room to Jett. "Do you want to tell me why you've asked me here?"

He nodded and, taking my arm, he steered me across the room to a group of chairs round a low table. I took the chance to look around the large room. It was the size of a tennis court and was obviously a recent addition to the beautiful eighteenth-century mansion Jett had bought five years before. In one corner was a built-in bar, the only thing in the place that looked tacky. The long windows that looked out over the house's adjoining parkland had heavy shutters that could be drawn across to improve the room's acoustics. As well as the piano, there were banks of synthesizers, a few guitars, both acoustic and electric, a drum kit and an array of other percussion instruments. It was an impressive sight and I said so.

Jett smiled. "It's not bad, is it? I've turned part of the cellars into a recording studio. I mean, for a man who can't tell Château Margaux from Country Manor, it was a hell of a lot of wasted space."

Kevin walked across to join us. Jett ignored him and leaned on the bar, staring intently into my eyes. "I want you to find someone for me. I knew as soon as we met that I could trust you, Kate. I had the feeling that we'd met before. In a previous life."

My heart sank. I really wasn't in the mood for some rehashed New Age philosophy. The last thing I needed right now was a loop for a client.

"It's the flux. When I really needed someone to do this job for me, our paths crossed. I realize this isn't the kind of thing you usually take on, but you have to do this one." Jett patted my hand.

"So tell me about it," I stalled, sipping my drink.

"When I started out, I had a partner. I suppose you know about that, huh? Moira was my soul mate, the one person I was meant to be with. We wrote all the songs on the first two albums together, we were magic. But we blew it. I didn't look after her needs, and she couldn't take the pressures without my support. So she went. I was too full of my success to realize what a fool I was to let her go. And she left enough of her energy with me for me to keep going a long time without noticing how much I'd needed her." His eyes were shining with tears, but Jett showed no embarrassment at baring his soul in front of so motley a crew.

"I don't need to tell you that I've run out of that energy. My last two albums have been shit." He looked up defiantly at Kevin, who shrugged. "You know it's true. I just can't cut it any more. It's not just my music. It's my whole life. That's why I need you to find Moira for me."

I congratulated myself silently on having guessed correctly. "I don't know, Jett," I hedged. "Missing persons takes a lot of time. And if Moira doesn't want to be found, no amount of work will bring her back to you."

Kevin, who had been bursting to interrupt, could contain himself no longer. "That's exactly what I said, Jett," he said triumphantly. "I told you it would be nothing but grief. You don't know that she'd want to see you. You sure as hell don't know if she can still write lyrics the way she used to. Kate's right. It's a waste of time."

"Don't tell me that shit," Jett roared. I nearly fell off my stool with the shock of the sound wave. "You're all the goddamn same," he carried on shouting. "You're all shit-scared of what will happen if she comes back. Neil's the only one of you who agrees with me. But just for once, Kevin, I'm going to have what I want. And Kate's going to get it for me."

The silence after his outburst was more deafening than the noise. I shook my head to clear it. I had to admit that Kevin's opposition had aroused the contrary side of me. I almost wanted to take it on just to spite him. I took a deep breath and said,

"I'd need a lot more information before I could decide if this is a case we can take on."

"You got it," Jett said.

"Just a minute," Kevin said. "Before we get into this, we should know what we're getting into. What's it going to cost?"

I named a price that was double our normal daily rate. If we were going to get embroiled in the search for Moira, they were going to have to pay for the privilege. Jett didn't bat an eyelid, but Kevin drew his breath in sharply. "That's a bit heavy," he complained.

"You pay peanuts, you get monkeys," I replied.

"Getting Moira back would be cheap if it cost me everything I own," Jett said softly. Kevin looked as if he was going to have a stroke.

Neil's smile had grown even broader during the last exchange. The prospect of me finding a major primary source for his book was obviously one that cheered him up. He got to his feet, slightly unsteady, and raised the glass of whisky he'd been nursing. "I'd like to propose a toast," he said. "To Kate's success."

I don't know if my smile looked as sick as Kevin's, but I hope I'm a better actress than that. I tucked my hand under Jett's elbow and steered him away from the others. "Is there somewhere we can sit down quietly and you can fill me in on the details I'll need about Moira?" I asked softly.

He turned to face me and patted my shoulder paternally. "OK, guys," he said. "Me and Kate have got some business to do. Neil, I'll catch up with you later, OK? You too, Kevin."

"But Jett," Kevin protested. "I should be here if it's business."

Jett was surprisingly adamant. Clearly, he had the boundaries between business and personal well defined in his own mind. In business matters, like who was going to ghost Jett's autobiography, Kevin's word was obviously law. But when it came to his own business, Jett could stand up for himself. It was an interesting split that I filed away for future reference.

Neil headed for the door, turning back on the threshold to wave his glass cheerily at us. "Good hunting!" he called as he left.

Grumbling under his breath, Kevin picked up a filofax and a mobile phone from the bar and stomped down the room without a farewell. As I watched his departing back, fury written large across his slouched shoulders, I remarked, "I'm surprised you chose a woman for a job like this, Jett. I thought you were a great believer in a woman's place being in the home."

He looked a little suspiciously at me, as if he wasn't certain whether or not I was at the wind-up. "I don't believe in working wives and mothers, if that's what you're getting at. But single women like you—well, you got to make a living, haven't you? And it's not like I'm asking you to do anything dangerous like catch a criminal, now, is it? And you women, you like talking, gossiping, swapping stories. If anyone can track down my Moira, it's another woman."

"You want her back so you can work with her or so you can marry her?" I asked, out of genuine curiosity.

He shrugged. "I always wanted to marry her. It was her didn't want to. My mother brought me up strict, to respect women. She taught me the way the Bible teaches. Now, I've studied a lot of different philosophies and ideas since then, but I have never come across anything that makes sense to me like the idea of a family where the woman loves and nurtures her children and her husband. So, yes, I wanted Moira to be the mother of my children, wanted that more than anything. I don't know if that feeling's still there, so I can't answer you."

I nearly got up and walked out right then. But I don't think it would have changed anything if I had. Certainly not Jett's neolithic view of women. I couldn't understand how a man of some intelligence and sensitivity, judging by his music, could still hold views like that in the last decade of the twentieth century. I swallowed the nasty taste in my mouth and got down to business. "About Moira," I began.

Two hours later, I was back in my own office. I'd just spent a quarter of an hour persuading Bill that we should take on the case. I was far from convinced that we could get a result, but I thought the chances were better than evens. It would earn us a tasty fee, and if I did pull it off word would get around. Record companies have a lot of money to throw around, and they're notoriously litigious. Going to law and winning requires solid evidence, and private investigators are very good at amassing that evidence.

Now I'd pitched Bill into accepting the case, I had some work to do. Once I'd prised Jett away from Kevin and Neil I'd managed to get a substantial amount of background on Moira. The difficulty had been getting him to shut up. Now I needed to arrange my thoughts, so I booted up my database and started filling in all I knew about Moira.

Moira Xaviera Pollock was thirty-two years old, a Pisces with Cancer rising and a Sagittarius moon, according to Jett. I felt sure that piece of knowledge would help enormously in my task. They had been kids together in Moss Side, Manchester's black ghetto, where growing up without a drug habit or a criminal record is an achievement in itself. Moira's mother had three children by different fathers, none of them in wedlock. Moira was the youngest, and her father had been a Spanish Catholic called Xavier Perez, hence the unusual middle name that was such a godsend to an investigator. In the photographs Jett had given me, she looked both beautiful and vulnerable. Her skin was the colour of vanilla fudge and her huge brown eyes made her look like a nervous bambi peeping out from a halo of frizzy brown curls.

Jett and Moira had started dating in their early teens and they'd soon discovered that they both enjoyed writing songs. Moira wrote the poignant and enigmatic lyrics, Jett put them to music. She had never wanted to perform, seeing no need to compete with Jett's unique voice, but she'd done her best to organize gigs for him. He'd played a couple of local clubs, then she'd managed to get him a regular weekly spot in a new city centre wine bar. That had been the break they needed. Kevin, who'd bought the wine bar as a diversion from the family wholesale fashion business, immediately saw Jett's potential and informed the pair that he was going to manage them and to hell with the rag trade.

Seeing Jett now, it was hard to imagine what an enormous change it must have been for the two of them. Suddenly they were being wined and dined by Kevin Kleinman, a man who had a suit for every day of the week and then some left over.

Height, five foot, four inches, I typed in. She'd had a good figure too. The snapshots taken before Jett hit the top of the charts looked positively voluptuous. But later, she'd lost weight and her clothes had hung unbecomingly on her. Cutting through Jett's self-reproach, it seemed that Moira had felt increasingly insignificant as Jett became the idol of millions.

So she had fallen for the scourge of the music industry. I could see how it had happened. Drugs are everywhere in rock, from the fans at the concerts to the recording studios. With Moira, it had all started when Kevin was piling on the pressure for more songs for the third album. She'd started taking speed to stay awake, working through the night with Jett on new songs. Soon she'd moved on to the more intense but shorter high of coke. Then she'd started freebasing coke and before too long she'd been chasing the dragon. Jett hadn't had a clue how to cope, so he'd just ignored it and tried to lose himself in his music.

Then one night, he'd come home and she hadn't been there. She'd just packed her bags and gone. He'd looked for her in a half-hearted way, asking around her family and friends, but I suspected that deep down he'd felt a kind of relief at not having to deal with her mood swings and erratic behaviour any longer. Now, his fear of falling into musical oblivion had spurred him into taking action. I could see why his entourage were nervous.

The Return of the Junkie was not a feature eagerly awaited at
Colcutt Manor.

I finished inputting all my notes, and checked my watch.
Half-past six. If I was lucky, I might just be able to short circuit some of the tedium of tracing Moira. Her unusual middle
name made the search through any computerized records a lot
easier. I picked up the phone and rang Josh, a friend of mine
who's a financial broker. In exchange for a slap-up meal every
few months, he obligingly does credit checks on individuals for
Mortensen and Brannigan.

His job gives him access to computerized credit records
for almost everyone in the British Isles. These records tell him
what credit cards they hold, whether they have ever defaulted
on a loan, and whether there have ever been County Court
judgements against them for debt. Also, if you supply him with
a person's full name and date of birth, he can usually come up
with an address. Very handy. We could probably hack into the
system and do it ourselves, but we do like to keep things semi-
legal when we can. Besides, I like having dinner with Josh.

The next call I made was to ask for something strictly illegal. One of my neighbours on the estate is a detective constable
with the vice squad. He's always happy to earn the twenty-five
pounds I slip him for checking people out on the police national
computer. If Moira had any kind of criminal record, I'd know
by morning.

There was nothing more I could do that night to trace
Moira Pollock. It had been a hell of a day. All I wanted was to go
out and kick the shit out of someone. So I decided to do just that.

6

I shook my head to clear the sunburst of stars that filled my vision, trying to dodge the next blow. The woman who was bearing down on me was a good three inches taller and twenty pounds heavier than me and there was a mean look in her eyes. I tried to match her glare and circled her warily. She feinted a punch at me, but that opened up her defences and I swung my leg up and round in a short, fast arc. It caught her in the ribs. Even through her body protector, it winded her. She crashed at my feet, and I felt the last of the day's tensions flow out of me.

It was a burglar who got me into Thai boxing three years ago. Dennis O'Brien is what I like to think of as an honest villain. Although he feeds and clothes his wife and kids with the proceeds of other people's hard work, he's got his own rigid moral code that he adheres to more firmly than most of the supposedly honest citizens I know. Dennis would never rob an old lady, never use shooters, and he only steals from people he thinks can afford to be robbed. He never indulges in mindless vandalism, and always tries to leave houses as tidy as possible. He'd never grass a mate, and the one thing he hates more than anything else is a bent copper. After all, if you can't trust the police, who can you trust?

I'd been having a drink with Dennis one evening, asking his advice about an office I needed to have a quiet little look round. In return, I was answering his questions about how I work. He'd been outraged when I'd revealed I had no self-defence skills.

"You want your head mending," he exploded. "There's a lot of very naughty people out there. They're not all like me, you know. Plenty of villains don't think twice about hitting a woman."

I'd laughed and said, "Dennis, I deal in white-collar crime. The sort of people I'm chasing don't think their fists have the answers."

He'd interrupted, saying, "Bollocks, Kate. Never mind work, living where you live, you need martial arts. I wouldn't bring the milk off the doorstep in your street without a black belt. Tell you what, you meet me tomorrow night and I'll have you sorted in no time."

"Sorted" meant taking me to the club where his own teenage daughter was junior Thai boxing champion. I'd had a good look around, decided that the showers and the changing rooms were places where I'd be prepared to take my clothes off, and signed up there and then. I've never regretted it. It keeps me fit and gives me confidence when I'm up against the wall. And time has shown that just because a man has a fifty grand salary and a company Scorpio it doesn't mean he won't resort to violence when he's cornered. As long as the British government never takes us down the criminally insane road of the USA, where every two-bit mugger totes a gun, I guess it's all I'll need to keep me alive.

Tonight, I'd got what I came for. As I showered afterwards, my whole body felt loose and relaxed. I knew I could go home and listen sympathetically to Richard without biting his head off. And I knew that in the morning I'd be raring to go on the trail of Billy Smart and Moira Pollock.

I got home just after nine with a carrier bag bursting with goodies from the Leen Hong in Chinatown. I let myself into

Richard's house via the conservatory and found him sprawled on the sofa watching *A Fish Called Wanda* for what must have been the sixth time, a tall glass of Southern Comfort and soda beside him on the floor. Judging by the ashtray, he'd smoked a joint in tribute to each time he'd seen the movie. On the other hand, maybe he just hadn't emptied it for a week.

"Hi, Brannigan," he greeted me without moving. "Is the world still out there?"

"The important bits of it are in here," I reported, waving the bag in the air. "Fancy some salt and pepper ribs?"

That got a reaction. It's depressing to think that a Chinese takeaway provokes more excitement in my lover than my arrival. Richard jumped off the sofa and hugged me. "What a woman," he exclaimed. "You really know what to give a man when he's down."

He let me go and seized the bag from my hand. I went to his kitchen for some plates, but as soon as I looked in and saw the mound of dirty dishes in the sink, I gave up the idea. How Richard can live like this is beyond me, but I've learned the hard way that his priorities are different from mine. A dishwasher is never going to win a contest with an Armani suit. And I refuse to fall into the trap of washing his dishes for him. So I simply took a couple of pairs of chopsticks from a drawer, picked up the kitchen roll and headed back for the living room before Richard polished off all the food. I know from bitter experience just how fast he can go through Chinese food when the dope-induced raging munchies get him in their grip.

I was pissed off that I couldn't tell him about my assignment from Jett, because I really needed to pick his brains. However, Richard was still smarting from his humiliation the previous evening, and it didn't take much prompting from me to put some more flesh on the bare bones of my information. The only hard part was getting him off the subject of Neil Webster.

"I just don't understand it," he kept saying. "Neil Webster, for God's sake. Nobody, I mean nobody, in the business has

got a good word for the guy. He's ripped off more people than
I've had hot spring rolls. He got fired from the *Daily Clarion* for
fiddling expenses, you know. And when you think that every
journalist in the history of newspapers has fiddled their expenses,
you begin to realize just what a dickhead the guy must be.

"He's been in more barroom brawls than anybody else I
know. And he treats people like shit. Rumour was, his first wife
had a lot more black eyes than hot dinners from him. After he
got the bullet from the *Clarion*, he set up as a freelance agency
in Liverpool. He was bonking this really nice woman who
worked for the local paper there. He persuaded her to bankroll
him in his new venture. He even promised to marry her. On
the day of the wedding, he left her standing like a pillock at
the register office. That's when he took off to Spain. After he'd
gone, she discovered he'd left her with a five grand phone bill,
not to mention a load of other debts. Then her boss found out
she'd been putting him down in the credits book for payments
for jobs he hadn't actually done, so she got the boot. That's the
kind of guy that Kevin thinks is right for the job." He stopped
speaking to attack another rib.

"Maybe Kevin's got something on Neil, something to keep
him in line with," I suggested.

"Dunno," Richard mumbled through his Chinese. He
swallowed. "I guess it was just that Jett wasn't bothered enough
about who did it to hold out for me."

"Perhaps Kevin wants to make sure it's a whitewash job,"
I tried.

Richard snorted with laughter. "You mean he thinks he
can keep Neil on a leash? He thinks he can tell Neil exactly
what to do and Neil will do it? Shit, he's in for a rude awaken-
ing. Neil will feather his own nest, regardless of Kevin laying
down the law."

"Yes, but at the end of the day, Neil's not a rock journalist.
You know exactly what stones to turn over, where to start looking if you wanted to dish some dirt, to get behind the headlines

to the real story. But Neil doesn't even know where to start, so to some extent, he's going to have to go with whatever Kevin feeds him. And they've got him right where they want him, you know. According to Jett, Neil's got an office and everything right there at Colcutt. He's actually living there while he does the book."

"That's exactly what I mean," Richard pounced. "Looking after number one. And he's the only one who will come out of this on the up, I'd put money on it. Kevin might think he can control Neil more than he could me, but I'd give you odds that Neil will end up biting the hand that feeds him, just you wait and see."

"Sounds like a bad deal for Jett."

"Wouldn't be the first time Kevin's done that. And it won't be the last."

That sounded fascinating. And it was a good way to get off Neil and on to the other members of Jett's entourage. "How do you mean?" I asked sweetly, helping myself to more vermicelli before it all disappeared into the human dustbin.

"Always seems to me that Jett has to work a lot harder than other people at his level in the business. I'd love to pin Kevin down as to why that is."

"Maybe he just likes it," I suggested.

Richard shook his head. "Not the amount of stuff he does," he said. "He's always on the road for a couple of circuits a year. He should be able to get away with one tour, fewer venues, that sort of thing. On top of that, he's doing an album a year. And even though he hates it, Kevin's always plugging him into chat shows. He even had him doing local radio slots earlier this year, can you believe it? Jett has hardly had any time off, I mean proper time off, for the last four years. He shouldn't have to do that. And the tour merchandise—they really push that stuff. There's nothing laid back about Kevin's operation, and somebody should be asking why. Maybe it is just bad deals, bad judgement. Or maybe they're making sure that when they retire they'll never have to lift a finger again. But if I was Jett, I'd be looking for a new manager."

I put some of the lyrics down to sour grapes, but I filed the general melody away for future reference. As Richard tore into the spicy pork, I tried another strategy. "Couldn't you go ahead anyway and write the unauthorized biography, warts and all?" I asked. "You must know a lot about the things that Jett wouldn't necessarily want to make public. Like the split with . . . Moira, wasn't it?"

"Sure, I could spill any amount of beans," Richard agreed. "But I don't know if I want to do that. I mean, Jett's a mate."

"He's got a funny way of showing it," I mumbled through a mouthful of beef koon po.

"It would be the last exclusive I got from him."

"There are plenty more people in the rock business who trust you," I replied.

"But an awful lot of them wouldn't be happy about talking to me if I'd dropped Jett in it," Richard reasoned.

"Surely they'd understand why you'd done it?" We were going down a side alley that wasn't taking me any further, but I couldn't help myself. Offering support to Richard was a lot more important to me than helping Jett.

Richard shrugged. "I don't know. But anyway, there wouldn't be enough of a market for two books. Jett's not quite in the international megastar league."

I got up and helped myself to a bottle of Perrier from the executive drinks fridge Richard keeps in the living room. It had been a birthday present from a friendly roadie who'd stolen it from a Hilton room. "What if . . ." I said slowly. "What if you wrote a story for one of the Sunday tabloids. The things you won't be reading in Jett's autobiography, that kind of thing? You must have plenty up your sleeve like that."

Wonders will never cease. Richard stopped eating. "You know, Brannigan, you just might have something there . . . If

I flogged it on the quiet, they could put a staff reporter's byline on it and that would protect my other contacts."

That was enough to open the floodgates. I knew that when he was sober in the cold light of morning, Richard would have changed his mind about plastering Jett across the front pages of the gutter press. But by the time we made our amorous way to bed a couple of hours later, as far as Jett and his entourage were concerned, I had picked Richard's brains as clean as he'd picked the salt and pepper ribs.

7

The following morning, the sun was shining and I was full enough of the joys of spring to cycle into work. I was in the office even before Shelley, keying in all the information Richard had unwittingly given me the night before. I couldn't imagine how it could be relevant, but I'd rather have it neatly stored in my database just in case. It's a hell of a lot more reliable than my memory, especially when you consider how many brain cells shuffle off this mortal coil with every vodka and grapefruit juice. God help me if my computer ever gets the taste for Stolichnaya.

A few minutes after nine, Shelley put a call through to me. It was my friendly neighbourhood copper. Derek's a career constable. He doesn't like the hassle that his seniors have to live with, so he tries to keep his head down whenever promotion is suggested. He does, however, like the vice squad. It makes him feel virtuous and he likes the perks. I've yet to meet a thirsty vice cop.

"Hi, Kate," Derek greeted me cheerfully. "I popped round to the house, but I couldn't get a reply, so I thought I'd try a long shot and call you at the office."

"Very funny," I replied. "Sorry I missed you, but some of us have to work long hours keeping the streets safe."

He chuckled. "With your respect for the police, Kate, you really should have stuck to being a lawyer. Any road, I've got what you wanted. Your young lady does indeed have a record. First was five years ago. Soliciting. Fifty pound fine. There are three others for soliciting, ending up with two years' probation just over a year ago. There's also Class A possession charge. A small amount of heroin, personal use. She got a three hundred pound fine for that, but the fine must have been paid because there's no record of a warrant for non-payment."

I scribbled frantically to keep up with his sad recital of what had become of the talented writer of Jett's best lyrics. "What address have you got?"

"I've got as many addresses as there are offences. All in the Chapeltown area of Leeds."

Just what I needed. I didn't know Leeds well, but I knew enough to know that this was bedsitterland. The kind of area where junkies and prostitutes rub shoulders with the chronically poor and students who try to convince themselves there's something glamorous about such Bohemian surroundings. It isn't an easy belief to sustain, especially after the murderous depredations of the Yorkshire Ripper ten years ago. I copied down the three latest addresses as Derek read them out at dictation speed. I had no real hopes of them but at least I now knew that when Moira had fled from Jett she'd headed over the Pennines. It was a start.

I thanked Derek and promised to drop his money in that evening. It looked like I was going to have to go over to Leeds, which meant I wouldn't be looking after the Smart brothers for another day. That didn't worry me as much as it perhaps should have, because they'd followed an identical pattern on the two previous Thursdays. The days I still needed to keep watch were Mondays and Tuesdays when they did most of their irregular deliveries. I knew if Bill was worried about their surveillance he could bring in one of the freelances that we occasionally use for routine jobs when we're overstretched. The extra cash we were making on Jett would more than cover the outlay.

Before I left, I gave Josh a quick call to see if his computer searches had come up with anything. Like Derek, all he had for me was bad news. When she left Jett, Moira had had a five-star credit rating. Within two years of her departure, she'd run up a string of bad debts that made me wince. She owed everybody— credit cards, store accounts, hire purchase, two major bank loans. There were several County Court judgements against her, and a handful more still pending. The court hadn't been able to find her to serve the papers. That really filled me with confidence. But it also explained why she'd not been staying at any one address for too long.

I left the office by half-past nine and cycled home, where I changed into a pair of jogging pants that were past their best and a green Simply Red road crew sweatshirt, one of the few donations from Richard that hadn't been despatched straight back next door. If I was going down those mean streets, then I wanted to make damn sure I looked a bit mean myself. I pulled on a pair of hi-top Reeboks and a padded leather jacket that was a bit scuffed round the edges. I picked up the last bottle of mineral water from the fridge and threw a packet of fresh pasta with yesterday's sell-by date into the bin. I made a mental note to hit the supermarket on my way home.

I didn't want to risk getting snarled up in the crosstown traffic, so I took the longer but faster motorway route out to the western edge of the C-shaped almost-orbital motorway and picked up the M62 to cross the bleak moors. Within the hour, I was driving out of Leeds city centre north into Chapeltown, singing along with Pat Benatar's *Best Shots* to lift my spirits.

I cruised slowly around the dirty streets, attracting some equally dirty looks when the whores who were already out working moved forward to proposition me, only to discover a woman driver. I found the last address that Derek had given me without too much difficulty. Like so many of the Yorkshire stone houses in the area, it had obviously once been the home of a prosperous burgher. It was a big Victorian property, stand- ing close to its neighbours. Behind the scabby paintwork of the window frames there was an assortment of grubby curtains, no two rooms matching. In front of the house, what had once been the garden had been badly asphalted over, with weeds sprouting through the cracks in the tarmac. I got out of the car and carefully set the alarm.

I climbed the four steps up to a front door that looked as if it had been kicked in a few times and examined an array of a dozen bells. Only a couple had names by them, and neither was Moira's. Sighing deeply, I rang the bottom bell. Nothing happened, and I started working my way systematically up the bells till I reached the fifth. I heard the sound of a window being opened and I stepped back and looked up. To my left, on the first floor, a black woman wearing a faded blue towelling dressing gown was leaning out. "What d'you want?" she demanded aggressively.

I debated whether to apologize for troubling her, but decided that I didn't want to sound like the social services department. "I'm looking for Moira Pollock. She still living here?"

The woman scowled suspiciously. "Why d'you want Moira?"

"We used to be in the same line of business," I lied, hoping I looked like a possible candidate for the meat rack.

"Well, she ain't here. She moved out, must be more'n a year ago." The woman moved back and started to close the window.

"Hang on a minute. Where would I find her? Do you know?"

She paused. "I ain't seen her around in a long while. Your best bet's that pub down Chapeltown Road, the 'Ambleton. She used to drink there."

My thanks were drowned by the screech of the sash window as the woman slammed it back down. I walked back to the car, shifted a large black and white cat which had already taken up residence on the warm bonnet, and set off to find the pub.

The Hambleton Hotel was about a mile and a half away from Moira's last known address. It was roadhouse style, in grimy yellow and red brick with the mock-Tudor gables much beloved by 1930s pub architects. The inside looked as if it hadn't been cleaned since then. Even at half-past eleven in the morning, it was fairly lively. A couple of black men were playing the fruit machine, and a youth was dropping coins into a jukebox which was currently playing Jive Bunny. By the bar was a small knot of women who were already dressed for work in short skirts and low-cut sweaters. Their exposed flesh looked pale and unappetizing, but at least it lacked the bluish tinge that ten minutes' exposure to the cold spring air would lend it.

I walked up to the bar, aware of the eyes on me, and ordered a half of lager. Something told me that a Perrier wouldn't do much for my cover story. The blowsy barmaid looked me up and down as she poured my drink. As I paid, I told her to take one herself. She shook her head and muttered, "Too early for me." I was taken aback. Before I could ask her about Moira, I felt a hand on my shoulder.

I tensed and turned round slowly. One of the black men who'd been playing the fruit machine was standing behind me with a frown on his face. He was nearly six feet tall, slim and elegant in chinos and a shiny black satin shirt under a dove grey full length Italian lambskin coat that looked like it cost six months of my mortgage. His hair was cut in a perfect flat-top, accentuating his high cheek-bones and strong jaw. His eyes were bloodshot and I could smell minty breath-spray as he leaned forward into my face and breathed, "I hear you been looking for a friend of mine."

"News travels fast," I responded, trying to move away from his hot breath, but failing thanks to the bar behind me.

"What d'you want with Moira?" There was a note of menace in his voice that pissed me off. I controlled the urge to kick him across the bar and said nothing as he leaned even closer. "Don't try telling me you're on the game. And don't try telling me you're a cop. Those fuckers only come down here mobhanded. So who are you, and what d'you want with Moira?"

I know when the time for games is past. I reached into my pocket and produced a business card. I handed it to the pimp who was giving me a severe case of claustrophobia. It worked. He backed off a good six inches. "It's nothing heavy. It's an old friend of hers who wants to make contact. If it works out, there could be good money in it for her."

He studied the card and glared at me. "Private Investigator," he sneered. "Well, baby, you're not gonna find Moira here. She checked out a long time ago."

My heart did that funny kind of flip it does when I get bad news. Two days ago, I couldn't have cared less if Moira were alive or dead. Now I was surprised to find that I cared a lot. "You don't mean . . . ?"

His lip curled in a sneer again. I suspected he'd perfected it in front of a mirror at the age of twelve and hadn't progressed to anything more adult. "She was still alive when she left here. But the way she was pumping heroin into her veins, you'll be lucky to find her like that now. I kicked her out a year ago. She was no use to anybody. All she cared about was getting another fix into her."

"Any idea where she went?" I asked with sinking heart. He shrugged. "That depends on how much it's worth." "And that depends on how good the information is." He smiled crookedly. "Well, you're not going to know that till you check it out, are you? And I don't give credit. A hundred to tell you where she went."

"Do you seriously think I'd carry that kind of cash in a shit pit like this? Fifty."

He shook his head. "No way. Fancy bit of skirt like you, you'll have a hole-in-the-wall card. Come back here in half an hour with a oner and I'll tell you where she went. And don't think you'll get the word off somebody else. Nobody round here's going to cross George."

I knew when I was beaten. Whoever George was, he clearly had his patch sewn up tight. Wearily, I nodded and headed back towards the car.

8

The short drive from Leeds to its neighbouring city of Bradford is like traversing a continent. Crossing the city boundary, I found myself driving through a traditional Muslim community. Little girls were covered from head to foot, the only flesh on display their pale brown faces and hands. All the women who walked down the pavements with a leisurely rolling gait had their heads covered, and several were veiled. In contrast, most of the men dressed in western clothes, though many of the older ones wore the traditional white cotton baggy trousers and loose tops with incongruously heavy winter coats over them, greying beards spilling down their fronts. I passed a newly erected mosque, its bright red brick and toytown minarets a sharp contrast to the grubby terraces that surrounded it. Most of the grocery shops had signs in Arabic, and the butchers announced Hal-al meat for sale. It almost came as a culture shock to see signs in English directing me to the city centre.

I stopped at a garage to buy a street directory. There were three Asian men standing around inside the shop, and another behind the counter. I felt like a piece of meat as they eyed me up and down and made comments to each other. I didn't need to speak the language to catch their drift.

Back in the car, I looked up my destination in the map's index and worked out the best way to get there. George's information represented the worst value for money I'd had in a long time, but I wasn't in any position to stick around and argue the toss. All he'd been able to tell me was that Moira had moved to Bradford and was working the streets of the red light district round Manningham Lane. He either didn't know or wouldn't tell the name of her pimp, though he claimed that she was working for a black guy rather than an Asian.

It was just after one when I parked in a quiet side street off Manningham Lane. As I got out of the car, the smell of curry spices hit me and I realized I was ravenous. It had been a long time since last night's Chinese, and I had to start my inquiries somewhere. I went into the first eating place I came to, a small café on the corner. Three of the half dozen formica-topped tables were occupied. The clientele was a mixture of Asian men, working girls and a couple of lads who looked like building labourers. I went up to the counter, where a teenager in a grubby chef's jacket was standing behind a cluster of pans on a hotplate. On the wall was a whiteboard, which offered Lamb Rogan Josh, Chicken Madras, Mattar Panir and Chicken Jalfrezi. I ordered the lamb, and the youth ladled a generous helping into a bowl, opened a hot cupboard and handed me three chapatis. A couple of weeks before, their hygiene standards would have driven me out the door a lot faster than I'd come in. However, on the Smart surveillance, I'd learned that hunger has an interesting effect on the eyesight. After the greasy spoons I'd been forced to feed in up and down the country, I couldn't claim the cleanliness standards of an Egon Ronay any longer. And this café was a long way from the bottom of my current list.

I sat down at the table next to the prostitutes and helped myself to one of the spoons rammed into a drinking tumbler on the table. The first mouthful made me realize just how hungry I'd been. The curry was rich and tasty, the meat tender and plentiful.

And all for less than the price of a motorway sandwich. I'd heard before that the best places to eat in Bradford were the Asian cafés and restaurants, but I'd always written it off as the inverse snobbery of pretentious foodies. For once, I was glad to be proved wrong.

I wiped my bowl clean with the last of the chapatis, and pulled out the most recent photograph I had of Moira. I shifted in my chair till I was facing the prostitutes, who were enjoying a last cigarette before they went out to brave an afternoon's trade. The café was so small I was practically sitting among them. I flipped the photograph on to the table and cut through their desultory chatter. "I'm looking for her," I explained. "I'm not Old Bill, and I'm not after her money either. I just want a chat. An old friend wants to get in touch. Nothing heavy. But if she wants to stay out of touch, that's up to her." I dropped one of my business cards on the table by the picture.

The youngest of the three women, a tired-looking Eurasian, looked me up and down and said, "Fuck off."

I raised my eyebrows and remarked. "Only asking. You're sure you don't know where I'll find her? It could be a nice little earner, helping me out."

The other two looked uncertainly at each other, but the tough little Eurasian got to her feet and retorted angrily, "Stuff your money up your arse. We don't like pigs round here, whether they're private pigs or ones in uniform. Why don't you just fuck off back to Manchester before you get hurt?" She turned to her companions and snarled, "Come on, girls, I don't like the smell in here."

The three departed, teetering on their high heels, and I picked up the photo and my card with a sigh. I hadn't really expected much co-operation, but I'd been a bit surprised by the vehemence of their reaction. Clearly the pimps in Bradford had drilled their employees in the perils of talking to strange women. I was going to have to do this the hard way, out on the streets and in the pubs till I found someone who was prepared to take the risk of talking to me.

I left the café and went back to move the car. I didn't feel happy about leaving it parked in such a quiet street for any length of time. I'd look for a nice big pub car park fronting on the main drag for a bit more security. As I started the engine, I was aware of a flash of movement at the edge of my peripheral vision and the passenger door was wrenched open. Bloody central locking, I cursed silently. My mouth dried with fear, and I thrust the car into gear, hoping to dislodge my assailant.

With a flurry of legs and curses, a woman threw herself into the passenger seat and slammed the door. I almost stalled in my surprise. "Just keep fucking driving," she yelled at me.

I obeyed, of course. It seemed the only sensible thing to do. If she was carrying a blade, I wasn't going to win a close encounter inside my Nova. I flashed a glance at her and recognized one of the women who'd been in the café. But she gave me no chance to ask questions. At the end of the street, she shouted at me to turn left, then right. About a mile from the café, she stopped shouting and muttered, "OK, you can stop now."

I pulled in to the kerb and demanded, "What the hell is going on?"

She looked nervously behind us, then visibly relaxed. "I didn't want anybody to see me talking to you. Kim would shop me soon as look at me."

"OK," I nodded. "So why were you so keen to talk to me?"

"Is it true, what you said back there? You're not after Moira for anything?" There was a look in her pale blue eyes as if she desperately wanted to trust someone and wasn't sure if I was the right person. Her skin looked muddy and dead, and there was a nest of pimples round her nose. She had the look of one of life's professional victims.

"I'm not bringing her trouble," I promised. "But I need to find her. If she tells me she doesn't want to make contact with her friend, that's fine by me."

The woman, who in truth didn't look much older than nineteen, nervously chewed a hangnail. I was beginning to wish she'd light a cigarette so I'd have an excuse to open the window—the smell of her cheap perfume was making me gag. As if reading my thoughts, she lit up and exhaled luxuriously, asking, "You're not working for her pimp, then?"

"Absolutely not. Do you know where I can find her?" I wound down the window and gulped in fresh air as unobtrusively as possible.

The girl shook her head and her bleached blonde hair crackled like a forest fire. "Nobody's seen her for about six months. She just disappeared. She was doin' a lot of smack and she was out of it most of the time. She was workin' for this Jamaican guy called Stick, and he was really pissed off with her 'cos she wasn't workin' half the time 'cos she was out of her head. Then one day she just wasn't around no more. One of the girls asked Stick where she'd gone and he just smacked her and told her to keep her nose out."

"Where would I find Stick?" I asked.

The girl shrugged. "Be down the snooker hall most afternoons. There or the video shop down Lumb Lane. But you don't want to mess with Stick. He don't take shit from nobody."

"Thanks for the advice," I said sincerely. "Why are you telling me all this?" I added, taking thirty pounds out of my wallet.

The notes vanished with a speed Paul Daniels would have been proud of. "I liked Moira. She was nice to me when I had my abortion. I think she maybe needs help. You find her, you tell her Gina said hello," the girl said, opening the car door.

"Will do," I said to the empty air as she slammed the door and clattered off down the pavement.

It took me ten minutes to find the snooker hall off Manningham Lane. It occupied the first floor above a row of small shops. Although it was just after two, most of the dozen or so tables were occupied. I barely merited a glance from most of the players as I walked in. I stood for a few minutes just watching. Curls of smoke spiralled upwards under the strong overhead table lights, and the atmosphere was one of masculine seriousness.

This wasn't the place for a few frivolous frames with the boys after work.

As I looked on, a burly white man with tattoos snaking up both his bare arms came over to me. "Hello, doll. You look like you're looking for a man. Will I do?" he asked jocularly.

"Not unless you've had your skin bleached," I told him. He looked confused. "I'm looking for Stick," I explained.

He raised his eyebrows. "A nice girl like you? I don't think you're his type, doll."

"We'll let Stick be the judge of that, shall we? Can you point him out to me?" I demanded. It seemed like a waste of time to tell this ape that I was neither nice, nor a girl, nor a doll.

He pointed down the hall. "He's on the last table on the left. If he's not interested, doll, I'll be waiting right here."

I bit back my retort and headed down the aisle between the three-quarter-sized tables. At the end of the room, there were four competition-sized tables. A chunky black man was bending over the last table on the left. Behind him, in the shadows, was the man I took to be Stick. I could see how he'd earned the name. He was over six feet tall, but skinny as his cue. He looked like a stick insect, with long, thin arms protruding from a white t-shirt and twig-like legs encased in tight leather trousers. His head was hidden in the shadows, but as I approached, he emerged and I could see a gaunt face with hollow cheeks and sunken eyes surrounded by black curly hair grown in a thick halo to counteract the pinhead impression he'd otherwise have given.

At the edge of the light, I stopped and waited till the man at the table made his stroke. The red ball he'd been aiming for shuddered in the jaws of the pocket before coming to rest against one cushion. With an expression of disgust, he moved away, chalking his cue. The thin man walked up to line up his shot and I stepped forward into the light.

He frowned up at me, and I met his eyes. They were like bottomless pools, without any discernible expression. It was like looking into a can of treacle. I swallowed and said, "George from Leeds said I should talk to you."

Stick straightened up, but the frown stayed in place. "I know a George from Leeds?"

"George from the Hambleton Hotel. He said you could help me."

Stick made a great show of carefully chalking his cue, but I could tell he was sizing me up from under his heavy eyebrows. Eventually he put his cue on the table and said to his opponent, "Be right back. Do not move a fucking ball. I have total recall."

He strode across the hall and I followed him as he unlocked a side door and entered a stuffy, windowless office. He settled down in a scruffy armchair behind a scratched wooden desk and waved me to one of the three plastic chairs set against the wall.

He pulled a silver toothpick from his pocket and placed it in his mouth. "I'm not like George," he said, the traces of a Caribbean accent still strong in his voice. "I don't usually talk to strangers."

"So what's this? A job interview?"

He smiled. Even his teeth were narrow and pointed, like a cat's. "You too little for a cop," he said. "You wearing too much for a whore. You not twitchy enough for a pusher. Sweatshirt like that, maybe you a roadie's lady looking for some merchandise for the band. I don't think I've got anything to be afraid of, lady."

I couldn't help smiling. In spite of myself, I felt a sneaking liking for Stick. "I hear you might be able to help me. I'm looking for somebody I think you know."

"What's your interest?" he demanded, caution suddenly closing his face like a slammed door.

I'd given the matter of what to say to Stick some thought on the way there. I took a deep breath and said, "I'm a private inquiry agent. I'm trying to get in touch with this woman." Again, I took out the photograph of Moira and handed it over.

He glanced at it without a flicker of recognition. "Who she?"

"Her name is Moira Pollock. Until recently, she was working the streets round here. I'm told you might know where she went."

Stick shrugged. "I don't know where you get your information, but I don't think I can help you, lady. Matter of interest, what you want her for?"

In spite of his nonchalant appearance, I could see Stick had taken the bait. I reeled out my prepared speech. "Some years back, she was in the rock business. Then she dropped out of sight. But all those years, her work's been earning her money. The record company held on to it and they won't hand it over to anyone. Now her family badly need that money. They want to sue the record company. But to do that, they either need to prove Moira's dead or get her to agree."

"Sounds like a lot of bread to me, if it's worth paying you to find out. So you working for this Moira's family?"

"A family friend," I hedged.

He nodded, as if satisfied. "Seems to me I might have heard her name. This family friend . . . They pay your expenses?"

I sighed. This job was turning into a cash-flow nightmare. And none of my payees were the kind to hand out receipts. "How much?" I groaned.

Stick flashed his smile again and took a joint out of the desk drawer. He lit it with a gold Dunhill and took a deep drag. "A monkey," he drawled.

"You what?" I spluttered with genuine surprise. He had to be kidding. He couldn't really think I would pay five hundred pounds for a lead on Moira's whereabouts.

"That's the price, take it or leave it. Lot of money involved, it's got to be worth it," Stick said calmly.

I shook my head. "Forget it," I replied. "You told me yourself, you don't even know the woman. So anything you can tell me has got to be pretty chancy."

He scowled. He'd forgotten the pit his caution had dug for him. "Maybe I was just being careful," he argued.

"Yeah, and maybe you're blagging me now," I retorted. "Look, I've had an expensive day. I can give you a hundred now, without consulting my client. Anything more and I have to take advice, and I don't think I'll get the go-ahead to pay five hundred pounds to someone who didn't even know Moira. You can take it or leave it, Stick. A definite oner now, or a probable zero later."

He leaned back in his chair and gave a low chuckle. "You got a business card, lady?" he asked.

Puzzled, I nodded and handed one over. He studied it, then tucked it in his pocket. "You one tough lady, Kate Brannigan. A man never knows when he might need a private eye. OK, let me see the colour of your money."

I counted out five twenties on the desk top, but kept my hand on the cash. "Moira's address?" I demanded.

"She left the streets about six months ago. She checked in at the Seagull Project. It's a laundry."

"A what?" I had a bizarre vision of Moira loading table-cloths into washing machines.

Stick grinned. "A place where they clean you up. A drug project."

That sounded more like it. "Where is this Seagull Project?" I asked.

"It's on one of those side streets behind the photography museum. I can't remember the name of it, but it's the third or fourth on the left as you go up the hill. A couple of terraced houses knocked together."

I got to my feet. "Thanks, Stick."

"No problem. You find Moira and she gets her bread, you tell her she owes Stick the other four hundred pounds for information received."

9

I parked the car in a pay and display behind the National Film and Television Museum. I walked round to the museum foyer and found a telephone booth which miraculously contained a phone book. I looked up the Seagull Project, and copied its address and number into my notebook. I checked my watch and decided I deserved a coffee, so I walked upstairs to the coffee bar and settled myself down in a window seat looking out over the city centre.

The pale spring sun had broken through the grey clouds, and the old Victorian buildings looked positively romantic. Built on the sweatshops of the wool industry, the once prosperous city had fought its urban decay and depression by jumping on the tourism bandwagon that's turning England into one gigantic theme park. Now that the nearby Yorkshire countryside had been translated into The Brontë Country, Bradford had seized its opportunity with both hands. Even the biscuits in the tearooms and snack bars are called Brontë. But it was the Asian community who'd really revitalized the city's slum areas, producing oases of industrial and wholesaling prosperity. I'd been around a few of those in the past few weeks, hot on the trail of Billy Smart's personal mobile circus.

I tore my eyes away from the view and looked up the Seagull Project's address in my street directory. Stick's information was sound so far. The street was third on the left, off the hill that climbed up the side of the Alhambra Theatre. I finished my coffee and set out on foot.

Five minutes later, I was outside two three-storey stone-built terraced houses that had been knocked together with a board on the front proclaiming "Seagull Project." I stood around uncertainly for a few minutes, not at all sure what was the best way to play it. The one thing I was sure about was that introducing myself and explaining my mission was the certain route to failure. Bitter experience has taught me that voluntary organizations make the Trappists look like blabbermouths.

I eventually settled on my course of action. More lies. If my childhood Sunday School teacher ever finds out about me, she'll put me straight to the top of the list for the burning fire. I walked up the path and turned the door handle. I walked into a clean, airy hallway painted white with grey carpeting. A large sign pointing to the left read "All visitors please report to reception."

For once, I did as I was told and walked into a small, tidy office. Behind a wide desk, a mop of carrot red hair was bent over a pile of papers so high it almost hid its owner from view. I felt a pang of sympathy. I knew just how she felt. My own hatred of paperwork is so strong that I ignore it till Shelley practically locks me in my office with dire threats of what she'll do to me if I dare to emerge before it's finished. It's just the same at home; if I didn't force myself to sit down once a month and pay all the bills, the bailiffs would be a permanent fixture on the doorstep.

As the reception door closed behind me, a pale, freckled face looked up. "Hi, can I help you?" she asked in a tired voice.

"I don't know, but I hope so," I replied with my most ingratiating smile. "I was wondering if you needed any volunteer workers here right now?"

The tiredness evaporated from her face and she grinned. "Music to my ears!" she exclaimed. "Those are the first good words I've heard today. Sit down, make yourself comfortable."

She gestured expansively at the two worn office chairs on my side of the desk. As I settled on the less dilapidated one, she introduced herself. "I'm Jude. I'm one of the project's three full-time employees. We're always desperate for volunteers and fund-raisers." She opened a drawer and took out a long form. "Do you mind if I fill this out while we talk? I know I'm being quick off the mark, but it saves time in the long run if you do decide to help us."

I shook my head. "No problem. My name's Kate Barclay." I knew Richard wouldn't mind me borrowing his name. After all, he knew I'd never be making the loan permanent.

"And where do you live, Kate?" Jude asked, scribbling furiously. I plucked a number out of the air and attached it to Leeds Road, which I knew was long enough to reduce the chances of her knowing a near neighbour.

We went through the formalities quickly. I told her I'd been working abroad as a teacher and that I'd just moved to Bradford with my boyfriend. I explained I'd heard about the project from the city council's voluntary services unit and had come along to offer my services. All the while, Jude nodded and wrote on her form. At the end of my recital, she looked up and said, "Have you any experience with this kind of work?"

"Yes. That's why I came to you. We've been living in Antwerp for the last three years and I did some work with a drug rehabilitation charity there," I lied fluently.

"Right," said Jude. "I'd no idea they ran something like that in Antwerp."

I smiled sweetly and refrained from saying that that's why I'd chosen the Belgian city. No one in Britain has ever been to Antwerp, though I don't know why. It's more attractive, interesting and friendly than almost any other city I've ever been to. It's where Bill's parents came from originally and he still has a tribe of aunts, uncles and cousins there that he visits regularly. I've been over with him a couple of times, and fell in love with it at first sight. I always use Antwerp now for obscure cover stories.

No one ever questions it. Jude was no exception. She swallowed my story, made a note on her form then got to her feet.

"What I'll do is show you round now, to let you see exactly what we've got going here. Then I suggest you come to our weekly collective meeting tomorrow evening and see if you feel you'll fit in with us, and we feel we'll fit in with you," she added, moving towards the door.

My heart sank. The thought of enduring a meeting of the Seagull Project's collective filled me with gloom. I hate the endless circular debate of collectives. I like decisions to be made logically, with the pros and cons neatly laid out. I know all the theory about how consensus is supposed to make everyone feel they have a stake in the decisionmaking. But in my experience, it usually ends up with everyone feeling they've been hard done by. I couldn't imagine any reason why the Seagull Project would be any different.

I hid my despair behind a cheerful smile and followed Jude on her tour of the building. My target was clearly the second room we entered. There were filing cabinets the length of one wall and an IBM PC clone on one of the two desks. As well as its hard disc drive, I noted a slot for 5.25" floppies. A man in his early thirties was sitting at the computer keyboard, and Jude introduced him as Andy.

Andy looked up and grinned vaguely at me before returning to his keyboard.

"The filing cabinets hold details of all the clients we've had through here, all the other agencies we work with, and all our workers. We're trying to transfer all our records to computer, most recent cases first, but it's going to take a while," Jude explained as we left Andy to his task. I noticed that the only lock on the door was a simple Yale.

The other office on the ground floor was the fund-raising office. Jude explained that Seagull was kept on the wing by a mixture of local authority and national grants and charitable donations. The staff consisted of herself as administrator, a psychiatrist and a qualified nurse. They had an arrangement with a local inner-city group practice, and there were always a few biomedical sciences students from the university who were glad to help.

The first floor contained a couple of consulting rooms, two meeting rooms and a common room for the addicts who were living in. On the top floor, addicts in the early stages of kicking heroin sweated and moaned through the first weeks of their agony. If they made it through that, they moved on to a halfway house owned by the project, which tried to find them permanent jobs and homes well away from the temptations of their old stamping grounds. The whole place seemed clean and cheerful, if threadbare, and I thought that Moira could have done a lot worse for herself.

"We run an open door policy here," Jude explained as we made our way back downstairs. "We have to. As it is, we have to turn more away than we can treat. But they're free to go any time. That way, if they make it they know they've done it themselves and not had a cure imposed on them. We believe it makes them less likely to fall into the habit again."

I knew better than to ask about their success rate. It would only depress Jude to talk about it, and she seemed so happy to have a new volunteer on her hands I didn't want to disappoint her any more than I was going to have to do anyway. As we reached the front door, I shook Jude's hand and asked when I should turn up the following evening.

"Come about half-past eight," she said. "The meeting starts at seven, but we have a lot of confidential stuff to get through first. You'll have to ring the bell when you get here because the front door's locked at six."

"Open door policy?" I queried.

"To keep people out, not in," Jude pointed out with a wry smile. "See you then."

"I can hardly wait," I muttered under my breath as I walked down the path and headed back to the car. I felt a complete shit,

having raised her hopes of finding another volunteer. Maybe
I could pitch Jett into giving them a substantial donation once
I'd reunited him with Moira. After all, he'd said he'd be happy
to give everything he owned to get her back.

It was just after eight when I drew up at the foot of the car-
riage turning-circle outside Colcutt Manor. On the way back
to Manchester, I'd dictated a report for Shelley to type up and
fax to Jett so he'd know I wasn't just sitting around collecting
my daily retainer. I pulled off the motorway to hit the ASDA
superstore. I wandered around the aisles trying to fill my trolley
with only the essential items on my mental shopping list, but I
fell by the wayside at the deli counter, as usual, and loaded up
with a dozen little treats to cheer myself up. Then I called the
manor to ask for the fax number. I asked to speak to Jett. That
was my first mistake.

"I'm sorry, Jett's unavailable at present," Gloria informed
me, unable to keep the spark of pleasure from her voice.

"Gloria," I warned, "I haven't got the energy to play games
right now. Let me speak to him, please."

"He really is unavailable," she protested, her voice going
from silky to sulky. "They're in the recording studio. But he
left a message for you," she admitted grudgingly.

"And are you going to tell me or are we going to play
twenty questions?"

"Jett said that he wants you to come round and give him
a progress report."

"I have a progress report right here. I'm about to drop it
off in my secretary's in-tray. It'll be on your desk tomorrow
morning," I told her.

"He wants you here in person," she retorted smugly.

I sighed. "I'll be there in an hour." I dropped the phone
back in the cradle and stomped back to the car. Unfortunately,
the trolley wouldn't go in a straight line, so the effect wasn't

quite what I'd had in mind. Luckily there were no small children around to laugh. That saved me the aggravation of an assault charge.

I really wasn't in the mood for trekking over to Colcutt. Apart from anything else, my carton of double choc chip ice-cream would have melted by the time I got home. But I couldn't see any alternative. If I refused, it would give Gloria more ammunition than she'd need to see me off. Besides, we were charging Jett such astronomical fees I could hardly deny him a face-to-face. Maybe I could ask permission to put my ice-cream in their freezer.

At least Gloria had grown out of the silly childishness with the entryphone. This time she let me in right away. I was surprised to find the circle in front of the house crammed with the kind of motors the likes of me don't even know the price of. Top of the range Mercs, BMWs, even a couple of Porsches. It looked like a march past of Billy Smart's hire cars. For somebody who was working hard only an hour ago, Jett sure knew how to throw an impromptu party I thought as I opened the front door to a blast of Queen.

I looked uncertainly round the hall, not sure where to start a search for Jett. The music seemed to be coming from everywhere rather than one specific room, though the noise of raised voices was definitely on the left somewhere. I'd just set off on the long walk to what was probably once the ballroom when Tamar practically flattened me as she bounced out of a loo tucked under the stairs.

She giggled tipsily as I grabbed at her to steady myself. "Well, well, well," she gurgled. "If it isn't our very own Sherlock Holmes. Come to check your burglar alarms, have you? Well, you've picked the wrong night."

I pasted a smile on my tired face. "Why's that, Tamar?"

"Celebration. World and his dog all celebrating the fact that we've finally got one bastard track that everyone's happy with. Jett's actually managed to write something that hasn't put the entire household to sleep." She hiccuped and pulled away from me to head unsteadily towards the din. "Whoops," she muttered. "Not supposed to say that to the hired help. Anyway, what exactly are you doing here?" she added, pirouetting so that her sequinned jacket sparkled, and fixing me with a bleary stare.

"Jett wanted to see me," I said. Well, it was more or less true.

"About burglar alarms? At this time of night? Today?" Then the incredulity vanished from her voice, replaced by suspicion. "You're not really installing a new alarm, are you?"

I shrugged. It wasn't my job to tell her my business. Apart from the rules of confidentiality, if Jett hadn't told her what I was doing, I certainly wasn't about to bring her wrath down on my head. "That fucking bitch," she swore under her breath. She tossed her expensively tousled hair back from her forehead and stormed down the hall. Curious, I followed her back towards the front door and into the office, where Gloria sat at her word processor, apparently doing the housekeeping accounts, judging by the pile of bills beside her. She glanced up at Tamar, then coolly carried on typing.

"You told me she was here to sort out a burglar alarm," Tamar accused Gloria, a mottled flush rising from her neck to her cheeks.

Gloria's fingers didn't even falter. "And that's what I'll tell you now if you ask properly instead of barging in here like a spoilt child," she said primly. She stopped typing and ran a hand over her blonde hair, pulled back so tightly that in the light from her desk lamp it looked like it had been painted on.

"She's looking for Moira, isn't she?" Tamar raged.

"Why don't you ask Jett? He'll tell you anything he wants you to know," Gloria replied insultingly. I almost wished Tamar would flatten her. It would have made my day, and I wouldn't mind betting I wouldn't have been alone.

Instead, Tamar, who seemed to have sobered up under the influence of so much adrenalin, pushed past me and went back up the hall at a speed I wouldn't have believed possible on four-inch stilettos. I threw a vague smile in Gloria's direction and followed her. The cabaret was worth the trip.

I caught up with Tamar on the threshold of what looked like it had once been a Regency ballroom. The plaster swags were still in place. But everything had been painted gold and black. It would have given the National Trust an apoplexy, or a surfeit, or one of those other things they were always dying of way back then. There were no Regency bucks there tonight, however, just a couple of dozen ageing rockers with a fascinating array of bimbettes on their knees, arms or various other parts of their anatomy. It was hard to tell in the dim light.

Jett was leaning on the gilded mantelpiece, his arm round Kevin in a friendly sort of way. As we approached, I could see the unfocused look of a man who is on his way to being seriously drunk. It was quite an achievement for someone who had been in the studio just over an hour before. It must have been some track he'd just laid down. Tamar landed like a cloudburst on his parade.

"Why didn't you tell me she was looking for Moira?" she hissed.

Jett turned away from us and stared bleakly at the wall. Tamar grabbed his arm and repeated her question. Kevin quickly moved behind her, gripped her tightly above both elbows and stepped back. She had no choice but to move with him. Using the same grip, he turned her round and frogmarched her out of the door. She was so astonished she didn't say a word till they were halfway across the room. But then her yells caused less of a stir than a mugging in Moss-side. As far as everyone else was concerned, it was just a bit of good clean fun.

I moved closer to Jett. "You wanted a report," I said. "I'm making progress. I know where she was a few months ago. By tomorrow night, I should have a current address."

He turned his head to face me. When I got a whiff of the alcohol on his breath, I wished he hadn't bothered. "Is she all right?" he slurred.

There wasn't a way to soften the blow. I called it like I saw it. "She might be. She was on the streets, Jett. She was doing smack as well. But she'd checked into a clinic to clean herself up. Like I say, I'll know more tomorrow. I'll fax you a full update in the morning." He didn't look like he was in the mood for details now.

He nodded. "Thanks," he mumbled. I felt like the last of the great party poopers as I trudged across the room. I found Tamar halfway up the stairs, just where they split into two. Tears had done serious damage to her make-up. She looked like an aerial shot of a war zone. "Don't bring her back," she pleaded with me. "You'll spoil everything."

I sat down beside her. "What makes you think that?"

"You wouldn't understand," she said, pushing herself upright. She ran a hand through her hair like a tragedy queen. "Your kind never do. You just create havoc and walk away. Well, I'm telling you nobody wants Moira back. Not even Jett, not deep down. He doesn't want her back out of love, or out of his desperation to make a good album. He wants her back so he can play the lead in the parable of the prodigal son," she complained cynically. "The thing he needs most of all right now is to feel good about himself, and she's the perfect vehicle. I mean, where's the kick in getting it on with me? I don't need saving, I don't need putting on track in my karmic journey. Moira's a fucking godsend, literally."

She looked as if she was going to say more, but Kevin appeared at the head of the stairs. "For God's sake, Tamar, pull yourself together. I don't bloody want it any more than you do. But at least if you keep him happy, maybe he won't fall for her shit again. OK?"

He glared at me as he came downstairs. "Thanks for your contribution to the celebrations," he said sarcastically. "Have you found her yet?"

I shook my head.

"Good," he commented bitterly. "Take as long as you like. I'd rather pay your exorbitant fees for six months than have her back here." That made me realize just how serious Kevin was about Moira.

Tamar sighed and headed upstairs. I followed Kevin down to the hall, in time to see Gloria lock her office behind her and head towards the ballroom. Good old Gloria. Nothing could make everyone's life a misery like her literal interpretation of the boss's instructions. Now she'd be able to toddle off and offer the hero a shoulder to cry on. He sure as hell wouldn't be getting any offers of comfort from Tamar tonight.

10

I dropped the tape off in Shelley's in-tray and headed home, determined to have some time to myself. I was in luck. Richard had gone to sit in on an Inspiral Carpets rehearsal session. The first time he'd come home talking about the band, I couldn't believe my ears. Thought he'd finally started taking an interest in interior design. Silly me.

After a languid bath, I booted up the computer. Until I met Bill, I'd always thought people who played computer games were intellectual pygmies. But Bill introduced me to role-playing adventures, so different from arcade shoot-em-ups that I can hardly bring myself to mention them in the same breath. The way the games work is that the player takes on the role of a character in the story, explores locations, achieves tasks, and solves complex puzzles. A really good game can take me up to a couple of months to complete. From there, I discovered strategy simulations, and that was the end of my relationship with the television set. Can't say it shows signs of missing me.

I loaded up Sierra's Leisure Suit Larry and spent a bawdy hour as the eponymous medallion man in the white polyester suit, looking for love in all the wrong places, from a whore's boudoir to a filthy toilet. I've played the game half a dozen times, but it's one of the old favourites I always go back to whenever

I want to relax rather than stretch my mind on a fresh set of puzzles. By the time I went to bed, I was feeling more laid back than any carpet, inspiral or otherwise. I almost didn't mind when the alarm went off at six, catapulting me into another wonderful day of chasing the Smarts. We'd been to Glasgow and back by mid-afternoon, when I abandoned them to the delights of a late lunch in Chinatown and headed back to the office with a takeaway pizza, calabrese with onion and extra cheese. Shelley gave me a filthy look as the smell filled her office, so I skulked off to my own cubbyhole where I tried to type up my surveillance report without getting mozzarella on the keys.

The drive back to Bradford to the strains of Tina Turner almost seemed relaxing after the stresses of chasing Billy and Gary up the motorway. But I couldn't afford to let myself become too confident. The hardest part of the day still lay ahead. I sat in the car till half-past seven, then walked up the path to the Seagull Project. I rang the bell and waited.

After a few minutes, I heard feet thundering down the stairs and the door was opened by Andy. He looked surprised to see me. "I've come for the meeting," I told him. "I know I'm early, but I was in the area, and I thought I could wait inside rather than go to the pub on my own." I gave him the full hundred-watt smile.

He shrugged and said, "I don't see a problem with that. Come on in. You can wait in Jude's office." I followed him through and sat down, pulling a Marge Piercy novel out of my bag and trying to look as if I were settled for the evening.

"Help yourself to a coffee," he said, gesturing towards a tray containing all the paraphernalia for brewing up. "Someone'll come down for you when we're ready. I'm afraid it'll be about three quarters of an hour at least."

"Thanks," I said absently, already appearing immersed in my book. I waited till I heard his footsteps reach the top of the stairs, then I counted a hundred elephants. I put my book away and moved quietly across the room. I inched the door open and listened. There was a distant hum of conversation, too low to make out individual voices.

I pulled the door further open and stuck my head into the hall. If I'd seen anyone, I was looking for the loo. But the coast was clear. There was no one in the hall or on the stairs. I crept out of the room, closing the door quietly behind me, and moved quickly across the hall and down the side of the stairs towards the room where the records were kept. I paused outside the door.

My hands were slippery with nervous sweat, so I wiped them on my trousers before taking an out-of-date credit card from my pocket. I'm not bad at picking locks, thanks to Dennis the burglar, but with a simple Yale, the old credit card trick is quicker and leaves fewer traces if you're an amateur like me. I turned the door handle with one hand, and with the other, I slid the card between the door and the lintel. At first, it wouldn't budge and I could feel a trickle of sweat running down between my shoulder blades. I took the card out, took three deep breaths, listening all the time for noise from upstairs, then tried again.

This time, the lock slipped back and the door opened. I hurried into the room and closed the door behind me, flipping up the catch to double-lock it. I leaned against the door and found myself panting. I forced myself to breathe normally and took stock of my surroundings. First, I examined the filing cabinets. I soon found a drawer marked "Clients. O-R." It was locked.

Fortunately, the Seagull Project didn't just hand out charity. It had clearly been on the receiving end as far as the elderly filing cabinets were concerned. With new cabinets, you actually have to pick the locks. But with ones of this vintage, I could forget about the set of lock-picks I'd bought from Dennis. I inched the cabinet away from the wall and pushed the top, tipping it back. Cautiously, keeping it in place, I crouched down and slipped my hand underneath. I groped around till I found the lock bar and pushed it upwards. The sound of the bar releasing the locked drawers was sweet to my ears. I carefully let the cabinet down and pushed it back into place. It had taken me nearly five minutes. I flicked hastily through the files and found a cardboard folder marked "Pollock, M." I pulled it out. It was worryingly slim and when I opened it I discovered why. It contained only one sheet of paper. My heart sank as I read it. "Moira Pollock. File transferred to computer 16th February."

I swore under my breath and turned to the computer. The perfect end to a perfect day. I switched it on and sat down. As I'd expected, it wanted a password. I tried Seagull. No luck. Then Andrew. It's amazing how many people are stupid enough to use their own names as security passwords. Andy wasn't one of them. I thought hard. My next try had to be right. Like copy-protected games, most security programs only give you three attempts before they crash. I sat and stared into the screen, desperately racking my brains for inspiration.

Then it came to me. I crossed my fingers, said a swift prayer to the gods of the New Age and typed in JONATHAN. "Thank you, Richard Bach," I said softly as the menu appeared before me.

Once I was into the program, it didn't take me long to find Moira's records. I didn't have time to plough through them all then and there, but realizing I might have to steal some data from the computer, I'd taken the precaution of bringing a couple of blank floppies with me. I quickly made two copies of the file to be on the safe side, pocketed the discs and switched off the computer. So much for the Data Protection Act. I checked my watch and saw that it was nearly ten past eight. Time to get a move on.

At the door, I paused and listened. It seemed quiet, so I carefully released the lock catch and opened the door. I stepped into the hall with a sigh of relief and pulled the door to behind me. The noise of the lock snapping home sounded like a thunderclap. I didn't wait to see if that's how it sounded to anyone else. I raced down the hall and out of the front door. I didn't stop running till I got to the car.

I didn't like leaving the Seagull Project minus their new volunteer. But at least I'd managed to avoid the collective meeting.

Besides, I figured that now she'd flown the nest, Moira might need my help more than them.

I arrived home just as Richard was leaving. When he saw me, his face lit up in my favourite cute smile and he leapt across the low fence that separates our front gardens. He pulled me into his arms in a comforting hug. Until I tried to relax into him, I hadn't realized how tense I still was after my burglary at Seagull.

"Hey, Brannigan!" he exclaimed. "I'd given you up for dead. Come on, get your glad rags on and we'll go and paint the town."

It was a tempting offer. I didn't keep the full range of software at home that we have in the office, and I knew that I couldn't read the disc I'd copied at the Seagull Project with what I had on my machine. I certainly couldn't face going into the office this late. Besides, it was Friday night and I felt entitled to time off for bad behaviour. "Sounds like a good game," I agreed.

I took a quick shower and blissfully pulled on a pair of clean toffee-coloured silk trousers that were my bargain of the year—a tenner in a reject shop. I added a cream camisole and a linen jacket, and half an hour after I got home, I was climbing into the passenger seat of Richard's hot pink Beetle convertible. I wriggled uncomfortably, then pulled out a handful of scrunched up papers from under me and tossed them on to the rest of the detritus in the back seat.

"This car's a health hazard," I grumbled as I kicked Diet Coke cans, old newspapers and cigarette packets aside in a bid to find some floor space for my feet.

"It's my office," he replied, as if that was some kind of reason for driving round in a dustbin.

"You leave it sitting around with the top down, and some-body's going to come along and mistake it for a skip. You'll come out one morning to find a mattress and a pile of builder's rubble in it," I teased him, only half-joking.

Luckily for my eardrums, Richard was having a night off, so we avoided anywhere with live music. We ended up dancing the night away at one of the city's more intimate clubs. Afterwards, we went for a late Chinese, so it was after three when we finally crawled into bed, hungry for one thing only. And I don't mean sex.

11

I woke around noon to the electronic music of a computer game, and found Richard sitting naked in front of the screen playing Tetris. It's a game that sounds simple, but isn't. The object is to build a solid wall out of a random succession of differently shaped coloured bricks. Sounds boring, but the game has outsold every other computer game ever invented. Richard, like half the high-powered traders in the City, is addicted to it. Unlike the City superstars, however, Tetris is about Richard's limit when it comes to computers.

I pried him away from the screen not with the temptations of my body but with the offer of a pub lunch. He got up eagerly and went off to his house to have a shower, a shave and a change of clothes. What I had omitted to mention was that this was to be a working lunch. A couple of weeks ago, I had followed one of Billy Smart's customers to a pub on the outskirts of Manchester. I wanted to take a look and see what was going on there. But a woman on her own would be both conspicuous and a target for the kind of assholes who think that a woman alone is desperate for their company. What better camouflage in a trendy young people's fun pub than Richard?

We took my car, partly on environmental health grounds and partly so that Richard could have a drink. It took about twenty minutes to drive out to the pub in Worsley, a large 1950s tavern with a bowling green and a beer garden that ran down to the canal. The car park told me all I needed to know. Every car had its string of poser's initials—GTI, XR3i, Turbo. I felt like a second-class citizen with a mere SR. Inside was no better. The interior had been completely revamped according to the chapter of the brewery bible headed "fun pub." My first impression as we walked through the door was of pink neon and chrome. It looked like a tacky version of every New York bar featured in the teen movies of the last decade. I half-expected to find Tom Cruise throwing bottles around behind the bar.

I was out of luck. The barman who shimmied up to serve us looked more like a cruiserweight. While Richard ordered the drinks, I took a good look around. The pub was busy for a lunchtime. "Plenty of Traceys," Richard commented as he glanced round.

He wasn't wrong. The women looked as if collectively they might just scrape together enough neurons for a synapse. The men looked as if they desperately wanted to be taken for readers of GQ magazine. One day, I'm going to find a pub where I feel equally comfortable with the staff, the decor, the clientele and the menu. I rate the chances of that as high as coming home to find Richard doing the spring-cleaning.

Richard handed me my orange juice and soda and I steered him over to a crowded corner of the lounge where I'd spotted my man. I'd briefed Richard on the way so he was happy to oblige. We sat down a few yards away at a table that gave me a good view of what my target was up to. He was sitting at a table with a bunch of eager young men and women around him. There was nothing particularly discreet about his operation. For a start, he was wearing a bright green Sergio Tacchini shell suit. In front of him on the table were half a dozen watches. I could identify the fake Rolexes and Guccis from that distance. Within minutes, all of them had been bought. He appeared to be charging fifty pounds a time, and getting it without a quibble. But he didn't seem to be passing them off as the real thing. Realistically, though, anyone trying that routine would have to be a lot more discreet, dealing one on one to make it look like an exclusive.

Another half dozen watches appeared from Billy's contact's pockets, and most of them vanished as quickly as the others. He shuffled the remaining two back into his jacket then burrowed under the table. He surfaced with three cellophane packets containing shell suits. Surprise surprise. The suit he was wearing was a schneid.

"Sometimes this job is a pain in the arse," I muttered to Richard.

He looked surprised. "Did I hear right?" he asked in tones of wonderment. "Did I hear you say you were less than one hundred per cent thrilled with your life in crime?"

"Piss off," I quipped wittily. "Just look at those shell suits! They're the business. If this wasn't a surveillance operation, I'd be over there right now buying those suits. Take a look at the colours!" I couldn't take my eyes off two of the suits, one gold, one teal blue. I just knew I'd look wonderful in those colours.

Richard got to his feet. "Poor old Brannigan," he teased. "But I'm not working." He moved towards the neighbouring table.

"Richard!" I wailed. A couple of heads turned and I lowered my voice to a piercing whisper. "Don't you dare!"

He shrugged. "Who's to know? Anybody asks you, I bought them for you as a present. You didn't have to know they were copies, did you?"

"That's not the point," I hissed. "I *do* know. Sit down right now before you blow me out of the water."

Richard reluctantly did as I asked him. His face had sulk written all over it. "I thought you wanted one," he muttered.

"Of course I do. I also want a Cartier tank watch, but I can't afford the real thing. I dare say if Dennis had offered me a copy before I got involved in this assignment, I'd have bought it. But this job changes things. I'm sorry, Richard, I know you were trying to please me. And if you want one for yourself, I won't mind."

Richard shook his head. "You and your bloody morals," he commented darkly.

"Oh, come on! Who was it who read me a lecture a couple of months ago about how immoral it is to make tapes of my albums for my friends when it means taking the bread out of the mouths of poor, starving rockstars like Jett?" I reminded him.

He grinned. "OK, Brannigan, you win. Now, have you seen enough, or do I have to spend the whole day in this dump?"

I glanced over at the next table. The man had got to his feet, empty-handed, and was heading over towards the door, followed by most of his audience. I guessed the rest of his stock was in his car outside. "I'm nearly done," I told him. "Let's just tag along with the kids and see what he's got hiding in his boot."

We trailed behind at a discreet distance, and I managed to get a good look as we passed. The boot was full of shell suits in a wide choice of colours, but there were no rolls of watches that I could see. Nevertheless, it had been worth the trip, I pointed out as I drove Richard home. And there was a bonus too. If we pulled off the watches job, we might well be able to interest Sergio Tacchini in doing something similar for them. I'd been surprised to see the suits. I knew that schneid designer clothing was big business, but it was the first time I'd come across it connected, however tangentially, to the Smarts' business. I said as much to Richard.

"There's a lot of it about," he said, to my surprise. "I've seen all sorts of stuff on sale at gigs in the clubs. Anyway, I'm glad it worked out. Always happy to oblige the Sam Spade of Chorlton-on-Medlock."

Poor sod, I thought. In reality, we live in Ardwick, one of those addresses that makes insurance companies blench. But Richard still believes the propaganda that the property developers came up with to convince us that we were moving somewhere select. "Ardwick," I corrected him absently. He ignored me and asked what my plans were for the afternoon. "Work, I'm afraid. And this evening too, probably. Why?"

"Just wondered," he said, too innocently for my liking.

"Tell, Barclay. Or else I'll tidy your study," I threatened.

"Oh no, not that!" he pleaded. "It's just that I've got the chance of a ticket for this afternoon's match at Old Trafford. But if you were free, I was going to suggest we went to the movies."

The scale of the sacrifice made me realize he really does love me. I pulled up at the lights and impulsively leaned across to kiss him. "Greater love has no man," I remarked as I drove off.

"So will you drop me at that pub opposite the ground? I said I'd meet the lads there if I could make it," he asked.

How could I refuse?

Moira's file made fascinating reading. The first interesting nugget came under the heading of "Referral." The entry read, "Brought in by unidentified black male, who made donation of £500 and described her as a former employee in need of urgent help." It sounded as if Stick had a bigger heart than he wanted anyone to know about. It also explained why he wanted five hundred pounds for his information.

Moira had apparently reached the point in her addiction where she realized that she wasn't going to have too many more last chances to kick the smack and change her life. As a result she'd been a model patient. She had opted to go down the hardest road, kicking the drug with minimal maintenance doses of methadone. After her cold turkey, she had been extremely co-operative, joining in willingly with group therapy and responding well in personal counselling. After a four-week stay at the project, she had signed herself out, but had continued to turn up for her therapy appointments.

The sting in the tail for me came at the very end. Instead of going to the halfway house after her initial intensive treatment, she had moved in with a woman called Maggie Rossiter.

The notes on the file said that Maggie Rossiter was a social worker with Leeds City Council and a volunteer worker at the Seagull Project.

That was unusual enough to raise my eyebrows. But a separate report by Seagull's full-time psychiatrist was even more revealing. According to Dr Briggs, Maggie and Moira had formed a highly charged emotional attachment while Moira was still at Seagull. Following her discharge, they had become lovers and were now living together as a couple. In the doctor's opinion, this relationship was a significant contributory factor in Moira's commitment to staying off heroin.

Jett was going to love this, I thought to myself as I made a note of Maggie Rossiter's address. It's one thing to know with your head that a lot of whores prefer relationships with women. I can't say I blame them. If the only men I ever encountered were johns or pimps, I'd probably feel the same way. But when the woman concerned was your former soul mate . . . That was a whole different ball game.

I reluctantly called Colcutt Manor to give Jett an up-to-date report, but Gloria informed me gleefully that he was out. No, she didn't know where he could be reached. No, she didn't know when he'd be back. Yes, he would be back that night. I was almost relieved that I'd missed him. I felt sure that once he knew I had Moira's address he'd want to come with me himself. I couldn't help thinking that would be the messiest possible way to handle things. All that raw emotion would get us nowhere. I settled for typing up a current report and faxed it through to Gloria for her to pass it on to Jett as soon as he returned.

I copied Moira's files on to the disc where I was storing Jett's information, then switched off the computer. The office seemed unnaturally quiet, not just because I was alone in it, but because all the other offices in the building are occupied by sensible people who think working from Monday to Friday is quite enough to be going on with. I locked up behind me and walked down to the ground floor. Luckily, I emerged on Oxford

Road just before the afternoon matinee at the Palace Theatre
spilled its crowds on to the pavement. I'd left the car at home
since parking near the office is impossible thanks to Saturday
afternoon theatregoers and shoppers. Besides, the walk would
do me good, I'd thought. That was before the rain came on.

I plodded up past the BBC and headed across to Upper
Brook Street. By the time I got home, I was wet through. I
hoped Richard had been sitting far enough back in the stands
to avoid a soaking. I had a quick shower to warm me up, then I
stood in front of the wardrobe wondering which outfit would
be the key that would get me across Maggie Rossiter's doorstep.

I settled on my favourite Levis and a cream lambswool
cowl-necked sweater. Thoroughly inoffensive, making no statement that a lesbian social worker could disagree with, I hoped. I
went through to the kitchen to fix myself a plate of snacks from
my supermarket blitz, and washed it down with a small vodka
and grapefruit juice. I was in no real hurry. I was aiming to get
to Maggie's home in Bradford between six thirty and seven. With
any luck I'd catch them before they went out for the evening.

As it turned out, my timing was diabolical. I found Maggie's house easily enough, a neat brick terrace in a quiet street
only a mile away from the motorway. I parked outside with a
sinking heart as I registered that the house was in darkness. I
walked up the crazy paved path and knocked on the stripped
pine front door anyway. There was, of course, no response.

As I walked back down the path, a small calico cat rubbed
itself against my legs. I crouched down to stroke it. "Don't suppose you know where they've gone, do you?" I asked softly.

"Darsett Trades and Labour Club," a deep male voice said
from behind me. I nearly fell over in shock.

I stood up hastily and stared in the direction of the voice. A
tall dark hunk was standing by the gate with a box of groceries.
"I'm sorry?" I asked inadequately.

"I'm the one who should be sorry, startling you like that,"
he apologized with a smile that lit up twinkling eyes. I shrugged.

Eyes like that I'd forgive most things. "If you're looking for Maggie and Moira, they've gone to Darsett Trades and Labour Club," he said.

"Oh, right," I hedged. "I didn't realize they were out tonight. I'll catch up with them later."

"You a friend of theirs?" the hunk asked.

"Friend of a friend, really," I replied, walking down the path towards him. "I know Maggie from Seagull."

"I'm Gavin," he said. "I live next door. We would have been going with them tonight except that we've got people coming for dinner. Still, I'm sure there will be plenty more chances to hear Moira sing in public"

My heart jolted. Moira was singing? I swallowed hard and spoke before Gavin's helpful garrulity gave out. "I didn't know it was tonight," I improvised.

"Oh yeah, the big night. Her first engagement. She's going to be a big success. I should know, I hear her rehearsing enough!"

I smiled politely and thanked him for his help. "I'll catch them another time," I said, getting back into my car. Gavin sketched a half-wave from under his box and turned into the next house. I pulled out my atlas. I groaned. Darsett was a good twenty miles away. With a sigh, I headed back towards the motorway.

12

Within three minutes of entering Darsett Trades and Labour Club, I knew that not even double rates could compensate me for spending Saturday night there. I don't know enough about the northern club circuit to know if it's typical, but if it is, then my heartfelt sympathy goes out to the poor sods who make their living performing there. The building itself was a 1960s concrete box with all the charm of a dead dog. I parked among an assortment of old Cortinas and Datsuns and headed for the brightly lit entrance.

Being a woman, I already had problems on my hands. In their infinite wisdom, working men's clubs don't allow women to be members in their own right. Strange women trying to get in alone are a complete no-no. The doorman, face marked with the blue hairline scars of a miner, wasn't impressed with my story that I was an agent there to see Moira perform, not even when I produced the business card that carefully doesn't specify what Mortensen and Brannigan are. Eventually, he grudgingly called the club secretary, who finally agreed to let me in, after informing me at great length that I would not be able to purchase alcoholic beverages.

I regretted this rule and the fact that I was driving as soon as I crossed the threshold. The only way to make an evening at

Darsett Trades and Labour Club tolerable was to be so pissed I wouldn't notice it. The bar, on my left, was brightly lit, packed and already blue with smoke. It sounded like a riot was in progress, an impression increased by the rugby scrum at the bar.

I carried on through double doors under a blue neon sign that said Cabaret Room. Like the bar, the room shimmered under the glare of lights and the haze of cigarette smoke. It was crammed with small, round tables, two-thirds of which were occupied with chattering groups of men and women. Their gaiety was infectious, and I mentally ticked myself off for my patronizing response to the club.

At the far end of the room was a small stage. A trio of electronic organ, drums and bass were listlessly playing "The Girl From Ipanema." No one was listening. I looked around intently, trying to pick out Maggie in the crowd. At first, I couldn't see any woman on her own, but on the second sweep of the room, I spotted her.

She was standing in the shadows right at the edge of the room about halfway back. Her clothes as much as her isolation marked her out. Unlike the other women in the room apart from me, she wasn't dressed up to the nines in teetering heels and a bright dress. Maggie wore jeans, a chambray shirt and a pair of trainers. From where I was standing, it looked like she had also avoided the cosmetic excesses of the rest of the room. She was about my height, with curly, shoulder-length pepper and salt hair. She was carrying about ten pounds overweight, but she looked sturdy rather than flabby.

For a moment, I toyed with the idea of making the first approach to her, but decided against it. I suspected she'd leap immediately to Moira's defence and give me the elbow without actually weighing up what I had to say, and I couldn't blame her for that. Even if I'd been going to approach her, I was cut off at the pass. The organist finished the Stan Getz piece with a flourish and played a fanfare. A burly man leapt on to the stage and peppered the audience with a few risqué jokes, then announced, "Ladies and animals, put your hands together for tonight's star attraction, a young lady who's going all the way to the top. Let's hear it for Moira Moore!"

With another fanfare on the organ, he vanished into the wings. The band played the opening chords of "To Be With You Tonight" and Moira walked out on to the stage. As she moved forward into the fixed spotlight, she looked nervously from side to side, as if searching for an escape route that wasn't there. She was wearing a tight blue lurex dress which came to just above her knees. She looked painfully thin.

As the band finished the intro, Moira leaned forward to the mike and began to sing. To say I was astonished would be putting it mildly. Could this really be the woman who'd been happy to take a backseat lyricist's role because her voice wasn't up to scratch? OK, she didn't have the silky richness of Jett, but by any other standards Moira's was quite a voice. Slightly husky, almost bluesy, she hit the notes perfectly, and the nerves that were obvious in her body language didn't transmit themselves into her singing. Even the louts in the audience shut up to listen to Moira sing.

She followed Jett's first hit with an unadventurous selection of torch songs, ending up with a version of "Who Will I Turn To" that almost had tough old Brannigan in tears. The audience loved it, clapping and cheering and demanding more. Moira looked dazed and surprised by her reception, and after a few minutes of applause, she turned and asked the organist something inaudible. He nodded and she launched into Tina Turner's whore's anthem, "Private Dancer," with the kind of bitter attack that could only come from experience. The crowd went wild. If it had been up to them, she would have been there all night, but she looked exhausted by the end of the song and escaped gratefully to the wings.

Like the audience, I'd been mesmerized by Moira and when I looked back to where Maggie had been standing, I realized I'd been letting pleasure interfere with work. Maggie had gone.

Furious with myself, I hurried down the side of the room and through a pass door at the side of the stage.

I was in a narrow corridor. Two doors on the left were marked Ladies and Gents, and on my right were steps leading up to the stage. Round a corner, I found three more doors. No reply to my knock on the first. Same with the second. On the third attempt, I hit pay dirt. The door opened six inches and Maggie's face appeared in the crack. Close up, she was a pretty woman. She had small, neat features and intelligent blue eyes with laughter lines at the corners. I put her in the mid thirties. "Can I help you?" she asked pleasantly.

I smiled. "You must be Maggie. Hi. I'd like to see Moira."

She frowned. "I'm sorry, have we met?" Without waiting for a reply, she went on. "Look, she's too tired. If it's an autograph you want, I can get her to sign one for you."

I shook my head. "Thanks, but I need to see her. It's a personal matter," I stated calmly.

"Who is it?" a voice from inside the room called out.

"No one we know," Maggie remarked over her shoulder. She turned back to me and said, "Look, this is not a good time. She's just done a show, and she needs to rest."

"What I have to say won't take long. I don't like to be difficult, but I'm not going till I've spoken to Moira." I spoke firmly, with more confidence than I actually felt. I was in no doubt that Maggie could have me thrown out of there so fast my feet wouldn't touch the sticky carpets. However, to do that, she'd have to leave Moira. I couldn't see Darsett Trades and Labour Club being the kind of place that had a house phone in the star dressing room.

"What the hell's going on?" Moira demanded, pulling the door open and staring belligerently at me. It should have been a moment of triumph for me, to come face to face with my quarry like this, but any satisfaction was destroyed by the irritation in her voice. "Are you deaf or what? She told you, I'm too tired to talk to anybody."

"I'm sorry it's a bad time, but I need to talk to you," I apologized. "It's taken me a long time to find you, and it's important for you that you listen to what I have to say." I tried a conciliatory smile which produced a scowl from Maggie, standing like a bulldog in front of Moira.

Moira sighed and pulled her white bathrobe more tightly round her. "You're damn right, it's a bad time. I suppose you'd better come in. Let me tell you, sister, this better not be bad news."

I waited for Maggie to move reluctantly away from the door before I entered the tiny dressing room. There were two small formica topped tables in front of mirrors, a corner sink unit, three chairs and several hooks on the wall. Moira sat down in one chair facing a mirror and carried on removing her make-up. Maggie leaned against the wall, arms folded.

I pulled a chair over beside Moira and sat down. "I don't think it's bad news, but that's for you to decide. My name's Kate Brannigan and I'm a private investigator." Moira flashed a quick look at me, fear in her eyes, then forced herself to look back in the mirror.

"So what's your interest in me?" she challenged.

"Jett asked me to find you," I told her, watching for her reaction. The hand with the make-up removal pad shook and she quickly lowered it to the table.

"I don't know what you're talking about," she said in a low voice.

"He wants to work with you again. He bitterly regrets what happened all those years ago," I tried. My instincts told me that with Maggie in the room, I should steer well clear of the emotional arguments.

Moira shrugged. "I haven't a clue what you're on about."

"I think you should go now," Maggie piped up.

I ignored her. "Look, Moira, Jett is desperate to reach you. He says his work has gone down the tube since the two of you stopped writing songs together. As a fan, I have to agree with him. And I bet you do, too. He just wants to meet you, to talk about the possibilities of making music together again. That's all. No strings."

Moira laughed, a harsh bark. "Oh yeah? And what's Kevin going to say about that? If you've been looking for me, you know what my life's been like the last few years. I'd be too much of a skeleton in the cupboard for Mr Clean. Never mind what Jett will think."

"Jett knows all about it. And he didn't tell me to stop looking just because you'd been on the game, or on smack. He wants to talk to you. He doesn't care what's happened in between," I argued as fiercely as I could.

Moira ran a hand through her short curls. "I don't think so," she said softly. "Too much water under the bridge."

"You heard her," Maggie interjected. "I really think you'd better go now before you upset her any more."

I shrugged. "If that's what Moira wants, I'll go. I told Jett he might be wasting his money, asking me to find you. I told him you might not want to be found. But he's not going to be satisfied with that. And the next private eye he hires might not do things my way."

"Don't you threaten us!" Maggie exploded.

"I'm not threatening you," I flashed back. "I'm simply trying to be straight with you. Jett wants to find you. Whatever that takes. You might do a runner after tonight, but you've got to leave traces. Someone else will track you down, just like I did. And next time, it could be Jett knocking on your door. Don't you think it would be better to meet him on your terms, when you're prepared for it, rather than have him catching you by surprise?"

Moira's head dropped into her hands. "You say he knows already?" she mumbled.

"He knows about everything except the singing." And I don't think that's going to give him the screaming habdabs, I thought wryly.

Moira's head came up and she stared at her face in the mirror. "I don't know," she said doubtfully, lighting up a pungent Gauloise.

Maggie crossed the room, all two paces of it, and put a protective arm round Moira. "You don't need him any more," she declared. "Where was he when you really needed help? If he'd been so bloody keen to find you, why didn't he do it when you left? He's just being selfish. His career's a disaster area, and he wants you to get him out of the shit. You don't owe him anything, Moira."

"Oh, I see," I remarked. "There's a statute of limitations on feeling guilty now, is there? Just because Jett didn't act right away, then he can only be out for himself? Is that it?"

Maggie glowered at me, but Moira actually smiled as she reached up to squeeze her lover's hand. "He's really not like that, Maggie. He's one of the good guys. I didn't expect him to come after me. I'd been doing his head in for so long he must have been glad of the peace."

"So what's it to be?" I asked. "Will you at least listen to what he's got to say?"

Moira took a deep drag on her cigarette. Maggie looked as if she was holding her breath and praying. Moira blew two streams of smoke down her nose and nodded at me. "I'll listen. When can you set it up?"

"The sooner the better. He's at home working on his new album. Believe me, he needs your help yesterday."

Moira smiled, a wide grin that lit up her whole face and took ten years off her. "I'll bet," she said. "What about tonight? Might as well get it over with."

"But it's past ten o'clock!" Maggie protested. "You can't go off there now."

"Maggie, unless Jett has had a personality transplant, he'll be up watching videos and listening to music till three or four o'clock. He doesn't get up to listen to the Archers omnibus on Sunday mornings," Moira replied, a gentle tease in her voice.

Maggie flushed. "I still think you should leave it till tomorrow," she said stubbornly. "You're tired. You need a night's rest after the show."

She still had a lot to learn, I thought sadly. Every performer I've ever met is so high after a show that they need half the night to come down to a point where sleep's possible. That's why so many of them get hooked on a mixture of uppers and downers.

As if reading my thoughts, Moira said, "No, Maggie. Right now, I'm on a high. All that applause! Tonight, I feel like I could meet Jett as an equal. And if I sleep on it, I'll probably bottle out. Or else I'll let you talk me out of it."

Moira got to her feet and put an arm round Maggie's waist. "Kate, if you'll give me ten minutes, we'll meet you in the car park. Ours is the red 2CV. I'll have to go home and change into something more suitable," she added, waving at her blue lurex dress and a jogging suit. "If you follow us back there, then you can take me over to see Jett. If that's OK with you."

"Fine by me," I confirmed, feeling exultant. There's no better feeling in the world than the moment when you know you've cracked a difficult job. Moira wasn't the only one who was on a high.

An hour later, Moira and I were heading back down the motorway towards Manchester. "I feel like I've spent more time on this motorway in the last couple of weeks than I've spent in my own bed," I muttered to break the silence that had fallen on us since Maggie had waved a mournful farewell on the doorstep.

Moira chuckled. "I'm sorry I've given you so much trouble," she remarked.

"Oh, it's not just you. It's another case I've been working on. A team that's flooding the country with fake watches. You know, Rolex copies, all that sort of thing."

Moira nodded. "I know exactly what you mean. A lot of the guys in Bradford are into that kind of thing. It's a nice little earner. They do a lot of fake jogging suits and t-shirts. You know, any big thing like the Batman movie, or the Teenage

Mutant Turtles. They just copy the legit stuff and flog it round the pubs and the markets. The guy I worked for in Bradford even had us selling fake perfume to johns for their wives, can you believe it?"

I laughed. "Wonderful. I love the psychology." I put Everything But The Girl's *Language Of Life* in the cassette and we both settled in a companionable silence to listen to Tracy Thorn's sensuous tones.

"So how did you track me down?" Moira asked finally as I turned on to the M6, heading south towards Jett's mansion. The home she'd never seen, I reminded myself.

When I got to the bit about Stick asking for his four hundred pounds, she laughed out loud. "You know," she said, "if this does work out, I might just pay him back. Mind you, he'd die of embarrassment if word got out that he took me to Seagull. Stick the hard man! He'd never live it down."

I turned into the gateway of Colcutt Manor and wound down the window and leaned out to press the intercom button. When it crackled back at me, I said clearly, "It's Kate Brannigan to see Jett. Don't fuck with me, Gloria, let me in."

As the gates opened, I caught Moira's expression out of the corner of my eye. She looked stunned. I headed up the long drive, and the house appeared in my headlights. "Shit," she breathed. "You might have warned me, Kate."

I pulled up at the foot of the steps that led up to the front door and said, "You ready?"

Moira took a deep breath and said, "Ready as I'll ever be."

We got out of the car and I led the way up towards the door. Three steps from the top, it opened and a pool of light flooded out. Jett himself stood silhouetted in the doorway. It took only a moment for him to realize I wasn't alone. Then he saw who my companion was. "Moira?" he said in tones of wonder, as if he couldn't believe his eyes.

I paused, and she walked past me. "Hi, babe," she said, stopping a few feet short of him.

Jett's hesitation was only momentary. Then he stepped forward and folded her into his arms. Moira buried her head in his shoulder.

Me, I headed back into the night, trying to start the car as quietly as possible. Some things don't need witnesses. Besides, I had a huge invoice to dictate before I could sleep.

PART II

13

The sound of the phone jerked me awake. "Kate? It's Jett. It's an emergency. Get over here right away." Then the phone slammed down. The clock said 01:32. Happy Monday. I leapt out of bed and dressed on automatic pilot. I was halfway to the car before I remembered it had been six weeks since I'd stopped working for Jett. What the hell was he playing at? By then, I was awake anyway, so I figured I might as well drive out and see.

The gates stood open, and Jett was waiting for me on the doorstep. He looked stoned out of his box. I asked what was going on and he simply handed me the key and said, "The rehearsal room."

It was my first dead body. The private eyes in books fall over corpses every other day, but Manchester's a long way from Chicago in more ways than one. My first reaction was to get out of the room as fast as my legs would carry me and keep on running till I was safe inside my car.

Instead, I tried to fight my nausea by breathing in deeply. That was my second mistake. Nobody ever told me that freshly spilled blood has such a strong smell. My only experience with the stuff was when half a pound of liver leaked all over my cheque book. That hadn't been too pleasant either.

I tried to behave like a professional and forget that I knew the person who was lying dead on the polished wooden floor. If I was going to get through this experience, I'd have to convince myself it was no more real than the Kensington Gore in a Hammer Horror film.

Moira's body lay a few yards inside the door of the rehearsal room. Her limbs were splayed at angles too awkward for comfort. That alone would have been enough to show something was badly wrong. But there was more. The back of her head was matted with blood, which had trickled into a congealed pool behind her. A few yards away lay a tenor sax, its gleaming golden horn smeared with blood. I left it alone. My only direct experience with murder weapons was Cluedo, but even I knew enough not to mess with it.

I walked cautiously towards the body, and noticed that her face looked mildly surprised. I crouched down, forcing myself not to think of this as Moira, and noticed that her hands were empty, palms upwards. No clues there. Feeling foolish because I couldn't think of anything else to do, I picked up her wrist and felt vainly for a pulse. Nothing. Her skin felt warmish—not quite normal temperature, but not cold either. I got to my feet and glanced at my watch. It was forty minutes since Jett had woken me. What the hell was keeping the police?

With a deep sigh, I left the room and locked it behind me. I found Jett in the blue drawing room, huddled in a corner of the sofa. I sat down beside him and put a hand on his shoulder. His skin felt cold and clammy through the thin silk shirt.

His eyes were frightened. I realized now he was in shock rather than stoned.

"She's dead, isn't she?" he whispered hoarsely.

"I'm afraid so."

He nodded, and kept on nodding as if he had a tic. "I should never have brought her here," he muttered.

"What happened, Jett?" I asked as gently as I could. It looked pretty obvious even to me, but I wanted to hear it from his own lips.

"I don't know," he replied, his voice breaking like a teenager. "We were supposed to be working on a new song tonight, and when I went in, she was lying there." He cleared his throat and sniffed. "So I came out and locked the door and called you."

Gee, thanks. "Did you try her pulse?" I asked.

"No need. The spirit had left. I knew that right away."

Thank you, Dr Kildare. "Why aren't the police here yet?" I asked, refraining from pointing out that she just might have been still alive when he made his New Age diagnosis.

"I didn't call the police. I only called you. I thought you'd know what to do."

I couldn't credit what I was hearing. He'd found his ex-lover's murdered body in his house and he hadn't called the police? If Jett wanted to throw suspicion on himself, the only way he could have made a better job of it would have been to call his lawyer as well. "You'll have to call them now, Jett. You should have done that first, before you called me."

He shook his head obstinately. "No. I want you to handle it. I can trust you."

"Jett, you can't hush up a murder. You have to call the police. Look, I'll make the call if you don't feel up to it," I offered desperately. The last thing I needed was for the police to get it into their heads that I was involved in concealing a crime.

He shrugged. "Please yourself. But I want you to handle it."

"We'll talk about it in a minute." I stood up. There was a phone in the room, but I wanted some privacy to gather my thoughts so I headed for Gloria's office down the hall. Neil was coming down the stairs as I reached the door. He looked as surprised to see me as I was to see him. "Kate!" he exclaimed. "I didn't know you were here."

"Jett needed a meeting," I offered lamely, not feeling up to breaking the news.

"Maybe see you later," he said, sketching a wave as he walked down the corridor into the far wing. Clearly he saw nothing odd about business meetings in the small hours.

I closed Gloria's door behind me, picked up the phone and dialled 999. I was quickly connected to the police emergency line. "I'm calling to report a murder," I said. To my amazement, I could feel a giggle welling up inside me. I must have been more shocked than I'd realized.

The copper on the other end of the phone wasn't amused. "Is this some kind of hoax?" he demanded.

I pulled myself together and said, "I'm sorry. Unfortunately not. A woman has been killed at Colcutt Manor, just outside Colcutt village."

"When did this happen, Madam?" His voice was hard and cool.

"We're not sure. The body's only just been discovered." I gave him the details. It seemed to take forever. When I returned, Jett was sitting exactly as I'd left him, hugging himself and rocking gently to and fro. What he needed was a cup of strong, sweet tea, but I didn't rate my chances of finding my way to the kitchen and back again without a ball of string or a map. Instead, I sat down and put an arm round him. "Jett," I said softly. "We're going to have to get our story straight or the cops are going to get very heavy with you. Listen. I was passing on my way home from a job and I dropped in for a drink. We were talking for the best part of an hour, then you went down to the rehearsal room to get Moira to join us, and that's when you found the body. I was already here. Understand?" I could only pray that the pathologist wouldn't come up with a time of death that made a nonsense of the alibi I was handing him.

"I got nothing to say to the cops," he informed me.

"Jett, unless you want to spend tonight in a cell you're going to have to stick to our story. In their eyes, you're the number one suspect, especially if we tell them the truth. Promise me you'll keep to my version." I repeated the tale to him and made him recite it back to me.

We were interrupted by the distant sound of the gate intercom. Jett showed no signs of moving, so I headed back towards the hall. Gloria had beaten me to it. She was wearing a heavy red silk kimono with, appropriately enough, black and gold dragons embroidered all over it. Either she had ears like a bat or she'd been on her way downstairs anyway when the intercom sounded. She was carrying out her usual friendly interrogation over the entryphone when I butted in and said curtly, "Let them in. Jett knows all about it."

She pressed the gate release button then turned furiously towards me. "I don't know what you think you're playing at, police in the middle of the night. I suppose Moira's doing drugs or something. I wish he'd never hired you in the first place. Then we would all have been happy."

I already felt put upon, which is the only excuse I can offer for snapping back at her, "Moira won't be doing drugs or anything else ever again. Somebody made very sure of that tonight. Moira's dead."

Before I could properly judge her reaction, there was a tattoo of knocks on the front door. I pushed past Gloria and opened the door. Two uniformed officers stood on the doorstep, the flashing blue light on top of their car washing them in an eerie glow. "Miss Brannigan, is it?" the older of the two asked politely.

"That's me. You'd better come in. Are the CID on their way?"

"That's right Miss," he said as they walked into the hall, looking around them curiously. They'd drink out on this for months, murder in the rock star's den. "Can you show me where the uhh . . ."

"You'd better wait here, Gloria," I said loftily. "Someone will have to let the other officers in."

As I turned away to lead them to the rehearsal room, a man's voice echoed down the stairwell. "What the fuck is going down?" I glanced up to see Kevin leaning over the gilt banister, looking as spruce as if he was heading for a meeting with his bank manager. Didn't anybody ever sleep in this house?

"You'd better get yourself down here," I called back.

"What the hell are you doing here, Brannigan?" he ranted as he turned the corner of the stairs. Then he saw the cops and stopped dead. "Oh shit, what are they doing here? What's going on?"

"Moira's been killed," I blurted out before anyone else could speak.

Kevin missed a step and almost tumbled to the foot of the stairs, just catching himself in time on the banister. "You what?" he gasped. "There's got to be some mistake. Gloria, what's she playing at?"

"I don't know, Kevin. I just came downstairs and found her here."

"No mistake, I'm afraid," I interrupted. "I've seen the body. You'd better go and sit with Jett. He's in the drawing room."

Kevin shook his head like a man who thinks he's trapped in a bad dream and moved across the hall towards the door. Gloria took a couple of steps after him, then hesitated. The policemen conferred almost inaudibly, then the younger one stepped back towards the front door. "I'll have to ask you not to leave the building, Sir," he said to Kevin.

"Listen, sonny, I'm not going anywhere. I've got an artiste to look after," he said self-importantly. "I've got a right to be here. Why don't you ask her what the hell she's doing on the premises? She's the outsider here," he complained sharply, pointing to me.

The older policeman looked exasperated. All he wanted to do was get to the murder scene before the CID arrived and started treating him like a turnip. At this rate, he'd end up looking like a complete wally who hadn't even managed to keep tabs on the occupants of the house. Ignoring Kevin's histrionic gesture, he said, "Miss, if you could just show me the way?"

I led him to the door. Wild horses wouldn't have dragged me across the threshold again. I handed him the key and nodded at the door. "In there. I checked for a pulse, but there wasn't one."

"Touch anything else, miss?" he asked as he unlocked the door.

"No." I leaned against the wall as he let himself in. All I wanted was to climb back into bed and pull the duvet over my head. It didn't seem to be an available option. Wearily, I pushed myself back into action. Apart from the young constable, whose radio was crackling like an egg in a hot frying pan, the front hall was empty. I didn't feel up to Kevin and Gloria, so I sat on the bottom step of the stairs and wondered gloomily why I'd already stuck my neck out to protect Jett. He wasn't a friend, simply a client who'd paid his bill promptly. I know that's rarer than a socialist at a Labour Party meeting, but it still wasn't reason enough for my quixotic behaviour.

The sound of the intercom brought Gloria scuttling back from the drawing room. This time, the door opened to reveal two plain clothes officers, a uniformed sergeant and an inspector. They hadn't wasted any time. They had a brief conference with the officer on the door, and the CID disappeared in the direction of the rehearsal room. The inspector went off to the drawing room. The sergeant turned to Gloria and me, pulled out his notebook and asked, "Who else is in the house?"

I shrugged and Gloria pursed her mouth in a self-satisfied smirk. She didn't care if it took murder to keep me in my place. Then she rattled off efficiently, "Jett is in the drawing room with his manager, Mr Kleinman. Mr Webster, Jett's official biographer, will either be in his office or in bed. Miss Spenser, Jett's companion, is in her room upstairs."

"Thank you," the officer interjected, desperately trying to keep up with her flow. He scribbled on for a moment then said, "And you ladies are . . . ?"

"I'm Gloria Seward, Jett's personal assistant and private secretary. And this is Kate Brannigan," she added, her tone spelling out that I was an insignificant menial, there to make up the numbers. I held my tongue. The time to reveal my profession would come soon enough. Once they knew I was a private eye, it would be straight into quarantine for me, and I wasn't ready for that yet.

The sergeant, a hard-eyed man in his late thirties, finished writing and said, "So that's everyone, is it?"

Gloria ran through her mental checklist, then her hand flew to her mouth. I really didn't think anyone did that any more. "I forgot Micky," she wailed. "I'm sorry. Micky Hampton is Jett's record producer. He'll probably be in the studio—that's in the cellar."

"Don't worry, it's hard to remember everything at a time like this. You've obviously had a bit of a shock. I'm sorry to ask this, but we're going to have to interview everyone as soon as possible. I'd appreciate it if one of you ladies could get everyone together," he said.

"I'll go," I piped up. "I think Gloria should be with Jett right now."

The look she shot at me was pure poison, but there was really nothing she could do about it. After all, she was the one who'd set herself up as Jett's little helper. The policeman nodded and I swiftly got directions from Gloria. Jett clearly wasn't going to let me walk away from this murder. And if I was going to have to investigate these choice specimens, I at least wanted to see how they reacted to the news.

14

Tamar was my first target. For obvious reasons, her reaction to
Moira's death was the one that interested me most. I didn't know
what had been happening at Colcutt Manor in the six weeks
since I'd dutifully delivered Moira, but the corpse downstairs
told me plenty. Not everyone had been as thrilled by her return
as Jett. At least one person had taken extreme measures to try to
return things to the status quo ante. (I love legalese. Sometimes
it sums things up so beautifully.) And even if Jett and Moira had
no longer been an item, it can't have been Easy Street for Tamar
having Jett's alleged soul mate under the same roof.

I knocked sharply on the panelled door Gloria had directed
me to and didn't wait for a reply. Crossing the threshold gave
me the answer to one question at least. Jett and Tamar might
be lovers, but he was clearly a man who liked his own sleeping
space. This room was Tamar's, no question.

It looked like a guest room where someone was camping
out. The only light came from a flickering TV screen, but it
was enough to show me the room was decorated in white and
gold, with some very nasty still-life oils on the walls. Lots of
dead pheasants and fruit. It was furnished in Louis Quinze style.
The only straight edges were on the television, which was even

housed in a hideous gilt cabinet. If someone had put me up there, I think I would have preferred to sleep in the bath.

Tamar was lying on one of the twin beds wearing a pair of silk lounging pyjamas. She hadn't noticed my entrance because she was glued to the television, watching a video of *9½ Weeks*. A pair of headphones were clamped to her head as she studied Kim Basinger and Mickey Rourke indulging in the ultimate nice work if you can get it. I walked across her line of vision and she sat bolt upright in annoyance.

She pulled the headphones off and snapped the bedside lamp on. More gilt horror.

"What the hell do you think you're doing, walking into my bedroom?" she snapped.

"Sorry to butt in on you," I apologized insincerely.

"So you bloody should be. What are you doing here, anyway?"

I was beginning to get the message. Maybe I should change my deodorant. "I'm afraid I've got bad news for you," I said.

She scowled and pushed her tangled blonde hair back from her face. "OK," she sighed, swinging her legs over the side of the bed and standing up. "Message received and understood. He means it this time." She walked across the room and dramatically pulled open a wardrobe door. "I was getting pissed off with having to be a little goody two shoes anyway. I'm too old to be sneaking off to the loo every time I want a joint." She rattled the hangers noisily.

Then she turned back to me and shouted, "So what are you hanging around for? Enjoying the cabaret, are you? My God, he didn't have to send you to do his dirty work."

Crossed wires are, in my experience, the kind that provide most illumination. Unfortunately, it looked like this set had finally short-circuited. "I think we're at cross purposes, Tamar. It's not Jett who asked me to come and get you. It's the police."

"The police?" The puzzlement on her face looked genuine. "What d'you mean?"

"Like I said, I've got some bad news. Moira's dead," I said.

It was as if I'd pressed the freeze-frame button. Tamar stopped dead, her face immobile. At first, she said nothing. Then a slow smile curled her lips. "Well, what a shame," she said sarcastically. "I suppose she just couldn't stay away from the stuff."

Tamar might have been a blonde, but I was far from convinced that she was dumb. And if she was guilty, she was choosing a very clever way of hiding it.

"You're right off track," I commented. "Moira's been murdered. In the rehearsal room."

That got a reaction. Tamar flushed scarlet. "I . . . I don't understand," she whispered.

"I don't know any more than that myself," I said. "I called in to see Jett, and he went to fetch Moira. He discovered the body, and we called the police. They're waiting downstairs. You'd better get down there now. Everyone's in the blue drawing room." I know I'm not going to win any points from bereavement counsellors for my attitude, but as far as I was concerned, Tamar lost all rights to my sympathy with that smile.

I moved towards the door. "Wait," she called. I turned back. "Do you know who did it?" she asked.

I shook my head. "Not up to me, Tamar. It's the police who work that sort of thing out. And they want to see you now," I added, twisting the knife as I closed the door behind me.

I didn't hang around to see if she was following me. I tripped back down the curving stairs, half-expecting a Busby Berkeley chorus to break into song. But all I could hear was the police radio chatter. As I reached the hall, the intercom sounded again. This time, the constable on the door dealt with it so I made my way to the cellar door at the end of a short side-passage. I opened the door which led to a tiny vestibule with a flight of steps. I descended and found myself facing a heavy steel door. Above it was a red light. I know what happens in computer games if you ignore warnings like that, but I thought the chances of being zapped by an android were pretty remote, so I opened the door. Just shows how wrong you can be.

I was in a large recording studio, walls and ceiling covered in acoustic tiling. Keyboards, drum machines and mikes filled most of the available space. At the far end of the room there was a wall of glass. Behind it, a man sat hunched over a series of control consoles, a cigarette hanging out of one corner of his mouth. I could actually feel in my chest and stomach the throbbing bass line that emerged from tall speakers. I walked down the studio and waved to catch his attention. Abruptly the music stopped and a deafening voice yelled over the intercom, "Get the fuck out of here! You blind, or what?"

I didn't know if he could hear me, but I spoke anyway. "I'm sorry to interrupt, but you have to come upstairs." I was beginning to wish I'd left this to Gloria.

"Look, sweetheart, it might have escaped your obviously limited intelligence, but I'm working. I don't stop on the say-so of anybody's bimbo, so just fuck off and find someone else to bug," he snarled back at me, stubbing out his cigarette and immediately lighting another.

"Please yourself," I said angrily. "The next interruption you'll get will be the cops. They don't like being pissed about by little boys with expensive toys when they're investigating a murder." I turned on my heel and marched off towards the door, feeling strangely satisfied with my childish response. Two steps later, I regretted it. I'd thrown away the chance of watching his reaction to my news. I turned back quickly and saw he'd stood up.

The resemblance to a chimp was overwhelming. The long arms, the jutting jaw, the flat nose all gave Micky Hampton a startlingly simian appearance. His blond-streaked hair had been carefully cut, but it couldn't altogether hide the Prince Charles ears. He'd have made a wonderful extra for *Planet of the Apes*. At least the make-up department wouldn't have had much work to do.

As I watched, he disappeared from my sight then emerged from a small door at the back of the studio. "Wait a minute," he said. "You'd better explain yourself. For a kick-off, who the hell are you?"

"I'm Kate Brannigan."

Understanding flooded his face. His soft brown eyes were unexpectedly intelligent. "You're the one who dug Moira up," he acknowledged. "What did you mean about a murder?"

"Moira's been killed. I'm sorry to be the bearer of bad tidings, but the police want to see everyone who was in the house tonight," I parroted.

Micky's eyebrows shot up. "They're wasting their time with me. A bomb could drop up there and I wouldn't know. I've worked in top-class studios the world over and I've never found one that was better soundproofed than this."

His concern for Moira was overwhelming. I hid my contempt and simply said, "Nevertheless, they want to see everyone. The blue drawing room," I added as I left him.

The hall had suddenly begun to resemble a police station. The scene-of-crime team had arrived with their cameras and fingerprint cases. Half a dozen uniformed constables were being directed to search the outside of the house and the grounds, to check for any signs of a break-in and to cover all exits. No one seemed to be paying any attention to me, so I slipped past them and crossed the hall. I headed down the corridor to Neil's domain. According to Gloria, he'd been given an office on the ground floor near the dining room.

I knocked on his door and heard him call, "Come in, open all hours." I closed the door behind me and leaned against it. The wood panelling obviously deadened any noise from outside. The small room looked remarkably like Richard's study. I wondered if journalists are born untidy or if they think the appearance of complete chaos is a necessary part of the image. Neil sat at the eye of the storm of paper, facing a computer screen, a small tape recorder beside him. He leaned back in his chair and grinned at me. "Kate! Glad you could find the time to pop in on a humble scribe. Sorted out your business with Jett?"

"I'm afraid this isn't just a social call," I said. "I've been asked to come and fetch you."

His hooded eyes half-closed as a guarded expression crossed his face. "Fetch me?" he queried. "Who wants me?"

"The police," I said.

I could see the muscles in his jaw clench. "What's all this about, Kate?" he forced out in a light tone.

"Bad news. Moira's dead."

His eyes opened wide in horror. "Oh no!" he exclaimed. "Moira? Dead? How? What happened? Has there been an accident?" His questions spilled out, the professional habit attaching itself to his obvious personal shock.

"No accident, I'm afraid. Look, Neil, you'd better get along to the blue drawing room. The police want to see everyone who was in the house. They'll be able to fill you in on the details."

"You mean, it happened here?"

"Why? Where did you think it had happened?"

"I don't know. She said something earlier about going down to the village to see someone. I suppose I assumed she was attacked on her way back or something. Oh God, poor Jett. He must be in a hell of a state." At last, someone had finally spared a thought for the boss. Neil jumped to his feet and pushed past me to the door. "The blue room, you said?" he demanded as he pulled it open.

"That's right," I replied as I followed him.

As I re-emerged in the hall, a plain clothes policeman pounced. "Kate Brannigan?" he demanded.

"That's me," I agreed.

"You didn't tell us you're a private investigator," he accused.

"No one asked me," I replied, unable to resist. I don't know why I get this urge to be a smartass round coppers.

"The inspector wants to see you right now," he told me, steering me down the hall into a smaller room next to the blue drawing room. It was wood panelled and stuffed with leather chairs. It looked like I've always imagined a gentlemen's club to be. A small writing desk had been moved away from the wall, and behind it sat a slim, dark-haired man in his mid thirties, his eyes indistinct behind a pair of glasses with tinted lenses. He was the last man in England wearing a pale blue shirt with white collar and cuffs under his dark blue suit. His striped tie was neatly knotted. He didn't look as if he'd been called out of bed in the middle of the night, but equally, he didn't look crumpled enough to have been on duty.

"I'm Inspector Cliff Jackson," he introduced himself. "And you must be our elusive private eye."

"Good morning, Inspector," I replied politely. "I'm Kate Brannigan, of Mortensen and Brannigan."

"I know exactly who you are, Miss Brannigan," he countered, a note of irritation in his gravelly Lancashire voice. "What I want to know is why you felt it necessary to go round interfering with witnesses."

"I haven't been interfering with anyone," I returned. "If you mean rounding up the inhabitants, I was simply doing what your sergeant asked."

"As you well know, he wouldn't have let you near one of them if he'd known the way you earn a living."

"Inspector, if anyone had bothered to ask what I do, I'd have been happy to tell them. Don't give me a bad time because one of your lads didn't do his job properly. I really don't want to fall out with you."

"That's the first sensible thing you've said so far," he grumbled as he made a note on his pad. We went through the formal routine that prefaces the taking of a statement, then he pushed his glasses up and massaged the bridge of his nose with surprisingly well-manicured fingers. "So, what were you doing here tonight?" he asked.

"It was a social call. We did a job for Jett some time ago, and he told me to drop in whenever I was passing. So I did." It sounded thin, even to me, but I could only hope he thought I was a bit starstruck.

"You were just passing at this time of night?" he challenged sarcastically, letting his glasses slip back into place. "You normally drop in on people this late?"

"Of course not," I countered. "But I knew Jett keeps late hours. I'd been working and I was wide awake, so rather than go home and bounce off the walls I thought I'd stop off for a coffee. Besides, it wasn't that late when I got here. It can't have been that much after midnight."

He clearly wasn't happy with the scenario, but he didn't have anything to contradict it yet, so he let it go for now. I outlined the version of events I'd agreed with Jett, hoping he'd remembered what he was supposed to say. I had plenty of time to think between sentences, since the detective who'd collared me was carefully writing it into a statement.

After we'd exhausted the subject of the discovery of the body, Jackson asked plenty of questions about the household and their movements, but I didn't have any answers. Frustrated, he gave up on that line and asked, "What was the nature of this job your firm did for Jett?"

I'd hoped we wouldn't get to that till I'd had a chance to discuss the matter with Bill. I took a deep breath and recited, "The nature of our business is confidential. I am afraid that is a private matter between Mortensen and Brannigan and our client."

Jackson pushed his glasses up and rubbed the bridge of his nose again. It looked like he had a sinus headache, and I began to feel the slight stirrings of sympathy. He wouldn't be getting much sleep over the next few days unless they got a very lucky break. However, my sympathy didn't override my professional ethics.

"You are withholding information that could be material to a murder inquiry," he sighed.

I was waiting with bated breath for him to say something, anything, that wasn't a cliché. I was destined for another disappointment.

"I don't have to tell you that it's an offence to obstruct the police. Frankly, I could do without the hassle of charging you, Miss Brannigan, but you make it very tempting."

"I could do without the hassle too, Inspector. If it's any help, the answer will be the same whether you charge me or not." I tried not to sound as defiant as I felt. A night in the cells would be both uncomfortable and bad for business.

"Get her out of my sight, Sergeant Bradley," Jackson said, getting to his feet. "Get her to sign her statement first," he continued as he crossed the room and left.

The sergeant proffered the sheets of my statement and I read through it quickly. It never ceases to amaze me that no matter what you actually say in a police statement, it always comes out in a strangulated officialese. In spite of the jargon, Sergeant Bradley appeared to have got the gist of what I'd said, so I signed dutifully.

I was escorted back to the hall, where Jackson was earnestly talking to the uniformed sergeant. When he saw me, he scowled and said, "Miss Brannigan's leaving now, sergeant. Get one of the lads to see her off the premises. And I mean right off." Then he turned to me and said, "I don't want you discussing the circumstances of this case with anyone. And I don't just mean the press. I mean you are not to talk to anyone about the method or timing of this incident. Is that understood?" I nodded. Then he added, "We'll let you know when we want to see you again. And keep your nose out. Leave this to the professionals."

I'd be only too happy to do just that, I thought as I drove down the drive. But somehow, I had the feeling Jett wasn't going to give me that option.

It was just after three a.m. when the electronic gates opened silently before me and I drove out into the lane, waving goodbye to the patrol car that had followed me down the drive. I slowed down as I approached Colcutt village, searching in the glove box for something more soothing than Tina Turner. As I hit the bend, a figure appeared in my headlights. It froze momentarily, then disappeared into the darkness of the verge.

I braked the car to a halt and jumped out. I ran back the few yards to where the figure had disappeared. There was no trace of anyone. The only sound to break the silence of the night was the soft mutter of my engine. I might have been dreaming, but I didn't think so. I had only seen Moira's lover once, but I'd have recognized Maggie Rossiter anywhere.

15

When people find out what I do for a living, they always ask if it's dangerous. They usually seem disappointed when I confess that the hardest thing to deal with is lack of sleep. I get very ratty if I'm kept away from my bed. I'd been asleep for a mere four hours after my run-in with Jackson when the phone rang insistently.

I picked up the phone. "Who is it?" I growled.

"Good morning to you, too," Shelley replied. "Bill wants to talk to you. Are you coming in or do you want to speak to him now?"

"Both," I replied. Bill's no stickler for regular office hours, and he knows me well enough to know that if I'm not in the office at nine there's a good reason. So for him to get Shelley to roust me out of bed, it had to be important.

"Kate," his voice boomed in my ear as Shelley connected us. "What's this you've been up to now?"

"How did you get to hear about it?" I asked wearily, climbing out of bed and heading for the kitchen.

"The news about Moira was on the radio this morning, and I got into the office to find a string of increasingly hysterical messages from Jett and a demand for a meeting from a pompous

asshole called Inspector Cliff Jackson. It didn't take a lot of working out," he reported.

"What did Jett want?"

"You, basically. A lot of moaning about why did you run
out on him when he needed you and instructions to get yourself
back over there asap. I think you'd better come in and brief me
on what's been going on before we decide whether we want to
have any further involvement. OK?" It was the nearest Bill was
ever going to get to a direct order.

Twenty minutes later, I was filling him in. When I got to
the bit about the story I'd concocted for the police about the
body's discovery, he shifted uneasily in his chair. "I don't think
that was one of your brightest moves, Kate," he complained.

"I know. But anything else made Jett look like the killer."

"And how do you know he wasn't?" Bill challenged me.

"I saw the state he was in. It wasn't the kind of reaction
I'd expect from a man who had just killed his so-called soul
mate. It was more like he couldn't believe it till someone else
had confirmed it. Besides, if I'd told the truth, Jett wouldn't
have been cluttering up our answering machine all night. He'd
be down the nick in an interrogation room." I knew it sounded
weak even as I told it, but the strength of my own gut feeling
about Jett's innocence didn't allow for compromise.

"I trust your instincts, Kate. But the cops sure as hell won't.
We'll have to make damn sure they don't find out the truth.
And I suppose that means you'll have to stay close to whatever's
going on," he added. He chewed his beard restlessly, a sure sign
that he's worried.

"At least Jett seems to want that," I tried. It wasn't much
of a consolation, but it was the only one I could see right then.

"Jett might, but I don't," Bill flashed back. "We don't do
murders, Kate. We do white-collar crime. We're not geared
up to compete with the police on something like this. Besides,
I'm not happy about putting you in the front line when there's
someone out there killing people."

"I can handle myself," I replied huffily.

"I know you can. It's the other poor fuckers I'm worried about," he said with a tired smile. "Seriously, though. I really wish you hadn't got us involved. But now we are, you'd better brief me fully."

I gave him a quick résumé of events, leaving out only my glimpse of Maggie. I don't know why I held that back; maybe I was worried about her being the obvious scapegoat, even to a supposedly new man like Bill.

"Jackson wanted to know the nature of the job we did for Jett," I finished up. "I hid behind client confidentiality."

"You did right. Leave Jackson to me. You'd better have a listen to Jett's messages then get yourself over to Colcutt."

It was after eleven when I drew up outside the electronic gates. Half a dozen cars were parked along the verge, and I recognized a couple of national newspaper reporters. The news of Moira's death had broken too late for that morning's editions, but they were determined to make up for lost time. As I pulled up to speak to the police constable, who looked cold and miserable in the thin drizzle of rain, car doors suddenly opened and the pack descended. Luckily, Jett had had the sense to tell the police I should be admitted. He'd also remembered to leave me the security code for the gate in one of his messages. I was halfway through the gates before the first journalist reached me. I put my foot down and left him shaking off the spray from my tyres.

At the house, another freezing copper let me in. There was no one in sight, but the constable on duty at the door of the rehearsal room grudgingly told me that Jett was in the kitchen. I found him there alone, slumped at an old pine farmhouse table, a mug of tea sitting in front of him. He barely glanced at me when I crossed the room to the kettle. I put it on to boil and picked up his mug. Nothing like making yourself at home. His untouched tea was stone cold, so I made us both fresh.

"You shouldn't have gone," he greeted me. "I wanted you here."

"I didn't have any choice," I explained patiently, like I would to Davy, Richard's five-year-old. "The cops bounced me as soon as they found out who I was."

Jett lifted his mug to his lips, but lowered it untasted. His skin had taken on a strange dullness, the colour of slate. His eyes were bloodshot, but not puffy with tears. "You liked her, didn't you?" he asked.

"Moira? I hardly knew her, but yes, I liked what I saw of her. She had courage, and a sense of humour," I replied.

He nodded, as if I'd confirmed something. "That's why I want you to find out who killed her. Somebody in this house, somebody I trusted, took her life away. You're going to find out who."

I felt like I'd stumbled on to the set of an episode of *Murder, She Wrote*. I took a deep breath and tried to bring the conversation down to earth. "Don't you think you should leave this to the police? They've got the manpower and the facilities to investigate murder, Jett. I haven't."

He warmed his hands on the mug. "You don't understand, Kate. This isn't going to be solved by fingerprints and alibis. This is going to be solved by understanding people. The Old Bill, they didn't know Moira. And they sure as hell don't understand any of us. The people in this house, we don't talk the same language as these cops. Not even Mr Respectable Kevin. But you're different. You live with Richard, you know this life. You can speak to them, make them open up like they won't to the Old Bill." It was a long speech for a man as close to the edge as Jett obviously was. He leaned back in his chair and squeezed his eyes shut.

"I don't know, Jett. I've never had to investigate a murder before."

His eyes opened abruptly and he stared at me, brows drawn down in a scowl. "Listen, Kate. To those cops, I'm just a piece of black shit. A rich piece, but still shit. Moira was just a junkie hooker to them. They'd love to pin this on me and walk away, because that would fit. I grew up in the Moss, I know how their minds work. I don't trust them and they sure as hell won't trust me. There's only you between me and the nick, Kate, and I need your help to stay out of it." His bottom lip thrust out defiantly.

I pushed my mug away and reached out for his hand. "OK, Jett. No promises, but I'll give it my best shot."

He clasped my hand in both of his. There were tears shining in his eyes. "That's good enough for me." A single tear trickled down his cheek and he brushed it away as impatiently as if it were a troublesome fly.

"What happened after I left?" I asked.

"They kept us all shut up together till gone four o'clock. Didn't leave us alone for a minute, though. They had a kid copper keeping his ears open. That guy Jackson, he told me to say nothing about how I found her, or anything else. They all wanted to know, though," he added bitterly.

"They'll be hoping they can trip up the killer," I explained. "You know, someone knowing more than they're supposed to." Amazing that the police still rely on that after they spent three years barking up the wrong tree on the Yorkshire Ripper investigation because of a hoax tape that revealed details only the killer should supposedly have known.

"What time is it?" he asked incongruously.

I glanced at my watch. "Five to twelve."

Jett got to his feet and swallowed most of his tea in a oner. "I told them all to be in the blue room at twelve. I knew you'd be here. You have an intuitive spirit. I knew you'd know I needed you."

I refrained from pointing out that it had more to do with the office answering machine than my psychic powers. "I'm going to have to talk to you about the last six weeks, Jett," I protested as he walked out of the room.

"You're going to have to talk to all of us about the last six weeks," he said over his shoulder as I followed him. "I just want them all to know they have to co-operate with you. They can be as bloody-minded as they like with the cops, but it's me that puts the bread in their mouths and they'll do what I tell them."

It was strange to see how quickly his natural authority had returned to him. I couldn't believe it was my agreeing to work for him that had done the trick. If he was capable of such mercurial mood shifts, maybe my initial assessment of his innocence had been way off-beam.

Jett threw open the drawing room door just on the stroke of twelve. They were all there except Neil. None of them looked as if they'd had much sleep. Equally, none of them looked like they'd shed too many tears.

As I entered behind Jett, Kevin groaned. "Oh God, Jett, I told you to leave her out of this. We don't need an extra nosy parker round here. The cops have already turned this place into a goldfish bowl."

"He's right, Jett," Gloria chipped in. "You need to come to terms with your grief. Having her around the place isn't going to help."

Jett threw himself into a spindly-legged chair. Miraculously, it withstood the impact. "I can't be doing any grieving while I know Moira's killer is under my roof, eating my food and drinking my booze. Kate's here to find out which one of you is my enemy. Any of you that doesn't want to be part of my team, you can go now. But you want to stick around, then you co-operate with Kate one hundred per cent. She'll be reporting directly to me, and I don't want her interfered with. Is that clear?"

Kevin cast his eyes up to heaven and muttered, "Give me strength!" I knew exactly how he felt. Melodrama was never my favourite art form. But it was Tamar who was right on the ball. She crossed the room and hugged him. "Whatever you need is all right by me, Jett." I tried not to vomit, but it was hard.

Before anyone else could chip in with their tuppence worth, Neil came in. "Sorry I'm late, Jett," he apologized. "I've been issuing full press statements to all the nationals, and it took longer than I thought."

"Enter stage left, the in-house vulture," Micky sneered.

"Somebody's got to handle them," Neil replied mildly. "Better that it's someone who can string two sentences together."

"Meaning what?" Micky demanded belligerently.

"My God, can't you two stop bickering for once? Have some respect for the dead," Tamar shouted. Her shameless hypocrisy left me gasping, but no one else seemed to notice. Micky mumbled an apology and walked over to the window to watch the rain falling.

"You on the payroll, then?" Neil asked me *sotto voce.* I nodded. He smiled conspiratorially. "Glad I'm not the only one making a shilling out of Moira's death."

I'd only been there an hour and already I was heartily sick of the lot of them. Some jobs should come stamped with a government health warning. Something like: "You lie down with dogs, you get up with fleas."

I decided it was time to start asking questions. But in the great tradition of the best-laid plans, I was thwarted by the arrival of Inspector Jackson and his merry men. Jackson marched in as if he'd taken a long lease on the place. He'd found time for a fresh suit and shirt, though the tie was the same. Maybe it held some Masonic significance I didn't recognize. Hot on his heels was an older man, who moved to Jackson's side and announced, "Good day, ladies and gentlemen. I am Detective Superintendent Ron Arbuthnot and I will be in overall charge of this inquiry. I know some of you have given my officers initial statements, but we will be requiring you for further interviews in the course of the day. Please arrange to keep yourselves available." The Royal Command having been delivered, Arbuthnot wheeled his tubby body round past Jackson and left us.

As soon as he'd gone, Jackson turned on me. "Have you got some kind of death wish, Brannigan?" he hissed as he took me by the arm and led me to the door. "I've already thrown you out of here once. Is business so bad you've got to come touting?"

"I was invited here," I told him through clenched teeth. "Get your hands off me. Now."

He reluctantly let me go, then opened the door and tried to usher me through it. I stood my ground. Jett called, "You OK, Kate? The lady's a friend, Inspector. I want her here."

Jackson turned to Jett and flashed an insincere smile. "I'm afraid that won't be possible, Mr Franklin. We have some questions for Miss Brannigan, and after that, we'll be needing to talk to you again. Perhaps it would be better if she came back tomorrow."

Jett glared at Jackson. I wasn't sure if that was on my account or because Jackson had used his real name. Jett doesn't like to be reminded of its patriotic overtones. Let's face it, which of us outside the Tory Cabinet would like to be saddled with Winston Gladstone Franklin?

"It's OK, Jett," I said reassuringly. "I'll come back tomorrow morning, OK?" There were things I wanted to do, and none of this lot were going anywhere. They would keep. Maggie Rossiter might not be so keen to talk if I waited till she'd got her emotions under control.

16

I was in the Colcutt Arms by half-past twelve. It turned out that the only questions Jackson had for me related to what I was doing back at the manor and what I'd done for Jett in the past, nudge nudge, wink wink. I didn't like his innuendoes, and suspected he was trying to needle me into an admission of some sort. Obviously, he'd got no more change out of Bill than he had out of me. At least he wasn't challenging my version of the discovery of the body yet.

It wasn't just relief that drove me to the local pub. I was after information. I spotted the members of Her Majesty's Gutter Press in the lounge bar, and gave it a body-swerve. What the saloon bar lacked in creature comforts it made up for by the complete absence of journos. If I was going to go into my chatty passing-motorist act, I didn't want an audience.

The harried barmaid who served me seemed as glad to escape from them as I was. She bustled through from the lounge when I pressed a bell on the bar and pushed a strand of bottle blonde hair from her forehead. She was in her forties, and looked shell-shocked to find herself in the throes of a lunchtime rush.

"Busy today," I said sympathetically as she poured me a Saint Clement's.

"You're not wrong," she replied. "Ice?" I nodded. "Last time we were this busy of a dinner time was Boxing Day."

"Bad business up the road," I remarked as I sipped my drink. She was happily leaning against the bar, relieved to escape the clod-hopping probings of the press. I hoped my questions fitted in the category of Great British Pub Gossip.

"That poor woman!" she exclaimed. "Do you know, she was in here last night with a friend of hers, sitting in a corner of my lounge bar! And next thing you know, she's murdered in her own home. You're not safe anywhere these days. You'd think with all the security they've got up there they'd be all right. I said to my Geoff, it's like Fort Knox up there, and they're not safe. Makes you wonder."

My ears pricked up at the news of Moira's meeting in the pub, but I didn't want to pounce too eagerly. "I sometimes wonder if it's all the security that attracts them," I responded, playing along with the Passing Vagabond theory. "You know, like a challenge or something."

"Well, all I can say is we've never had any trouble in this village till we had so-called rock stars living here." Her mouth pursed, revealing a nest of wrinkles she'd have been mortified to see in a mirror.

"Do they come in here much?" I asked casually.

"One or two of them. They've got a journalist living up there, writing some book about Jett, he's never out of here normally. I don't know when he gets his writing done. He's in here for a couple of hours most dinner times and he gets through half a dozen pints every session. Not that I'm complaining—I'm glad of the custom in the winter months. Sometimes I wonder why we bother opening up in the middle of the day. What we take across the bar hardly covers the electricity," she grumbled.

"Nice place, though," I complimented her. "Been here long?"

"Five years. My husband used to be a mining engineer, but we got tired of living abroad, so we bought this place. It's hard work, especially doing the bed and breakfast, but it's better than living with a load of foreigners," she replied. Before I could ask more, the bell from the lounge summoned her.

To ensure her return, I called, "Do you do food?"

"Just sandwiches."

I ordered a round of roast beef, and when she returned, I said, "It must have been a shock for you, one of your regulars getting murdered."

"Well, she wasn't exactly a regular. She's been in a few times the last couple of days when her friend was staying here. But she'd only been in the once before that, with a crowd of them. The only way I knew it was her was with her being black. Not that I'm racist," she added hastily. "It's just that we don't get many of them round here."

I could believe her. I remembered only too well how the police inspector in one of the nearby Cheshire towns had defended his policy of arresting any blacks he saw on the street by announcing, "None of them live around here so if they're walking our streets they're probably up to no good."

"Her friend must have been in a hell of a state when she heard the news," I tried, checking the gender of the friend. I was pretty sure it must have been Maggie, but it would be nice to make sure. I took a bite out of the sandwich. Even without the information about Moira's visit, the trip had been worthwhile. The bread was fresh and crusty, the meat pink, sliced wafer thin and piled thick, with a generous smear of horseradish. I nearly choked on it when I heard her reply.

"I don't even know if she has heard the news," the land-lady replied. "When I got up this morning, there was an envelope on the hall table with the money she owed and a note saying she'd had to leave early. I knew she was checking out today, but I didn't expect her to be off at the crack of dawn."

She sounded slightly aggrieved, as if she'd been done out of a good piece of drama.

"You mean she just cleared off in the middle of the night? Funny, that," I remarked, trying not to sound like a private eye who's one happy step ahead of the police.

"No, not the middle of the night. She didn't actually leave till about half-past six. Our bedroom's at the back, you see. The car woke me up, and I got up because I thought she might have gone off without paying. I didn't even know about the murder myself then." She clearly saw nothing suspicious in Maggie's behaviour, and I was grateful for that. There would be at least one suspect I'd get to before the police.

"Perhaps she had a phone call or something," I hazarded.

"Not while she was here," the landlady replied positively. "I'd have known. I think she probably just woke up early and decided to get an early start. To be honest, I was surprised she wasn't staying at the manor. Their friends don't usually put up here."

I could have come up with a couple of good reasons why Maggie Rossiter hadn't been willing to accept Jett's hospitality, but I wasn't about to share them. I finished my sandwich, exchanged a few routine complaints about the weather, and set off for Leeds.

It was still drizzling when I pulled up outside Maggie's terraced house. Crossing the Pennines hadn't worked its usual trick of transforming the weather. Through the drift of rain, the house looked miserable and unwelcoming. There were no lights on to combat the gloom. Mind you, if my lover was lying dead in a morgue somewhere, I don't think I'd feel like a hundred watt glare.

Maggie took her time answering the door. I'd just decided she wasn't home when the door opened. When she saw me, she started to close it again. I moved forward quickly enough to insinuate my shoulder in the gap.

"What the hell do you think you're playing at?" she demanded feebly, her voice cracked and shaky.

"We need to talk, Maggie," I said. "I know it's the last thing you feel like, but I think I can help."

"Help? You do resurrections?" Her voice was bitter, and tears shone in her red-rimmed eyes. My professional satisfaction at getting to her first withered in the face of her obvious grief.

"I'm trying to find out who killed Moira," I told her.

"What's the use? It's not going to bring her back, is it?" Maggie rubbed her eyes impatiently with her free hand, as if she hated showing me her humanity.

"No, it's not. But you've got to grieve. You know that. And finding out what happened is the first step in the process. Maggie, let me come in and talk to you."

Her straight shoulders seemed to sag and she stood back from the door. It opened straight on to her living room, and I sat down before she could change her mind. Behind me, Maggie closed the door firmly and went through to the kitchen. I could hear the sound of a kettle being filled. I took the chance to take stock of the room. It was large, occupying most of the ground floor of the house. One of the alcoves by the chimney breast held an assortment of books, from science fiction to sociology texts. The other held a small TV and a stereo system with a collection of tapes, CDs and LPs. The only decoration on the walls was a large reproduction of Klimt's Judith. The room contained two sofas and, in the bay, a small pine dining table with four chairs. It looked like home, but only one person's idea of it.

She came through with a pot of tea on a tray with two mugs, a bottle of milk and a bowl of sugar. "I've got this terrible thirst. I can't seem to stop drinking tea," she said absently as she poured. Her hair looked dishevelled, as did the sweatshirt and jeans she was wearing. The room was unbearably warm, the gas fire on full, yet Maggie shivered as she lifted her mug to her lips.

"I'm sorry," I said, knowing how hollow it would sound, but feeling the need nevertheless. "I hardly knew her, but I liked what I did know."

Maggie walked over to the window and stared out at the silent rain falling on the grey roofs. "Let's get one thing straight, Kate," she observed. "I am not going to discuss my feelings with you. I have friends for that. I'll tell you anything I can about what happened after she left with you that night, but our feelings for each other and the way I feel right now is nothing to do with you."

"That's fine by me," I said, feeling like I'd been reprieved. After Jett's histrionics, I didn't know how much more I could take.

She turned back into the room and sat on the other sofa, as far from me as it was possible to be. "I suppose Jett's hired you to discover I did it?" she challenged.

"I'm working for Jett, but he hasn't pointed the finger at anyone. I think he's still too upset to have given it much thought. It was him who found the body, you know."

"I didn't know," she sighed. "You should never have tried to find her. If Jett had let the past rest in peace, she'd still be here now."

I couldn't deny it. And I saw no point in trying to justify my own part in the process. "Suppose we go back to the beginning and work forward?" I asked. "What happened after I took her over to see Jett?"

Maggie sighed again. She pulled a small tin out of her pocket and with trembling fingers rolled a cigarette. "She rang the morning after. She said that she and Jett had had a long talk." A half-smile flickered across her lips as she went on. "She'd learned the hard way not to take any prisoners. She went in there with an agenda, and she wasn't prepared to make any compromises. She said she'd work with him on the songs for his new album, and if that worked out, then she'd consider future collaborations. But that was it. No going back to their old relationship. She wanted a room of her own, all the back royalties that were due to her, and a new deal for the new album. She wanted a percentage share of the profits as well as her songwriting royalties. After all, he'd be doing well out of it too." Maggie paused, looking to me for a response.

"It doesn't sound unreasonable to me. I'd guess that Jett could afford it," I agreed.

"Jett was over the moon, according to Moira. He said she'd have to work out the money details with Kevin, but it was fine by him. She was laughing, you know? She said he'd got into all this New Age stuff, and kept telling her they were soul mates and must be together. She'd told him that only extended to work and he could forget sex. Then he went all huffy and started on about spiritual love. She was very funny about it all." Memories overwhelmed Maggie suddenly and she looked away.

Awkwardly, I said, "I liked her sense of humour, too. Maggie, did she say anything about the reactions of the others at the manor to her arrival?"

Maggie relit her cigarette and took a deep drag. "Not then. But she had plenty to say later. Only Neil seemed really pleased that she was there. He seemed to think she'd be able to fill in any gaps from the early days. I know he talked to her about what it was like before Jett hit the big time. She said Gloria was always trying to bust up their conversations. She wanted to come across as the only significant person in Jett's life. Pathetic, really."

"Tamar hated her on sight, of course. Her and Jett have been having this on-off relationship for a few months now, and I guess she saw Moira as a threat. Moira couldn't stand her, thought she was just a stupid bimbo, and she told me she used to wind her up by flirting with Jett when Tamar was around. But there was nothing in it. She told me that, and I believe her. I trust . . ." she gulped. "I trusted her."

"What about Kevin? How did he take it?" I probed.

"She said he wasn't thrilled, but that she wasn't surprised because the idea of parting with any money, even if it's not his own, gives him a physical pain. She said if he gave you his shit for fertilizer he'd want the roses. And there was a lot of money coming to her. All those years of royalties from the first three albums."

"Did she get the money?" I suspected I knew the answer before I asked the question.

"Not yet. Kevin said it was tied up in some account where he had to wait three months before he could get access to it."

I'd been right. Moira had died before she'd cost anyone a penny. I wondered if anyone would ever be able to untangle things now she was dead. "Do you happen to know if she left a will?" I asked.

Maggie's mouth twisted into an ironic smile. "Jett tell you to ask that? Yes, she left a will. We both made wills in favour of each other about two months ago."

"Do you mind if I ask you why?"

"Because a friend of mine was killed in a car crash and she hadn't left a will. The house was in her name, and her family kicked her lover out on the street the day before the funeral. Gay couples don't have any rights. We have to make our own. That's why we made the wills. At that point, Moira didn't even think she had anything to leave," Maggie said bitterly.

But when she'd died, it had been a different picture. I knew I'd want to come back to this, but I needed to hear more from other people before I'd have any useful leverage. So I changed the subject. "Surely Micky was pleased? He must have been happy that they were all working together again, just like the good old days?"

"You'd have thought so, wouldn't you? But not according to Moira. She said he was always nit-picking. She thought he wanted to take all the credit for Jett's great comeback album—they hadn't worked together for the last four, you see."

"I'm beginning to wonder why she stuck it," I remarked.

"I wondered myself. But she really enjoyed the work she was doing with Jett. She loved the writing. And she was even doing some of the backing vocals. She kept telling me that when the money came rolling in, I could give up work and we'd go and live in the sun somewhere." Maggie's face crumpled and she pulled a soggy handkerchief out of her pocket. She blew her nose. "If she hadn't been doing it for us, maybe she'd never have been tempted to stay."

"Had you seen her much in the last few weeks?" I asked.

"Not really. She hasn't been home at all. We had a couple of weekends in a hotel in Manchester. Jett had gone to Paris with Tamar, and he'd given her some money and told her to show me a good time." Her eyes lit up, then the light died. "We had a good time, too," she said softly.

"Why did you go to Colcutt this week?" I asked.

She looked at me in surprise. "What do you mean?"

"I saw you. I was driving the car that nearly ran you over in the early hours of the morning. The landlady at the Colcutt Arms told me you'd been staying there. I just wondered, you know? With you two not having seen very much of each other lately." I let my words hang in the air. Maggie was no fool. She must have realized it would only be a matter of time before the police would be at her door.

"Now I see why you wanted to talk to me," she accused. "You really are trying to pin it on me."

I shook my head. "Maggie, I'm not trying to pin it on anybody. I'm trying to find Moira's killer."

"If that's true, you'd be better off back in Colcutt," she said angrily. "Someone there had it in for her. That's why I went over to see her, to try to persuade her to come home with me."

"What do you mean?" I asked. My antennae were quivering. I had the feeling we were really getting somewhere at last.

"Someone there wanted her dead. They'd already tried once."

17

I took a deep breath and said very slowly, "What do you mean, they'd already tried?"

"I don't know how much you know about heroin addiction," Maggie replied.

"Lay person's knowledge only. Assume I'm ignorant."

"OK. Coming off is hell. But once an addict is off, they often get a strange kind of confidence that one little hit wouldn't do any harm. Like the smoker who's been stopped for three years and fancies a fag at a party. Only with heroin addicts, that can be fatal a lot faster than with smokers. Anyway, someone at Colcutt Manor kept leaving a set of works in Moira's room. Every couple of days, she'd come upstairs to find a nice little hit sitting there waiting for her." Maggie stopped dead, her anger making her voice a growl.

"That is evil," I breathed.

"So now you see why I wanted her to leave. So far, she'd just flushed the smack down the loo and shoved the syringes in the bin. But sooner or later there was going to come a time when she'd be low, when she couldn't ring me up for reassurance, when she was going to go for it. I couldn't stand the thought of it."

I swallowed hard. Now for the nasty question. "So why did you leave when you did? In the middle of the night like that?"

Maggie rolled another cigarette while she pondered my question. I couldn't help feeling she was using me as the rehearsal for the harder interrogation she knew was on the horizon. "We'd had a drink together that evening in the pub. Moira promised me that her work would be over in another two weeks and then we'd go on holiday together. She said she could hold out, and begged me not to make her choose. I gave in, God help me."

"Afterwards, we went up to my room and made love. She left about eleven, saying she was going back to work with Jett. I tried to sleep, but I couldn't. I know it sounds pathetic, but I had a dreadful feeling in the pit of my stomach that something terrible was going to happen. Eventually, I got up and went for a walk. Then I saw all those police cars up at the manor and I panicked. Whatever was going on, I knew I would only be in Moira's way if I turned up on the doorstep, so I went back to the pub. That's when you nearly ran me over." Maggie lit her cigarette and ran a hand through her greying curls.

"I tried to ring from the phone in the pub, but it was constantly engaged. I didn't know what else to do, so I set off for home. Moira knew I was coming home today, and I knew she'd call me as soon as she could. The first I knew she was dead was when I heard the news on Radio One at half-past nine." She couldn't hold the tears back any longer, and they streamed down her face. Her shoulders shook.

I got up and tentatively put a hand on her arm, but she shook me off and huddled into a ball. Feeling helpless, I retreated to the sofa. While I waited for her to compose herself, I thought about what I'd heard. It sounded incredibly thin to me. I couldn't imagine any circumstances in which I'd behave as Maggie had done unless I was running from something. But equally, I couldn't see why she'd have killed Moira if she was telling the truth about their relationship.

After a few minutes, Maggie managed to find the strength from somewhere to dry her tears, clear her throat and look me in the eye. "I didn't kill her. I'd have cheerfully killed the bastard who was trying to destroy her with the smack, but not Moira. Never Moira."

Her denial was vehement. But I've heard good performances before. I didn't have enough information to try to get beyond that right now, but if I uncovered it, I'd be back. This was one case where I couldn't let sentiment get in the way. "I believe you," I said, almost convinced. "Is there anything else, however trivial, that Moira said that might shed some light on what happened?"

Maggie got up and poured herself another mug of tea. She leaned against the table, eyebrows twisted in concentration. "There was one thing," she said uncertainly.

"Yes?" I asked expectantly.

"It's probably nothing, but last night in the pub, she asked me about one of the guys she used to know in Bradford. A bloke called Fat Freddy. She wanted me to ask around and see what he was into just now that might be connected to Jett in some way," Maggie said hesitantly.

"Did she say why?"

Maggie shrugged. "To be honest, I wasn't paying a lot of attention. She said something like, she'd seen him talking to someone from the manor who shouldn't be mixing with small-time villains like Fat Freddy."

The whiff of red herring was getting pretty strong. If I'd been trying to divert suspicion away from myself, that was exactly the kind of unprovable line I'd come up with.

"Did she say who it was she'd seen with this Fat Freddy?" I asked cautiously.

Maggie shook her head. "I'm sorry, she didn't. She said she wanted to find out what the connection was before she said anything more."

I felt frustrated. Why couldn't Maggie have shown a bit more interest in something other than her own relationship with Moira? Had she no natural curiosity? If I'd dropped something like that on Richard, he'd have been on it like a rat up a drain, demanding chapter and verse on everything I'd seen and heard. "What do you know about Fat Freddy?" I asked without much hope.

"He's a bit of a wide-boy. Moira knew him from when she was working in Bradford. She told me he was into buying and selling—whatever came along. I met him once. Moira bought a couple of jogging suits from him."

"Would you know where to find him?"

Maggie pulled a face. "Not really. Why? Do you think it might be important?"

"Yes, I do. I don't know how yet, but it could be."

"OK. I'll see if I can find out what he's up to and get in touch with you. It's what Moira asked me to do."

I tried not to show my surprise at her co-operation, and fished a card out of my wallet. I wrote my home number on the back. "If you remember anything more or come up with something on Fat Freddy, give me a call any time, day or night." I got to my feet. "Thanks for being so helpful. I know it can't have been easy."

"Believe me, the worst is yet to come. And I'm not talking about the police." Maggie's face had frozen into a cold mask. "There's no framework for grief when you're gay."

"I'm sorry," I said inadequately.

"Spare me the bleeding-heart liberal shit," Maggie flashed back, suddenly angry. "Just leave me alone."

It wasn't hard to do exactly as she asked.

I spent what was left of the afternoon back at the office. I'd recorded my notes on tape on the way back from Leeds, so I didn't even have that to keep me occupied. I hate those spells in an investigation where everything is stalled. I didn't want to go back to the manor for another confrontation with Jackson. I'd rather wait till tomorrow, when the police presence would have eased off, and the initial shock would have worn off for the inhabitants.

So I did the paperwork on the Smart brothers that had been hanging over me for the last couple of weeks since our clients had passed our dossier on to the police. I was providing them with more details on my surveillance, so they'd be fully prepared for the raid they were planning for some unspecified date in the future when they got their act together. I ploughed through my diary for the relevant weeks, and there, in the middle of it all, I found the notes of my search for Moira. I couldn't help agreeing with Maggie that it was a pity I'd ever found her. Bill had been right. Missing persons' jobs produce more trouble than they're worth.

Before I left the office, I helped myself to a couple of Raymond Chandlers and a Dashiell Hammett from Bill's bookcase. I was going to need all the help I could get, and somehow I had the feeling that wandering down to Waterstone's for a book on how to solve a murder wasn't going to be a lot of use.

I got home just after six. For once, my heart sank when I saw Richard's car outside the house. I wasn't looking forward to telling him about the secrets I'd been keeping. But I couldn't hide my involvement in the murder investigation, not without moving out while it went on. There would be too many incoming phone calls and answering-machine messages from people connected to the case.

I decided to get it over with as quickly as possible, so I poured myself a drink and crossed the conservatory. Halfway across, Jett's first album hit me right between the ears. Richard's living room was empty, so I followed the music down to his study. He was so absorbed in the screen of his word processor that he didn't hear me enter.

Over his shoulder, I read, "Moira got her second chance at the dream ticket just six weeks ago when she turned up at Jett's luxury mansion, a world away from the mean streets where they started off." I don't know, even the journalists I trust can't get their facts right.

I tapped him gently on the shoulder and he glanced up at me with a distracted smile. "Hiya, Brannigan."

I leaned over and kissed him. "Busy?"

"Ten minutes. You hear about Moira Pollock?" I nodded. "I'm doing a piece for the *Sunday Tribune*—you know, wringing their withers, lots of colour, plenty of topspin. Be right with you."

I left him to it. True to his word, ten minutes later he joined me in the conservatory, where I was watching the rain on the glass making rivers against the darkness. Richard threw himself into a basket chair and popped the top of a Michelob Dry.

"I have a confession to make," I announced.

Richard's eyebrows rose and he gave me his cute smile. "You wore the same clothes two days running? You forgot to hoover the lounge before you went out this morning? You ate a yoghurt that was two days past its sell-by date?"

I don't know who told him he was funny. It certainly wasn't me. "This is serious," I explained.

"Oh, shit! You left a ring round the bath!" he teased.

Sometimes I wish I lived with a grown-up.

"Moira Pollock didn't just turn up on Jett's doorstep out of the blue," I announced bluntly. It was the only way to get his attention.

"How d'you know that?" he demanded, suddenly serious now his professional world was involved.

"Because it was me who drove her there."

I had the momentary satisfaction of seeing his jaw drop. "You what?" he exclaimed.

"I'm sorry. I couldn't tell you about it at the time. Jett swore me to secrecy, with particular reference to you. He hired us to find Moira for him. So I did. And now he's hired me to find Moira's killer."

I'd dropped my bombshell, and it seemed to have left Richard momentarily speechless. He just stared at me, mouth open like a drunken actor who's forgotten his lines. Eventually, he closed his mouth, swallowed hard and said, "You're at the wind-up."

"Never been more serious."

He looked at me suspiciously. "So how come you're telling me now? How come client confidentiality goes out the window at this precise moment?"

"Because when murder's on the agenda, I'm entitled to grab all the extra help I can get," I explained.

"Shee-it," he drawled. Then the journalist in him jumped out like a jack-in-the-box. "That's great. You'll be able to give me the inside track on the story."

I shook my head wonderingly. "That's not the idea, Richard. We'll happily pay you a consultancy fee, but I don't let the cat out of the bag for anyone except my client. And besides, whatever I could give you would be old hat anyway. Your old mate Neil Webster is sitting there in Colcutt Manor, feeding the world what it wants to hear, straight from the horses' mouths."

He covered his disappointment with a wry grin. "Anybody should have been murdered up there, it should have been that piece of shit," he complained. "OK, Brannigan. You got it. Any help I can give you, it's yours. So why don't you take me right back to the beginning and tell me how you tracked Moira down. Surely you can at least give me that teensy weensy exclusive?"

I grinned back at him. One day I'm going to learn how to put up a resistance to his charms. With any luck, it's a long way off.

18

There was still a policeman at the gates of Colcutt Manor when I arrived the following morning. But half-past ten was too early for the press, who, judging by the number of cars in the pub car park, had invaded the guest rooms of the Colcutt Arms and were still sleeping off their expense account excesses.

It was also too early for the household. Now the bulk of the police had left, life was slowly returning to normal. The kitchen was empty, as was the blue drawing room, the television room, the dining room, the billiard room and Neil's office. I was beginning to feel like a National Trust curator on a rainy Wednesday as I trudged back to the hall. This time, one of the crew of the Marie Celeste had appeared.

Gloria was just walking out of her office when she heard my heels clattering on the terrazzo tiles and turned sharply round. "Oh, it's you," she said with her usual grace and charm. She ignored me and carried on walking, closing the door behind her.

Undaunted, I followed her down the hall to the rear porch. As she pulled on a tan leather blouson, she eyed me warily, and I returned the compliment. I know that white is the colour of mourning in oriental cultures, but I've never encountered the civilization where they show their feelings for the departed in coral and cream jogging suits. I guess Valkyries do things differently.

"I'm busy," she informed me, opening the back door and heading for the stable block.

"Must be a lot to do," I said. "Organizing the funeral and all."

She had the good grace to blush, a reaction that strangely did nothing for her English Rose colouring. She zapped the up-and-over garage door with the little black box on her keyring and the door slid quietly open.

"That's being arranged by Moira's mother. We decided Jett was in no fit state to cope with it," she informed me.

And Ms Pollock indubitably will be, I thought, but didn't say. There was already enough animosity between us. "In that case," I insisted, following her to the driver's door of a Volkswagen Golf, "I'm sure you can find a few minutes of your time to answer a few questions." She climbed in the car, ignoring me, and started the engine. I had to jump back to avoid her rear wheels amputating my toes.

"Bitch," I yelled as the GTi shot out of the garage, leaving me gagging on her exhaust fumes. I hesitated for a moment, then my anger got the better of me. I raced back to the house, clattered down the hall and jumped behind the wheel of my Nova. I hit the drive at fifty, and reached the gates in time to see Gloria turn right.

By the time I got through the gates, she was out of sight. I put my foot to the floor and screamed down the winding lane, standing on my brakes like a boy racer. I prayed she hadn't taken one of the narrow lanes that turned off at irregular intervals. I was nearly at the main road when I caught a glimpse of her across the angle of a field. She was heading for Wilmslow.

"Gotcha," I yelled triumphantly as I shot across the oncoming traffic to make a right turn and get on her tail. I assumed she didn't know my car, but hung back a little just in case.

She seemed to know where she was going, moving between lanes with no hesitation. Just before she hit the town centre, she suddenly swung left without indicating, leaving me to make a hair-raising manoeuvre, cutting up a coach who was really too big to argue with. I found myself in a narrow street of terraced houses. I drove down as fast as I dared, slowing at the junctions to check she hadn't turned off. I was almost at the end when she headed back down the street, well in excess of the speed limit. I had to swerve to avoid her.

She clearly wasn't afraid to let me know she'd spotted me. I wrenched the wheel round in a tight turn, hitting the pavement as I went. Another thousand miles off the tyres. I screeched back after her, reaching the junction in time to see her continue on her way to Wilmslow. I sat at the corner long enough to see her turn right down the side of Sainsbury's. I followed, and found a space in the car park near the back entrance to the supermarket. I was afraid I'd lost her, but I picked her up by the Pay and Display ticket machine and got back on her tail.

I felt like a complete moron when she walked into Sainsbury's and helped herself to a trolley. I tried to console myself that she'd spotted me and was trying to throw me off the scent again, but by the time she'd reached the breakfast cereals and her trolley was almost full, I had to concede I'd overreacted. I strolled alongside as she grabbed a packet of Weetabix.

"I said I wanted you to answer a few questions," I remarked casually. She nearly jumped out of her skin, so I added, "Just like Jett invited you to yesterday."

She was torn between the desire to piss me off in good style, and the sure and certain knowledge that if she did, I'd go straight to Jett, reporting on the merry dance she'd just led me. Her adulation of the boss won. "You've got till the check out," she said, trying to sound tough and almost succeeding.

"It may take longer than that, but I'll be as quick as I can," I replied calmly. "Where were you between eleven and two the night before last?"

"I've already told the police all this," she complained, moving ahead down the aisle.

"I'm sure you have. So it should all be clear in your mind."

Gloria's blue eyes narrowed in a glare. If looks could kill, the corn-fed chicken would have been well past its sell-by date. "I was in the TV room watching *The Late Show* on BBC2 till quarter to midnight. Then I came into the office to check the answering machine. There were no messages, so I went straight up to bed. I was reading till the sound of the intercom disturbed me."

"You got there very quickly," I commented.

"My bedroom is right at the top of the stairs," she replied defensively.

"I thought you'd have a TV in your room," I said.

"I do. But it doesn't have stereo speakers and there was a band performing that I wanted to listen to. And before you ask, I didn't see anyone except Kevin. He came into the TV room and watched the band with me, then he left. Now, if that's all, I've got stuff to do."

I shook my head. "It's a long way short of being all, Gloria. Why did you hate Moira so much?"

"I didn't hate her," she blurted out. The woman standing next to her having the mental washing-powder debate was so riveted she began to follow us before she was withered by Gloria's hard stare and her muttered, "Do you *mind*?"

A few feet further on, she said, "I just didn't like the effect she had on everyone. We were all happy here together before she arrived. Since she got here, everyone's been bickering. And whatever anyone else says, she made Jett edgy with her constant demands. Everything had to be just the way she wanted it."

"So you're not exactly sorry she's dead?"

Gloria banged her fabric conditioner on the side of the trolley. "That's not what I said!" she flared. "Just because I didn't think she was good for Jett doesn't mean I'm not upset about the way she died. I know you don't like me, Miss Brannigan, but don't think you can pick on me!"

I felt a pang of sympathy for her then. She was too young to be setting herself up as the devoted handmaiden to the great man. She should have been out there enjoying life, not stuck with a bunch of piranhas who fed off each other's emotions and talents. I mean, for God's sake, who sends a qualified secretary round the supermarket these days? Apart from anything else, it would be cheaper to hire a woman from the village.

"How long have you been with Jett?" I asked, hoping to defuse her anger.

"Three years and five months," she replied, unable to keep a note of pride out of her voice. "I was working at his record company, and I heard he needed a secretary. Of course, the job has grown a lot since I took over. Now I organize his schedule completely."

This time my sympathy was all for Jett. Again, I switched the subject, hoping to catch her off guard. "When I told you about Moira, you seemed convinced that she was doing drugs. Why did you think that?"

Gloria refused to meet my eyes. "Everyone knew she'd been a drug addict," she mumbled. "It was the obvious conclusion. We all knew she'd be back on the drugs again as soon as she got half a chance."

"And did you help to give her that half a chance?" I demanded, leaning over Gloria to study the assorted nuts, so close I could smell her fresh lemony perfume.

"No!" she cried desperately.

"Somebody did, Gloria," I insisted.

"Well, it wasn't me. You've got to believe me," she pleaded. "If she was doing drugs, she was doing it of her own free will. Why else would she steal my syringes?"

19

I just stood staring at Gloria, who looked back at me with a mixture of triumph and defiance in her eyes. "What do you mean?" I finally gasped.

"Somebody has been stealing my syringes over the last four weeks or so," she said.

"What syringes?" I almost howled in my frustration. The snacks section had never seen drama like this.

"I'm a diabetic. I have to inject myself with insulin. I keep a supply of disposable syringes in my room. On three or four occasions, I've noticed that there were a couple missing. I have to keep a close eye on them, because I daren't run out."

I took a deep breath. "So why did you assume that Moira was responsible?"

She shrugged. The shopping was forgotten now. We'd gravitated to the end of the aisle, and neither of us was showing any inclination to hit the soft drinks.

Gloria dropped her voice and said, "Well, who else would want needles except a drug addict? And in spite of what you might think about the rock business, nobody in the house is a junkie. Jett just wouldn't stand for it. He's got very strict views on the subject. I know some of the others sneak away and do some

coke, but none of them are stupid enough to get into heroin.
Especially after what happened when Moira got hooked."

"Any other reason why you were sure it was Moira?" I
asked.

"Well, for one thing, they'd never gone missing before she
moved in. Then one day I came upstairs and caught her with
her hand on my doorknob. She said she'd just knocked to see if
she could borrow a book, but I wasn't falling for that. I knew
by then what she was after."

"And did she borrow a book?"

"Yes," Gloria acknowledged reluctantly. "The new Judith
Krantz."

"Was she in the habit of borrowing books from you?"

Gloria shrugged. "She'd done it a couple of times."

"And did she know you were a diabetic?" I asked.

"There's no secret about it. She never actually discussed it
with me, if that's what you're getting at."

The next question was obvious, though I knew she wouldn't
like it. That was just tough luck. "Who else comes into your
room either regularly or occasionally?" I demanded.

I was right. "Just what are you trying to suggest?" Gloria
flashed back, outraged.

"I'm not trying to suggest anything. I asked a straightforward question, and I'd appreciate a straightforward answer."

Gloria pointedly turned away from my stare. "No one uses
my room except me," she mumbled. "Moira was the only person
apart from the cleaner who's been in there."

I took pity on her. I couldn't see being madly in love with
Jett as an emotionally rewarding pastime, and I didn't want to
rub in the fruitlessness of her passion. "Given that it wasn't a
drug overdose that killed her, have you any ideas about who
might have wanted rid of Moira?"

"How should I know?" Gloria snapped.

"I would have thought there was no one better placed to
have a few theories," I replied. "You're right at the nerve centre

of the household. You're in Jett's confidence. I can't imagine there's much goes on around here that you don't know about." When in doubt, flatter.

Gloria rose to the bait. "If I had to choose one person, I'd pick Tamar," she bitched right back at me. "If Jett wasn't such a nice guy, she'd have been out of here weeks ago. They've been rowing for ages, and when Moira arrived, Tamar's nose was put right out of joint. Jett needs a woman who understands him, who really appreciates how demanding his work is. But Tamar just wants to have a good time, and Jett's just the means to that end for her. When Moira turned up, he saw how many of his needs weren't being met by Tamar, and it was obvious he didn't have much time for her any more. And now Moira's dead, Tamar's been all over him, trying to get back in his good books."

It was a long speech for Gloria, and her efforts to make it sound objective rather than vitriolic would have been funny under any other circumstances. I nodded sagely, and said, "I see what you mean. But do you really think she's capable of a crime of violence like that?"

"She's capable of anything," Gloria retorted. "She saw her position under threat, and I think she acted on the spur of the moment to protect herself."

"What about the others? Micky? Kevin?" I inquired.

"Kevin wasn't thrilled that she was back. He was worried about the press getting hold of the details of her past and using that to smear Jett. And she was always chasing him about money, as if he was trying to do her out of her share, which is just ridiculous. I mean, if Kevin was dishonest, Jett would have found out and got rid of him years ago. He had nothing to fear from Moira's silly allegations, so why would he kill her? All her murder's achieved is to stir up the very stuff he wanted kept quiet," Gloria informed me.

"And Micky?"

"You wouldn't be very thrilled if someone who had been out of the business for years came along and started telling you how to do your job, would you? She was very pushy, you know. She had her own ideas and God help anyone who didn't go along with them. I felt really sorry for Micky. She was always pushing Jett into taking her side over the album, and he was so scared that she'd take off again that he went along with her. But Micky wouldn't have killed her. I mean, she might have been driving him demented, but she couldn't do his career any damage," Gloria stated. She pointedly made for the check-out queue. In her eyes, she'd clearly decided she'd told me all I was going to get.

I cut round in front of her, making her brake sharply. "One last question," I promised. "You said cocaine was the drug of choice around Colcutt. Who uses it?"

"It's not my place to say," she replied huffily, her eyes on the display of cookery books beside us.

"If you don't tell me, someone else will. And if no one else will, I'll just have to go to Jett," I retaliated, fed up with fencing.

Gloria gave me a look that should have reduced me to a smouldering heap of ashes. Clearly she thought threats were as pleasant a form of communication as I did. "Ask Micky about it," she finally offered.

"I'll do just that," I replied. "Thanks for your help, Gloria. I'll mention to Jett how co-operative you've been." I smiled sweetly and walked away. If I were a store detective, I'd never have let me out of there without a body search. There can't be that many complete weirdos walking around looking like they're rehearsing scenes from *Inspector Morse* in Sainsbury's in a nice *Country Life* town like Wilmslow.

Back in the car park, I found that an officious traffic warden had decided to make my day. Peeling off the ticket, I crumpled it into a ball and tossed it on the floor of the car. Clearly Richard's disgusting motoring habits were beginning to rub off on me. Grumbling quietly in a highly satisfactory sort of way, I eased the car into the traffic and headed back towards Colcutt.

I was stopped at the lights when I spotted Kevin. He was coming out of the bank, and I nearly peeped the horn to let

him know I was there. Luckily, my reflexes were a little slow
that morning. He was joined immediately by a burly guy in a
padded leather body warmer over a navy blue rugby shirt. His
Levi's were tight enough to show he wasn't wearing boxer shorts.
I grabbed my tape recorder, depressed the record button and
said, "White male, mid-forties, straight grey hair, thinning on
top, neatly cut. Wide mouth, plump cheeks and chin, beer gut."
The lights changed and I had to go with the flow. What I did
see as I drove off, apart from the bulky gold flash of a Rolex on
Kevin's pal's wrist, was the thick manila envelope that changed
hands on the steps of the bank. I could think of a dozen reasons
why Kevin should be paying someone off in cash. At least half
of them made me feel very uncomfortable indeed.

I swung the car right into a narrow side street and doubled
back towards the lights. At the junction, I paused, eyes flicking
from side to side, trying to spot Kevin's contact. I caught sight of
him as he rounded the arcade of shops opposite, heading for the
leisure centre car park. An impatient driver behind me sounded
his horn, so I committed myself to a left turn, then turned off for
the leisure centre. I reversed the car into a side turn and waited.
I'd made the right gamble, not keeping my quarry in sight every
inch of the way. A couple of minutes later, a red XJS shot past
my turning. The driver was unmistakably Kevin's contact. I
waited till he'd moved out into the traffic heading back towards
Manchester, then I slipped out behind him and took up station
a couple of cars behind.

The guy was the worst kind of driver to tail. He was a
show-off determined that everyone sharing the same bit of road
as him would see he was a big man with a flashy Jag. Never
mind that it was four years old, it was the real thing, not some
souped-up piece of Jap crap. I could just hear him laying down
the law in the wine bar. I reckoned he and Kevin were probably
a pair out of the same box.

He drove like a man with serious sexual problems, cutting
people up, overtaking in the craziest places, flashing his lights like

the Blackpool illuminations. Interestingly, I drove no differently from normal, and I was never in any danger of losing him. As we shot through the lights on the dual carriageway at Cheadle, he made a kamikaze run across three lanes of traffic to hit the motorway intersection. I said one of those words that men like my dad think women shouldn't know and followed, praying he wasn't keeping too close an eye on his rear-view mirror.

Out on the motorway he let rip. He either wasn't a local or he didn't give a toss about the video cameras mounted every couple of miles along the motorway to catch the speeders. I was forced into the kind of driving that terrifies me, never mind the rest of the drivers on the road, zooming right up behind lorries, nipping into the outside lane to overtake, then cutting back in as soon as I was clear of their front bumper. It made for an interesting journey.

Then the volume of traffic built up and things got a little less traumatic. By the time we were heading east on the M62, I had stopped sweating and started breathing again. I slid Sinead O'Connor into the cassette deck and had a little wonder to myself about my friend in the XJS with the envelope full of readies. He looked definitely iffy to me, but not the sort of bad lad who carries out hits. On the other hand, he might well know a man who could . . . As we headed up Hartshead Moor, I checked my fuel gauge and started sweating again. I'd be OK if Bradford was the destination. I might just make Leeds. But if we were heading for Wakefield or Hull, I'd be making the acquaintance of roadside assistance.

For once, my luck was holding well. He repeated his suicide run across the lanes again to take the Bradford exit. But this time I was prepared, hiding in the inside lane. I stayed with him in the heavy traffic round the ring road, skirting the city centre and out towards Bingley. Then I lost him. He jumped an amber as it turned red and shot off, leaving me law abiding at the lights. I watched helplessly as he hung a right about half a mile ahead. Of course, by the time I made it to that corner, he was long gone. I drove back to the nearest petrol station in a seriously bad mood and filled up.

I signalled to turn back in the direction of the motorway, then I changed my mind. What the hell was I playing at? I'd schlepped all the way over the Pennines, taken more risks behind the wheel in one morning than I normally handle in a week, and I was even thinking about leaving it at that? I swear to God, two days in the world of sax 'n' drugs 'n' rock 'n' roll and my brain was getting as soft as theirs.

I went straight back to the street corner where I'd lost him and started the slow cruise. Within a few yards of the main road, I was in the kind of tangle of narrow streets where the wide-boys operate. Terraced houses, small warehouses, the odd little sweatshop factory, corner grocers converted into auto spares shops, lock-up garages filled with everything except cars. It was the kind of district I'd become familiar with recently, thanks to the Smart brothers. I didn't need a map to have a pretty clear idea of how the streets would be laid out, and I carefully started to quarter them, eyes peeled for the scarlet Jag.

As it was, I nearly missed it. I was taking it slowly when I caught a flash of red on the edge of my peripheral vision. I'd overshot the narrow alley before it registered properly. I parked up and strolled back along the street. On the corner of the alley, I stopped and glanced down. The Jag blocked the whole alley-way, barely leaving enough room for someone to sidle past it. It was parked outside the back entrance to a two-storey building. I counted from the end of the alleyway down to it, then walked on to the next corner.

The building had once been a double-fronted shop. Now, the windows were whitewashed over, and the signboards over them were weathered illegible. A transit van with its doors open was parked outside. I turned the corner and continued my leisurely stroll. Before I drew level, the door opened and a youth waddled uncomfortably in the general direction of the van. He couldn't actually see it since he was struggling to balance four cardboard cartons stacked on top of each other. "Left a bit," I suggested.

He threw a grateful half-smile at me, sidestepped and swivelled on one heel. The top box started to slide, and I moved forward to grab it as it fell.

"Cheers, love," he gasped as he leaned forward to tip the boxes into the van. He stepped back, hands on hips, head dropping forward.

"What you got in there anyway? Bricks?" I said as I stowed the other box for him.

He looked up at me and gave me the once over. "Designer gear, love. Top-class stuff. None of your market stall rubbish. Hang on a minute, I'll get you a sample. Just a little thank you." He winked and headed back to the door. I followed him and stood in the doorway. To my right, cardboard boxes were stacked ceiling high. Beyond them, a couple of women stood at long tables, folding shell suits, putting them in plastic bags and filling more boxes with the bags.

On my left, two machines clattered. The further one seemed to be printing t-shirts, while the other was embroidering shell suits. Before I could get a closer look, the van driver drew everyone's attention to me. "Oy, Freddy," he shouted.

From a small office at the back of the warehouse, my quarry emerged. "Do what, Dazza?" he asked in a deep voice, the cockney revealing itself even in those couple of words.

"T-shirt for the lady," Dazza said, waving an arm at me. "Saved my stock from the gutter."

"Pity she couldn't do the same for you," Freddy grunted. He gave me an appraising look, then picked out a white t-shirt from a pile on a trestle table by his cubbyhole. He threw it at Dazza, then turned on his heel and pulled his flimsy door shut behind him.

"I see he's been to the Mike Tyson school of charm and diplomacy," I remarked as Dazza returned.

"Don't pay no never mind to Fat Freddy," he said. "He don't take to strangers. Here you are, love."

I reached out for the t-shirt. I picked it up by the neck and let the folds drop out. His face gazed moodily into mine. Across the chest, in vivid electric blue was the *Midnight Stranger* logo, straight from the last album and the tour promotional posters. Jett was alive and well and being ripped off in Bradford.

20

I sat in the car and stared at the t-shirt. I wasn't quite sure what it amounted to. If Kevin was responsible for official merchandising, there was no reason why he shouldn't farm it out to Fat Freddy, even if some of the guy's other business was well on the wrong side of the legal borderline. What I needed to find out was whether this particular t-shirt was the real thing.

I also owed Maggie the courtesy of letting her know I didn't need her to do my legwork any longer. I thought of phoning, but decided against it. Face to face, there was always a chance that she'd come across with some more information, and her house was only a twenty-minute drive away.

The house looked much the same, except that a sheaf of cream and red tulips had suddenly bloomed by the front door. For some reason, it made me think of Moira, something I'd been determinedly avoiding. I didn't think I could get through this job if I allowed myself to dwell on my own anger and the guilty fear that I'd delivered her to her killer. The vivid memory of her singing "Private Dancer" filled my head. The grip of her voice on my mind didn't make it any easier to walk up the path to face her lover.

I rang the bell and waited. Then I knocked and waited. Then I peered through the letter box. No lights, no sign of life.

I thought about writing a note and decided to try the neighbours instead. Next door there was someone home. I could
hear the operatic screeching five feet from the door. I had no
confidence that whoever was inside would hear the doorbell
above the earsplitting soprano that was going through my head
like cheesewire.

Abruptly the music stopped, though the ringing in my ears
continued. The door opened to reveal the twinkling blue eyes
of the neighbour I'd encountered before. He frowned at me, in
spite of my smile.

"Hi," I said. "It's Gavin, isn't it?" I amaze myself sometimes.

He nodded, and the frown deepened into a scowl. "You're
the private eye," he said. It wasn't a question. Obviously the
jungle drums had been busy after my first visit.

There didn't seem a lot of point in getting into a debate
about it. "That's right. I'm looking for Maggie. I just wondered
if you happened to know when she'll be back."

"You're too late," he said.

"I'm sorry?"

"The cops took her off about two hours ago. They let
her come round and tell me, so I could feed the cat if she's not
back. But the policewoman who was with her didn't make any
reassuring noises about her getting home in a hurry. Looks like
your friends in the cops have gone for the easy option," Gavin
said angrily.

There were things I wanted to say. Like the cops aren't my
friends. Like did she know a good criminal lawyer. Instead, I
gambled that Maggie would have picked on a nice, reliable chap
like Gavin as the concerned person who would be informed of
her whereabouts. So I simply asked, "Do you know where she's
being held?"

He nodded grudgingly. "They rang me about half an hour
ago. They've got her at Macclesfield cop shop. I asked about lawyers, but they said they would be arranging that with Maggie."

"Thanks. I'll make sure she's got a good one."

"Don't you think you've done enough?" he said bitterly. There didn't seem much I could say to that, so I turned and walked back down the path.

I made good time back over the motorway. I'd rung Macclesfield police station from the motorway services. I regretted the impulse as soon as I was connected to Cliff Jackson.

"I'm glad you rang," he growled. He didn't sound it. "I want a word with you."

"How can I help, Inspector?" I said. It's a lot easier to sound sweet and helpful when there's forty miles of road between you.

"There's nothing gets on my threepennies more than people like you who think there's something clever about obstructing the police. One more stroke like this, Ms Brannigan, and you're going to be in a cell. And if you remember your law, under PACE I can keep you there for thirty-six hours before I have to get round to charging you with obstructing my investigation." Now he'd got that off his chest, I hoped he felt better. I sure as hell didn't.

"If I knew what you were referring to, Inspector, I might be able to offer you some reassurance as to my future conduct." He really brought out the lawyer in me.

"The way you conveniently forgot to mention that Maggie Rossiter was not only in the vicinity of Colcutt Manor at the time of Moira Pollock's death but was also out and about in the highways and by-ways of Cheshire at the relevant time," he snarled.

"Well, for one thing, Inspector, I wasn't even sure what the relevant time was. The fact that she was in the lane a good hour after Jett and I discovered the body didn't seem especially revelant to me, I have to admit."

"Don't try to be clever with me, Ms Brannigan. I'm not making idle threats here. If you interfere with the course of my investigation again, or if I find you've been withholding evidence, I'm going to come down on you so hard it'll make your eyes water. Do I make myself plain?"

"As the proverbial pikestaff, Inspector."

"Right. And I think I'll be wanting another word with you about your version of events around the time of the murder. You seem rather more hazy than I'd expect from someone who thinks she's as sharp as you do. I'd appreciate it if you could come into my office tomorrow morning at nine."

Before I could refuse, the line went dead. Going back to Colcutt could only be an improvement on the day.

"Kate!" Neil exclaimed as I stuck my head round the door of his office. "Come in!" I'd caught a glimpse of his retreating back as I'd entered the manor and followed him.

He was standing by his desk pouring a mug of coffee from a Thermos jug. His face had the bleary, unfocused look of a hangover. "Fancy a cuppa? I've no milk here, I'm afraid."

"Black's fine," I replied. He opened his desk drawer and took out a second mug, which he filled and handed to me.

"Fancy a little something to keep the cold out?" he asked. I shook my head with a mental shudder, and watched in revulsion as he pulled a bottle of Grouse from his desk drawer and poured a generous slug into his mug. He took a long swallow of the brew, and as it went down, his face seemed to regain definition. "Aah," he sighed comfortably. "That's better."

Neil slouched across the room and collapsed into a leather armchair in a corner. "So," he said with a crooked smile, "how's Hawkshaw the Detective getting on? Ready to finger the culprit yet?"

"Hardly," I replied, sitting down on the typist's chair in front of the desk. I was in two minds whether or not to tell him about Maggie's arrest. On the one hand, I didn't want to help him earn a shilling out of selling the story. But on the other, I was convinced Jackson was so far off-beam that I wanted him to end up looking like the fool he was. In the end, I decided I wanted to get my own back on Neil more than I did on Jackson, so I kept the news to myself.

"I've only just started my inquiries," I said. "And if Gloria's anything to go by, I'd have more joy panning for gold in the Mersey than extracting information out of you lot."

Neil pulled a face. "I don't envy you the lovely Gloria. But if it's good gossip you're after, you've come to the right place. My encyclopaedic knowledge of the occupants of Colcutt Manor is entirely at your disposal. Fire away." My relief must have shown in my face, for Neil chuckled. "Bit of a shock to the system, eh, finding someone who actually wants to talk."

"Just a bit," I said. "Before we get down to the serious gossip, though, I have to do the proper detective bit. You know, where were you on the night of, etc."

He lit a cigarette and blew out a cloud of smoke with an appreciative smile. "Eat your heart out, Miss Marple. Well, I'd been nattering to Kevin earlier, then about ten I went down the local pub for a few sherbets before closing time. I must have got back about half-past eleven, then I came through here and did a couple of hours' work, transcribing tapes and knocking them into shape. I went up to bed around half-past one. Didn't see a soul, before you ask." It was hard to gauge his truthfulness from his hooded eyes. Like most journalists I know, he'd carefully cultivated the appearance of total sincerity to encourage the public to fly in the face of all the evidence and trust him.

I asked a few more questions, and soon elicited the fact that he hadn't seen Moira in the pub. Presumably she and Maggie had gone up to her room before he'd arrived. I decided to change to a more profitable line of questioning. "So, if you were a gambling man, who would you be putting money on?"

His eyes crinkled up in concentration for a moment, then he rattled off the odds: "2–1 Tamar, 3–1 Gloria and Kevin, 7–2 Jett, 4–1 Micky and 10–1 the girlfriend."

I couldn't help smiling. I hadn't expected such a literal answer. "And what about you?"

Neil stroked his moustache. "Me? I'm the dark horse. An outsider in more ways than one. You'd have to put me down at 100–1. After all, I was the only one who had nothing to gain and everything to lose from her death."

I was intrigued. On the face of it, what he said was plausible. But since my only experience of murder is in the pages of Agatha Christie, that made him number one suspect in my book. I said as much.

He roared with laughter, and got up to refill his mug. This time, the tot of whisky was noticeably smaller. "Sorry to disappoint you, Kate," he remarked, "but I meant what I said. Moira was the best possible source for early material on Jett. I mean, we all know how showbiz biogs steer well clear of scandal. And Jett's life has been well-documented. The only genuinely new angle I could hope for was finally lifting the lid on what happened between Jett and Moira all those years ago. I couldn't get an on-the-record word out of anybody about the reasons for the partnership splitting up. Her arrival on the scene was a godsend. She was willing to talk, and we'd only just begun to get into it. So I had a vested interest in her being around to talk to me. Forget the doctrine of the 'least likely person'."

"OK. So you didn't have a motive. But you obviously think the others did. Suppose you run them past me?" I flipped my bag open and on the pretext of getting my notebook out, I switched on my tape recorder. I'd meant to tape all my interviews, but finding a strategy to deal with Gloria had driven the thought from my mind.

Neil stretched out in his chair and crossed his legs at the ankle, revealing odd socks above his scuffed leather loafers. "First, Tamar," he said, a note of relish in his tone that made me feel slightly uncomfortable. Life with Richard has shown me that journalists are the biggest bitches on two legs, but I still can't get off on listening to them dishing the dirt. "They were on the rocks long before you found Moira. She'd actually taken a walk a week or two before that gig when I met you, but when Jett didn't chase her, she came back off her own bat. If he hadn't been so distracted with the work on the album, she'd have been on her bike a long time ago. But she was putting a lot of work in on making herself indispensable. When Moira turned up, Tamar could see all that good work going down the tubes."

"What d'you mean, good work? All I've seen her do so far is doss around," I interrupted.

Neil grinned. "I mean, 'Yes, Jett, no, Jett, three bags full, Jett'. And all those evenings in the kitchen rustling up tasty little gourmet dinners for her hard-working man. Not to mention the horizontal work. Once Moira arrived, she used to wind Tamar up something rotten, flirting with Jett whenever Tamar was around. As long as Moira was around, Tamar was living on borrowed time. And hell hath no fury. But now Moira's gone, Tamar's wasting no time consolidating her position. As you no doubt noticed for yourself yesterday."

"I can't see Tamar choosing a tenor sax as her murder weapon," I objected.

Neil crushed out his cigarette. "All the more reason for her to use it," he countered. "Though I agree it is a bizarre image."

We both paused for a moment to contemplate the idea. For me, it didn't work, but judging by the satisfied smirk on Neil's face, he was having less trouble with it. "Next," I demanded. "Gloria at 3–1."

"Obvious motive. She is obsessive about Jett. Madly in love with him, and all she is to him is a housekeeper with word-processing skills. She didn't approve of Moira's presence, reckoned she was disruptive and ultimately bad news for Jett, trapping him in a time warp. And if she thought Moira was going to spill any dirt on her idol, Gloria would have a double motive for getting her out of the way," Neil summed up with an air of having said all there was to be said on the subject.

"And you think Kevin's motive is as strong?" I challenged him.

"We-ell, that depends on how straight you think he is. There's been a lot of argument in this house over the past few weeks about money and contracts. Jett was pissed off with Kevin for signing me up, you know. He wanted your boyfriend."

"I know," I said stiffly. That had already tagged Kevin in my mind as a shit. I had to be careful not to let my personal reactions interfere with my professional judgement, something which Neil seemed to be deliberately trying to provoke. "But I hardly think that would give Kevin a motive for killing Moira."

"Well, there was a lot more going down between the three of them than that. Moira was convinced that Kevin had been systematically ripping Jett off. She kept egging him on to straighten out his finances, to get Kevin to give him a detailed breakdown of his earnings and his assets. Kevin was being awkward about it. Now, whether that is because he genuinely had something to hide or because Moira just pissed him off and made him stubborn, I don't know. I do know that she was having a hell of a lot of trouble getting her hands on all her back royalties." That confirmed what Maggie had already told me. Things were beginning to fall into place. Nothing like a bit of corroboration, though.

"There were a lot of rows about touring, too," Neil added. "Moira kept telling Jett that he shouldn't be having to do so much touring, that he should be concentrating on short tours of big venues like Wembley and the NEC. Kevin was furious. He seemed to think that she didn't know what she was talking about, and she had no right to interfere after being away for so long. She really was making his life a misery. If I'd been in his shoes, I'd probably have taken a meat axe to her weeks ago."

Neil certainly wasn't stinting himself when it came to putting the poison in. In spite of my misgivings, I knew I had to milk it for all it was worth. "Micky?" I asked, leaning over to pour myself the last cup of coffee.

"Micky produced Jett's first four albums, and that was the springboard that put him on the map as a producer." Neil paused to light another cigarette, and I had time to reflect that he even spoke like a tabloid newspaper. "But the last two years have seen him plummet from the top of the tree, thanks to the old nose candy."

"Coke?" I asked.

"The same. Just like Jett, Micky's had too many flops for comfort, and he knows it. The collaboration was supposed to work the old magic and produce a classic album. Till Moira came along, it was shaping up to be classic dross. She encouraged Jett to shout Micky down and go back to their old style. Micky kept ranting that they were five years out of date. But then, as Moira sweetly pointed out, so are most of Jett's fans. She also wasn't scared of badmouthing him over his habit. Given Jett's views on drugs, that was a serious no-no for him."

"You're not seriously trying to tell me Jett doesn't know about Micky?" That I couldn't believe.

"Yes and no. I mean, theoretically, he probably does. But Micky's very careful to keep it under wraps. You won't ever walk into a room here and find somebody doing a line or two. It's all behind-locked-doors stuff. Everybody goes along with Jett's little fantasies about this being a clean house. Moira was using that as a lever to put pressure on Kevin to make her joint producer. Micky was really running scared."

"Scared enough to kill her?" I asked. Maybe I'm too naïve for this game, but even my naturally suspicious mind was having trouble getting round that idea.

Neil shrugged. "Coke makes you very paranoid. It's a fact."

"And the girlfriend? What exactly do you mean?" I demanded.

"I'm presuming you knew Moira had become a dyke, since it was you who tracked her down? Well, she'd been shacked up with some social worker called Maggie over in Bradford. The girlfriend wasn't exactly chuffed as little mint balls when Moira

upped sticks and moved in here. According to Moira, Maggie
was constantly kicking off about it, sending out ultimata in every
post. So, Moira told her it was Good night, Vienna," Neil replied.

"And you think being given the big E is a motive for murder?" I said sceptically.

"If she thought Moira was packing her in to go back to
Jett, yeah. Helluva blow to the ego. And she's the only outsider
you could reasonably expect Moira to let into the house."

And she stood to inherit a substantial amount of money.
I could see why Jackson was in love with the idea of Maggie.
"You seemed to think Jett had a motive. But he has an alibi. He
was with me, remember?"

"And I am Marie of Romania! Come on, Kate, I know
that was all bullshit. And I know you believe he couldn't have
had anything to do with it. But just think on. Moira had turned
his comfortable life on its head. That might have been OK if
they had been lovers. But she wasn't having any, and he really
wasn't handling that. I mean, you've heard all his New Age
stuff about them being soul mates destined for each other. He
wanted them to be together and make babies, for God's sake.
Maybe she just turned him down once too often. I mean, the
guy has got one helluva quick temper. Maybe he thought that
if he couldn't have her, then no one else would. In spite of the
front he puts up, he's no pussycat."

"One big happy family," I remarked ironically. "All for
one and one for all."

"I tell you, if I wasn't working for Jett, I could make a
fortune with the shit I've picked up round here in the last few
weeks."

I got to my feet. I might still be able to learn more from
Neil, but I'd had enough for one helping. "Thanks for the info,"
I said. "You've given me a lot to think about." I wasn't bullshit-
ting, either. Neil's reminder of Jett's quick mood changes niggled
in my mind like biscuit crumbs in the bed. I almost missed his
parting remarks.

"You sound like you're surprised by the catalogue of motives. Listen, I thought journos were backstabbers till I got into rock. Just don't run into any of them in a dark alley."

With Neil's gypsy warning ringing in my ears, I stood in the hall and wondered which one of Moira's enemies I should go after next. Before I could take another step, the pager went off. In the echoing stillness of the hall at Colcutt Manor it sounded like the four-minute warning. I pulled it out of my pocket and hit the button that silenced it. The message said, "Back to base. Double Urgent."

That's not the kind of message you argue with. Not if your boss is a foot taller than you.

21

I made it back to the office in record time. The driver of the traffic car I'd zipped past at 110 m.p.h. had clearly been convinced he'd been hallucinating since he didn't get on my tail with sirens blasting. I dumped the car on a single yellow outside the chemist's shop, left the note that says, "picking up urgent prescription" on the dashboard and hit the stairs running.

I burst through the outer door, red-faced and sweating. Very chic. Shelley looked me up and down and shook her head in a mockery of disapproving motherhood. "Three deep breaths," she told me. "Then you're wanted in there." She gestured with her head at Bill's closed office door.

"What's going on?" I demanded in a stage whisper. I know just how thin the walls in this place are.

"The cops raided Billy Smart's warehouse this morning. The place was clean as a whistle," Shelley replied, her voice so low I had to lean close and risk my crowns on her Rasta beads.

"Oh shit," I sighed. "So who . . . ?"

"Bill's having a post-mortem with Clive Abercrombie from the jewellers' group and DI Redfern. He's been stalling them till you got here."

Some days I wish I did something simple for a living. Like brain surgery. I flashed a hopeless smile at Shelley, made a throat-cutting gesture and headed for the Spanish Inquisition.

Tony Redfern was sitting on the broad window sill, looking more like a depressed golden retriever than ever. Wavy blond hair, soulful brown eyes, drooping mouth. For all I knew, a wet nose too. He nodded gloomily as I entered. Clive Abercrombie leapt smartly to his feet and inclined his head towards me, every inch the Eton and New College gentleman. You'd never have guessed he was actually educated at a secondary modern in Blackpool followed by Salford Tech.

"Sorry to drag you back, Kate," Bill said. "But we really did need your expertise here." Translation: Someone's going to come out of this looking like a prize asshole, and it's not going to be us.

"I was only down the road. Just routine," I said.

Tony grinned. "Giving Cliff Jackson a headache, so I hear."

"The feeling's mutual, Tony," I replied, returning the grin. I've known Tony since he was a DS on the burglary squad. He's one of the few coppers I have any professional respect for. "Is there some kind of a problem with the Smarts?"

"That would be one way of putting it," said Clive, stuffy as ever. "It would appear that when Inspector Redfern and his colleagues from the Trading Standards department executed their warrant on Mr Smart's warehouse premises, they drew a blank." See what I mean? You'd never guess.

I looked questioningly at Tony. He nodded, looking as if he'd just lost the five closest members of his family. "He's not wrong. We'd had a team watching the place all day, and not a sausage came out that front door. There's no back entrance, no side entrance. The place was clean, Kate. Billy and Gary stood there watching us with a grin on their faces like a pair of Cheshire cats. I don't know where you got your info, but it's a duffy."

I couldn't believe it. "We were hoping you would be able to furnish us with some explanation, Miss Brannigan," Clive said icily. "You had mounted surveillance personally for some time, I believe."

"Over a period of four weeks, to be precise," Bill weighed in. "Averaging a sixteen-hour day. You were sent our detailed reports, including photographs, Clive." There was a warning note in Bill's voice. I hoped Clive was alert to it. It's hell getting bloodstains out of grey carpet.

"I don't understand it," I said, going for the note of genuine puzzlement. "Unless they've changed warehouses. But there's no reason why they should." I frowned. "Tony, how long have you had someone on them? Could they have cottoned on and shifted the gear?"

Tony shook his head. "Nice try, Kate. But we didn't move on them till yesterday morning, and all we did was put a team outside the warehouse. They couldn't have cleared the stuff since then."

"Perhaps there is a leak inside your organization, Mr Mortensen?" Clive suggested.

I thought Bill was going to explode. He leaned forward in his chair, put his rather large hands flat on the desk and snarled, "No way, Clive. If there is a leak, it's not from here. People in glass houses, Clive. I've always wondered how the thieves knew exactly which cupboard wasn't wired."

Clive looked petulant. "That's an outrageous suggestion," he complained. "Besides, it was your company that installed the alarm system."

"Bickering isn't going to get us anywhere," I said, my reflexes geared as ever to stopping the boys squabbling. But I couldn't help feeling Clive had a point about a leak. Unless there had been a tip-off, I couldn't see how Billy and Gary had got away with it. And until I did, Mortensen and Brannigan were going to be the fall guys, that much was clear. "Look, something has clearly gone down here that needs looking into. Will you give me twenty-four hours to see what I can come up with?"

Clive looked triumphant. "This will of course be at your own expense?"

Bill scowled. "I don't see why it should be."

I stepped in again. They were like a pair of stags in the rut. "The reward when the Smarts are convicted will more than pay for a day of my time," I said sweetly. Out of the corner of my eye, I could see Tony grin.

"I can't pull my team off," he said, "but I won't pursue any active line for another twenty-four hours." It wasn't much, but it was a small concession. At least I wouldn't be falling over PC Plod on every street corner.

Now the deal was struck, our guests couldn't get out of the door fast enough.

"The guy's a toad," Bill grumbled loudly as the door closed behind them. I knew he didn't mean Tony. "None of us is in Billy Smart's pocket. So, what are we going to do?"

"To be honest, I'm not sure. I thought I'd just go walkabout and see what I can dig up. The Smarts are going to be on their guard after last night, so God knows if I'll get anywhere. But I had to say something to stop Clive sniping away at us."

Bill nodded. "Noted and appreciated. What are you going to do about the murder investigation? D'you need anything from me?"

"Cliff Jackson and his merry men have pulled in Maggie Rossiter. It might be worth checking whether she's sorted with a good lawyer. If not, maybe you could give Diana Russell a bell? Jackson also wants to see me tomorrow morning, but I can handle it. Other than that, put it on hold. If Jett calls, tell him I'm pursuing some leads among the people she was hanging out with before she came back to the manor. OK?"

"No problem. I really am sorry to have dragged you back like that, but it was one of those situations where you have to put on a show of strength. Besides, if you hadn't been there, that shithead Clive would have spent the whole time putting the knife into you."

I knew Bill had enough on his plate right now without having to put up with Clive whingeing for England, so I gave him a reassuring smile and said, "As my grannie always said, if they're talking about me, they're leaving some other poor soul alone. I'll let you know when I get somewhere, OK?"

He looked relieved. "Thanks, Kate. And, by the way—Clive's full of shit. I know you did that job properly. If anyone fucked up, it wasn't you."

Now all I had to do was prove that.

I spotted Tony Redfern's surveillance team on my first pass of the Smarts' warehouse. In that area, any child over two and a half would have clocked them straight off. Newish Cavalier, base model, with a whiplash radio aerial. Two clowns in suits trying to look tough. Pathetic. They blended in like Dolly Parton in a Masonic lodge.

I cruised round the block. Tony had been right about the absence of other obvious exits. The Smarts' warehouse was flanked by two others. All three of them backed on to one big warehouse that was now a tyre and exhaust outlet, staffed by a constantly changing team of no-hopers in really practical sunshine yellow overalls. I slowed down, but studying the Fastfit premises told me nothing.

I pulled up near the corner and studied the layout in my rear-view mirror. As I watched, a Transit van reversed into Fastfit's loading area. The driver opened his door and got out. For some reason, I wasn't too surprised to see it was Gary Smart.

Three minutes later, my car was in one of Fastfit's bays, while I did the foreman's head in with a series of inquiries about the prices of tyres, shock absorbers and exhausts for my Nova. And my boyfriend's Beetle. And my dad's Montego. And, incidentally, while I got a good look at what Gary was up to.

Cardboard cartons about the size of a case of wine were being unloaded from the back of the van, then carried down between the stacks of tyres to the foot of a flight of wooden steps leading up to the exhaust storage area. I began to see a tiny glimmer of light.

Stopping the foreman in mid-sentence, I thanked him pro-
fusely, and climbed back behind the wheel. I couldn't help admiring
Billy Smart's forward planning. I drove about half a mile through
the back streets before I found what I was looking for. I took my
camera case out of the boot and walked into the block of council
flats and headed for the lifts. I was in luck. I had to wait nearly
three minutes, but at least the lift was working. I got in, trying
to breathe through my mouth only, and got out on the top floor.

It took me a moment to get my bearings, then I chose my
door. I knocked politely, and breathed a sigh of relief when an
elderly woman answered the door. It opened three inches on the
chain and she looked out suspiciously. "Yes?" she said.

I gave her the uncertain smile. "I'm terribly sorry to trouble
you," I started. "I'm a photography student at the Poly and I'm
doing a project for my finals. I've got to get photographs of the
Manchester city centre skyline from lots of different angles, and
this block is just perfect for me. I know it's a terrible imposition,
but I wondered if I could possibly step out on your balcony for
five minutes to do some pictures?" I looked hopeful.

She looked suspicious and craned her neck to see past me.
I stepped back obligingly so she could see I was alone. "I could
pay you a small fee," I said, deliberately sounding reluctant.

"How small?" she asked belligerently.

"I could manage ten pounds," I replied hesitantly, taking
my wallet from my pocket and opening it.

The money made her decision for her, and I could see why
as soon as I stepped inside. The whole place was threadbare—
carpets, curtains, furniture. Even her cardigan was darned on
the elbows. There was a pervasive smell of staleness, as if fresh
air cost as much as every other commodity that made life worth
living. I didn't like deceiving her, but consoled myself that it
was in a good cause, and besides, she was a tenner richer than
she'd been this morning.

She offered me a cup of tea, but I declined and waited
patiently while she unfastened the two locks on the balcony

door. Maybe she'd been watching too much television and really
believed in Spiderman.

The balcony was perfect. I opened my case and took out
a 400mm lens. I twisted it into my Nikon body and leaned the
heavy assembly on the balcony rail. I looked through the view-
finder. Perfect. Now I could see exactly how it had been done.
I started shooting, then, to prove the gods were really smiling
on me, Gary Smart appeared in shot. I kept my finger on the
trigger and let the motor drive do the work.

An hour later, I was surveying the results with a feeling of deep
satisfaction. I marched through to Bill with a sheaf of prints and
dumped them on his desk.

"Elementary, my dear Mortensen," I announced.

Bill tore himself away from his screen and picked up the
pictures. He thumbed through them with a puzzled frown, then,
as he reached the ones with Gary, he laughed out loud.

"Bang to rights, Kate," he chuckled. "Tony Redfern will
be kicking some arses tonight." He picked up the phone and
said, "Shelley, can you get me Tony Redfern, please." He covered the mouthpiece and said, "Well done, Kate. After I've put
Tony in the picture, I'm going round to see Clive and tell him
myself. I can't wait to see the grief on his face . . . Hello, Tony?
Bill Mortensen.

"Kate's just walked through the door with your answer."
I knew Tony would be squirming at the glee in Bill's voice.
"Listen to this for a scam. The Smarts' warehouse is the middle
one of three, right? They all have pitched roofs, right? And all
three back on to Fastfit. Which has a flat roof behind a para-
pet so you can't see it from the street. Still with me? The gear
comes out of the window in the gable end of the warehouse,
on to the Fastfit roof, down to the Fastfit loading bay then over
the hills and far away . . . Yes, Kate has it all on film. They've

been moving gear back in today. They must have spotted your surveillance team and shifted everything out in advance of the raid. And of course, you wouldn't be moving on them again till you saw something going in. And long before you did, you'd lose interest."

Nothing like making someone's day. I headed back for Colcutt hoping that someone would make mine.

22

By the time I got to Colcutt, the buzz of tracking the Smarts' scam had worn off and my stomach seemed to think it was time for something a little more substantial than black coffee. I headed for the kitchen, planning to take some of my wages in kind. On the way, I noticed that the rehearsal room was taped up with police seals. I wondered how long it would be before Jett felt like making music again.

I poked around in the kitchen, checking out the fridge, the freezer and the cupboards. I opened a can of Heinz tomato soup, the ultimate comfort food, emptied it into a bowl and put it in the microwave. I'd only managed to get a couple of spoonfuls down when the door leading into the stable yard opened and Micky walked in, shaking the drops of rain off his waxed jacket. It was the first time I've ever seen anyone with arms so long their wrists actually stuck out of the sleeves of a Barbour.

He nodded at me and headed for the kettle, pulling off a tweed cap which had left a circular impression on his thin blond-streaked brown hair. The effect was quite bizarre. "Bloody awful weather," he complained, the cigarette in the corner of his mouth bobbing up and down like a conductor's baton.

"You're not wrong. You wouldn't have caught me out in it unless I'd been working," I fished. He didn't rise. All I got for my pains was a grunt that fitted well with his simian features. I tried again. "Have you got a minute? I need to ask you some questions."

Micky sighed deeply and tossed his cigarette end into the sink. "It's doing my head in, this business. Questions, questions, questions. And Plod all over the sodding place. All I want to do is get on with my job. Some of us have got deadlines to meet," he grumbled.

"Inconsiderate of Moira, really," I replied. "But the sooner you answer my questions, the sooner it'll all be sorted," I added with a confidence I didn't feel.

"Might as well get it over and done with," he muttered irritably, tossing a teabag into a mug and swirling it around viciously with a teaspoon. He removed his jacket and threw it over a chair, then brought his tea over to the table. He perched on the edge of a chair and immediately lit another cigarette which he continuously dabbed nervously at his lips. Apart from the cigarette, he looked just like those chimps they dress up for the PG Tips adverts. I half-expected him to answer my questions in Donald Sinden's fruity tones.

"I need to know your movements around the time of Moira's death," I said bluntly.

"I didn't make any," he replied belligerently, his fingers beating a silent tattoo on the side of the mug. I gave him the benefit of my quizzical look. I couldn't do words because I had a mouthful of soup. "I was in the studio all evening," he finally volunteered.

"Doing what, exactly?" I pursued.

"Doing what I do, exactly. Jett and Moira had been in earlier, around eight, listening to what we'd been working on that afternoon. Moira was full of bright ideas about the mixing, and some synth effects she wanted me to lay down. I was fiddling around with a couple of tracks, trying various things. I wanted to have a selection of versions for them to hear the next day. Time passes fast when you've got your head down." Micky took a swig of tea and sniffed loudly as the steam hit his cold nose. It was far from incontrovertible evidence of what Gloria had suggested and Neil had confirmed.

Even the cloud of smoke slowly filling the kitchen couldn't put me off my soup. I finished it, and the sound of my spoon scraping on the bottom of the bowl made him wince. "I understand Moira had pretty firm ideas on what she wanted the album to be like," I remarked.

He crushed out his cigarette, swallowed some more tea, sniffed again, blew his nose on a large, paisley patterned handkerchief and lit another cigarette before he answered. "She was a royal pain," Micky informed me. "Let's try it this way, no, maybe not, let's go back to what you wanted to do in the first place," he mimicked with cruel accuracy. "She'd been out of the game too long to have a bloody clue what she was talking about."

"Doesn't sound like you're too sorry that she's dead," I said.

The look of astonishment that crossed his face came as a genuine surprise to me.

"Of course I'm bloody sorry," he shouted. "She was a bloody great songwriter. Just because she couldn't do my job doesn't mean I didn't respect the way she did hers. She might have been bloody difficult to work with, but at least she gave you something you could get your teeth into in the first place." He subsided as quickly as he'd erupted and slouched even deeper in the chair. "For fuck's sake," he muttered.

"I'm sorry," I said, meaning it. "Did anyone else come down to the studio while you were there?"

He rubbed the bridge of his nose with his fingers, screwing up his eyes in concentration. "Kevin came in. I've been trying to remember if it was once or twice, but I'm not sure. He wanted to hear how it was going, but I wasn't really in the mood. I was into the music you know? I didn't have a lot left over for small talk."

"Screws your memory up, doesn't it?" I said sympathetically.

"What d'you mean?"

"Charlie. Destroys the short-term memory."

"I don't know what you're on about," came the reflex answer.

"Coke. And I don't mean the brown fizzy stuff. It's OK, Micky, I'm not a copper's nark. I don't give a shit what you do to yourself. Everybody's got the right to go to hell in the handcart of their choice. I'm just concerned about finding out what happened to Moira. And if you were out of your box, your evidence on Kevin's movements isn't worth a damn," I informed him, aware even as I spoke how bloody sanctimonious I sounded. At least I'd managed to restrain myself from dishing out the standard Brannigan anti-drugs sermon.

"So I do the odd line. So what? I'd had a bit, but I wasn't flying. I just don't remember if he came in once or twice, OK?" The belligerent edge was back in his voice.

"You ever use heroin?"

"No way. I've seen too many talented kids go down that road. No, all I do is a bit of recreational coke."

"But you'd know where to get heroin if someone else wanted it?"

He shook his head in wide, disbelieving sweeps. "Oh no, you don't pin that one on me. I don't deal, not for anybody, not for my nearest and dearest. Personal use, that's all."

"But you'd know where to get it?" I persisted.

"I'd have a shrewd idea who to ask. If you work in this business, you get to hear things like that. But if you're nosing into heroin dealers, I'm not the one you should be asking." Micky lit his next cigarette. I was beginning to feel like a herring in a smokehouse. I'd be a kipper before morning if I hung around Micky.

"So who should I be asking?"

He shrugged, and a malicious gleam crept into his eyes. "A certain little lady who's got nothing better to do with her time. Ask her why she was so fascinated by Paki Paulie at the Hassy the other week."

He obviously meant Tamar. The description certainly didn't fit Gloria. And where better to meet a dealer than the Hacienda, full as it always is of kids looking for the next kick? I filed the hint away for further investigation.

"Have you got any idea who killed Moira?" I asked.

"I can't imagine any of them having the bottle, frankly," Micky said contemptuously. "Except Neil. That bastard would do anything for a few bob. He must have made a fucking fortune out of her death already, all the stories he's been selling to the papers. Fucking vulture." The venom in his voice was shocking.

"Sounds like there's not a lot of love lost between the two of you," I observed. When it comes to spotting the obvious, I'm an Olympic contender.

"Let's just say he's not the person I'd choose to write my biography."

"Why's that?"

"He's too fond of seeing his name in big letters in the papers. He turned over my brother-in-law, you know. Years ago, it was, but Des's never recovered. OK, Des was a bit dodgy, he ripped a few people off, but he wasn't a bad lad, not a proper villain, not when you compare him to those City bastards who rip people off to the tune of millions. Thanks to Neil fucking Webster, Des ended up inside for eighteen months. He used to have his own business, you know, but now he's just a bloody brickie working for buttons. Tell you what, an' all," Micky continued, his accent losing its classlessness and becoming pure East End, "That fucker Webster won't have given him another thought. I bet he doesn't even realize why I hate his guts."

All this was deeply fascinating, but I couldn't see its relevance. In spite of Micky's obvious conviction, I couldn't see Neil cold bloodedly planning murder for the sake of a byline. Before I could divert the conversation down more profitable paths, the door from the house opened and a wave of Giorgio cut through the smoky air.

I turned in my chair to watch Tamar sweep across the room in her silk pyjamas. Without a word of greeting, she made for the fridge. She bent over to peer inside, then slammed it shut with an air of bad temper. She started for the cupboards on the other side of the kitchen and caught Micky's eyes on her. "Stop letching, sleazeball," she threw at him on her way to the Weetabix.

Micky scrambled to his feet and hurried out of the room, grabbing his coat as he went. Thanks a bunch, Tamar, I thought to myself as I watched her tip two bars into a bowl and drench them with sugar. On her way back to the fridge, I remarked, "Sleep well?"

"What the hell business is it of yours?" she grumbled as she poured milk on her cereal and perched on a stool at the breakfast bar. If she was always this charming first thing in the evening, it wasn't so surprising that Jett preferred to wake up alone.

"You can always tell good breeding," I said airily. "Plebs like me, we can never aspire to the courtesy of the moneyed classes."

To my surprise, she spluttered with laughter, spraying the worktop with gobbets of coconut matting. "OK, I'm sorry, Kate," she conceded. It was the first time I'd seen a side of her that explained why Jett had put up with her for more than five minutes. "I'm always a complete shit until I've had something to eat. I think I get low blood sugar in the night. I guess all this business over Moira is just making it worse. And breakfast with Bonzo there was a prospect too dire for words." Her upper-class drawl exaggerated her words, made them seem more amusing than they were.

"So what's the daughter of a baronet doing among the Neanderthals, then?" I asked, trying to pick up the tone of her own remarks. Richard's background info was still coming in handy.

She gave an ironic smile. "Depends who you want to believe. According to my mother, I'm indulging in a belated teenage rebellion, having a bit of rough before I settle down.

According to the lovely Gloria, I'm a gold-digger who likes having her name linked in the gossip columns with Jett. According to Kevin, I was useful in the early days because I kept Jett amused, but now I'm a pain because we keep rowing."

"And according to you?"

"Me? I'm still here because I'm crazy about the guy. I'll admit that when I first met him, I thought he might be fun to play with for a while. But that changed. In a matter of days, that changed. I'm here because I love him and I want to make it work. In spite of all the efforts of his so-called friends to put a spanner in the works," she added, with an edge of bitterness that nullified the light tone of her earlier remarks.

"Was Moira one of those?" I asked, getting up to make myself some coffee.

She nodded. "In spades. Sorry, an unfortunate turn of phrase, but maybe not so inaccurate. She treated me like a brainless bimbo to the point where I felt like having my degree framed and hung on my door. Did you know I have an upper second in modern languages from Exeter?" she asked defensively. I waved an empty mug at Tamar and she nodded. "Black, one sugar. Moira seemed to think that since I wasn't a black, working-class musician then I could have nothing to offer Jett. It was ironic. She didn't want him any more, but she was damned if she was going to let anyone else be part of his life."

I was almost beginning to feel sorry for Tamar myself. Then I remembered the display in the drawing room the previous morning, and how insincere I'd instinctively felt it to be. "Well, she won't be around to throw any more spanners," I responded heartlessly.

"And if I'm being honest, I'd have to say I'm glad. If I'd heard one more sentimental conversation about 'our roots' I think I'd have screamed. But I didn't kill her. You can't get away from the fact that they made good music together. And I wouldn't have taken that away from him. I know how much his work means to him." Tamar stirred her coffee demurely. I nearly believed her. Then I remembered Micky's hints and their implications. Someone had been shoving heroin at Moira, and it looked like Tamar. I decided to wait till I had more evidence to hit her with, rather than waste the talkative mood she was in today. It hadn't escaped me that the reason for her co-operation might be nothing more than a desire to stay in Jett's good books.

"I hate to be a bore, but I have to ask you what you were doing on the night Moira was killed," I said. "I know you'll have run through it already with the police, but I have to go through the motions." I gave what was supposed to be a winning smile.

Tamar ran a hand through her tousled hair and pulled a face. "Bor-ring is right. OK. I'd been shopping in town all afternoon, then I met my sister Candida for a coffee in the Conservatory, you know, just off St Anne's Square. I got back around half-past seven. I bumped into Jett and Moira in the hall on their way down to the studio. Jett said they'd be about half an hour, and I decided to cook dinner.

"I did steaks in brandy and cream sauce with new potatoes and mangetout, and Jett and I ate in the TV room. I drank most of a bottle of burgundy, Jett had his usual Smirnoff Blue Label and Diet Coke. We watched the new Harrison Ford movie on video, then I went upstairs and had a bath. Jett came up and joined me just after ten. We made love in my room, then he went off downstairs some time after eleven. He said he was going to do some work with Moira. I couldn't sleep, so I read for a while then I started to watch the video. That's when you walked in."

It all came out a bit too pat. I used to have a boyfriend who continually confounded me by his ability to remember the most trivial remarks weeks later. So when he lied to me, his stories were always so detailed it never crossed my mind to doubt their veracity. When I think of that, I thank God that Richard can barely recall what he ate for dinner the night before. Unless it impinges on his professional life, information passes through Richard's head without leaving a trace. But Tamar was trying to impress me very forcibly with her candour and her excellent memory. I didn't trust her an inch.

I tried the tired old question. "So who do you think killed Moira?"

Tamar's eyes widened. "Well, it wasn't Jett. But then, you know that, don't you?" she added, her voice heavy with irony.

"Leaving Jett aside, you must have given the matter some thought," I pressed her.

She got to her feet and dumped her dishes in the dishwasher. With her back to me, she said, "Gloria is a very stupid woman, you know. Stupid enough to think she's bright enough to get away with murder, if you understand me." I caught the reflection of Tamar's face in the kitchen window. There was a tight smile on her lips.

She turned back to face me, her expression wiped clean. "Why don't you ask her what she was doing running upstairs just before one o'clock?"

I could feel the pulse in my throat. "What do you mean?"

"I heard someone running upstairs. I was coming through from my bathroom, so I stuck my head round the door. I saw Gloria's door closing. What was she up to? You're the detective. Maybe you should ask her."

23

Tamar swept off to make herself fit for company after that final pleasantry, leaving me rejoicing at the prospect of another friendly little chat with Gloria. Luckily, I didn't have to scour the shopping centres of the north west for her. She was in her office, beating up her word processor as if the keyboard had my face on it.

"Sorry to interrupt," I said. "I just wondered where I might find Kevin."

"He's got a suite in the west wing," she said pompously, not even breaking her rhythm. "Bedroom, bathroom, lounge and office. Turn left at the top of the stairs, then left again. The office is the double doors on the right. But you probably won't find him there at this time of day. He's more likely to be out and about."

"Thanks. Oh, one other thing. When I asked you about your movements, you didn't mention that you'd gone downstairs again after you went up to bed."

That brought her frenzied typing to a halt. "I never did," Gloria denied vehemently, her chin thrust out like a defiant child. "Anyone who says I did is a liar." She'd gone that ugly puce again.

"Are you sure?" I asked mildly.

Her lips seemed to tighten and shrink. "Are you accusing me of lying?" she challenged.

"No. I simply wondered if it might have slipped your mind."

"It couldn't have slipped my mind if I'd never done it, could it?"

I shrugged and said, "See you around, Gloria." I walked slowly up the stairs, pondering on her reaction. If I were Neil, I'd be laying odds of 2–1 that she'd been lying. Which meant one of two things. Either she was the killer, or she thought she was protecting the killer. And the only person I could imagine Gloria protecting was Jett.

I followed Gloria's instructions to the letter, but there was no reply when I knocked on the double doors. I tried each handle in turn. They moved, but both doors were locked. On the off chance that someone had been careless, I tried the pair of them together. The doors swung apart, the small gilt bolt in one grazing the pile of the carpet. Oh dear, someone hadn't fastened it properly. I remedied the oversight, carefully sliding the bolt into place as I shut the doors behind me. The lock clicked sharply into place. The Ramblers' Association would have been proud of me.

The contents of Kevin's office were a set of clichés that sat in that beautifully proportioned room like a Big Mac on Sèvres china. The walls were mushroom—sorry, taupe!—decorated with framed gold discs and photographs of Kevin with everyone from Mick Jagger to Margaret Thatcher. There was a Georgian repro stereo cabinet, and lots of those tricksy little repro low-level cupboards and sets of drawers. His desk was roughly the size of a championship snooker table. On top of it, two telephones flanked a Nintendo console. Naff toys for mindless boys. I laid a small bet with myself that he couldn't get beyond level two of Super Mario Brothers. Behind the desk was an executive swivel chair upholstered in glossy chestnut leather, and against the walls there were a couple of those deep sofas that leave your feet waving in the air like a toddler.

I wasn't sure what I was looking for, but that's never stopped me before. I started with the desk itself. It held few surprises. Top drawer, pens and executive gadgets, right down to the aerobasic calculator. (I only knew what it was because they sell them in the Science Museum's mail order goodie book, and I'm a catalogaholic.) Second drawer, scratch pads and packs of adhesive memos with album and record company logos on them. Also, black leather desk diary and telephone book. Bottom drawer, current issues of the music press, and men's mags from the navel-gazing *Esquire* to the nipple-gazing *Penthouse*.

I turned my attention to the nasty furniture. The unit immediately behind the desk looked like it had two drawers. But when I pulled it open, I realized they were fakes, disguising a file drawer. I quickly flipped through it, but as far as I could tell, it was a file of routine correspondence with record companies, promoters and tour venues. There was nothing at all relating to merchandising. The second looked more promising, if only because it was locked. I was assessing my chances of getting into it undetected when my worst nightmares came true. I heard voices outside the door.

It's amazing how quickly your mouth can get really dry. I straightened up as the key fumbled noisily into the lock. There weren't too many options. Under the desk was a sure way to be discovered inside thirty seconds. No room behind the sofas. That only left the door on the far wall. It could lead to a cupboard or a bedroom. As I shot across the room, grateful for the ostentation that had required ankle-risking deep-pile carpet, I prayed it wasn't locked. I yanked the door open and hit the threshold running. I hauled the door shut behind me, in time to see the office door opening.

Gloria's voice reached me across the office and through the door. "If you'd just like to take a seat, Inspector, Mr Kleinman will be back in about ten minutes. If you see that Miss Brannigan, would you tell her that? She was looking for him a few minutes ago, but she's obviously found something more interesting to do than wait. Can I get you some tea?"

"No thanks, Miss. The constable and me are awash with tea. We'll keep an eye out for Miss Brannigan, though." There was no mistaking that voice. It grated like an emery board on my nails. Cliff Jackson was sitting on the other side of the door, in the room I'd illegally entered not quarter of an hour before.

I looked around the room I'd registered subconsciously was a bathroom. That old villain Lord Elgin would have had it away on his toes with the whole room. Walls, floor and even the ceiling were marble. Not that cold, white marble with the grey veins. This was soft, pinky, with dark red veins running through it like a drinker's nose. The bath looked as if it had been hollowed out of a single lump of the stuff, with monstrous gold dolphins for taps. You could never be sure you'd got it really clean, that was for sure.

Luckily for me, there was another door on the far side. I slipped off my heels and tiptoed across the room. That was where my luck ran out. The door wouldn't budge. I crouched down, applying my eye to the crack. Situation hopeless. It was bolted on the far side. That left me two alternatives. Either I could sit it out and hope that no one would be caught short. Or I could brazen it out. If I was going to do that, better sooner rather than later. It would be a lot easier to talk my way out of it before Kevin arrived and started asking awkward questions about what I was doing in his office.

I tiptoed back to the loo and put my shoes back on. Then, very noisily, I stood up, flushed the loo and clattered loudly over to the sink, where I committed an arrestable offence with the dolphin till I got a loud gush of water out of it. Then I made great play of fiddling with the door lock before I emerged.

I managed to stop short in the doorway with every appearance of surprise. "Inspector Jackson!" I exclaimed as his head swivelled round to face me. Those tinted glasses of his were really sinister when the light was behind him.

"And what exactly are you doing here, Miss Brannigan?" he demanded, a note of weary irritation in his voice.

"Pretty much the same as you, by the looks of it. Waiting for Kevin. I heard he'd be back soon." Well, it was true, sort of.

"And how, exactly, did you get through a locked door?" His voice was oilier than I'd have imagined possible. It's the voice they use, cops, when they think they've got you bang to rights. Doesn't matter if it's speeding or murder. I think they learn it in training.

"Locked? You must be mistaken, Inspector. I just turned the handle and walked through. After all, if I'd effected an illegal entry, I'd hardly be powdering my nose and touching up my mascara, now would I?"

Me and my big mouth. Jackson's hands moved up to the knot of his immaculate paisley tie and tightened the precise knot a fraction. I had the irresistible feeling he wanted to tighten his hands round my neck. "And is Mr Kleinman expecting you?" he said through stiff lips.

"Only in the most general way. He knows I'll be wanting to talk to him sometime. Nothing urgent. I'll pop back another time, when I'm not in your way." I headed for the door, doing the confident routine.

"While you're here, let's you and me have a little chat while we're waiting," he commanded.

"Fine by me," I said. "It'll save me having to get up early tomorrow for our little chat." I can't help myself, I swear. Every time I run up against a copper who thinks he's in the last days of his apprenticeship to God, I get one on me. I walked over to the desk and leaned against it. Jackson squirmed forward on the sofa to try and get in a commanding position. I could have told him it was a waste of effort. "Ask away, Inspector," I invited him.

"In your statement, you said you'd been here, quote, about an hour, unquote, before you and Mr Franklin went in search of Miss Pollock."

"That's right," I confirmed.

"You can't be more precise than that? I'm sorry, but I find that very hard to believe, Miss Brannigan. I thought you private eyes prided yourselves on being accurate." Had to get his little dig in, didn't he?

I shrugged. "Don't you find that's so often the way it is, Inspector? People's memories are incredibly inconvenient. I'm constantly surprised when I'm interviewing people by the things they manage to be vague about."

"Perhaps we can be more precise if we work backwards. Where did you come from? And what time did you leave there?"

"I had been working near Warrington. I finished there about half an hour after midnight, and decided that since I was only ten minutes or so away from Colcutt, I'd pop in for a nightcap." Time to go on the offensive, I decided. I really couldn't afford to get into a detailed analysis of time and place. "What's the big deal, anyway, Inspector? Still trying to get Jett in the frame? I'd have thought there wasn't a lot of point in that now you've got someone in custody."

He pushed his glasses up and rubbed the bridge of his nose in an exasperated gesture. "Why don't you just leave us to do the job we're paid to do, Miss Brannigan?"

"Are you denying you've arrested Maggie Rossiter?"

"If you're so keen to find out what we're up to, you should send that boyfriend of yours along to our press conferences," he said sarcastically. Pity the police aren't as good at catching villains as they are at gossiping. "At least that way you'd get hold of the right end of the stick. You still haven't answered me. What time was it when you got here?"

"I told you, I can't be sure. We chatted for about an hour, I'd guess, then Jett went to fetch Moira."

"Why did he wait that long? Why didn't he go and get her before then?"

I took a deep breath. "He went to get her then because they'd arranged to meet for a working session in the rehearsal room and he didn't want her hanging around waiting for him. I guess he didn't go and get her before because he didn't know where she was."

"How long was he away?"

"A couple of minutes. Not long enough to kill her, if that's what you're trying to get at. Besides, I felt her skin temperature when I tried for a pulse. She was a lot cooler than she could have got in three or four minutes."

"Don't tell me," Jackson said sarcastically. "Let me guess. And she wasn't as cold as she would have been if she'd been dead an hour, am I right?"

"That would be my judgement, yes," I replied.

"I'm sure our pathologist will be fascinated by your expert opinion," Jackson sighed. "When you saw the girlfriend—was she going towards the house or away from it?"

"I can't be certain, but I think she was heading back towards the village."

Jackson nodded. "And she looked what? Startled? Afraid? Upset?"

"She looked pretty startled. But who wouldn't, nearly being run over in the small hours?"

"And when you went rushing off to interview her, did she happen to mention how Moira Pollock met her end?"

"No." That I was sure about.

"And did you?" He was probing more firmly now. I began to wonder why he wasn't back at the station giving Maggie the third degree.

"No. You told me not to, remember?"

"And you always do what you're told? Spare me, Miss Brannigan."

I pushed myself away from the desk. "I don't know where this is getting us, Inspector, but I've got more important things to do with my time than sit here being insulted. If you've got some genuine questions to put to me, fine, we'll talk. But if you're just going over old ground, and trying to get me to change my testimony to incriminate my client, then you're wasting your time as well as mine." I was halfway to the door as I finished. But Jackson was faster than me.

He blocked the doors, standing with his back to them. "Not so fast," he began. Then he stumbled forward, nearly cannoning into me as someone pushed the door behind him.

Kevin looked furious as he stomped into his office. "What the hell is going on here?" he started. "What is this? Why's everybody playing cops and robbers in my office?"

"I was just leaving," I said haughtily, skirting the pair of them. "I'll catch up with you another time, Kevin," I threw over my shoulder as I pulled the door shut firmly behind me. Time to do some work on my timetables.

24

I found Jett in his private sitting room, on the opposite side of the house to Kevin's suite. I walked in through the open door, then paused till he noticed me. He was sitting on a tall stool by the window, picking out fragments of old melodies on a twelve string Yamaha. After a few minutes, he turned his head towards me and nodded. He reached the end of a phrase of "Crying In The Sun," one of their collaborations from the second album, then stood up abruptly. "Kate," he said softly. It was impossible to see the expression on his face, silhouetted against the light as he was.

I sat down on a chaise longue and said, "How're you doing?"

Jett carefully leaned the guitar against the wall then folded himself into the lotus position on the floor a few feet away from me. "It's the hardest thing I've ever known," he replied, his voice curiously lacking in its usual resonance. "It's like losing half of myself. The better half. I've tried everything I know—meditation, self-hypnosis, booze. Even sex. But nothing makes it go away. I keep getting flashbacks of her lying there like that."

I didn't have anything useful to say. Bereavement isn't something I've had a lot to do with. We sat in silence for a few moments, then Jett said, "Do you know who killed her yet?"

I shook my head. "I'm afraid not. I've asked a lot of questions, but I'm not a whole lot further forward. Anyone could
have done it, and nearly everyone seems to have some kind of
motive. But I've got a few interesting leads that I need to follow
up. Then I might have a clearer idea."

"You've got to find who did it, Kate. There's a really bad
atmosphere round here. Everybody suspects everybody else.
They might not admit it, but they do. It's poisoning everything."

"I know. I'm doing my best, Jett. It would help if I could
ask you a few questions." I was treading gently. I didn't know
how close to the edge he was and I didn't want to be the one to
push him over. Besides, he was the client, therefore not up for
any kind of badgering.

He sighed, and forced out a half smile that looked grotesque
on his haggard features. "I laid you on, so I guess I have to pay
the price. Look, I have to go see Moira's mother. Why don't you
drive me into town and we can talk on the way."

"How will you get home?" I asked. Trust me to find the
completely irrelevant question.

He shrugged. "Gloria'll come and pick me up. Or Tamar.
It's not a problem."

I followed him out the door and down the stairs. On the
front steps, he paused and said, "You can ask me anything you
want, you know. Don't worry about sparing my feelings."

"Thanks." I unlocked the car and kept an anxious eye on
him as he squeezed into the passenger seat. The briefest of smiles
flickered on his face as he strapped himself in.

"I've got too used to flash motors," he remarked.

I revved the engine and headed off down the long drive.
The tyres hissed on the wet road, the wipers struggled to keep
the screen clear. "Weather looks like I feel," Jett said. "OK, Kate,
what d'you want to know?"

"Can you run through your own movements from about
eight? I particularly want to know where and when you saw
anyone else."

Out of the corner of my eye, I saw Jett massage the back of his neck with one hand, then rotate his head a few times. "Tamar came back from one of her shopping sprees, and said she'd cook us some dinner."

"Was that usual?" I butted in.

He shrugged. "We don't stick to formal routines round meals here. Everybody kind of fends for themselves, except for Sunday. Gloria always cooks a proper Sunday dinner and we all get together then. But Tamar often cooks for the two of us. Moira did dinner a few times the first couple of weeks she was here, but once we'd really got stuck into the work, she didn't bother."

"Right. So what did you do then?" I opened the window and pressed the gate release button. A flurry of rain stung my face before the electric window could wind up again.

Ignoring the invasion of the weather, Jett said, "Moira and I went down to the studio to see Micky about a couple of tracks we weren't happy with. He wanted to do some fancy stuff with drum machines and stuff, but we weren't thrilled with the idea. So we discussed it, and then I went up to have dinner with Tamar."

"Did you and Moira come back upstairs together?"

Jett thought for a moment. "No," he eventually said. "She was still there when I left, but she was upstairs a few minutes later, because I saw her going towards the front door as I came through from the kitchen. I thought she was going off to meet Maggie."

"So you knew Maggie was staying in the village?" I asked, with a vague gesture in the general direction of the pub.

"Sure I knew," he replied in surprise. "Moira didn't broadcast it, but she had to tell me. I'd have been worried, you see, if I'd been looking for her and I hadn't been able to find her. I told her to bring Maggie up to the house to stay, but she wasn't having any of that. Said she didn't see why Maggie should have to put up with the shit she was getting from all sides."

"OK, so after Moira left, what then?"

"We ate our steaks, and watched *Regarding Henry* on the video. Tamar went off to have a bath just before ten, and I came up here to make a couple of phone calls. There were a couple of session musicians I wanted for next week, and I needed to check they were available. Usually, Micky does that, but he's got such strong ideas about this album that I didn't trust him not to come back to me pretending they couldn't make the sessions. After that, I went along to Tamar's room and we went to bed together." His voice dropped and he came to a halt.

"What exactly is the score between you and Tamar?" I prompted.

"That's a question I don't have the answer to. I'm fond of her, but sometimes she drives me crazy. She's so materialistic, so empty compared to Moira. I keep thinking I'll end it, then we go to bed together one last time and I remember all the good times and I can't let go. Maybe if Moira and me had been able to get it together in bed again, I'd have been able to free myself."

You mean Tamar's a great lay, and you won't say goodbye till something better comes along, I thought cynically. "I see," was all I said. "So where did you go after you left Tamar's room?"

"I went back to my room and had a shower. Then I went down to the rehearsal room. That must have been some time between half-eleven and midnight. Moira and I had planned to do a couple of hours' work on a couple of new songs, but we weren't meeting till half-past one."

I said nothing for a moment, concentrating on the road junction ahead. The traffic comes down that main A56 like it was a German autobahn and speed limits hadn't been invented. I spotted a gap in the cars and went for it. Thank God for the Nova's acceleration. It took Jett by surprise, I noticed. He was thrust back into his tight-fitting sports seat with a look of serious discomfort on his face.

"Isn't that a bit late to start work?" I asked.

Jett relaxed as my speed levelled out and the G-forces disappeared. His smile this time seemed genuine, though I couldn't see into his eyes. I adjusted the rear-view mirror slightly so I could see his face. "We always did our best work in the early hours," he told me. "Sometimes we'd still be tossing lyrics and tunes around at dawn. In the early days, we used to drive off to a greasy spoon around five in the morning and have bacon butties and tea to celebrate our new songs."

"So why did you go off to the rehearsal room so much earlier than you'd arranged?"

"I'd had a tune going round my head for a couple of hours, and I wanted to fiddle around with it a bit before Moira arrived. So I'd have something new to show to her, I guess. I tinkered with it for a while, then I decided to fix myself a sandwich, so I went off to the kitchen. That must have been just before one, because the news came on the radio while I was eating." His speech had become noticeably more jerky as he got closer to the discovery of the body, his shoulders tense and hunched.

I slowed for the roundabout but still managed to hit the motorway slip road at fifty-five. This time, Jett made it to the grab handle in plenty of time.

"Did you see anyone at all?"

"No. But then I probably wouldn't have noticed anyone unless they'd actually spoken to me. My head was full of music, I wasn't paying attention much to anything else. I don't know how to explain it to someone who's not a musician. I don't even remember what was on the radio. They could've announced World War Three and I wouldn't have taken it in."

Which explained Gloria's behaviour. Great. I had a client in the right place at almost the right time. I had a witness who wasn't admitting it yet, but who could put him there. And it was my lies to the police which had given him his non-existent alibi. Never mind Inspector Jackson, Bill was going to love this.

"Did you go straight from the kitchen to the rehearsal room, then?"

Jett bowed his head in assent. "That's when I found her. I was only a room away, and I didn't hear a damn thing."

"Because the rehearsal room's so well soundproofed?"

"That's right. That's why the police had to believe you and me when we said we didn't hear a thing."

There was no point in questioning him about what he'd seen in the room. I'd seen it too and it hadn't told me anything except that Moira was battered to death with a tenor sax. Besides, he seemed to be retreating inside himself, and I figured I'd have to move the conversation into different channels if I wasn't to lose him altogether. "Who do you think it was, Jett?"

"I can't believe any of us did it," he said in a tone that lacked conviction. "Shit, we're always rowing in this business. Nobody ever got killed before."

"She'd been arguing with Kevin, hadn't she? Do you know what that was all about?"

"She thought he was ripping her off over her royalties. But that was only a little bit of it. She made me stand up to him to get the deal she wanted—you know, a profit percentage on the album, an increased royalty rate, and now she was pushing for a production credit too. She kept telling me I wasn't getting my share either, that Kevin was taking too much of a rake-off. And she kept going on about how I was being ripped off on the merchandising. She said there were loads of illicit copies of the tour merchandise all over the place, and Kevin should be doing something to put a stop to it, and why wasn't he."

My ears pricked up. Moira knew about the schneids? I was so busy with my own thoughts I almost missed Jett's next comment. "She was even hinting we should get shot of Kevin and manage ourselves. She said it wouldn't take her long to get the job sussed, then we could ditch him. I didn't want to, but she made me promise that if she got evidence that he was ripping me off, I'd go along with her."

I took a deep breath. Could anyone be as naïve as Jett appeared to be? Here he was, handing me the strongest of motives on a plate, and he didn't even seem to notice.

"Did you know someone kept dropping heroin on Moira?" I asked. The motorway petered out into dual carriageway. I barely noticed, only my automatic-pilot reflexes making me slow to within ten miles an hour of the speed limit.

His face jerked up and his lips seemed to curl inwards in a snarl. "What the hell do you mean?" he demanded.

"Someone had been leaving fixes and syringes in her room, according to Maggie. And Gloria said she'd noticed some of her disposable syringes had gone missing."

"Jesus Christ!" he exploded. "What kind of bastard would do that? Why the hell didn't Gloria tell me?"

"I suppose because she thought it was Moira who was stealing them, and it was her own business."

"The stupid cow!" he howled, smashing his fist into the dashboard. "It's her fault Moira's dead. The silly bitch!"

I took a deep breath, then said, "I'm not convinced the two things are related. I've got an idea who was behind the heroin, and I don't think it was the murderer. It's a very different thing from being the passive supplier of the means of death and actually killing someone with your own hands."

"So who was giving her heroin?"

"I don't have any proof yet. And I'm not making wild accusations without proof."

"You got to tell me. I'm hiring you. You got to tell me, Kate." There was a note of desperation in his voice. Too late I realized he was desperate for a scapegoat, desperate to wreak his personal vengeance on Moira's killer. I'd have to learn to tread a lot more carefully with Jett than I had so far.

"When I find out for sure, you'll be the first to know," I promised him. We were on the fringes of Moss-side, only a few minutes away from Moira's mother's house. I'd decided to leave for now any questions about other people's motives. The last thing I wanted right now was to put any ideas into Jett's head and have him flying off at half-cock. "Can you give me some directions?"

In a dull monotone, he told me Ms Pollock's address and how to get there. I pulled up in front of a council maisonette. It was less than fifteen years old, but already the cement facings were streaked and crumbling. These buildings would be pulled down before we citizens of Manchester had even finished paying for them.

"Like I said, Jett, I've got a few leads I want to pursue." I leaned across him and opened the passenger door. "When you get back to Colcutt, make some music," I advised him. "Try not to brood on what you've lost. Concentrate on the positive things she brought you." If someone had said that to me, I'd probably have hit them. But it seemed to appeal to Jett's New Age philosophy.

"You're right," he sighed, his shoulders drooping. He left the car and bent down to give me a little wave as he closed the door. He didn't slam it either, not like most people do. I watched him till the door opened and a skinny woman let him in. Then I got into gear and headed for friendly territory.

I hadn't been lying to Jett when I'd told him I had leads to pursue. Maybe I'd exaggerated their quantity and quality, but that was my business. Paki Paulie was high on my agenda, but there was no point in even thinking about that till later on.

There was a fax waiting for me from Josh, my financial broker friend. I'd rung him that morning to ask for a fully detailed breakdown of Moira's financial history, in the vague hope that there might be something of interest there. But right now, I was more concerned with the little matter Jett had just raised. I needed the answers to some questions. And I knew just where to go for them.

25

The smell of sweat was the first thing that hit me as I walked into the club. Not stale sweat, but the honest smell of hardworking bodies. Various voices greeted me as I walked over to the ringside where two teenage girls were engaged in kicking shit out of each other in as technically perfect a way as possible. For once, I hadn't come to fight myself, though just watching made my body yearn for release.

The man I'd come to see was standing in a line-backer's crouch, his face distorted by yells of encouragement. "Go for it, Christine," he was screaming. And we think we've come a long way from the primeval ooze, I thought, as I tapped my friend Dennis the burglar on the shoulder. He whipped round and I took a nervous step backwards.

When he saw me, he straightened up and grinned. "Hiya, Kate. Just give me a minute. Our Christine'll be through to the semifinals in a couple of minutes." Then he spun back to face the ring and resumed his passionate cheerleading. Nothing comes before Dennis's family.

The bell sounded for the end of the round, and after a moment's conferring with the judges, the referee held Christine's gloved hand up in victory. Let's face it, with Dennis's reputation, there wasn't a judge in the place who wouldn't have given any benefit of the doubt to Christine. Not that she ever needed that, I had to admit.

Christine emerged from the ring to a bear hug from her father. Even her body protector wasn't enough to stop her wincing at the force of his embrace. She gave me a wry grin and said, "I'll soon be good enough to lick you, Kate."

"On that showing, you could do it now," I told her. I wasn't joking either. I turned to Dennis. "She's really got it."

"You're not wrong. She could go all the way, that kid. She's well sound. Now, what can I do for you, Kate?"

"I need your brains and your body, Dennis."

He faked a wicked leer. "I always said you'd never be able to resist my animal magnetism. Did you finally ditch the wimp, then?"

I didn't take offence. He affectionately calls Richard "The wimp" to his face. Richard returns the compliment by calling Dennis Neanderthal Man, and Dennis pretends not to understand what it means. They're all big kids, men. And just like kids, they're ruled by their appetites. Like Jett with Tamar.

"Sorry to disappoint you, Dennis, but it's just your muscle I'm after."

He pretended to be devastated by the news, clapping his hand to his forehead and saying, "How can I face tomorrow, Kate?" Then he became serious. "Is this going to take a while?"

"Couple of hours at the most."

"Let me take Christine home, and I'll meet you in half an hour at your place. OK?"

Dennis was true to his word. Exactly half an hour later, my doorbell rang. I had the kettle boiled in readiness. He likes to stay in shape, does Dennis. He seldom drinks alcohol, never touches drugs, and runs six miles every morning, rain or shine. His only vice, apart from burglary and GBH, is cigarettes. I greeted him with a cup of sweet milky coffee, placed an ashtray by his feet and settled down with my vodka and grapefruit.

"Schneids," I announced.

"I told you all I could about the Smarts," he said, wagging a finger at me. He was right. He'd given me a head start in my inquiries. He's a great source, is Dennis, as long as the people I'm after have no connection to his friends or family. Well, those of his extended family that he's on speaking terms with at any given time. And sometimes, he spontaneously brings me little gems if he owes someone a bad turn. His moral code is stricter than that of a Jesuit priest, and not a lot easier to figure out.

"It's not the Smarts I'm interested in right now, I don't think. It's a guy in Bradford called Fat Freddy. Mean anything to you?"

Dennis frowned. "I think I've heard the name, but I can't put a face to it. He's not connected locally."

"He's in the schneid merchandising area—t-shirts, pirate cassettes. Anyway, there's a tie-in to another case I'm working. What I'm trying to get at is why someone who's legitimately involved in the merchandising business would have anything to do with a schneid merchant."

Dennis lit a cigarette and flicked a trace of ash off his shell suit bottoms. "S'easy, Kate. Say I'm licensed to produce the straight gear for a top band like Dead Babies, and I'm a bit bent myself. I find out who's doing the schneids and I offer them a deal. I won't shop them if they cut me in on their scam. I mean, a couple of years ago, shopping someone was no big deal. They just got raided and their gear confiscated. But now they've changed the law, you can go down for these trademark jobs. So it's a real threat. Also, if I was double bent, I'd offer my schneid merchant advance copies of the designs I was going to put out next, so he'd have a head start against the competition." He sat back and blew smoke rings, well pleased with himself. It made a lot of sense.

"I like it. Thanks, Dennis. That was the brain bit. Now the muscle bit. You know a dealer called Paki Paulie?"

Dennis scowled. He hates dealers more than he hates bent coppers. I think it's something to do with having two young kids. He once broke the legs of a pusher who was hanging round the local school gates, after the local police had failed to arrest the guy. There were a dozen mums who saw Dennis go berserk with a baseball bat, but not one of them ID'd Dennis when the cops arrived. They're used to rough justice round there. "Yeah," he growled. "I know that scumbag."

"I need to know if he sold any heroin to one of the people involved in this case I'm on. I've got a funny feeling he's not going to roll over for me. That's why I need a bit of muscle. You game?"

"When do we start?" Dennis asked. He drained his coffee mug and leaned forward expectantly.

❦

We found Paki Paulie an hour later in a seedy bar in Cheetham Hill. The front bar looked like any other run down pub, its clientele mainly middle-aged, poor and defeated. But the back bar was like walking into another world. In the dim light, a handful of guys in expensive suits held court at the tables lining the walls, accompanied by their muscle. Scruffy kids meandered in and out, pausing by one table or another for muttered conversation. Sometimes cash was passed over fairly discreetly in exchange for dope. More often, the dealer got up and accompanied his punter out of the bar's back door into the car park.

On my own, I'd have been scared I'd be taken for a cop. But with Dennis by my side, there was no danger of that. He nodded towards one of the corner tables while we waited for our drinks.

"That him?" I asked, trying to keep my glance casual. Dennis nodded.

Paki Paulie wore a shimmering silver grey double-breasted suit over an open-necked cobalt blue shirt. The clothes were obviously expensive but he looked cheap as a bag of sherbet lemons. He was leaning back in his chair, gazing at a point on the ceiling as if his only worry in the world was what to drink next. Next to him, a hard-looking white youth stared gloomily into an almost-empty pint pot.

Dennis picked up his glass and strolled over to the table, with me in his wake. "All right, Paulie?" he said.

"Dennis," Paulie acknowledged with a regal nod.

"How's business?"

"Not good. It's the interest rates, you know?" Paulie replied, twitching his mouth into a smile. That was all I needed. A smack dealer with a smart mouth.

"A word, Paulie," Dennis said softly.

"Dennis, you can have as many words as you want." Paulie's urbanity was firing on all four cylinders now, but it wasn't polished enough to cover the quick flicker of concern in his eyes.

"You heard about Jack the Smack?" Dennis asked innocently. Paulie's eyebrows rose. He clearly knew all about Dennis's little vigilante action. "Bad time for accidents in your line of business," Dennis went on conversationally. "State of the health service these days, nobody in their right mind'd want to end up in hospital."

Paulie's protection seemed to gather himself together and shifted forward in his seat. "You want to . . ." was all he got out before Paulie snapped, "Shut it." He turned back to Dennis and said, "I hear what you're saying, Dennis."

Dennis gestured towards me with his glass. "This is a friend of mine. She's looking for some information. She's not the law, and if you're straight with her, there's no comeback."

Paulie looked directly at me. "How do I know I can trust you?"

"The company I keep," I answered.

Dennis put his glass down and cracked his knuckles dramatically. Paulie's eyes flicked from me to Dennis and back again. I took a photograph of Tamar out of my bag. It was one I'd clipped from the papers that morning, with Jett cut out of it. "Has this woman ever bought anything from you?"

He barely glanced at it and shrugged. "Maybe. How do I know? I serve a lot of punters."

"I can't believe you've got a lot of punters like this, Paulie. Natural blonde, doesn't dress out of a catalogue, accent like Princess Di? Come on, you can do better than that."

Paulie picked up the picture and studied it. "I seen her down the Hassy," he finally conceded.

"How much did you sell her, then?" Dennis butted in, thrusting his face forwards till it was only inches from the dealer's.

"Who said I sold her anything? Shit, man, what is this? You joined the drugs squad?"

Dennis's head snapped back, like a cobra ready to strike. Before he could complete the manoeuvre that would spread Paulie's nose over his face, the dealer shouted, "Wait!" Dennis paused. The sound level in the room had dropped to an ominous level. A sheen of sweat had appeared above Paulie's top lip. His hand fluttered at his bodyguard who was straining at an invisible leash. "It's OK," he said loudly.

Gradually, the noise picked up. Paulie wiped his face with a paisley silk handkerchief. "OK," he sighed. "About a month ago, this tart came up to me in the Hassy saying she wanted some smack. She didn't seem to know what she wanted or how much. She told me she wanted it for a coming home present for a friend, enough for a dozen hits. I thought she was full of shit, but what the hell? I don't give a monkey's what they do with it. So I sold her ten grammes. I never saw her again. And that's the truth."

I believed him. It wasn't so much the threat of Dennis breaking his nose that had changed his mind. It was the thought of what would happen to him if the O'Brien brothers came looking for him. Even bodyguards have to sleep.

The thing that bothered me was that Dennis's methods hadn't bothered me. Maybe I'd been reading the wrong books. Perhaps tonight I should tuck myself up with an Agatha Christie and a few balls of pink wool.

26

I was thirty pages into *The Murder At The Vicarage* when Richard breezed in through the conservatory. "Sorry to interrupt you while you're working," he teased. I put the book down as he sat down beside me and pulled me into his arms. It was a long kiss, as if to make up for the little time we'd spent together in the previous few days.

"Fancy an early night?" Richard whispered.

"That's the nicest thing anybody's said to me today," I replied, snuggling into him. "How in God's name do you manage to put up with your job? If I had to spend my time with assholes like that lot, I'd slit my wrists."

"You just tune it out. I always treat it like I'm watching *Dynasty* or the *South Bank Show*. You know, it's either glitz or pretension. I never let myself believe it's the real world. Sometimes I feel like David Attenborough, sitting in a hide watching the habits of a strange species," he told me. "It's fascinating. And I like most of the music, so I try to forgive them their worst excesses."

"Like murder?"

"Maybe not murder," he conceded. "Though I'd have to say I think that someone like Jett is a bigger contributor to the quality of life than your average copper."

"He's not contributing much to the quality of my life right now. This job is mission impossible. A house full of people and not a decent alibi among them. And everybody has some kind of a motive. Except for Neil, who seems to be the only person who had a vested interest in her staying alive."

Richard snorted. "Him? I wouldn't put it past him to have bumped her off just to stir up a bit of scandal for his book."

"That's outrageous!" I protested. "Besides, she was an important source for him on Jett's early days in the business."

"Yeah, well maybe he milked her dry then bumped her off. From what I hear, he's been talking to the world since she died." Richard sounded mean and spiteful, which isn't like him.

I tried to show him he was just talking out of blind prejudice, explaining that Kevin had asked Neil to handle all the press liaison. "So of course he's had to talk to people."

"It's not just all the copy he's been flogging," Richard replied, still peeved. "He's been doing the hard sell on this biography too, telling people that there's going to be stuff in there that no one else even guessed at before."

I was puzzled. I remembered Neil telling me that his biggest problem with the book was that there were no new, exciting revelations. However, that had been before Moira had reappeared on the scene. "Maybe he's just talking it up," I suggested.

"I don't think so. I suppose he could just be trying to cash in on the interest in Moira's death by trying to stitch up a serialization deal sight unseen, but most feature desks won't play unless they've got a bloody good idea what they're getting for their money. Everybody's under the cosh financially these days. The golden age when you could talk a story up and still get paid when the end product didn't match up to expectations is long gone. The emperor's new clothes trick just doesn't work any more. Now they want to talk to the tailor." Richard shifted away from me and got up. "I need a beer," he said, heading for the kitchen.

While he was off examining his collection of exotic beers of the world, I thought about what he'd said. I still couldn't believe he seriously thought Neil would have killed Moira for a few headlines. But I know from Richard that there is still big money to be made in the seedy world of newspaper exposes. I began to wonder just what Moira had told Neil. I'd have to ask him some more questions. The trouble with this investigation was that I just didn't know the right things to ask. It wasn't like insurance fraud or software piracy, where I knew who knew exactly what I needed to know. I was floundering, and I knew it.

Richard came back with a can of Budweiser and leaned against the door jamb. "Am I drinking this on the couch, or are you still in the market for an early night?"

An hour later, I felt different again. It's amazing how good sex with someone you love puts everything back into proportion. If I didn't discover who had killed Moira, it wouldn't be the end of the world. I'd have given it my best shot, and that was all anyone could demand from me. Richard wouldn't think any the less of me, and I sure as hell wasn't going to beat myself up for not being clairvoyant.

I pulled my arm out from under Richard's shoulders as I felt the tingle of pins and needles. It disturbed his little post-coital reverie and he turned on his side to plant a soft kiss on my nipple. I felt warm and languorous, and kind of sorry for Miss Marple.

"What's happening about your schneids case, by the way?" Richard asked, with all his usual tact and sensitivity.

"You pick your moments, don't you?" I complained. "The police and the Trading Standards guys are planning another raid some time in the next few days, I think. They probably won't tell us till it's all over, if they even bother then. They're a bit embarrassed about us doing their work for them."

"So they should be. You'd think they'd be a bit more grateful that you're there to hand them the stuff on a plate."

"It doesn't work like that. There's still a fair few of them who think that proper coppers shouldn't be spending their time on things like trade mark infringements," I told him ruefully.

"Well, they can't catch burglars or car thieves. They should be glad somebody's doing something that gets a conviction or two."

Sometimes I think Richard's spent so long in the cloud cuckoo land of rock that he's lost touch with the real world. But what he'd said about schneids had reminded me of something I wanted to ask him. "Is there a lot of schneid merchandising around on the rock scene just now? You know, sweatshirts and all that?"

"You wouldn't believe the half of it," he assured me. He was wrong. After the day I'd had, nothing would stretch my credulity. "It's an epidemic. Top name acts are losing a fortune from it. Do you know, sometimes the schneid gear even ends up on sale at the official stall at gigs? God knows how they get away with it."

My ears pricked up. "You mean, it's an inside job?"

"Depends. It can be done one of two ways. Either they hire a couple of kids locally to run the stall and they're doing it as a bit of private enterprise, if the schneids are good enough. Or else somebody high up in the organization is slipping them in and not putting them through the books. I don't really know how it would work, but that's the word on the street."

I needed the answer to one more question. "Do you happen to know if Jett's been having any problems like that?"

"If he wasn't, he'd be unique. But I don't know for sure. Why don't you ask him?"

I did just that. I rolled over, picked up the phone and dialled Jett's private line. Tamar answered, and called to Jett that it was for him. A couple of moments later, he was on the line.

"Hi, Jett. Just a quick query. You know you told me Moira thought you were having problems with merchandising rip-offs?

I mean copycat versions of your tour t-shirts and sweatshirts, that kind of thing? Did she give you anything specific?"

"Well, she didn't exactly, but there was a load of fake stuff around on the last tour. I got Kevin to call in the cops, but they apparently couldn't find anything. But what's that got to do with Moira?"

"It may have nothing to do with her murder at all, but I believe she had some information connecting the fake merchandise to someone who works for you," I said cautiously.

There was a long silence from the other end of the phone. I almost thought we'd been cut off when Jett finally said, "She should have come straight to me. She knows I wouldn't stand on for that. Do you know who it was?"

"Not yet," I stalled.

"Well, find out, and when you do, you let me know. You hear?"

"Will do, Jett. Good night."

He put the phone down. Before I untucked the receiver from my chin, I heard the sound of another phone clicking into place. Interesting. Someone had been listening in.

It all fitted. Moira had told Maggie that she'd seen someone from the manor talking to Fat Freddy. Fat Freddy was doing schneids of Jett's gear. Kevin had handed Fat Freddy an envelope on the steps of the bank. And the only person at the manor in a position to exploit that relationship was Kevin.

Then I remembered something that hadn't registered at the time. When Kevin had appeared on the landing after the police arrived, he'd been suited up. Not even his tie had been loosened. Now, I know people who fall into bed with their clothes on, but Kevin didn't strike me as one of them.

"Penny for them, Brannigan," Richard said. The sound of his voice startled me. I'd almost forgotten he was there.

I lay down beside him and thought about sharing my ideas with him. By the time I'd decided it wouldn't be a bad idea, his soft, regular breathing told me that the only information

I'd be getting into his head would be subliminal. Richard was out for the count.

I couldn't believe it when the phone woke me up yet again. Blearily, I disentangled myself from Richard and grabbed the phone, checking the clock. Five past seven. This was getting silly.

"Kate Brannigan," I barked.

"All right, kid? Sorry to wake you. It's Alexis here."

She didn't need to announce herself. I'd recognize Alexis Lee's voice anywhere. The combination of Scotch, cigarettes and Liverpool have produced a unique Scouse growl. Alexis is the crime reporter on the *Manchester Evening Chronicle*, and we've done each other a few favours in the past. I didn't count waking me up as one of them.

"What the hell is so urgent you need to call me at this time in the morning?" I moaned as I dragged myself into a sitting position. Richard mumbled in his sleep and turned over. Lucky bastard.

"Jack, known as Billy, and Gary Smart," Alexis said. "A little bird told me you could give me the SP on their little operation."

"You woke me up for that? Listen, Alexis, I can't tell you a damn thing about the Smarts. If it's not already *sub judice* it soon will be."

"I thought you were half a lawyer, Kate. You should know you can't charge dead men."

"You what?"

"The cops raided their warehouse in the early hours. Billy and Gary did a runner in a hired Porsche. They got as far as Mancunian Way, then Gary lost it and they went off the elevated section. Car ended up the thickness of a club sandwich on Upper Brook Street. I'm surprised you didn't hear the bang round your place. Anyway . . ."

"Hang on a minute," I protested. "I need to take this in. So they're both dead? You're sure?"

"Believe me, Kate, I saw the wreckage. A gerbil would have struggled to make it out alive. So that's why I'm picking your brains. I thought it would make a nice little plug for Mortensen and Brannigan. Efficiency in contrast to the boys in blue."

"Look, Alexis, I'd love to help, but I've not even had a cup of coffee yet."

"No problem. Get some clothes on and meet me in the office canteen in quarter of an hour. Breakfast on me."

People think private eyes are hardnosed. They sure as hell don't know any journalists. I sighed and bowed to the inevitable. Better than having Alexis round here discussing my latest case with Richard. "Make it half an hour."

Now I knew I was never going to have to visit another disgusting greasy spoon on the tail of Billy and Gary Smart, bacon, eggs and fried bread held a strange appeal, even in the subterranean gloom of the *Chronicle* canteen. I tucked into breakfast while Alexis filled in the gaps in our telephone conversation. I couldn't believe how bright and bouncy she was at that time in the morning. And she'd been up a couple of hours before me, after a tip-off from a contact in the police control room.

I first met Alexis a week after I started working for Bill. One of her contacts had told her there was a new woman PI in town, and she'd come along to try to persuade me into a profile in the paper. I'd refused, not wanting to run the risk of being recognized on the job. But we'd hit it off, and over the years she'd become the kind of friend I could go shopping with and count on to tell me when an outfit made me look like a candidate for Crufts. And her girlfriend Chris is the best architect in town. I know—I've got the conservatory to prove it.

But this morning, she wasn't interested in my latest discoveries in skin care. She was being professional. Her untamable mop of thick black hair was growing more unruly by the minute as she ran one hand through it while taking notes with the other. After half an hour, she knew almost as much about the Smarts as I did.

The surprise of her news had worn off, and I'd begun to feel sorry for Billy and Gary. OK, they'd been villains, but they hadn't been the kind of villains who cause individuals pain. They hadn't been burglars, or armed robbers or killers. They hadn't deserved to die like that just for ripping off a few big companies who would barely notice the hole in their balance sheets. I said as much to Alexis, albeit off the record.

"Yeah, I know. We're going to run a reaction piece about the number of people who die as a result of police chases. It's well out of order. Mind you, I think I'm going to have to give Richard a warning," Alexis added, her blue eyes giving a twinkle as she smiled. I swear she practises that twinkle in front of the mirror to charm cops and victims of crime alike.

"A warning? What about?"

"Well, there seems to be a lot of death and destruction hanging around you these days." Alexis lit a Silk Cut and blew a plume of smoke over her shoulder. She's always had interesting manners.

"I don't know what you're talking about," I lied. I drained my polystyrene cup of coffee-flavoured dishwater and tried to look innocent.

"Come on, supersleuth. It's me you're talking to. Everybody knows you're working on Moira Pollock's murder. I'll admit, I was surprised to find you off your usual white-collar beat, but then I heard on the grapevine that it was you that found the body. Care to go on the record about it?" Alexis's voice was offhand, but her eyes were hard.

I shook my head. "No way. Sorry. I can't even confirm what you've just suggested, on or off the record."

Alexis shrugged. "Oh well, it was worth a try. We'll just have to make do with Neil Webster's copy. Not that I've any

complaints on that score. It's been remarkably detailed for supposedly official stuff. Would you believe, he's even pitched us
into paying him for it? He actually managed to persuade the
newsdesk that he wasn't just issuing press releases, but operating
as a freelance inside Jett's camp."

"Really?" I was interested, in spite of my desire to keep
Alexis's nose out of my business for once.

"You can come upstairs and have a read through it if you
want. That'll keep you quiet while I write my copy, because
I know you'll want to check it. After all this time, I'd have
thought you'd trust me to spell Brannigan," she grumbled
good-naturedly.

I jumped at the chance. Neil was more accustomed to
interrogating people than I was. Maybe there was something in
his reports that I'd missed. Either way, as Alexis said, it would
pass the time.

27

Alexis hadn't exaggerated, for once. Neil's copy was all she'd claimed for it. Dramatic, detailed and accurate. That was what puzzled me. "Alexis?" I interrupted the rush of her fingers over the keyboard at the next terminal.

"Mmm?" she paused, keeping her eyes on the screen.

"Are these stories arranged in the order they came in?"

"Probably. They arrive in a special directory for electronically transmitted copy, and then whoever is on the newsdesk sends a copy of anything crime related into my electronic desk. The dates on the files refer to the last time I entered it, but the order they're listed in is the order in which they were put there," she explained, pointing out what she meant with her pen.

"This first batch of copy from Neil. When did it arrive?" I asked.

"Not sure. It was waiting in the transmission desk when the day staff came on duty, that's all I know."

"What time would that be?"

"The early newsdesk guy comes in at half-past six. I was in around half-past seven myself that morning. He told me the copy had come in overnight. I helped myself to a printout and went over to Colcutt. Got bloody nowhere, of course. I'm busy telling my desk that nobody's talking, nobody's even reachable, and he seems to think that I can fly over the gates and pick up all the stuff Neil isn't telling."

"Poor you," I sympathized absently. "Is there any way of telling exactly when Neil's copy arrived in your transmission desk?"

Alexis ran a hand through her hair. The effect would have frightened small children. "Not that I know of. Not at this end. Maybe he date-stamps his files, but we don't keep any copy trail that gives that kind of info. That all you wanted to know?"

I nodded, and she returned to her story. I wondered how exactly I could get the information I needed. It seemed to me that a lot of the details in Neil's copy were only generally known at the manor much later than he'd transmitted them. I needed to know who'd given him that information, for as far as I was aware, it was known only to me, Jett and the killer. If Jett had told him, there was no problem. If it had come from anyone else, then I'd have my killer. Unless, of course, Jett was the killer. God, this was all so complicated. I yearned for a nice, clear set of fraudulent accounts.

Alexis hit a key with a flourish and swivelled her chair to face me. "All done. Want a look?"

I read the copy. It was good. It made Mortensen and Brannigan look efficient and subtle, as opposed to the police, who came out smelling of the stuff you put on roses. I pointed out a couple of minor corrections, to keep Alexis on her toes. Muttering about "nit pickers anonymous," she made the changes.

As I got to my feet, she said, "When you've got anything to report on Moira's murder, give us a tip-off, eh? And if you're going to point the finger and get the cops to make an arrest, my edition time's ten a.m."

I was still smiling when I parked outside the office ten minutes later. I was first in, by five minutes. Shelley looked shocked to find me at my desk when she walked in at five to nine. I winked and said, "We never sleep."

"I can tell," she replied. "Next time you kindly grant me a holiday, remind me to borrow those bags under your eyes."

I was desperate to get back to the manor and ask more questions, but I knew it would be too early for the night owls. Instead, I decided to ring DI Tony Redfern to ask what they'd found in the Smarts' lock-up.

Tony sounded almost relieved that someone wanted to talk to him about anything other than the fatal car chase, so he gave me all the details I needed to write my report. I'd only just put the phone down on him when Shelley buzzed me. "I've got Inspector Jackson on the line for you," she said. "He sounds like he's just been stung by a wasp."

"Thanks for the warning. Put him through, would you?" My heart sank. The events of the morning had put my appointment with Jackson right out of my mind. Besides, I couldn't imagine what more he thought he could get out of me than he'd done the previous afternoon.

"Good morning, Inspector," I greeted him.

"Why am I speaking to you over the phone instead of face to face?" he demanded.

"I thought we covered the ground yesterday afternoon, Inspector. Besides, I've been a little busy this morning with your colleagues in the Greater Manchester force. If you'd like to check with Detective Inspector Redfern . . ."

"I'm a busy man, Miss Brannigan, and I'm in the middle of a murder inquiry. When I make appointments, I expect them to be kept."

His dignity had obviously taken more of a bruising than I'd realized after Kevin's entry yesterday. Time to smarm. "I appreciate that, Inspector. Perhaps we could make it another time?"

"How soon can you get round here?"

"I'm really sorry, Inspector. But I'm tied up for the rest of the day. Perhaps tomorrow?"

"Tomorrow morning, same time," he snapped. Obviously he didn't feel he could push it. I suppose I should have felt relieved I wasn't actually a suspect.

"That's a date," I promised. "Sorry about today, it went clean out of my mind with the other business. By the way, have you charged Maggie Rossiter yet?"

There was a silence. Then he said stiffly, "Miss Rossiter was released at eight-thirty this morning." The line went dead.

Surprise, surprise. They'd had their hands on Maggie for thirty-six hours and they hadn't been able to manufacture enough of a case to hang on to her. I flicked open my notebook and called her number. She answered on the third ring. "Maggie? Kate Brannigan here. I've just heard that you'd been released, and I wanted to tell you how pleased I was."

She cut in, her voice remote and cool. "Yes, well, I owe that to Moira."

"I'm sorry?"

"My next-door neighbour, Gavin, picked up the post this morning. He noticed a letter to me in Moira's handwriting. It was posted second class the night she was killed. She must have dropped it in the box on her way to meet me. She was like that, you know. Thoughtful, romantic, even. Take it from me, it's not the letter of someone who's splitting up with her lover."

"So Gavin got it to your solicitor, did he?"

"That's right. He's got a friend with a fax machine, so he opened it and sent it straight over to my solicitor. She brought it round to the police station right away."

And of course, with no motive, the police case collapsed. They had nothing at all to base a charge on. No wonder Jackson was looking for someone to kick.

"Thank God that's over," I said.

"Don't be too sure," she replied glumly. "I got the distinct impression that they haven't given up on the idea of pinning it on me. Let's face it, if they can't stick it on the dyke or the black, they'll be less than happy. I'd make sure you're covering your client's back, if I was you, Kate."

The phone went dead, before I even had the chance to tell her about Fat Freddy. I decided I'd try her again in the evening, once she'd had a bit of time to get used to being home alone again. I used the rest of the morning to type up a report for Bill and our clients about the morning's events. It was a sorry ending to a successful investigation.

I was putting a new pack of microcassettes in my handbag when I caught sight of the detailed info Josh had faxed me about Moira's financial problems. In the recent chaos, I'd completely forgotten to look at it. I smoothed it out and started to read.

The very first debt, for £175, caught my eye immediately. The County Court judgement on it dated from a few months after she'd left Jett. The creditors were an outfit called Cullen Holdings in Bradford. The name rang a vague bell. I went through to Shelley's office for the Bradford phone directory and looked it up. There was no listing for Cullen Holdings, but there was a listing for The Cullen Clinic. That was what had rung the bell. Before I'd joined Bill full-time, I'd done a company search on The Cullen Clinic for a client in the same line of business who was looking for traces of financial shenanigans. Or any other kind of dirt.

Shelley found the relevant records disc and I loaded it into my computer. The Cullen Clinic was owned by Dr Theodore Donn. In spite of the title, he was no medical man. His degree was a Ph.D. in electrical engineering from Strathclyde University. He'd set up The Cullen Clinic for one reason only. To make money out of abortion. He'd been running the clinic at a substantial profit for nearly ten years. He'd even survived a Department of Health inquiry into the connection between his business and a pregnancy advisory service owned by his sister, which referred their unhappily pregnant clients to The Cullen Clinic for terminations. Very cosy. And they'd sued Moira Pollock for the non-payment of a bill incurred just a week after she'd left Jett.

I closed my eyes and breathed deeply. I couldn't believe that Jett had known about that when he hired me to find her. If he'd found out after she'd come back, it gave him one hell of a motive. I knew his rigidly hostile views on abortion. I'd seen how mercurial he could be. I'd seen his rages. And above all, this crime was spontaneous, panicky and angry.

I changed discs, just to confirm what Josh's printout had told me, and called up Moira's medical records from the Seagull Project. Halfway down the page, there it was. VAT. Voluntary Assisted Termination. She must have been going through hell. Hooked on smack, pregnant, alone. It was a miracle she'd survived as well as she had. And all the more of a crime that someone had killed her when she'd finally got her life back together.

I leaned back in my chair and thought. If I'd been able to find out about Moira's abortion, the chances were that Neil could have too. Good journalists use exactly the same kinds of sources that investigators do. The only question for me was if Neil's sources in the financial sector were as efficient as mine. And if he'd told Jett about his discovery. That could be just the kind of scandal he'd been looking for to sell his book. Whether he'd still be getting any cooperation from Kevin and Jett if he'd told them he planned to use material like that was another matter entirely. It was time to ask Neil Webster a few more questions.

It was lunchtime for the world, breakfast time at the manor when I arrived. The atmosphere in the kitchen was less than welcoming. Jett looked up from the toast he was buttering to say hello, but no one else paid me a blind bit of notice. Kevin and Micky were sitting opposite Jett, both leaning forward earnestly over their cups of coffee. Tamar was shovelling down Weetabix, spluttering between mouthfuls that Jett ought to listen to Kevin and Micky, that they were right.

"Right about what?" Jett was paying me to poke my nose in, after all.

Micky's brow corrugated in a simian frown. Kevin delivered one of his ingratiating smiles and said, "We've just been telling Jett, the best thing for him is to get back to making music. Take his mind off things, let him work through his grief."

"How near is the album to completion?" I asked.

"It'll never be finished now," Jett replied morosely. "How can I even think about it?"

A look of irritation was chased off Kevin's features by a spuriously sympathetic expression. "Hey, I know you feel like that now, but you should think of this as a tribute to Moira. A way of making her spirit live on." I had to hand it to Kevin. He was shrewd when it came to manipulating Jett.

Jett looked doubtful. "I dunno, seems like bad taste, and her not even in her grave yet."

"That's just her body, Jett, you know that. Her spirit's free now. No fear, no hate, no pain, nothing to worry about. She came back because she wanted you to make music together. You owe it to her to finish that work." I cast my eyes heavenwards at Kevin's words. God, I'd be glad when this job was over.

Gloria swept into the room and headed straight for the kettle. "The police have released the rehearsal room," she announced. "We can use it whenever we want."

Jett shuddered. "No way. Kevin, I want my instruments moved out of there and up to my sitting room."

"But what about the piano? And the synths?"

"Them too. If I'm going to work, I can't do it in that room, with all the negative energies from her death."

Kevin nodded in resignation. "There's a couple of road crew live locally. I'll get them over to sort it out." He got to his feet and left, followed at a trot by Micky. Gloria finished making her herbal tea and turned to glare at Tamar, who was helping herself to a slice of Jett's toast. If I had my breakfast in an atmosphere like that, I'd be sucking Rennies for the rest of the day.

"While you're all here, can I ask when it was that you knew how Moira had been killed?" Time to get to work.

Gloria looked uncertainly at Jett. Tamar covered her toast with strawberry jam and said, "The first I knew was after I got up that morning. Jett was the only one who knew, and he wasn't in the mood for talking. Besides, PC Plod was standing over us in the drawing room till well after four o'clock. It really wasn't the atmosphere for cosy chats about murder methods."

"Gloria?" I asked.

"I knew before I went to bed," she admitted reluctantly. "I went to my office after they told us we could go to bed, and I overheard one of the policemen saying he'd never seen anyone battered to death with a saxophone before."

I couldn't disprove it, and she couldn't prove it. "Did you discuss it with anyone else?"

"Of course not," she retorted, back on her dignity.

"And was there anyone else in your office with you?"

"No. I just wanted to make sure everything was locked up securely before I went to bed."

"Jett, did you discuss the method of Moira's death with anyone at all apart from me?"

He shook his head. "Kate, I was too fucked up for conversation. No way did I want to talk about it. Also, you told me to keep my mouth shut, so I knew there had to be a good reason for it."

I thanked them all, and went off in search of Neil. He was in his office, battering the keyboard of his computer as if it were an old manual typewriter. I winced as I perched on the edge of his desk. "I can see you're not exactly familiar with the leading edge of modern technology," I said sarcastically.

He paused and grinned. "I know exactly as much as I need to do the job," he said.

"And if all else fails, read the manual?"

"You got it in one," he replied, still smiling.

"It's a shame," I said. "I always feel sorry for people who don't use their machines to their full potential."

"How do you mean?" he asked, finally intrigued enough to give me his full attention.

"Well, for example, you must have a comms setup here to send your copy, am I right?"

"You mean the modem and the Hermes Link?" he asked.
That answered one question. Now I knew which electronic
mail service he was hooked into. "That's right," I said. "But
have you ever used bulletin boards and public domain software?"

He looked at me as if I had lapsed into Mandarin. "Sorry,
Kate, I haven't a clue what you're on about."

I explained at mind-numbing length about communicat-
ing with other users through bulletin boards, about capturing
free software programs over the phone lines, and about game-
playing via modems. He looked just as dazed and confused as
I'd intended. "I bet you don't even do the things that make it
easy on yourself, like date-stamping your files."

That earned me a blank look. "Pardon?"

"You date-stamp your files, that way you can check when
they were sent and what mailbox they were sent to. A great
come-back when people haven't paid you and claim they never
had the copy."

"Oh, right," he said blankly.

"You want me to show you?" I asked, sidling over beside
him. "Just connect yourself to Hermes and I'll show you how."

Right according to plan, he connected his computer to the
telephone system. He had an autologon program, which only
revealed his mailbox number, not his ID and passwords. But
that was probably enough for what I had in mind. I memorized
the eight digit number, ran a routine quickly by him, then
exited from the link. "If you're interested, I'll come over one
afternoon after all this is finished and show you how to do it
for yourself," I offered.

He gave me a sly grin. "Be my guest. Maybe I can do you
a trade. I'm sure there's one or two things I could teach you."

How to slide under a stone without disturbing it, perhaps,
I thought. Time for a bit of hardball, I decided. "Neil? How did
you hear about the way Moira was killed?"

He shifted in his seat. "Why do you want to know?" he
asked.

"I'm just checking with everyone. Routine. I'm not very accustomed to investigating murder, and there were one or two things I forgot to ask last time around."

"Obviously, I was dying to find out exactly what had happened, but the cops told us not to talk about it while they had us cooped up in that bloody blue drawing room. Besides, the only person who seemed to know what was going on was Jett. Anyway, after the police told us we could go to bed, I collared Kevin. I told him the best way to control any bad publicity was for me to handle all the stories. I know, I know, it's earned me a few bob, but why not? Anyway, I asked him for the details, and he told me she'd been battered to death in the rehearsal room with a tenor sax." He smiled disarmingly. I wondered if he knew he'd just given me the last brick in my case.

28

Cracking a case is a unique feeling, a mixture of relief, self-congratulation and a curious sense of deflation. I felt all that and more at Neil's words, and I struggled not to show him any of it. Until the net was ready to close round Kevin, I didn't want anyone to know how much I had on him. I searched my mind for another question to ask Neil, so his last reply wouldn't stick in his mind as the thing that had sent me haring off. "Have you told Jett about the abortion yet?" I hazarded.

He froze, and a mottled flush spread up from his neck. "A-abortion," he stuttered.

I'd got him. Time for the major league bluff. "I know all about it, Neil. And I know you know. I just wondered if you'd told Jett yet."

He shook his head. "I don't know what you're on about, Kate, I swear."

"You can't bullshit me, Neil. Either you co-operate with me, or I go straight to Jett and tell him you're planning to drop that little bombshell in the public domain just to make yourself a shilling."

"You're a hard-faced bitch," he complained, his face the picture of petulance.

"Yeah, but I'm good at it. Now talk. When did you find out about the abortion?"

"A few days before Moira died," he admitted sulkily.

"Just as a matter of interest, how did you find out?"

"I ran a financial check on her, then I rang the clinic pretending to be Moira's accountant, saying she was now in a position to settle the outstanding amount, and could they send the account to me. I confirmed it was for a termination, and gave them a fake address to send it on to." He couldn't help himself. He looked smug as a Cheshire Conservative.

"So how did you plan to use the information?" I asked.

He shrugged. "I thought about telling Jett, but it didn't seem like a good idea when he and Moira were working so closely together. He's not exactly what you'd call a New Man when it comes to abortion and working wives, is he? It would have caused an almighty row, and God knows what would have happened. I decided to hang on and see what happened after the album was finished."

"You mean you were going to wait till the book came out, then sell it separately, and to hell with the damage it caused?"

His angry look told me I'd hit the nail right on the head. But he wasn't going to admit it. "Of course not," he said hotly. "What do you take me for?"

If I were American, I'd have pleaded the fifth. As it was, I just gave him my most contemptuous look and walked out.

Two doors down the hall from Neil's office, I found the dining room. It looked as if it got about as much use as Richard's vacuum cleaner. I sat down on an antique balloon-backed chair and inserted a fresh tape in my recorder. I dictated a report of the case to date, explaining the reasons for my conclusion that Kevin was the killer. The problem was that I still lacked any substantial proof. I had no doubt that would be easy enough for the police to find once he was arrested. A serious probe into his finances would be one place to start. But I had to produce enough evidence to convince the police to take that first step.

It seemed to me there were two ways to approach it. One was to "persuade" Fat Freddy to co-operate. The other was to try to flush Kevin out into the open. That was risky, but the results would be much more damning than anything a Bradford villain might have to say.

I found Jett in his sitting room, talking music with Kevin and Micky, who both looked less than thrilled to see me again. "Sorry to interrupt, but I've got something important to say," I announced.

Jett jumped to his feet and crossed the room in a rush. He gripped my upper arms so tightly I knew I'd have to forget sleeveless dresses for a few days. "You know who killed Moira? I sense it, Kate. You know!" he said intensely.

"I've got a pretty good idea," I said.

"Tell me," he shouted, shaking me.

I tried to wriggle out of his grasp, but he held on. "Jett, you're hurting! Let me go!" I demanded.

His hands fell to his sides and he slumped into the nearest chair, drained. "I'm sorry, Kate. I didn't mean to hurt you. You gotta tell me, though."

Micky lit a cigarette and inhaled deeply. "He's right. If you know, he's got a right to be told."

"I haven't got enough proof to start throwing accusations around yet," I said. "But I know where to go to find it. By this time tomorrow, I should know for sure. When I do, Jett, you'll know. What I want you to do is to get everyone together tomorrow at five. The blue drawing room's as good a place as any. I'll tell you everything I've learned then."

"For God's sake," Kevin exploded. "This is ridiculous. I never heard of anything so bloody silly. What do you think this is? Some crappy detective novel? Showdown in the drawing room? Why the hell can't you just tell Jett like you're paid to do?"

"Shut up, Kevin," Jett said forcefully. "I gave Kate a free hand. She'll handle it. She knows what she's doing."

"Thanks," I replied. "The reason I want you all together is that I have things to say that affect each and every one of you. And there are people who know more than they've told, for whatever reason. Once they know they're no longer suspects, they'll be more willing to give me the full picture."

"Can't you give us some idea now? I don't fancy spending another night under the same roof as a killer," Kevin protested.

I had to hand it to him. He had bottle. Either that or the arrogance of the criminal who thinks he's cleverer than the investigators. "No. All I will say is that Moira was killed because she knew too much. Someone in this house got greedy. They were trying to make a fast buck. And purely by chance, Moira found out. And once I've made a little trip across the Pennines tomorrow to talk to a certain businessman, I'll know everything Moira knew. And more. Now, if you'll excuse me, gentlemen, I've got work to do."

I didn't hang around waiting for a response. Within five minutes, I was heading back to town. I'd done my best to flush Kevin out. Now I was going to have to cover my back.

I double-tracked the busy line between Essen and Utrecht and monitored the effect on my station boxes. Railroad Tycoon, the ultimate computer strategy program, was doing the trick of taking my mind off the waiting game. It's not just little boys who like playing trains.

I'd been building my trans-European railroad for about an hour when the doorbell rang. I froze the game and went through to the hall. The security lights blazed down on a uncomfortable-looking Kevin. Surprise, surprise. I was a little taken aback by the full frontal approach, but if he'd been planning to take me by surprise, he would have been foiled by the lights as soon as he got within twenty yards of any of the windows. I must remember to tell clients that they're a great deterrent against potential murderers.

"Can we talk, Kate?" he said as soon as I opened the door.

"I was actually having an evening off, Kevin. Can't it wait till tomorrow?"

"We've got some things to clear up that won't wait."

"We do? You'd better come in then," I said grudgingly, leading the way back through to the living room. I gestured to one of the sofas, and he perched on the edge.

I sat down opposite him, deliberately not offering him a drink. I wanted to keep him edgy. "What did you want to talk to me about?" I inquired.

"You're setting me up," he said abruptly, lacing his fingers together tightly. "I didn't kill Moira, and you're trying to make it look like I did."

"I am? What makes you say that?" I asked coolly.

He cleared his throat and swallowed hard. "I overheard your conversation with Jett last night. I picked up the extension because I was waiting for a call."

"On Jett's private line? You'll have to try harder than that, Kevin."

He sighed. "All right, all right. I picked it up because I was nosy, OK? That suit you better?"

"Much better. I prefer it when people tell me the truth. You overheard our conversation. So?"

Kevin unlocked his fingers and massaged the back of his neck with one hand. "I'll come clean. I admit I've been doing one or two side deals that might not be strictly kosher."

"You mean you've been ripping Jett off with fake merchandise. Let's stick to plain English, Kevin."

He flinched. "OK, but that doesn't mean I killed Moira. I don't even think she knew anything about it."

"She didn't tell you she'd seen you and Fat Freddy together?" I was intrigued by the line he was taking. I had to admit what he was saying wasn't impossible. After all, at the time of Moira's death, Maggie still hadn't found out exactly what line of work Fat Freddy was currently in. For all Moira knew, it could have been nothing to do with Jett.

"No, she didn't. And if she'd known about it, do you really think she'd have kept her mouth shut? She was quick enough to badmouth me to Jett and to anyone else who'd listen about her bloody royalties money. She couldn't have resisted telling him anything she found to blacken my name with," Kevin protested.

The psychology sounded credible, I had to admit. But my belief in his guilt didn't just depend on one thing. I was torn between letting him stew till the following evening, and fronting him up with what I suspected, to see if I could nail him once and for all. Arrogance won, for a change. "You must have wanted rid pretty badly," I observed.

Kevin gave me an admiring smile, all expensive dentistry and insincerity. "Nice try, Kate. I'll admit that if she'd said she was leaving, I'd have carried her bags to the station. But murder? That's not my style."

"You had plenty of motive, though."

"Me?" Kevin threw his arms out in a gesture of supplication. "Kate, if I bumped off every musician who made my life difficult, I'd have been in Strangeways a long time ago."

"I hear Moira thought that's where you should be."

Kevin's eyelids fluttered as his body tensed. "Look, you keep making these innuendos, but I'd suggest you don't repeat them outside these four walls."

"I'm talking about money, Kevin. Not just the business with Fat Freddy, or Moira's back royalties. She was convinced you were doing some fancy footwork with Jett's cash. Otherwise, why would he be on the constant treadmill of tours and albums? Most people of his stature who've been in the game as long as he has take it a lot easier than him. A few big stadium dates, an album every eighteen months or so. But according to Moira, Jett had to keep working to keep paying the bills. So where was all the money?" I pinned him with a hard stare, and I was gratified to see his hands grip his knees tightly.

"Look, I told you. If she'd had any proof of anything like that, do you think I'd still be around?" he exploded. "She was full of shit! She loved to stir it. I told her a dozen times, her cash was all accounted for. It was tied up in a high interest investment account that I have to give three months' notice of withdrawal on. Out of that tiny, insignificant fact, she built a whole edifice of poisonous rumour. That shows you the kind of woman she was."

"Frankly, I'm amazed. I'd have expected you all to fall on her neck weeping tears of joy and gratitude, given the way Jett's career's been going of late," I retaliated.

Kevin's head seemed to shrink into his shoulders, like a tortoise in retreat. "Listen, Kate, I said when you started looking for Moira that we were looking at trouble. She was always a manipulative bitch. She loved playing us all off against each other, always had. OK, Jett's been going through a difficult patch in creative terms, but he would have come good again, with or without Moira. He just got this crazy obsession that he needed her. So we all got lumbered with her. She was only through the door five minutes when she had us all at each other's throats. I've told you already. We're not killers. We're putting an album together, that's the number one priority. No one would jeopardize that by making us the focus of all these shitty stories in the press," he added.

"I thought Neil was controlling the press for you."

Kevin snorted. "Might as well try to knit a bed jacket out of a mountain stream as try to control those toe-rags. Neil's done his best, but he's got an uphill struggle on his hands. God knows where they've got some of this stuff from. I mean, one of them's even got some tale about Moira and Tamar being at each other's throats. I've a good mind to sue, except that it would only cause more bad publicity."

"You'd have a job suing." I couldn't resist it.

"What d'you mean?" he asked indignantly.

"I don't think you'd have any grounds," I said sweetly. "But let's leave that aside for a minute," I continued. "Cast your mind back to the evening of Moira's death."

He butted in eagerly. "I suppose you want to know what I was doing when Moira bought it?"

I nodded. He nodded. We were like a pair of toy dogs on a car's parcel shelf. "No problem," he said. "I'd been over to Liverpool for a business meeting and I got back around nine. I stuck my head round the TV room door and said hi to Jett and Tamar. Then I nipped up to my office to make a few phone calls. Around ten, I went downstairs and made myself a steak sandwich, then I popped down to the studio for a word with Micky. That must have been getting on for eleven. He was up to his eyes in it, so I left him to it and went back up to the TV room. Gloria was watching Dead Babies on *The Late Show*, and I sat in for a while. I went back down to the studio about quarter to twelve, and listened to a couple of tracks with Micky, then I hit the sack. Next thing I knew, all hell was breaking loose."

It was just detailed enough to be credible, if a bit glib. "You don't have any problem with your memory, do you? Not like Micky?"

Kevin pulled a face. "Nose like mine, Kate, you don't mess about with it, if you catch my drift. Anything other than music goes out of Micky's head like water down a drain. Besides, I've already been through it once for the boys in blue. I was there twice, and he can't deny it."

"Did you see anyone near the rehearsal room?" I asked.

"Afraid not. The whole thing's a mystery to me. I can't accept it was one of us, you know. It must have been someone on the outside," Kevin told me confidently.

I ignored the pathetic attempt at a red herring. "You say you went up to bed after you'd spoken to Micky?"

"That's right. You saw me come downstairs yourself," he pointed out, his tone grievance incarnate.

"Precisely. And do you normally go to bed in a suit and tie?"

His eyes widened, and the fingers of one hand started to beat a nervous tattoo on his knee. "Just because I hadn't actually gone to bed yet doesn't mean a thing."

"You'd been upstairs nearly two hours. And you hadn't even loosened your tie, Kevin. That's not normal behaviour. And in a murder investigation, anything that's not normal behaviour is automatically suspicious. So what was going on?"

Kevin took a deep breath, leaned his elbows on his knees and rubbed his face. "If you must know," he said, his words curiously muffled, "I was going out. I haven't always shacked up in a grace and favour corner of Jett's house, you know. I've got a home of my own, Kate, a beautiful place down the road in Prestbury. Queen Anne style house, five bedrooms, gym, jacuzzi, swimming pool, the works. The wife lives there. When we split up, I moved in at Colcutt temporarily while I sorted things out. Only, my wife, she's screwing me for every penny she can get her hands on. And she's fucked off on a skiing holiday with her new boyfriend. I was going round to burgle the house." He raised his head and stared defiantly at me.

"In a suit and tie?" I blurted out incredulously.

"I thought it would be the least suspicious thing to be wearing if anyone saw me or if I got stopped by the police," he said lamely. "I know it sounds stupid, but she'd got me so wound up, I just wanted to get back at her."

"And make a few bob at the same time? That's some excuse, Kevin. God, you're pathetic"

"I might be pathetic in your eyes, but I'm not a bloody killer," he flared up.

This wasn't working out at all as I'd imagined. In my scenario, he was going to probe to find out what I knew then mount a murderous attack when he discovered I had him. Right now, he didn't look as if he could crush a daddy-long-legs.

I took a long swig of my drink and settled back to deliver the clincher. "Can you explain something to me, Kevin? If you didn't kill Moira, how is it that you knew exactly how she'd been murdered before the police told everyone?"

He looked completely nonplussed. Gotcha, I thought. Prematurely, as it turned out. "I don't know what you mean," he said with an air of bewilderment. "I knew the same time as everyone else. When the police interviewed me."

I shook my head. "Not what I've been told. According to my witness, you knew how Moira had died by the time the police released you from the blue drawing room, a couple of hours after the murder."

"That's not true," he cried, desperation in his voice. His eyes flicked from side to side, as if checking the escape routes. "Who told you that? They're lying! They're all lying. They're trying to discredit me." For the first time, his smart-alec composure had cracked wide open. He clearly hadn't been expecting this at all.

"You're the one who's lying, Kevin. You had means, motive and opportunity. You killed Moira, didn't you?"

"No," he shouted, jumping to his feet. "I didn't. You bitch, you're trying to set me up! Somebody's trying to push me out. First Moira, now someone else. Tell me who told you those lies!"

He lunged at me. I pushed myself sideways on the sofa. He crashed into the arm of the sofa, letting out an "oogh" of pain. But he kept coming at me, yelling, "Tell me, tell me."

I couldn't find enough space to use any of my boxing moves on him. He threw himself on me, gripping me by the throat. His paranoia seemed to lend him extra strength. I'd miscalculated. This was something I couldn't handle myself. Red spots danced in front of my eyes, and I could feel myself retching and fainting.

29

I opened my eyes to a huge, out-of-focus face inches from my own, like a sinister Hallowe'en mask. I blinked and shook my head, and realized it was Richard, his face a mixture of fear and concern. "You all right, Brannigan?" he demanded.

"Mmm," I groaned, carefully probing my tender, bruised neck. Richard sat down heavily beside me and hugged me. Looking over his shoulder, I could see Kevin's legs. The rest of him was hidden under Bill's bulk. My boss was sitting astride Kevin, looking triumphant.

"Would someone pass me the phone?" he said calmly. "I need to call the garbage disposal people." A muffled grunt escaped from the body under him. He obligingly shifted his position slightly.

"On the table, Richard," I told him, and he went to fetch it. Bill punched in a number and asked for Cliff Jackson.

"Inspector? This is Bill Mortensen of Mortensen and Brannigan. I'd like to report an attempted murder," he began when he was finally connected. "Yes, that's right, an attempted murder. Kevin Kleinman has just tried to strangle my partner, Miss Brannigan."

I wished I could have been a fly on the wall in Jackson's office. The news that someone had actually done what he'd been longing to do since the beginning of the case must have provoked a serious conflict of interest. "Well, of course it's connected," I heard Bill protest. "They were discussing the murder at the time of the attack . . . How do I know? Because I was listening at the door, man! Look, why don't you just get over here and we can sort it all out then?"

Richard, ignoring Bill's conversation, was fussing over me. "Thank God we were there," he kept repeating.

Losing patience, I said, "It had nothing to do with God and everything to do with the fact that I told you to be there." They had been my insurance policy; Richard crouching in the conservatory, Bill lurking in the hall. Arrogant I may be, stupid I'm not.

Richard grinned. "I thought that came to the same thing? You and God?"

"They're on their way," Bill interrupted, saving me the bother of having to think up a witty reply. "Inspector Jackson doesn't sound like a happy man." A muffled shout from under him indicated that Jackson wasn't the only one.

It took a couple of hours to sort everything out. They'd made Bill stop sitting on Kevin, and he'd immediately burst into a loud tirade of complaint. Jackson had shut him up briskly and removed him in a police car to Bootle Street nick. By the time he'd taken statements from all three of us, he grudgingly admitted that the assault on me gave him enough to hold Kevin while he made further inquiries into his financial background. I could see the whole episode hadn't improved his attitude to the private sector.

After he left, Richard found a couple of carefully hoarded bottles of Rolling Rock, his all-time favourite American beer. He and Bill toasted each other, boasting cheerfully about their rescue as small boys the world over will do. I poured myself a stiff vodka and said sweetly, "Don't you think we should save the celebrations for when we've nailed the murderer?"

They stopped in mid-swig and stared blankly at me. "I thought that was what we'd just done?" Richard said. "You said Kevin had done it."

"That's what I said. But now I'm not so sure."

Richard gave one of those sighs that seem to come from his socks. "I don't get it," he complained. "Two hours ago, you were accusing the guy of murder. Now you're not so sure?"

Bill shook his head, a wry smile lurking in his beard. "OK, Kate, let's have it."

I explained my theory, and he got to his feet, muttering about no rest for the wicked. "Let's go, then, Kate," he said resignedly. "I'll see what I can do."

"Can I come too?" Richard asked plaintively.

"You'll be bored out of your tree," Bill told him. "But you're welcome to come along if you want."

"You can always make the coffee," I added wickedly. I knew how to turn him off. And much as I love Richard, I didn't want him kicking his heels in boredom while we worked. I mean, would you take a four-year-old to the office with you?

My strategy worked. Richard shrugged and said, "I think I'll just stay home. I suppose I could earn myself a few bob putting out the story of Kevin's arrest. I mean, even if you think he didn't do it, he's still down the nick, isn't he?"

"Good thinking. Why should Neil Webster be the only one making a shilling out of Moira's murder?" I teased.

He poked his tongue out at me and gave me a farewell hug before he disappeared into the gloom of the conservatory.

"You think you can do it?" I asked Bill.

He shrugged. "Don't know till I try, do I? It won't be easy, but it shouldn't be impossible."

"Well, what are we hanging round here for?"

Bill's attempts at hacking still hadn't borne fruit by midnight, when the phone rang. From force of habit, I picked it up. "Mortensen and Brannigan," I announced automatically.

"Is that Kate Brannigan?" an unfamiliar voice asked.

"That's right. And you are?"

"My name is David Berman. I'm Kevin Kleinman's solicitor. I'm sorry to disturb you so late in the day, but my client was most insistent that I speak with you. Would it be possible for me to come round to your office? I'm only a couple of minutes away." His voice was soft and persuasive.

"Can you hold a second?" I asked him. I pressed the mute button and said, "Kevin's solicitor wants to come round. I don't think he's just after a decent cup of coffee."

Bill's eyebrows rose like a pair of blond caterpillars. "Let's see what the man has to say," he said. Sometimes I think I'd kill to be that laid back.

I reopened the channels of communication and said, "That would be fine, Mr Berman, I'll meet you downstairs in five minutes." I hung up and said, "Curiouser and curiouser."

"The time has come, the walrus said," Bill muttered in cryptic response as he tried out another password. I left him to it and put on a fresh pot of coffee before I went downstairs to meet David Berman.

When I got downstairs, a prosperous-looking yuppie was waiting on our doorstep. Dark grey self-stripe suit, pale-blue shirt and a subdued paisley pattern silk tie. Not a crease anywhere, except in his trousers, and that could have sliced salami. His dark hair was fashionably slicked back and a pair of horn-rimmed glasses perched on the bridge of his nose. He smiled confidently at me as I struggled with the four locks on the plate glass doors.

As soon as I opened them, his hand was thrust towards me. The handshake was cool, with the carefully measured amount of pressure that gives the message, "I could crush your hand if I wanted to, but who needs to be macho among friends?"

"Miss Brannigan? Pleased to meet you. David Berman," he said cheerfully. "I really appreciate you making time for me at this hour of the night."

He followed me up the stairs, avoiding small talk in a way that I found slightly unsettling. I suspected it was deliberate. I showed him into the main office, and offered him coffee. Bill didn't even look up from his screen, though I caught Berman peering nosily through the door of his office.

I sat down at Shelley's desk and said, "What makes you think we can help, Mr Berman?"

"It's a little difficult," he admitted. "I am well aware of the alleged attack earlier this evening, and I can appreciate that you might not be inclined to listen to what I have to propose."

"That's one way of putting it. Your client tried to strangle me tonight. He's right off my Christmas card list. But I'm always happy to listen. You'd be amazed the things you can pick up that way."

He smiled. He was meant to. "I take your point, Miss Brannigan," he acknowledged. "It's my understanding that you have been retained by one of my client's artistes to uncover the identity of the murderer of Moira Pollock. Is that correct?"

Why do lawyers always ask questions they know the answers to? It was one of the things that made me decide I preferred being a private investigator. Maybe you don't always come across as omniscient, but at least you get the occasional stimulating surprise. "Quite right," I reassured him.

He gave a curt nod. "And I understand that you made certain allegations against my client in this matter?"

"Right again." Had it really been worth trekking downstairs for this?

"My client has instructed me to pass certain information on to you, without prejudice," he said solemnly, as if he were handing me a gift of immense value and corresponding responsibilities. His glasses had slipped down, and he peered at me through them like a judge thirty years his senior.

"Indeed," I replied. All this legalese was causing serious linguistic regression.

"You alleged that my client had knowledge of the crime at a time when only the murderer could have known it. My client denies this strenuously, and has asked me to ascertain the source of this false information so that he can refute it," he said earnestly.

I should know better than to be surprised by the deviousness of lawyers. "It sounds like you're looking for information rather than handing it out," I told him. "If your client is a murderer, would it not be rather irresponsible of me to identify a witness against him?" More linguistic contagion.

"My client is going to be charged with attempted murder," Berman replied tartly, pushing his glasses up his nose. "I don't think he'll be in a position to pose a risk to anyone. The point is that my client strongly denies possessing the aforementioned information at the time you allege. He denies vigorously passing that information on to anyone, and believes he can produce witnesses to all his conversations up to the time when he returned to his room."

I felt a prickle of interest. Berman's words suggested there might be some corroboration of my fresh suspicions. Before I could reply, Bill's voice rang through the office like a demented *Sun* journalist. "Gotcha!" he cried.

"Excuse me," I mumbled as I jumped to my feet and shot through the door. "Have you cracked it?" I asked eagerly.

"Just a matter of time now. I've hacked into the accounts section, and it's just a case of working out how the files are organized and searching them," Bill said triumphantly.

I hugged him. People need hugs, especially when they've just saved your life then made your day. Then, aware of David Berman's gaze, I returned to the outer office, this time closing the door behind me. "Sorry about that," I said. "Bill's just cracked something we've been working on for a while now. If I can just go back to what you were saying. Has Kevin given you any account of what he said to whom?"

Berman compressed his lips, then said, "I'm not at liberty to say."

"Then it seems to me we're at an impasse. You can't tell me what he said, and I can't tell you who's making the claim."

"It'll all come out eventually," he said persuasively. "You must be aware that if my client is charged, we will have to be told the names of the witnesses against him. It would surely be in everyone's interest to clear the name of an innocent man so that the search for the guilty party can go on. If my client is charged, this thing will drag on for months, and people's memories will start to fade. When he is eventually cleared, it may be too late to trap the real killer."

It was a good argument. As I picked up my bag and told Bill I was going to Bootle Street with Berman, I tried to convince myself that it was the strength of his case that had persuaded me. After all, I thought sanctimoniously, even though Kevin was Mr Sleaze in my eyes, if I had wrongly accused him, I owed it to him to sort it out. Deep down, I knew otherwise. I had a theory, and I wanted to prove it to my own satisfaction.

It was nearly three when I got back to the office. After a lot of verbal ping-pong, with David Berman as the ball, I had obtained some very interesting material. As a result, I'd spent half an hour persuading Cliff Jackson that what I had to say to him was worth listening to. Credit where it's due, once he'd explained to me in graphic detail just why I was lower than a Salford sewer, he consented to pay attention. And instead of clambering on his high horse and ignoring what I had to say, he'd not only listened but had reluctantly agreed to give my suggestion a try. "You get one shot," he'd warned me. "If you screw up, I'll bang you up as well as your chum in the cells. No messing." I was so sure of myself I didn't feel I'd be risking that.

I found Bill leaning back in his chair, a look of deep satisfaction on his face as he puffed away on a Sherlock Holmes pipe filled with some noxious continental tobacco. "Any news?" he asked me.

I told him where we were up to, and he smiled. He looked just like the Big Bad Wolf, his lips pulled back over teeth that gripped the pipe stem. Then he showed me what he'd dug up.

We were making plans until four. This time, everything was going to go like clockwork. This time, I wasn't going to end up with a necklace of bruises. Meanwhile, I had things to do. Unfortunately, sleep wasn't one of them.

30

Jett was waiting for me on the steps when I arrived at half-past four. His shoulders were hunched and his face had a tight, pinched look around the mouth and nose. "You still going ahead with this showdown?" he greeted me.

"It has to be done, Jett," I told him as we walked into the empty hall together.

"Why? They arrested Kevin. The word is he tried to kill you because you found out he killed Moira." His tone was aggressive.

"I'm sorry, Jett. He did attack me."

"No need for *you* to be sorry. You were just doing the job, like I asked you to. I'm the one should be sorry. I trusted that man with my life. And now I find out he killed the woman I cared for more than anything in the world. So why d'you have to put us through more?"

Jett hurried ahead of me into the blue drawing room. I followed more slowly, wondering how to placate Jett without giving too much away. He was pouring himself a hefty drink when I entered. "Help yourself," he told me. With a moody scowl on his face, he moved over to the spindly-legged chair and threw himself into it again. If I'd been the man from the Pru, there's no way I'd have insured it.

I poured myself a weak vodka and topped it up with orange juice, in the absence of my usual. I didn't think this was a good time to demand a grapefruit juice. I positioned myself in front of the grate, where some logs were smouldering half-heartedly.

Jett took a gulp of his drink and started to say something. He was interrupted by a knock at the door, which opened before either of us could say "Come in." Cliff Jackson barged in with a face like a man with a bad case of piles. Gloria followed him, saying petulantly, "Sorry, Jett, he wouldn't wait till you'd finished with Kate."

"Never mind that," Jackson grunted. "Just what is going on here, Brannigan? You tell me last night that Kleinman was the killer, you set him up to assault you so we've got something to stick on him, then you leave messages all over town telling me to get up here if I want to find out the truth about Moira Pollock's murder. What the hell are you playing at?"

Jett got to his feet and shot me an angry look. "You didn't tell me he was coming," he protested. "This was supposed to be between us." Out of the corner of my eye, I spotted a complacent smile spreading across Gloria's face.

"What exactly was supposed to be between you?" Jackson demanded, rounding on Jett.

"Mind your own fucking business, pig," Jett yelled back at him. Jackson flushed dark scarlet and opened his mouth to retaliate.

"If we could all stop shouting at each other, I'll happily explain," I interjected forcefully.

"I'm all ears," Jackson snarled. "It better be good. I can feel an overwhelming desire to charge someone with wasting police time." I was impressed, I have to admit it. It made me wonder just how much of his routine bloody-mindedness was an act too.

"I know that you've charged Kevin with attempted murder after what he did last night, but there are still a few loose ends to be tied up. I asked you to come because I didn't want you to turn round and say things were being done behind your back."

I turned to Jett. "I know you didn't want him here, but things have gone too far to be kept in the family. I'm sure you don't want Moira's killer to get away with it just because you left it all to me and I couldn't deliver."

Jackson was shaking his head in disbelief. "You are unreal, Brannigan. I should nick you right now for this grandstanding."

"Give me half an hour, Inspector. Then you can throw the book at me if you're still so minded."

Jackson muttered something under his breath that I didn't catch. I don't think I was supposed to. He moved across the room to stare at an undistinguished oil landscape on the far wall.

Jett drained his glass and handed it to the hovering Gloria, who bustled over to the drinks. She threw a quick glance back at Jett as if to gauge what strength he needed, then poured. I noticed it was almost as large a measure as he'd poured for himself. Maybe I'd been underestimating Gloria.

The awkward silence was broken by Tamar and Micky, who entered together just on ten to five. Tamar ignored me and headed straight for Jett, who gave her a perfunctory kiss and steered her towards the sofa.

Micky moved to my side and touched my elbow. Through the cloud of cigarette smoke, I could see the worried look on his face. "When are they going to let Kevin out on bail?" he murmured.

"I doubt if they will. He's already facing one serious charge, and there's a possibility he'll be on a murder charge by morning," I explained softly.

He shook his head. "This couldn't have come at a worse time. We're at a crucial stage with the album. I don't know what we're going to do."

I was spared having to answer by Neil's entrance. He was positively bouncing with bonhomie as he crossed the room and greeted me with a kiss on the cheek. I was so surprised I couldn't move out of the line of fire fast enough. Micky moved away, disgust written all over his face.

"I know it's tasteless to say so," Neil whispered in my ear, "but Kevin's arrest is going to make my book a bestseller. I've been on to my publisher this afternoon, and we're going to have the book ready to roll as soon as the trial finishes."

"Why don't you get yourself a drink," I said through clenched teeth. The guy gave a whole new meaning to sleaze.

He winked at me and made his way over to the bar. The distant sound of the gate intercom buzzer caught everyone's attention and Gloria moved automatically towards the door to the hall.

"It's all right, Gloria, I'll get it," I said, moving swiftly across the room to head her off at the pass. I went out into the hall, closing the door behind me, and opened the gates for the final arrival.

I stood in the doorway and watched as the car slowly made its way up the drive. It pulled up at the foot of the steps, in a kind of defiance. Maggie Rossiter climbed out of the driver's seat and made her way up the steps towards me.

I cleared my throat and said, "People, if I could have your attention for a moment?" The murmur of conversation triggered off by Maggie's arrival ended as abruptly as if I'd pushed the mute button on their remote control. Jackson turned towards me and leaned against a marble topped pier table.

"You all know about Kevin's arrest, and I expect that most of you think that it's only a matter of time till he's charged with Moira's murder. But then, you already thought that about Maggie when she was arrested. However, I was hired to find a killer, and I suspect that most of you think that's exactly what I've done. But until I've cleared up some loose ends that are still remaining, I'm afraid I can't regard the case as being closed. That's why I've asked you all together. There are some inconsistencies in the stories I've been told, and I thought the best way to deal with them was to have you all together. It's a shame Kevin can't be here, but we'll just have to work around that." I looked around at their expressions, some hostile, some fascinated.

I took a deep breath and continued. "I hadn't been working the case for very long when I discovered that someone in this house had already been trying to get rid of Moira.

"Gloria, who is a diabetic, had noticed syringes going missing from her room. It was only a matter of time before she got round to telling Jett, who at the very least would have confronted Moira and accused her of returning to her old habits. But not content with that, the person who stole the syringes also purchased some heroin. According to Maggie, every few days some heroin and a syringe would appear in Moira's room, facing her with a temptation that most people in her shoes would have found it impossible to resist.

"But she did resist, and so the first thing I had to ask myself was if the killer was the same person who'd been trying to get rid of her earlier. But you weren't the killer, were you, Tamar?"

Tamar was on her feet. "You poisonous *bitch*," she screeched at me. "You poisonous, lying *bitch*!" Then she whirled round to face Jett, whose face was as cold as a marble statue. "She's lying, Jett, I swear she's lying."

"I can prove what I'm saying," I replied coldly. "The pusher who sold you the heroin identified your picture. You might have tried to get rid of Moira, but I'm satisfied you didn't kill her. There's a big difference between offering someone the option of death and actually facing up to your victim and caving her head in."

Tamar clutched Jett's arm and fell to her knees in a histrionic show of supplication. He shrugged her arm off roughly and hissed, "Get away from me, slag."

She collapsed on the floor and began to sob noisily. Micky moved across to her and jerked her to her feet. "For fuck's sake, get a grip," he shouted angrily, dragging her away and thrusting her into an armchair.

"Get on with it," Jett snapped.

"Gloria wasn't telling me the whole truth either," I reported. She looked startled and gazed at me with a terrified fascination.

"I don't know what you mean," she stammered. "I haven't lied to you."

"You came downstairs on the night of the murder and saw someone leaving the rehearsal room. You denied it, but there's only one person you'd lie to protect, and that's Jett. It was Jett you saw leaving the room, and you lied about it."

"I never," she shouted, like a small child who's been caught out lying about a broken piece of crockery. "I never did."

"What you didn't realize was that Jett had admitted to having been in the rehearsal room earlier. But that was before Moira arrived there. So there was no point in your lie."

Gloria collapsed into the nearest chair and buried her face in her hands. "Is there anything else you've lied to me about?" I asked gently.

She looked up, tears streaking her cheeks and shook her head mutely. I was inclined to believe her.

"Micky." As I said his name, he moved a couple of steps nearer to me, his long arms dangling at his sides like a caricature of a Western gunslinger. "I want to ask you about events in this room immediately after Moira died."

"I've already told you all I know," he said mutinously.

"All I want is some more detail," I said persuasively.

"Tell her what she wants to know," Jett growled.

Micky looked as if he wanted to argue, but he quickly remembered which side his bread was buttered. "OK, fire away," he complained.

"Can you tell me where you were sitting and who you were talking to?"

"I sat down on that chair over there," he said, pointing to the one where Tamar was currently leaving salt stains on the silk upholstery. "Kevin was stood next to me, by the bar. He poured me a drink, and we talked about Moira being killed. You know, what a shock it was, that kind of thing. He was worried about the effect it would have on Jett. Whether he'd be able to finish the album, whether the bad publicity would affect sales, the usual kind of Kevin shit."

"Did he say anything at all about how she'd been killed?"

"Only that nobody seemed to be telling exactly what had happened. He said it must have been a burglar, or somebody she'd brought back with her from the village."

I hoped to hell Jackson was keeping an eye on everyone. I was concentrating too hard on what I was doing to check the reactions around me. "Did Kevin talk to anyone else apart from you?"

Micky's forehead concertinaed as he thought for a moment. "Yeah," he eventually sighed. "Neil came over and asked what he wanted doing about the press. Kevin told him to deal with it, and to put out a story on it, just giving the bare bones of what had happened. He said he wanted it all handled in-house, and that Neil should make it clear that any other journalist who tried to get an interview would be wasting their time and his."

I felt that warm feeling in my gut that tells me I've cracked it. "And that's all he said?"

Micky nodded. "Yeah. Neil fixed himself a drink and kind of drifted off to the corner. He was sitting scribbling in a notebook. I suppose he was getting a story together."

"When did you and Kevin separate?" The crucial question.

Micky looked exasperated. "I don't know what this has got to do with anything," he stalled while he visibly cast his mind back. "Let me see . . . We came out of here together and walked up the stairs after the cops said we should all go to bed. I said good night to him outside his bedroom door. He looked as sick as a parrot. No wonder, after what he'd been up to."

I turned my head towards Neil. His eyes were calm and clear as they met mine, as if he were offering me some kind of challenge.

31

The temptation to go for the high melodrama was almost over-whelming till I looked at Jett. It didn't take much perception to see that the guy was near the end of his rope. So I didn't point dramatically and say, "Inspector, there is your murderer."

Instead, I took a swig of my drink and said casually, "Neil, why did you lie to me about what Kevin said to you?"

He smiled disarmingly and spread his hands out in a gesture of innocence. "But I didn't, Kate. You're surely not going to take Micky's word against mine? A cokehead who relies on Kevin for the pennies in his bank account? He's got every reason to lie to protect Kevin. But me? Why should I lie to you?"

"There's only one reason why, Neil. You killed Moira." A strange stillness seemed to have descended on the room. I'd certainly captured their attention now.

If I'd expected Neil to cave in, I was swiftly disappointed. He grinned and said, "I hope Mortensen and Brannigan have made a good profit this year. When I sue you for slander, I want it to be worth my while."

I returned his grin. "I know I only managed to complete two years of law school, but it's always been my understanding that truth is an absolute defence in slander actions."

"But you have to prove truth," Neil parried swiftly. "And I fail to see how you're going to provide proof of something I didn't do." His smile had a triumphant edge that almost made me doubt what I knew to be true.

"But there is proof, Neil. Right under this roof is all the proof I need."

He shook his head at me incredulously. "She's out to lunch and not coming back in a hurry," he said to the room at large.

Just then, Jackson moved forward into the room. "I'd be interested in seeing your idea of proof, even if no one else is," he said. I had an idea how much it cost him to utter those words, and I had to grant him a reluctant respect.

"If you'll follow me, Inspector, we need to make a little visit to Mr Webster's office," I said formally.

"Wait a minute," Neil said, showing traces of apprehension for the first time. "What the hell do you think you're going to find there?"

"My proof," I said, stalking out of the room. I didn't need to look back to know that I could easily have passed for the Pied Piper.

Neil overtook me on the threshold and snapped loudly enough for Jackson and everyone else to hear, "Just what the hell do you think you're playing at? All this because your precious boyfriend wasn't good enough to write Jett's biography?"

"This has got nothing to do with Richard," I informed him and everyone else within earshot. The tension was beginning to eat into me, and I didn't know how long I could maintain my cool façade.

"Oh no?" he sneered.

Ignoring him, I went straight to his computer, sat down in front of it and switched it on. Jackson leaned over my shoulder, while the others crowded round behind him. Neil hung back slightly, but his eyes were glued to the screen. I briefly looked through the text files in the directory where he stored his stories, then I moved over to his communications program and keyed into it. "For those of you who aren't familiar with computers," I said as I hit the keys, "This is a program that sends material over the telephone lines to another computer. Journalists use it to file copy electronically to newsdesks."

I chose the "Text edit" option and called up the first story he'd sent out about Moira's killing. I slowly scrolled through the story till only the last line remained off screen. "As you'll see, Neil had all the details of how Moira was killed. No problem with that if the story was filed after the police gave you all the details of how Moira was killed. Details which none of you who were shut up in the blue drawing room knew except Jett."

"Which it was," Neil blustered. "And you can't prove otherwise."

In silence, I brought the last line up on the screen. It gave the date-stamp on the story. 2.35 a.m.

"It's a set-up," Neil shouted wildly. "She's set this up, can't you see? She's the only one who knows enough about computers. She's framed me." His face was glossy with sweat and his eyes flicked nervously round the room.

"You can confirm that evidence with the company who transmit the electronic mail, I should imagine, Inspector," I said coldly.

"Neil Webster," Jackson intoned, pushing through the press of bodies. "I must warn you . . ."

The rest of his official caution was drowned by the sound of breaking glass as Neil threw himself through the window in a sparkling shower of splinters.

A soft kiss tickling the back of my neck woke me up. "I hear you nailed the bastard," Richard murmured into my ear. "Well done."

I groaned softly and rolled over on to my back. I could feel the warmth of his naked flesh next to mine, and the prospect of snuggling into him was more tempting than I wanted to admit. So I complained, "Couldn't it wait till morning?"

"I only just heard about it. I went into the *Mirror* to drop off some copy, and they told me Neil had been arrested, thanks to some nifty footwork by Mortensen and Brannigan," he said proudly.

"Mmm," I said. "That's about the size of it."

"So tell me all about it," he demanded enthusiastically. He moved away from me and I heard the soft pop and hiss of a champagne bottle being opened. There was no hope of catching up on sleep now. I sat up and switched on the bedside light.

Richard blinked in the unexpected glow, then gave me his cutest smile as he handed me a fizzing glass of pink champagne. "Every cough and spit," he demanded.

So I told him all about the showdown, and how Neil had been picked up within five minutes by the team Jackson had wisely stationed outside. He'd been taken to hospital where he'd been formally charged while the casualty staff sewed up his cuts.

"Great job," Richard said with as much satisfaction as if he'd been the prime mover. "But I still don't understand why he killed her. Surely it wasn't just to produce a scandal that would sell his book?"

"Not quite. I don't think he actually meant to kill her. There was nothing premeditated about it. He was just incredibly lucky that no one else had an alibi and everyone else had better motives."

"But why?" Richard howled in frustration.

I smiled sweetly and took a long, slow mouthful of champagne. "Can't tell you. It's all *sub judice*, and you journalists can never keep your mouths shut."

"Kate!" he wailed, his face a mixture of injured innocence and pure frustration.

I had to relent. "When Moira left Jett all those years ago, she was pregnant. She had nowhere to go, and not a lot of cash left, so she had an abortion. Jett never knew about it, and it's a pound to a gold clock that he would never have had her back if he had done. The guy's notoriously anti-abortion, and he'd never have forgiven her for killing his own kid. Anyway, Neil found out about the abortion, and he told Moira he knew. Maybe he was even trying a spot of blackmail. She didn't want a walking time-bomb like that around the place. I questioned Kevin about it last night, and it turns out that she was trying to do a deal with him where Neil would be kicked out. In exchange, Moira wouldn't tell Jett about Kevin's little games with the money. Once Neil was out the door, anything he said would be seen as sour grapes.

"She must have been crowing to him about it in the rehearsal room. The prospect of being deprived of what must have been his last chance of a meal ticket was too much for him. He snapped and picked up the nearest object and thumped her with it. Like I said, I don't think murder was part of his plans, but having done it, he did his damnedest to make sure he got away with it."

"And he would have done, too, if you hadn't known about the date-stamp on the files," Richard said. "Bloody clever of you."

"Mmm," I said. "I wouldn't have known what to look for if Bill hadn't been able to hack into the electronic mail company's records to check exactly when those files were sent." I carefully put my glass down on the bedside table and rolled over into Richard's arms. I deserved some fun after the last few days.

As my body started to tingle under Richard's familiar caresses, I made a mental note to burn the cassette of that earlier interview with Neil. It wouldn't do for Inspector Jackson to find out that Neil not only hadn't date-stamped his files. He hadn't even known how to.

KICK BACK

To Lavander Linoleum
Lovers Everywhere

ACKNOWLEDGMENTS

Writing is a solitary business, but there are always other people who have helped make a book. As far as Kick Back is concerned, I owe thanks to Diana Cooper, who guided me through the legal minefields as well as providing inspirations of various kinds; Stephen Gaskell, the man from Macclesfield who takes the pain out of conveyancing; Kirstie Blades from the Birkenhead Land Registry who took the time and trouble to make sure I understood what goes on there; Andrew at Information Technology Resource in Horwich; the Longsight cheque squad, who don't even know they helped; my editor, Julia Wisdom; and, as always, the team at Gregory and Radice. Any mistakes are uniquely mine.

"Property is theft"

Pierre Joseph Proudhon

1

The Case of the Missing Conservatories. Sounds like the Sherlock Holmes story Conan Doyle didn't get round to writing
because it was too boring. Let me tell you, I was with Conan
Doyle on this one. If it hadn't been for the fact that our secretary's love life was in desperate need of ECT, there's no way I'd
have got involved. Which, as it turned out, might have been
no bad thing.

I was crouched behind the heavy bulk of the elevator machinery,
holding my breath, desperately praying I'd pick the right moment
to make my move. I knew I wouldn't get a second chance with a
nasty bag of works like Vohaul's hit man. I caught sight of him
as he emerged from the stairwell. I leaped to my feet and threw
myself at one of the pair of heavy pulley attachments suspended
from the ceiling. It shot across the room towards my relentless
opponent. At the last minute he turned, spotted it and ducked,
letting it whistle over his head. My mouth dried with fear as he
caught sight of me and headed menacingly in my direction. I
dodged round the elevator machinery, trying to keep it between
us so I could make a dash for the stairs. As he rushed after me,
I desperately swung the other pulley towards him. It caught

him on the side of the head, the momentum plunging him over the lip of the lift shaft into the blackness below. I'd done it! I'd managed to stay alive!

I let my breath out in a slow sigh of relief and leaned back in the chair, hitting the key that offered me the "Save Game" option. A glance at my watch told me it was time to leave Space Quest III for the day. I'd had the half-hour lunch break that was all I could spare in my partner Bill's absence. Besides, I knew that our secretary Shelley would be returning from her own lunch break any minute now, and I didn't want her wandering in and catching me at it. While the cat's away, the mouse plays Space Quest, and all that, which isn't very businesslike behaviour for a partner in a security consultancy and private investigation agency. Even if I'm only the junior partner.

That particular week, I was the only show in town. Bill had abandoned ship for the fleshpots (or should that be lobster pots?) of the Channel Islands to run a computer security course for a merchant bank. Which meant that Kate Brannigan was the only functioning half of Mortensen and Brannigan, as far as the UK mainland was concerned. Say it fast like that and we sound like major players instead of a two-operative agency that handles a significant chunk of the white-collar crime in the North West of England.

I headed for the cupboard off my office that doubles as the ladies loo and office darkroom. I had a couple of films that needed processing from my weekend surveillance outside a pharmaceutical company's lab. PharmAce Supplies had been having some problems with their stock control. I'd spent a couple of days working on the inside as a temporary lab assistant, long enough to realize that the problem wasn't what went on in working hours. Someone was sneaking in when the lab was locked and helping himself or herself, then breaking into the computer stock records to doctor them. All I needed to discover was the identity of the hacker, which had been revealed after a couple of evenings sat cramped in the back of Mortensen and Brannigan's newest toy, a Little Rascal van that we'd fitted out specifically for stake-out work. Hopefully, the proof that incriminated the senior lab technician was in my hand, captured forever on the fastest film that money could buy.

I was looking forward to half an hour in the darkroom, away from phones that didn't seem to have stopped ringing since Bill left. No such luck. I'd barely closed the blackout curtain when the intercom buzzed at me like that horrible drill dentists use to smooth off a filling. The buzzing stopped and Shelley's distorted voice came at me like Donald Duck on helium. "Kate, I have a client for you," I deciphered.

I sighed. The Tooth Fairy's revenge for playing games on the office computer. "*I* was playing in my own time," I muttered, in the vain hope that would appease the old bag. "Kate? Can you hear me?" Shelley honked.

"There's no appointment in the book," I tried.

"It's an emergency. Can you come out of the darkroom, please?"

"I suppose so," I grumbled. I knew there was no point in refusing. Shelley is quite capable of letting a full minute pass, then hammering on the door claiming an urgent case of Montezuma's Revenge from the Mexican taco bar downstairs where she treats herself to lunch once a week. She always varies the days so I can never catch her out in a lie.

Still grumbling, I let myself back into my office. Before I'd taken the three steps back to my chair, Shelley was in the room, closing the door firmly behind her. She looked slightly agitated as she crossed to my desk, an expression about as familiar on her face as genuine compassion is on Baroness Thatcher's. She handed me a new-client form with the name filled in. Ted Barlow. "Tell me about it," I said, resigning myself.

"He owns a firm that builds and installs conservatories and his bank are calling in his loans, demanding repayment of his overdraft and refusing him credit. He needs us to find out why and to persuade his bank to change their minds," Shelley explained, slightly breathlessly. Well out of character. I was beginning to wonder just what had happened to her over lunch.

"Shelley," I groaned. "You know that's not our kind of thing. The guy's been up to some fiddle, the bank have cottoned on and he wants someone to pull him out of the shit. Simple as that. There's no money in it, there's no point."

"Kate, just talk to him, please?" Shelley as supplicant was a new role on me. She never pleads for anything. Even her demands for raises are detailed in precise, well-documented memos. "The guy's desperate, he really needs some help. He's not on the fiddle, I'd put money on it."

"If he's not on the fiddle, he's the only builder that hasn't been since Solomon built the temple," I said.

Shelley tossed her head, the beads woven into her plaits jangling like wind chimes. "What's the matter with you, Kate?" she challenged me. "You getting too high and mighty for the little people? You only deal with rock stars and company chairmen these days? You're always busy telling me how proud you are of your dad, working his way up to foreman from the production line at Cowley. If it was your dad out there with his little problem, would you be telling him to go away? This guy's not some big shot, he's just a working bloke who's got there the hard way, and now some faceless bank manager wants to take it all away from him. Come on, Kate, where's your heart?" Shelley stopped abruptly, looking shocked.

So she should have done. She was bang out of order. But she'd caught my attention, though not for the reason she'd thought. I decided I wanted to see Ted Barlow, not because I'd been guilt tripped. But I was fascinated to see the man who had catapulted Shelley into the role of a lioness protecting her cubs. Since her divorce, I hadn't seen any man raise her enviable cool by so much as a degree.

"Send him in, Shelley," I replied abruptly. "Let's hear what the man has to say for himself."

Shelley stalked over to the door and pulled it open. "Mr Barlow? Miss Brannigan will see you now." She simpered. I swear to God, this tough little woman who rules her two teenagers like Attila the Hun *simpered.*

The man who appeared in the doorway made Shelley look as fragile as a Giacometti sculpture. He topped six foot easily, and he looked as if a suit were as foreign to him as a Peruvian nose-flute. Not that he was bulky. His broad shoulders tapered through a deep chest to a narrow waist without a single strain in the seams of his off-the-peg suit. But you could see that he was solid muscle. As if that wasn't enough, his legs were long and slim. It was a body to die for.

Nice legs, shame about the face, though. Ted Barlow was no hunk from the neck up. His nose was too big, his ears stuck out, his eyebrows met in the middle. But his eyes looked kind, with laughter lines radiating out from them. I put him in his mid-thirties, and he didn't seem to have spent too many of those years in an office, if his body language was anything to go by. He stood awkwardly in the doorway, shifting his weight from one foot to the other, a nervous smile not making it as far as the gentle blue eyes.

"Come in, sit down," I said, standing up and gesturing towards the two exquisitely comfortable leather and wood chairs I'd bought for the clients in a moment of uncharacteristic kindness. He moved uncertainly into the office and stared at the chairs as if not entirely certain he would fit in to them. "Thank you, Shelley," I said pointedly as she continued to hang around by the door. She left, reluctantly for once.

Ted lowered himself into the chair and, surprised by the comfort, relaxed slightly. They always work, those chairs. Look like hell, feel like heaven. I pulled a new-client form towards me and said, "I need to take a few details, Mr Barlow, so we can see if we can give you the help you need." Shelley might be besotted, but I wasn't giving an inch without good cause. I got the phone numbers and the address—an industrial estate in Stockport—then asked how he'd come to hear of us. I prayed he'd picked us out of *Yellow Pages* so I could dump him without offending anyone except Shelley, but clearly, wiping out Vohaul's hit man was to be my sole success of the day.

"Mark Buckland at SecureSure said you'd sort me out," he said.

"You know Mark well, do you?" Foolishly, I was still hanging on to hope. Maybe he only knew Mark because SecureSure had fitted his burglar alarm. If so, I could still give him the kiss-off without upsetting the substantial discount that Mark gives us on all the hardware we order from him.

This time, Ted's smile lit up his face, revealing the same brand of boyish charm I get quite enough of at home, thank you. "We've been mates for years. We were at school together. We still play cricket together. Opening batsmen for Stockport Viaduct, would you believe?"

I swallowed the sigh and got down to it. "What exactly is the problem?"

"Well, it's the bank. I got this from them this morning," he said, tentatively holding out a folded sheet of paper.

I put him out of his misery and took it from him. He looked as if I'd taken the weight of the world off his broad shoulders. I opened it up and ploughed through the mangled verbiage. The bottom line was he had £74,587.34 outstanding on a £100,000 loan and an overdraft of £6,325.67. The Royal Pennine Bank wanted their money back pronto, or they'd seize his home and his business. And their associate finance company would be writing to him separately, basically to tell him his punters wouldn't be stiffing them for any more loans either. And I thought my bank manager wrote stroppy letters. I could see why Ted was looking gutted. "I see," I said. "And do you have any idea why they wrote this letter?"

He looked confused. "Well, I rang them up as soon as I got it, like you would. And they said they couldn't discuss it on the phone, would I come in to see them. So I said I'd go in this morning. It wasn't my local branch, you see; all the little branches come under the big branch in Stockport now, so I didn't know the bloke who'd signed the letter or anything." He paused, waiting for something.

I nodded and smiled encouragingly. That seemed to do the trick.

"Well, I went in, like I said, and I saw the chap that signed the letter. And I asked him what it was all about, and he said that if I checked my paperwork, I would see that he wasn't obliged to give me a reason. Right stuffed shirt, he was. Then he said he wasn't at liberty to discuss the bank's confidential reasons for their decision. Well, I wasn't happy with that, no way, because I've not missed a single payment on that loan, not in the four months I've had it, and I've reduced the overdraft by four grand over the last six months. I told him, I said, you're not being fair to me. And he just shrugged and said he was sorry." Ted's voice rose in outrage. I could see why.

"So what happened then?" I prompted.

"Well, I'm afraid I lost my rag a bit, you know? I told him he wasn't bloody sorry at all, and that I wasn't going to leave matters there. Then I walked out."

I struggled to keep a straight face. If that was Ted's idea of losing his rag a bit, I could see that someone like Shelley was just what he needed. "You must have some idea of what's behind this, Mr Barlow," I prodded.

He looked genuinely baffled as he shook his head. "I haven't a clue. I've always given the bank what they were due when it were due. This loan, I took it out so I could expand the business. We've just moved into a new industrial unit at Cheadle Heath, but I knew business was going well enough to pay back the loan on time."

"Are you sure your orders haven't dropped back because of the recession and the bank's not just taking safety precautions?" I hazarded.

He shook his head, his hand nervously heading for his jacket pocket. He stopped, guiltily. "Is it all right if I smoke?" he asked. "Go right ahead," I responded. I got up to fetch him an ashtray. "You were saying? About the effects of the recession?" He dabbed his cigarette nervously at his lips. "Well, to be honest, we've not seen it. I think what's happening is that people who've been trying to sell their houses have kind of given up on the idea and decided to go for some improvements to the places they're in already. You know, loft conversions for extra bedrooms, that kind of thing? Well, a lot of them go for conservatories, to give them an extra reception room, especially if they've got teenage kids. I mean, if a conservatory's double-glazed and you stick a radiator in, it's as warm as a room in the house in the winter. Our business is actually up on this time last year."

I dragged out of him that he specialized in attaching conservatories to newish properties on the kind of estates where double-glazing salesmen used to graze like cattle. That way, he only ever had to produce a handful of designs in a few standard sizes, thus cutting his overheads to a minimum. He also concentrated on a relatively compact area: the south-west side of Manchester and over to Warrington new town, the little boxes capital of the North West. The two salesmen he employed brought in more than enough orders to keep the factory busy, Ted insisted.

"And you're absolutely positive that the bank gave you no idea why they are foreclosing?" I demanded again, reluctant to believe they had been quite so bloody-minded.

He nodded, uncertainly, then said, "Well, he said something I didn't understand."

"Can you remember exactly what that was?" I asked in the tone of voice one uses with a particularly slow child.

He frowned as he struggled to remember. It was like watching an elephant crochet. "Well, he did say there was an unusual and unacceptably high default rate on the remortgages, but he wouldn't say any more than that."

"The remortgages?"

"People who can't sell their houses often remortgage to get their hands on their capital. They use the conservatory as the excuse for the remortgage. But I don't understand what that's got to do with me," he said plaintively.

I wasn't altogether sure that I did. But I knew a man who would. I wasn't excited by Ted Barlow's story, but I'd wrapped up the pharmaceuticals case in less time than I'd anticipated, so the week was looking slack. I thought it wouldn't kill me to play around with his problem for a day or two. I was about to ask Ted to let Shelley have a list of his clients over the last few months when he finally grabbed my attention.

"Well, I was that angry when I left the bank that I decided to go and see some of the people who had done a remortgage. I went back to the office and picked up the names and addresses and went over to Warrington. I went to four of the houses. Two of them were completely empty. And the other two had complete strangers living in them. But—and this is the really weird bit, Miss Brannigan—there were no conservatories there. They'd vanished. The conservatories had just disappeared."

2

I took a deep breath. I have noticed that there are some people in this world who are congenitally incapable of telling a story that runs in a straight line from the beginning through the middle to the end, incorporating all the relevant points. Some of them win the Booker Prize, and that's fine by me. I just wish they didn't end up in my office. "Disappeared?" I finally echoed, when it became clear Ted had shot his bolt.

He nodded. "That's right. They're just not there any more. And the people that are living in two of the houses swear blind there's never been a conservatory there, not since they moved in a few months ago. The whole thing's a complete mystery to me. That's why I thought you might be able to help." If Shelley had been in the room, she'd have rolled over on her back at the look of trusting supplication on Ted Barlow's face.

As it was, I was hooked. It's not often I get a client with a genuine mystery to solve. And this gave me the added bonus of getting my own back on Ms Supercool. Watching Shelley jumping through hoops for Ted Barlow was going to be the best cabaret in town.

I leaned back in my chair. "OK, Ted. We'll take a look at it. On one condition. I'm afraid that, since the bank's stopped your line of credit, I'm going to have to ask you for a cash retainer."

He'd been one step ahead of me. "Will a grand do?" he asked, pulling a thick envelope from his inside pocket.

It was my turn to nod helplessly. "I thought you'd want cash," he went on. "Us builders can always lay hands on a few bob in readies when we have to. Rainy day money. That way, you always make sure the important people get paid." He handed the envelope over. "Go ahead, count it, I won't be offended," he added.

I did as he said. It was all there, in used twenties. I pressed the intercom. "Shelley? Can you give Mr Barlow a receipt for one thousand pounds' cash on his way out? Thanks." I got to my feet. "I've got one or two things to sort out here, Ted, but I'd like to meet you later this afternoon at your office. Four o'clock OK?"

"That's great. Shall I leave the directions with your secretary?" He sounded almost eager. This could get to be a lot of fun, I thought to myself as I showed Ted out. He headed for Shelley's desk like a homing pigeon.

Much as I'd taken to Ted, I learned very early on in this game that liking someone is no guarantee of their honesty. So I picked up the phone and rang Mark Buck-land at SecureSure. His secretary didn't mess me about with tales of fictitious meetings since Mark's always pleased to hear from Mortensen and Brannigan. It usually means a nice little earner for him. SecureSure supply a lot of the hardware we recommend in our role as security consultants, and even with the substantial discount he offers us, Mark still makes a tidy profit.

"Hi, Kate!" he greeted me, his voice charged with its normal overdose of enthusiasm. "Now, don't tell me, let me guess. Ted Barlow, am I right?"

"You're right."

"I'm glad he took my advice, Kate. The guy is in deep shit, and he doesn't deserve it." Mark sounded sincere. But then, he always does. That's the main reason he can afford to drive around in seventy grand's worth of Mercedes coupé.

"That's what I was ringing you about. No disrespect, but I need to check out that the guy's kosher. I don't want to find myself three days down the road with this and some bank clerk giving me the hard word because our Mr Barlow's got a track record with more twists and turns than a sheep track," I said.

"He's kosher all right, Kate. The guy is completely straight. He's the kind that gets into trouble because he's too honest, if you know what I mean."

"Oh, come on, Mark. It's me you're talking to. The guy's a builder, for Christ's sake. He can lay his hands on a grand in cash, just like that. That's not straight, not in the normal definition of the word," I protested.

"OK, so maybe the taxman doesn't know about every shilling he makes. But that doesn't make you a bad person, now does it, Kate?"

"So give me the truth, not the advertising copy."

Mark sighed. "You're a hard woman, Brannigan." Tell me about it, I thought cynically. "Right. Ted Barlow is probably my oldest friend. He was my best man, first time round. I was an usher at his wedding. Unfortunately, he married a prize bitch. Fiona Barlow was a slut and the last guy to find out was Ted. He divorced her five years ago and since then he's become a workaholic. He started off as a one-man-band, doing a bit of replacement windows stuff. Then a couple of friends asked him if he could do them a conservatory. They lived in real punter property, you know, Wimpey, Barratt, something like that. They got Ted to create this Victorian-style conservatory, all stained glass and UPVC. Of course, monkey see, monkey want. Half the estate wanted one, and Ted was launched in the conservatory business. Now, he's got a really solid little firm, a substantial turnover, and he's done it the straight way. Which, as you know, is pretty bloody unusual in the home improvement game."

In spite of my natural scepticism, I was impressed. Whatever was going on with Ted Barlow's conservatories, it looked like it wasn't the man himself who was up to something. "What about his competitors? Would they be looking to put the shaft in?" I asked.

"Hmm," Mark mused. "I wouldn't have thought so. He's not serious enough to be a worry to any of the really big-time boys. He's strictly small, reputable and local. Whatever's going down here needs someone like you to sort it out. And if you do clear it up, because he's such a good friend, I'll even waive my ten per cent commission for sending him to you!"

"If I wasn't a lady, I'd tell you to go fuck yourself, Buckland. Ten per cent!" I snorted. "Just for that, I'm putting the lunch invitation on hold. Thanks for the backgrounder, anyway. I'll do my best for Ted."

"Thanks, Kate. You won't be sorry. You sort him out, he'll be your friend for life. Pity you've already got a conservatory, eh?" He was gone before I could get on my high horse. Just as well, really. It took me a good thirty seconds to realize he'd been at the wind-up and I'd fallen for it.

I wandered through to the outer office to give Shelley the new-client form and the cash, for banking. To my surprise, Ted Barlow was still there, standing awkwardly in front of Shelley's desk like a kid who's hung behind after class to talk to the teacher he has a crush on. As I entered, Shelley looked flustered and quickly said, "I'm sure Kate will have no trouble following these directions, Mr Barlow."

"Right, well, I'll be off then. I'll be seeing you later, Miss Brannigan."

"Kate," I corrected automatically. Miss Brannigan makes me feel like my spinster great aunt. She's not one of those indomitable old biddies with razor-sharp minds that we all want to be when we're old. She's a selfish, hypochondriacal, demanding old manipulator and I have this superstitious fear that if I let enough people call me Miss Brannigan, it might rub off on me.

"Kate," he acknowledged nervously. "Thank you very much, both of you." He backed through the door. Shelley was head down, fingers flying over the keyboard, before the door was even halfway closed.

"Amazing how long it takes to give a set of directions," I said sweetly, dropping the form in her in-tray.

"I was just sympathizing with the man," Shelley replied mildly. It's not always easy to tell with her coffee-coloured skin, but I'd swear she was blushing.

"Very commendable, too. There's a grand in this envelope. Can you pop down to the bank with it? I'd rather not leave it in the safe."

"You do right. You'd only spend it," Shelley retorted, getting her own back. I poked my tongue out at her and returned to my own office. I picked up the phone again. This time, I rang Josh Gilbert. Josh is a partner in a financial services company. They specialize in providing advice and information to the kind of people who are so paranoid about ending up as impoverished senior citizens that they cheerfully do without while they're young enough to enjoy it, just so they can sit back in comfort in their old age, muttering, "If I had my youth again, I could be waterskiing now . . ." Josh persuades them to settle their shekels in the bosoms of insurance companies and unit trusts, then sits back planning for his own retirement on the fat commissions he's just earned. Only difference is, Josh expects his retirement to begin at forty. He's thirty-six now, and tells me he's well on target. I hate him.

Of course, he was with a client. But I'd deliberately made my call at ten minutes to the hour. I figured that way he'd be able to call me back between appointments. Three minutes later, I was talking to him. I briefly outlined Ted Barlow's problem. Josh said, "Mmm," a lot. Eventually, he said, "I'll check your guy out. And I'll do some asking around, no names, no pack drill. OK?"

"Great. When can we get together on this?"

Over the phone, I could hear the sound of Josh turning the pages in his diary. "You hit me on a bad week," he said. "I suppose you need this stuff yesterday?"

"Afraid so. Sorry."

He sucked his breath in over his teeth, the way plumbers are trained to do when they look at your central-heating system. "Today's Tuesday. I'm snowed under today, but I can get to it tomorrow," he muttered, half to himself. "But my time's backed up solid Thursday, Friday I'm in London . . . Listen, can you do breakfast Thursday? I meant it when I said it was a bad week."

I took a deep breath. I'm never at my best first thing, but business is business. "Thursday breakfast is fine," I lied. "Where would you like?"

"You choose, it's your money," Josh replied.

We settled on the Portland at seven-thirty. They have this team of obliging hall porters who park your car for you, which in my opinion is a major advantage at that time of the morning. I checked my watch again. I didn't have time enough to develop and print my surveillance films. Instead, I settled for opening a file on Ted Barlow in my database.

Colonial Conservatories occupied the last unit before the industrial estate gave way to a sewage farm. What really caught the eye was the conservatory he'd built on the front of the unit. It was about ten foot deep and ran the whole thirty-foot width of the building. It had a brick foundation, and was separated into four distinct sections by thin brick pillars. The first section was classic Victorian Crystal Palace style, complete with plastic replica finials on the roof. Next was the Country Diary of an Edwardian Lady school of conservatory, a riot of stained panels whose inaccuracies would give any botanist the screaming habdabs. Third in line was the Spartan conservatory. A bit like mine, in fact. Finally, there was the Last Days of the Raj look—windows forming arches in a plastic veneer that gave the appearance, from a considerable distance, of being mahogany. Just the place to sit on your rattan furniture and summon the punkah wallah to cool you down. You get a lot of that in South Manchester.

Inside the conservatory, I could see Colonial Conservatories' offices. I sat in the car for a moment, taking in the set-up. Just inside the door was a C-shaped reception desk. Behind it, a woman was on the phone. She had a curly perm that looked like Charles I's spare wig. Occasionally, she tapped a key on her word processor and gave the screen a bored stare before returning to her conversation. Over to one side, there were two small desks, each equipped with a phone and a pile of clutter. No one was at either desk. On the back wall, a door led into the main building. Over in the far corner, a small office had been divided off with glass partitions. Ted Barlow was standing in shirtsleeves in this office, his tie hanging loose and the top button of his shirt open, slowly working his way through the contents of a filing cabinet drawer. The rest of the reception was taken up with display panels.

I walked into the conservatory. The receptionist said brightly into the phone, "Hold the line, please." She flicked a switch then turned her radiance on me. "How may I help you?" she asked in a little girl's voice.

"I have an appointment with Mr Barlow. My name's Brannigan. Kate Brannigan."

"One moment, please." She ran a finger down the page of her open desk diary. Her nail extensions mesmerized me. Just how could she type with those claws? She looked up and caught my stare, then smiled knowingly. "Yes," she said. "I'll just see if he's ready for you." She picked up a phone and buzzed through. Ted looked round him in a distracted way, saw me, ignored the phone and rushed across the reception area.

"Kate," he exclaimed. "Thanks for coming." The receptionist cast her eyes heavenwards. Clearly, in her view, the man had no idea how bosses are supposed to behave. "Now, what do you need to know?"

I steered him towards his office. I had no reason to suspect the receptionist of anything other than unrealistic aspirations, but it was too early in the investigation to trust anyone. "I need a list of addresses of all the conservatories you've fitted in the last six months where the customers have taken out remortgages to finance them. Do you keep track of that information?"

He nodded, then stopped abruptly just outside his office. He pointed to a display board that showed several houses with conservatories attached. The houses were roughly similar— medium-sized, mostly detached, modern, all obviously surrounded on every side by more of the same. Ted's face looked genuinely mournful. "That one, that one and that one," he said. "I had photographs taken of them after we built them because we were just about to do a new brochure. And when I went back today, they just weren't there any more."

I felt a frisson of relief. The one nagging doubt I had had about Ted's honesty was resolved. Nasty, suspicious person that I am, I'd been wondering if the conservatories had ever been there in the first place. Now I had some concrete evidence that they had been spirited away. "Can you give me the name of the photographer?" I asked, caution winning over my desire to believe in Ted.

"Yes, no problem. Listen, while I sort this stuff out for you, would you like me to get one of the lads to show you round the factory? See how we actually do the business?"

I declined politely. The construction of double-glazed conservatories wasn't a gap in my knowledge I felt the need to plug. I settled for the entertaining spectacle of watching Ted wrestle with his filing system. I sat down in his chair and picked up a leaflet about the joys of conservatories. I had the feeling this might be a long job.

The deathless prose of Ted's PR consultant stood no chance against the smartly dressed man who strode into the showroom, dumped a briefcase on one of the two small desks and walked into Ted's office, grinning at me like we were old friends.

"Hi," he said. "Jack McCafferty," he added, thrusting his hand out towards me. His handshake was firm and cool, just like the rest of the image he projected. His brown curly hair was cut close at the sides and longer on top, so he looked like a respectable version of Mick Hucknall. His eyes were blue and had the dull sheen of polished sodalite against the lightly tanned skin of his face. He wore an olive green double-breasted suit, a cream shirt and a burgundy silk tie. The ensemble looked about five hundred pounds' worth to me. I felt quite underdressed in my terracotta linen suit and mustard cowl-necked sweater.

"Kate, Jack's one of my salesmen," Ted said.

"Sales *team*," Jack put him right. From his air of amused patience, I gathered it was a regular correction. "And you are?"

"Kate Brannigan," I said. "I'm an accountant. I'm putting together a package with Ted. Pleased to meet you, Jack."

Ted looked astonished. Lying didn't seem to be his strong suit. Luckily, he was standing behind Jack. He cleared his throat and handed me a bulky blue folder. "Here are the details you wanted, Kate," he said. "If there's anything that's not clear, just give me a call."

"OK, Ted." I nodded. I had one or two questions I wanted to ask him, but not ones that fitted my exciting new persona of accountant. "Nice to meet you, Jack."

"Nice. That's a word. Not the one I would have used for meeting you, Kate," he replied, a suggestive lift to one eyebrow. As I walked back across the reception area and out to my car, I could feel his eyes on me. I felt pretty sure I wouldn't like what he was thinking.

3

I pulled up half a mile down the road and had a quick look through the file. Most of the properties seemed to be over in Warrington, so I decided to leave them till morning. The light was already starting to fade, and by the time I'd driven over there, there would be nothing to see. However, there were half a dozen properties nearby where Ted had fitted conservatories. He'd already visited one of them and discovered that the conservatory had gone. On my way home, I decided I might as well take a quick look at the others. I pulled my *A-Z* out of the glove box and mapped out the most efficient route that included them all.

The first was at the head of a cul-de-sac in a nasty sixties estate, one of a pair of almost-detached houses, linked only by their garages in a bizarre Siamese twinning. I rang the bell, but there was no response, so I walked down the narrow path between the house and the fence to the back garden. Surprise, surprise. There was no conservatory. I studied the plan so I could work out exactly where it had been. Then I crouched down and scrutinized the brickwork on the back wall. I didn't really expect to find anything, since I wasn't at all sure what I should even be looking for. However, even my untrained eye noticed a line of faint markings on the wall. It looked like someone had given it a going over with a wire brush—enough to shift the surface grime and weathering, that was all.

Intrigued, I stood up and headed for the next destination. 6 Wiltshire Copse and 19 Amundsen Avenue were almost identical. And they were both minus conservatories. However, the next two remortgages I visited still had their conservatories firmly anchored to the houses. I trekked back to my car for the fifth time, deeply depressed after too much exposure to the kind of horrid little houses that give modern a bad name. I thought of my own home, a bungalow built only three years before, but constructed by a builder who didn't feel the need to see how small a bedroom you could build before the human mind screams, "No!" My lounge is generous, I don't have to climb over anything to get in and out of bed and my second bedroom is big enough for me to use as an office, complete with sofa bed for unavoidable visitors. But most of these overgrown sheds looked as if they'd have been pressed to provide one decent-sized bedroom, never mind three.

The irony was that they were probably worth more than mine because they were situated on bijou developments in the suburbs. Whereas my little oasis, one of thirty "professional person's dwellings," was five minutes from every city centre amenity. The downside was that it was surrounded by the kind of inner-city housing they make earnest Channel 4 documentaries about. The locale had brought the price down far enough for me also to afford the necessary state-of-the-art alarm system.

I decided home was where I should head for. Darkness was falling, so I wouldn't be able to continue my fascinating study of late-twentieth-century bricklaying. Besides, people were getting home from work and I was beginning to feel a little conspicuous. It was only a matter of time before some overzealous Neighbourhood Watch vigilante called the cops, an embarrassment I could well do without. I drove out of the opposite end of the estate to the one I'd come in by, and suddenly realized I was only a couple of streets away from Alexis's house.

Alexis Lee is probably my best friend. She's the crime reporter on the *Manchester Evening Chronicle*. I guess the fact that we're both women who've broken into what is traditionally a male preserve helped build the bond between us. But apart from our common interest in things criminal, she's also saved me more money than anyone else I know. I can think of at least a dozen times when she's prevented me from making very costly mistakes in expensive dress shops. And, at the risk of making her sound like a stereotype, she's got that wonderful, rich Liverpudlian sense of humour that can find the funny side in the blackest tragedy. I couldn't think of anything that would cheer me up faster than a half-hour pit stop.

The earlier rain had turned the fallen leaves into a slick mush. As I braked gently to pull up outside Alexis's, I swear my Vauxhall Nova went sideways. Cursing the Highways Department, I slithered round the car and on to the safer ground of the driveway. I grabbed at a post to steady myself, then realized with a shock that this particular post wasn't a permanent fixture. It was supporting a For Sale sign. I was outraged. How dare they put the house on the market without consulting me? Time I found out what was going on here. I walked round to the back door, knocked and entered the kitchen.

Alexis's girlfriend Chris is a partner in a firm of community architects, which is why their kitchen looks like a Gothic cathedral, complete with flagged floor and vaulted ceiling with beams like whales' ribs. The plasterwork is stencilled with flower and fruit motifs, and there are plaster bas-relief bosses at regular intervals along the roof truss. It's an amazing sight.

Instead of the Quasimodo I always half-expect, Alexis was sitting at the pitch-pine table, a mug of tea at her elbow, some kind of catalogue open in front of her. As I came in, she looked up and grinned. "Kate! Hey, good to see you, kid! Grab yourself a cuppa, the pot's fresh," she said, waving at the multi-coloured knitted tea cosy by the kettle. I poured myself a mug of strong tea as Alexis asked, "What brings you round here? You been doing a job? Anything in it for me?"

"Never mind that," I said firmly, dropping into a chair. "You trying to avoid me? What's with the For Sale sign? You put the house on the market and you don't tell me?"

"Why? Were you thinking of buying it? Don't! Don't even let it cross your mind! There's barely enough room for me and Chris, and we agree on what's an acceptable degree of mess. You and Richard would kill within a week here," Alexis parried.

"Don't try to divert me," I said. "Richard and I are fine as we are. Next door neighbours is as close as I'm ever going to let it get."

"And how is your insignificant other?" Alexis interrupted.

"He sends you his love too." Alexis and the man I love have a relationship that seems to me to consist entirely of verbal abuse. In spite of appearances, however, I suspect they love each other dearly; once I actually came upon the two of them having a friendly drink together in a corner of the *Chronicle*'s local. They'd both looked extremely sheepish about it. "Now, about this For Sale board?"

"It's only been up a couple of days. It's all been a bit of a rush. You remember Chris and I talking about how we wanted to buy a piece of land and build our own dream home?"

I nodded. I could more easily have forgotten my own name. "You're planning on doing it as part of a self-build scheme; Chris is going to design the houses in exchange for other people giving you their labour, yes?" They'd been talking about it for as long as I'd known them. With a lot of people, I'd have written it off as dreaming. But Alexis and Chris were serious. They'd spent hundreds of hours poring over books, plans and their own drawings till they'd come up with their ideal home. All they'd been waiting for was the right plot of land at the right price in the right location. "The land?" I asked.

Alexis reached along the side of the table and pulled a drawer open. She tossed a packet of photographs at me. "Look at that, Kate. Isn't it stunning? Isn't it just brilliant?" She pushed her unruly black hair out of her eyes and gazed expectantly at me.

I studied the pictures. The first half-dozen showed a selection of views of an area of rough moorland grass that had sheep grazing all over it. "That's the land," Alexis enthused, unable to stay silent. I continued. The rest of the pictures were views of distant hills, woods and valleys. Not a Chinese takeaway in sight. "And those are the views. Amazing, isn't it? That's why I'm going through this." She waved the catalogue at me. I could see now it was a building supplies price list. Personally, I'd have preferred a night in with the phone book.

"Where on earth is it?" I asked. "It looks so . . . rural." That was the first word I could come up with that was truthful as well as sounding like I approved.

"It's really wild, isn't it? It's only three minutes away from the M66. It's just above Ramsbottom. I can be in the office in twenty minutes outside rush hour, but it's completely isolated from the hassle of city life."

If that had been me, I'd have ended the sentence six words sooner. If you're more than ten minutes away from a Marks & Spencer Food Hall (fifteen including legal parking), as far as I'm concerned, you're outside the civilized world. "Right," I said. "That's just what you wanted, isn't it?"

"Yeah, it's the business. As soon as we saw it advertised, we called a meeting of the other people we'll be building with, and we all went off to see it. We've agreed a price with the builder, but he wants a quick completion because someone else is interested. Or so he says, but if you ask me, he's just on the make. Anyway, we've put down a deposit of five thousand pounds on each plot, and it's looking good. So it's time to sell this place and get our hands on the readies we'll need to build the new house."

"But where are you going to live while you're building?" I asked.

"Well, Kate, it's funny you should mention that. We were wondering . . ." I nearly panicked. Then I saw the smile twitching at the corner of her mouth. "We're going to buy a caravan now, at the end of the season when it's cheap, live in it over the winter and sell it in the spring. The house should be just about habitable by then," Alexis told me cheerfully. I couldn't control the shiver that ran through me.

"Well, any time you need a bath, you're more than welcome," I said.

"Thanks. I might just take you up on that, you being so handy for the office," she said.

I drained my mug and got to my feet. "I've got to run."

"Don't tell me, you're off on some Deep Throat surveillance," Alexis teased.

"Wrong again. I can see why you just write about crime rather than detecting it. No, Richard and I are going ten-pin bowling." I said it quickly, but it didn't get past her.

"Tenpin bowling?" Alexis spluttered. "Tenpin bowling? Shit, Brannigan, it'll be snogging in the back row of the pictures next."

I left her giggling to herself. All through history, the pioneers have been mocked by lesser minds. All you can do is rise above it.

There are probably worse ways to spend a wet Wednesday in Warrington than wandering round modern housing developments talking to the local inhabitants. If so, I haven't discovered them. I got to the first address soon after nine, which wasn't bad considering it had taken me twice as long as usual to get ready that morning because of the painful stiffness in my right shoulder. I'd forgotten you shouldn't go tenpin bowling unless you've got the upper body fitness levels of an Olympic shot putter.

The first house was at the head of a cul-de-sac that spiralled round like a nautilus shell. I tried the doorbell of the neat semi, but got no response. I peered through the picture window into the lounge, which was furnished in spartan style, with no signs of current occupation. The clincher was the fact that there was no TV or video in sight. It looked as if my conservatory buyers had moved and were renting out their house. Most people who let their homes furnished tuck their expensive but highly portable electrical goods away into storage in case the letting agency don't do their homework properly and let the house to people of less than sterling honesty. Strangely, a couple of the houses I'd visited the previous evening had had a similar air of absence.

Round the back, there was more evidence of the missing conservatory than in the others I'd seen, where the concrete bases they'd been built on had simply looked like unfinished patios. Here, there was a square of red glazed quarry tiles extending out beyond the patio doors. Round the edge of the square was a little wall, two bricks deep, except for a door-sized gap. And the walls showed the now familiar traces of the mortar that had attached the extension to the house.

I'd noticed a car parked in the drive of the other half of the semi, so I made my way back round to the front and rang the doorbell, which serenaded me with an electronic "Yellow Rose of Texas." The woman who opened the door looked more like the Dandelion Clock of Cheshire. She had a halo of fluffy white hair that looked like it had been defying hairdressers for more than half a century. Grey-blue eyes loomed hazily through the thick lenses of gold-rimmed glasses as she sized me up. "Yes?" she demanded.

"I'm sorry to bother you," I lied. "But I was wondering if you could help me. I represent the company who sold next door their conservatory . . ."

Before I could complete my sentence, the woman cut in. "We don't want a conservatory. And we've already got double glazing and a burglar alarm." The door started to close.

"I'm not selling anything," I yelped, offended by her assumption. Great start to the day. Mistaken for a double-glazing canvasser. "I'm just trying to track down the people who used to live next door."

She stopped with the door still open a crack. "You're not selling anything?"

"Cross my heart and hope to die. I just wanted to pick your brains, that's all." I used the reassuring voice. The same one that usually works on guard dogs.

The door slowly opened again. I made a great show of consulting the file I was carrying in my bag. "It says here the conservatory was installed back in March."

"That would be about right," she interrupted. "It went up the week before Easter, and it was gone a week later. It just disappeared overnight." History had just been made. I'd dropped lucky at the first attempt.

"Overnight?"

"That was the really peculiar thing. One day it was there, the next day it wasn't. They must have taken it down during the night. We never heard or saw a thing. We just assumed there must have been some dispute about it. You know, perhaps she didn't like it, or she didn't pay or something? But then, you'd know all about that, if you represent the firm," she added with a belated note of caution.

"You know how it is, I'm not allowed to discuss things like that," I said. "But I am trying to track them down. Robinson, my file says."

She leaned against the door jamb, settling herself in for a good gossip. It was all right for her. I was between the cold north wind and the door. I jerked up the collar of my jacket and hated her quietly. "She wasn't what you'd call sociable. Not one for joining in, you might say. I invited her in for coffee or drinks several times and she never came once. And I wasn't the only one. We're very friendly here in the Grove, but she kept herself to herself."

I was slightly puzzled by the constant reference to the woman alone. The form in the file was in two names—Maureen and William Robinson. "What about her husband?" I asked.

The woman raised her eyebrows. "Husband? I'd have said he was somebody else's husband, myself."

I sighed mentally. "How long had you known Mrs Robinson?" I asked.

"Well, she only moved in in December," the woman said. "She was hardly here at all that first month, what with Christmas and everything. Most weeks she was away three or four nights. And she was always out during the day. She often didn't get home till gone eight. Then she moved out a couple of days after the conservatory went. My husband said she probably had to move suddenly, on account of her work, and maybe took the conservatory with her to a new house."

"Her work?"

"She told my Harry that she was a freelance computer expert. It takes her all over the world, you know. She said that's why she'd always rented the house out. There's been a string of tenants in there ever since we moved in five years ago. She told Harry this was the first time she'd actually had the chance to live in the house herself." There was a note of pride in her voice that her Harry had managed to get so much out of their mysterious neighbour.

"Can you describe her to me, Mrs—?"

She considered. "Green. Carole Green, with an e, on the Carole, not the Green. Well, she was taller than you." Not hard. Five three isn't exactly Amazonian. "Not much, though. Late twenties, I'd say. She had dark brown hair, in a full page-boy, really thick and glossy her hair was. Always nicely made up. And she was a nice dresser, you never saw her scruffy."

"And the man you mentioned?"

There was more than one, you know. Most nights when she was here, a car would pull up in the garage later on, about eleven. A couple of times, I saw them drive off the next morning. The first one had a blue Sierra, but he only lasted a couple of weeks. The next one had a silver Vauxhall Cavalier." She seemed very positive about the cars and I commented on it. "My Harry's in the motor trade," she informed me. "I might not have noticed the men, but I noticed the cars."

"And you haven't seen her since she moved out?"

The woman shook her head. "Not hide nor hair. Then the house was rented out again a fortnight after she moved. A young couple, just moved up from Kent. They left a month ago, bought a place of their own over towards Widnes. Lovely couple, they were. Don and Diane. Beautiful baby girl, Danni."

I almost pitied them. I bet they'd not thought fast enough to get out of the little social events of the Grove. I couldn't think of anything else to ask, so I made my excuses and left. I considered trying the other neighbours, but I didn't see how anyone could have succeeded where Carole with an e had failed.

Scarborough Walk was only a mile away as the crow flies. Clearly the crow has never inspired a town planner. Only a Minotaur fresh from the Cretan labyrinth would feel at home in the newer parts of Warrington. I negotiated yet another roundabout with my street map on my knees and entered yet another new development. Whitby Way encircled a dozen Walks, Closes and Groves like the covered wagons pulled up to repel the Indians. It was about as hard to breach. Eventually, second time round, I spotted the entrance to the development. Cleverly designed to look like a dead end, in fact it led straight into a maze that I managed to unravel by driving at 10 m.p.h. with one eye on the map. Sometimes I wonder how I cope with a job as glamorous, exciting and risky as this.

Again, there was no conservatory. The couple who lived there now had only been renting it for a couple of months, so the harried mother with the hyperactive toddler wasn't able to tell me anything about the people who'd actually bought the conservatory. But the woman next door but one had missed her way. She should have been on the *News of the World*'s investigative desk. By the time I escaped, I knew more than I could ever have dreamed possible about the inhabitants of Scarborough Walk. I even knew about the two couples who had moved out in 1988 after their wife-swapping had turned into a permanent transfer. However, I didn't know much about the former inhabitants of number six. They'd bought the house the previous November, and had moved out at the end of February because he'd got a job out in the Middle East somewhere and she'd gone with him. She'd been a nurse on permanent night duty, at one of the Liverpool hospitals, she thought. He'd been something in personnel. She'd had a blonde urchin cut, just like that Sally Webster on *Coronation Street*. He'd been tall, dark and handsome. She'd had some kind of little car, he'd had some kind of big car. He often worked late. They went out a lot when they weren't working. The perfect description to put out to Interpol.

The next house still had its conservatory. It also still had a satisfied customer, which I was grateful for. I really didn't need to be mistaken for the customer services department of Colonial Conservatories. I ploughed on through the list, and when I reached the end, I reckoned I was entitled to a treat for having spent so task-orientated a day. Four o'clock and I was back in Manchester, sitting in my favourite curry shop in Strangeways, tucking into a bowl of karahi lamb.

As I scoffed, I popped the earpiece of my miniature tape recorder in place and played back the verbal notes I'd made after each of my visits. Five out of the eight were victims of MCS (Missing Conservatory Syndrome, I'd christened it). The only common factor I could isolate was that, in each case, the couple concerned had only lived in the house for a few months after buying it, then they'd moved out and let the place via an agency. I couldn't make sense of it at all. Who were all these people? Two brunettes, one auburn, two blondes. Two with glasses, three without. All working women. Two drove red

Fiestas, one went everywhere by taxi, one drove a white Metro, one drove "something small." All the men were on the tall side and dark, ranging from "handsome" to "nowt special." A description that would cover about half the male population. Again, two wore glasses, three didn't. They all drove standard businessmen's cars—a couple had metallic Cavaliers, one had a red Sierra, one had a blue Sierra, one changed his car from "a big red one" to "a big white one." Not a single lead as to the whereabouts of any of them.

I had to admit I was completely baffled. I dictated my virtually non-existent conclusions, then checked in with Shelley. I answered half a dozen queries, discovered there was nothing urgent waiting for me, so I hit the supermarket. I fancied some more treats to reward me for the ironing pile that faced me at home. I had no intention of including myself in Richard's plans for the evening. I can think of more pleasurable ways of getting hearing damage than boogying on down to a double wicked hip hop rap band from Mostyn called PMT, or something similar. There's nothing like a quiet night in.

4

And that's exactly what I got. Nothing like a quiet night in. I'd gone back to the office after a quick hit on Sainsbury's and dropped off my cassette for Shelley to input in the morning. I was sure the thought that it was for Ted Barlow would make her fingers fly. Then I'd finally managed to find the peace and quiet to develop my surveillance films from PharmAce Supplies. As I stared at the film, I wished I hadn't. On the other hand, if you're going to have a major downer, I suppose it's as well to have it at the end of a day that's already been less than wonderful, rather than spoil a perfectly good one.

Where there ought to have been identifiable images of PharmAce's senior lab technician slipping in and out of the building in the middle of the night (timing superimposed on the pictures by my super-duper Nikon), there was only a foggy blur. Something had gone badly wrong. Since the commonest cause of fogged film is a camera problem, what I then had to do was to run a film through the camera I'd been using that night, and develop it to see if I could pinpoint the problem. That took another hour, and all it demonstrated was that there was nothing wrong with the camera. Which left either a faulty film or human error. And the chances were, whether I liked it or not, that human error was the reason. Which meant I was stuck with the prospect of another Saturday night in the back of the van with my eye glued to a long lens. Sometimes I really do wonder if I did the right thing when I gave up my law degree after the second year to come and work with Bill. Then I look at what my former fellow students are doing now, and I begin to be grateful I made the jump.

I binned the useless film, locked up and drove home in time to listen to *The Archers* on the waterproof radio in the shower. It was a birthday present from Richard; I can't help feeling there was a bit of Indian giving involved, considering how often I have to tune it back to Radio 4 from Key 103. I don't know why he can't just use his own bathroom for his ablutions. I'm not being as unreasonable as that sounds; although we've been lovers for over a year now, we don't actually live together as such. When Richard first crashed into my life—or rather, my car—he was living in a nasty rented flat in Chorlton. He claimed he liked a neighbourhood where he was surrounded by students, feminists and Green Party supporters, but when I pointed out that for much the same outlay he could have a spacious two-bedroomed bungalow three minutes' drive from his favourite Chinese restaurant, he instantly saw the advantages. The fact that it's next door to my own mirror-image bungalow was merely a bonus.

Of course, he wanted to knock the walls down and turn the pair into a kind of open-plan ranch-house. So I persuaded Chris to come round and deliver herself of the professional architect's opinion that if you removed the walls Richard wanted rid of, both houses would fall down. Instead, she designed a beautiful conservatory that runs the length of both properties, linking them along the back. That way, we have the best of both worlds. It removes most of the causes of friction, with the result that we spend our time together having fun rather than rows. I preserve my personal space, while Richard can be as rowdy as he likes with his rock band friends and his visiting son. It's not that I don't like Davy, the six-year-old who seems to be the only good thing that came out of Richard's disastrous marriage. It's just that, having reached the age of twenty-seven unencumbered (or enriched, according to some) by a child, I don't want to live with someone else's.

I was almost sorry that Richard was out working, since I could have done with a bit of cheering up. I got out of the shower, towelling my auburn hair as dry as I could get it. I couldn't be bothered blow-drying it. I pulled on an old jogging suit which was when I remembered my shopping was still in the car. I was dragging the carriers out of the hatchback of my Nova when a hand on my back made my heart bump wildly in my chest. I whirled round, going straight into the "Ready to attack" Thai boxing position. In inner-city neighbourhoods like ours, you don't take chances.

"Hang about, Bruce Lee, it's only me," Richard said, backing off, raising his palms in a placatory gesture. "Jesus, Brannigan, hold your fire," he added, as I moved menacingly towards him.

I bared my teeth and growled deep in my throat, just the way my coach Karen trains us to do. Richard looked momentarily terrified, then he gave that Cute Smile of his, the one that got me into this in the first place, the smile that still, I'm ashamed to admit, turns me into a slushy Mills and Boon heroine. I stopped growling and straightened up, slightly sheepishly. "I've told you before, sneak up on me outside and you risk a full set of broken ribs," I grouched. "Now you're here, give me a hand with this."

The effort of carrying two carrier bags and a case of Miller Lite was clearly too much for the poor lamb, who immediately slumped on one of my living-room sofas. "I thought you were doing your brains in to the sound of young black Manchester tonight?" I said.

"They decided they weren't ready to expose themselves to the fearless scrutiny of the music press," he said. "So they've put me off till next week. By which time, I hope one of them's had a brain transplant. You know, Brannigan, sometimes I wish the guy who invented the drum machine had been strangled at birth. He'd have saved the world a lot of brain ache." Richard shrugged his jacket off, kicked off his shoes and put his feet up.

"Haven't you got someone else to mither," I asked politely.

"Nope. I haven't even got any deadlines to meet. So I thought I might go and pick up a Chinese, bring it back here and litter your lounge with beansprouts out of sheer badness."

"Fine. As long as you promise you will not insinuate a single shirt into my ironing basket."

"Promise," he said.

An hour and a half later, I pressed my last pair of trousers. "Thank God," I sighed.

No response from the sofa. It wasn't surprising. He was on his third joint and it would have been hard to hear World War Three over the soundtrack of the Motley Crue video he was inflicting on me. What did penetrate, however, was the high-pitched electronic bleep of my phone. I grabbed the phone and the TV remote, hitting the mute button as I switched the phone to "Talk." That got a reaction. "Hey," he protested, then subsided immediately as he registered that I was using the phone.

"Hello," I said. Never give your name or number when you answer the phone, especially if you've got an ex-directory number. In these days of phones with last number re-dial buttons, you never know who you're talking to. I have a friend who discovered the name and number of her husband's mistress that way. I know I've got nothing to fear on that score, but I like to develop habits of caution. You never know when they'll come in necessary.

"Kate? It's Alexis." She sounded the kind of pissed off she gets when she's trying to put together a story against the clock and the news editor is standing behind her chair breathing down her neck. But the time was all wrong for her deadlines.

"Oh, hi. How's tricks?" I said.

"Is this a good time?"

"Good as any. I've eaten, I'm still under the limit and I still have my clothes on," I told her.

"We need your help, Kate. I don't like to ask, but I don't know who else would know where to begin."

This was no pick-your-brains business call. When Alexis wants my help with a story, she doesn't apologize. She knows that kind of professional help is a two-way street. "Tell me the score, I'll tell you if I can help."

"You know that piece of land we're supposed to be buying? The one I showed you the pics of yesterday? Yeah?"

"Yeah," I soothed. She sounded like she was about to explode.

"Well, you're not going to believe this. Chris went up there today to do some measurements. She figured that if she's going to be designing these houses, she needs to have a feel for the lie of the land so the properties can blend in with the flow of the landscape, right?"

"Right. So what's the problem?"

"The problem is, she gets up there to find a couple of surveyors marking out the plots. Well, she's a bit confused, you know, because as far as we know none of the other self-builders we're working with have asked anyone to start work yet, on account of we haven't completed on it yet. So, she parks up in the Land Rover and watches them for half an hour or so. Then it dawns on her that the plots they're marking out are different altogether from the plots we've been sold. So she goes over to them and gets into conversation. You know Chris, she's not like me. I'd have been out there gripping them by the throat demanding to know what the hell they thought they were up to." Alexis paused for breath, but not long enough for me to respond.

"But not Chris. She lets them tell her all about the land and how they're marking out the plots for the people who have bought them. Half a dozen have been bought by a local small builder, the rest by individuals, they tell her. Well, Chris is more than a little bewildered, on account of what they are telling her is completely at odds with the situation as we know it. So she tells them who she is and what she's doing there and asks them if they've got any proof of what they're saying, which of course they don't have, but they tell her the name of the solicitor who's acting for the purchasers."

This time, I managed to get in, "I'm with you so far," before the tide of Alexis's narrative swept back in. Richard was looking at me very curiously. He's not accustomed to hearing me take such a minor role in a telephone conversation.

"So Chris drives down to this solicitor's in Ramsbottom. She manages to convince their conveyancing partner that this is urgent, so he gives her five minutes. When she explains the situation, he says the land was sold by a builder and that the sales were all completed two days ago." Alexis stopped short, as if what she'd said should make everything clear.

"I'm sorry, Alexis, I suspect I'm being really stupid here, but what exactly do you mean?"

"I mean the land's already been sold!" she howled. "We handed over five grand for a piece of land that had already been sold. I just don't understand how it could have happened! And I don't even know where to start trying to find out." The anguish in her voice was heartbreaking. I knew how much she and Chris wanted this project to work, for all sorts of reasons. Now, it looked as if the money they'd saved to get their feet on the first rung of the ladder had been thrown away.

"OK, OK, I'll look into it," I soothed. "But I'm going to need some more info from you. What was the name of the solicitor in Ramsbottom that Chris saw?"

"Just a minute, I'll pass you over to Chris. She's got all the details. Thanks, Kate. I knew I could count on you."

There was a brief pause, then a very subdued Chris came on the line. Her voice sounded like she'd been crying. "Kate? Oh God, I can't believe this is happening to us. I just don't understand it, any of it." Then she proceeded to repeat everything Alexis had already told me.

I listened patiently, then said, "What was the name of the solicitor's you went to see in Ramsbottom?"

"Chapman and Gardner. I spoke to the conveyancing partner, Tim Pascoe. I asked him the name of the person who had
sold the land, but he wouldn't tell me. So I said, was it T. R.
Harris, and he gave me one of those lawyer's looks and said he
couldn't comment, only he said it in that kind of way that means
yes, you're right."

I looked at the names I'd scribbled on my pad. "So who
exactly is T. R. Harris?"

"T. R. Harris is the builder who was supposedly selling
the land to us." There was a note of exasperation in her voice,
which I couldn't help feeling was a bit unfair. After all, I'm not
a fully paid up member of the Psychic Society.

"And your solicitor is?"

"Martin Cheetham." She rattled off the address and phone
number.

"He your usual solicitor?" I asked.

"No. He specializes in conveyancing. One of the hacks on
the *Chronicle* was interviewing him about how the new conveyancing protocol is working out, and they got talking, and they
got on to the topic of builders catching a cold because they'd
bought land speculatively and the bottom had fallen out of the
market, and this hack said how one of his colleagues, i.e. Alexis,
was looking for a chunk big enough for ten people to do a self-
build scheme, and Cheetham said he knew of a colleague who
had a client who was a builder who had just the thing, so we
went to see Cheetham, and he said this T. R. Harris had bought
this land and couldn't afford to develop it himself so he was selling it off." Chris talks in sentences longer than the law lords.

"And did you ever meet this builder?"

"Of course. T. R. Harris, call me Tom, Mr Nice Guy. He
met us all out there, walked the land out with us, divided it up
into plots and gave us this sob story about how desperate he was
to keep his business afloat, how he had half a dozen sites where
the workers were depending on him to pay their wages, so could

we please see our way to coughing up five thousand apiece as a deposit to secure the land, otherwise he was going to have to keep on trying to find other buyers, which would be a real pity since it obviously suited our needs so well and he liked the idea of the land being used for a self-build if only because he wouldn't have the heartache of watching some other builder make a nice little earner out of such a prime site that he'd been really sick to have to let go. He was so convincing, Kate, it never crossed our minds that he was lying, and he obviously fooled Cheetham as well. Can you do something?" I couldn't ignore the pleading note in her voice, even supposing I'd wanted to.

"I don't really understand what's happened, but of course I'll do what I can to help. At the very least, we should be able to get your money back, though I think you'll have to kiss goodbye to that particular piece of land."

Chris groaned. "Don't, Kate. I know you're right, but I really don't want to think about it, we'd set our hearts on that site, it was just perfect, and I'd already got this really clear picture in my mind's eye of what the houses were going to look like." I could imagine. Eat your heart out, Portmeirion.

"I'll take a look at it tomorrow, promise. But I need something from you. You'll have to give me a couple of letters of authority so that your solicitor and anybody else official will talk to me. Could Alexis drop them off on her way to work tomorrow morning?"

We sorted out the details of what the letters should say, and I only had to listen to the tale once more before I managed to get off the phone. Then, of course, I had to go through it all for Richard.

"Somebody's been bang out of order here," he said, outraged. He summed up my feelings exactly. It was the next bit I wasn't so happy about. "You're going to have to get this one sorted out double urgent, aren't you?"

Sometimes, it's hard to escape the feeling that the whole world's ganging up on you.

5

I gave Alexis her second shock of the week next morning when she dropped off the letters of authority. It was just before seven when I heard her key in my front door. Her feet literally left the floor when she walked through the kitchen doorway and saw me sitting on a high stool with a glass of orange juice.

"Shit!" she yelled. I thought her black hair was standing on end with fright till I realized I was just unfamiliar with how untamed it looks first thing. She runs a hand through it approximately twice a minute. By late afternoon, it usually manages to look less like it's been dragged through a hedge backwards then sideways.

"Ssh," I admonished her. "You'll wake Sleeping Beauty."

"You're up!" she exclaimed. "Not only are you up, your mouth's moving. Hold the front page!"

"Very funny. I can do mornings when I have to," I said defensively. "I happen to have a breakfast meeting."

"Excuse me while I vomit," Alexis muttered. "I can't take yuppies without a caffeine inoculation. And I see that being conscious hasn't stretched to making a pot of coffee."

"I'm saving myself for the Portland," I said. "Help yourself to an instant. It's still better than that muck they serve in your canteen." I plucked the letters from her hand, tucked them in my bag and left her deliberating between the Blend 37 and the Alta Rica.

Josh was already deep in the *Financial Times* when I got to the Portland, even though I was four minutes early. Eyeing him up across the restaurant in his immaculate dark blue suit, gleaming white shirt and strident silk tie, I was glad I'd taken the trouble to get suited up myself in my Marks & Spencer olive green with a cream high-necked blouse. Very businesslike. He was too engrossed to notice till I was standing between the light and his paper.

He tore himself away from the mating habits of multi-national companies and gave me the hundred-watt smile, all twinkles, dimples and sincerity. It makes Robert Redford, whom he resembles slightly, look like an amateur. I'm convinced Josh developed it in front of the mirror for susceptible female clients, and now it's become a habit whenever a woman comes within three feet of him. The charm comes without patronage, however. He's one of those men who doesn't have a problem with the notion that women are equals. Except the ones he has relationships with. Them he treats like brainless bimbos. This makes for a quick turnover, since the ones who have a brain can't take it for more than a couple of months, and the ones who haven't bore him rigid after six weeks.

In spite of keeping his emotions in his underpants, when it comes to business he's one of the best financial consultants in Manchester. He's a walking database on anything relating to insurance, investments, trust funds, tax shelters and the Financial Services Act. Anything he doesn't know, he knows where to find out. We met when I was still a law student, eking out my grant by doing odd jobs for Bill. My first ever undercover was in Josh's office, posing as a temp to track down the person who was using the computer to divert one pound out of each client account into his own unit trust account. Because our relationship started on a professional footing, Josh never came on to me and it's stayed that way. Now, I take him out for a slap-up dinner every couple of months as a thank you for running credit checks for me. The rest of the work and advice, like this, he bills us for at his usual extortionate hourly rate, so I got straight to the point.

I outlined the problem facing Ted Barlow while we scoffed our bowls of fruit and cereal. Josh asked a couple of questions, then the scrambled eggs and bacon arrived. He frowned in concentration as he ate. I wasn't sure if that was because he was thinking about Ted's problem or appreciating the subtle pleasures of the scrambled eggs, but I decided not to interrupt anyway. Besides, I was enjoying the rare pleasure of hot food so early in the day.

Then he sat back, mopped his lips with the napkin and poured a fresh cup of coffee. "There's obviously some kind of fraud going on here," he said. With anyone else, I'd have made some sarcastic crack about stating the obvious, but Josh did his degree at Cambridge and he likes to establish the ground under his feet before he builds up the speculation, so I managed to keep my mouth zipped.

"Mmm," I said.

"I would say that the chances are the bank has a pretty shrewd idea of what that fraud is. They obviously think, however, that your Mr Barlow is the villain of the piece, and that is why they have taken the steps they've taken, and why they are refusing to discuss their detailed reasons with him. They don't want to alert him to the fact that they have worked out for themselves what he is up to, so they have shrouded it in generalizations." He paused and spread a cold triangle of toast thickly with butter. The way he was chugging the cholesterol, I didn't feel at all confident he'd live long enough to retire at forty. I don't know how he stays so trim. I suspect there's a portrait of an elephant in his attic.

"I'm not sure I follow you," I admitted.

"Sorry. I'll give you an example I came across a little time ago. I have a client who owns a double-glazing firm. They had a similar experience to that of your Mr Barlow—the bank closed down their credit and a few days later, the police were all over them. It turns out that there had been a spate of burglaries around the North West that all followed the same pattern. They were all houses that had a drive at the side with access to the rear of the house. The neighbours would see a double-glazing firm's van turn up. The workmen would start removing the ground floor windows, while one of them was removing the household valuables through the back or side of the house and loading them into the van. The neighbours, of course, thought the family were simply having replacement windows installed. They might wonder why the workmen disappeared at lunchtime and failed to return, leaving plastic sheeting over the window holes and the old windows sitting in the drive, but no one wondered enough to do anything about it.

"The common factor that all those houses shared, it eventually transpired, was that they had all been canvassed by the same double-glazing firm in the weeks previous to the burglary. And of course, the canvassers had established whether both husband and wife were working, thus uncovering which houses were empty during the day. The police suspected my client and paid a visit to his bankers. They, of course, were only too aware that after a grim spell my client's account had started to look very healthy again, and that much of his recent incomings had been in cash. After the police visit, they put two and two together and regrettably made a pig's ear of it. Partly the fault of my client, who had omitted to mention his recent investment in a couple of amusement arcades." Josh's sardonic tone told me all I needed to know about his opinion of slot machines as investments.

"It was, of course, all sorted out in the fullness of time. The burglaries were the brainchild of a couple of former employees, who paid backhanders to unemployed youths of their acquaintance to go and get jobs as canvassers with this double-glazing firm and report back to them. However, my client had an extremely sticky time in the interim. That experience leads me to suspect the bank think your Mr Barlow is the brains behind whatever is going on here. You said they mentioned a high default rate on remortgages?"

"That's about all they did say," I replied. "More toast?" Josh nodded. I waved the toast rack plaintively at a passing waitress and waited for Josh's next pearl of wisdom.

"If I were you, that's where I'd start looking." He sat back with the air of a conjuror who has just completed some amazing feat. I wasn't impressed, and I guess it showed.

He sighed. "Kate, if I were you, I'd ask my friendly financial wizard to run a credit check on all those good people who have taken out remortgages and whose conservatories have now vanished."

I still wasn't getting it. "But what would that show?" I asked.

"I don't know," Josh admitted. He didn't know? I waited for the sky to fall, but incredibly it didn't. "But whatever happens, you'll know a lot more about them than you do now. And I have that curious tingling in my stomach that tells me that's the right place to look."

I trust Josh's tingle. The last time I had personal experience of it, I quadrupled my savings by buying shares in a company he had a good feeling about. The truly convincing thing was that he told me to offload them a week before they crashed spectacularly following the arrest of their chairman for fraud. So I said, "OK. Go ahead. I'll fax you the names and addresses this morning."

"Splendid," he said. I wasn't sure if he was addressing me or the waitress placing a rack of fresh toast in front of him.

As he attacked the toast, I asked, "When will you have the info for me?"

"I'll fax it across to you as soon as I get it myself. Probably tomorrow. Mark it for Julia's attention when you send the details over. I'm hopelessly tied up today, but it's just routine, she can do it standing on her head. What I will also do is have a quiet word with a guy I know in Royal Pennine Bank's fraud section. No names, no pack drill, but he might be able to shed some light as to the general principle of the thing."

"Thanks, Josh. That'll be a big help." I gave my watch a surreptitious glance. Seven minutes till we got into the next billable hour. "So how's your love life?" I hazarded.

Martin Cheetham's office was in the old Corn Exchange, a beautiful golden sandstone building that, in aerial photographs, looks like a wedge of cheese, the windows pocking the surface like dozens of crumbly holes. The old exchange floor is now a sort of indoor flea market in bric-à-brac, antiques, books and records, while the rest of the building has been turned into offices. There are still a few of the traditional occupants—watch menders, electric razor repairers—but because of the unusual layout, the rest range from pressure groups who rent a cubbyhole to small legal firms who can rent a suite of offices that fit their needs exactly.

The office I was looking for was round the back. The reception room was small to the point of poky, but at least the receptionist had a fabulous view of Manchester Cathedral. I hoped she was into bullshit Gothic. She was in her late forties, the motherly type. Within three minutes, I was clutching a cup of tea and a promise that Mr Cheetham would be able to squeeze me in within the half-hour. She had waved away my apologies for not having an appointment. I couldn't understand how she kept her job, with all this being polite to the punters.

One of the reasons I wasn't sorry to quit my law degree was that after two years, I began to realize I'd stand all the way from Manchester to London rather than sit next to a lawyer on a train. There are, of course, notable exceptions, lovely people upon whose competence and honesty I'd stake my life. Unfortunately, Martin Cheetham wasn't one of them. For a start, I couldn't see how anyone could run an efficient practice when their paperwork was stacked chaotically everywhere. On the floor, on the desk, on the filing cabinets, even on top of the computer monitor. For all I could tell, there could be clients lurking underneath there somewhere. He waved me to one of the two surfaces in the room that wasn't stacked with bumf. I sat on the uncomfortable office chair, while he headed for the other, a luxurious black leather all-singing, all-dancing swivel recliner. I suppose that since most conveyancing specialists see very little of their clients he didn't place a high priority on their comfort. He obviously wasn't a fan of the cathedral either, since his chair faced into the room.

While he took his time with Alexis's letter, I took the chance to study him. He was around 5' 8", slim without being skinny. He was in shirtsleeves, the jacket of a chain-store suit on a hanger suspended from the side of a filing cabinet. He had dark, almost black hair, cut short but stylish, and soulful, liquid dark eyes. He had that skin that looks sallow and unhealthy if it goes without sun for more than a month or so, though right now he looked in the peak of health. He obviously lived on his nerves, for his neat, small feet and hands were twitching and tapping as he read the letter of authority. Eventually, he steepled his fingers and gave me a cautious smile. "I'm not exactly sure how you think I can help, Miss Brannigan," he said.

"I am," I told him. "What I have to do in the first instance is to track down T. R. Harris, the builder. Now, it was through you that Miss Lee and Miss Appleby heard this land was available. So, I think you must know something about Mr T. R. Harris. Also, I figure you must have an address for him since you handled the matter for Miss Lee and Miss Appleby and presumably had some correspondence with him."

Cheetham's smile flickered again. "I'm sorry to disappoint you, but I know very little about Mr Harris. I knew about the land because I saw it advertised in one of the local papers. And before you ask, I'm sorry, I can't remember which one. I see several every week and I don't keep back numbers." It looked like they were the only bits of pulped tree he didn't keep. "I have a client who is looking for something similar," he continued, "but when I made further inquiries, I realized this particular area was too large for him. I happened to mention it to Miss Lee's colleague, and matters proceeded from there."

"So you'd never met Harris before?"

"I've never met Mr Harris at all," he corrected me. "I communicated with his solicitor, a Mr Graves." He got up and chose a pile of papers, seemingly at random. He riffled through them and extracted a bundle fastened with a paper clip. He dumped them in front of me, covering the body text of the letter with a blank sheet. "That's Mr Graves' address and phone number."

I took out my pad and noted the details on the letterhead. "Had you actually exchanged contracts, then?"

Cheetham's eyes shifted away from mine. "Yes. That's when the deposits were handed over, of course."

"And you were quite convinced that everything was above board?"

He grabbed the papers back and headed for the haven behind his desk. "Of course. I mean, I wouldn't have proceeded unless I had been. What are you getting at, exactly, Miss Brannigan?" His left leg was jittering like a jelly on a spindryer.

I wasn't entirely sure. But the feeling that Martin Cheetham wasn't to be trusted was growing stronger by the minute. Maybe he was up to something, maybe he was just terrified I was going to make him look negligent, or maybe he just had the misfortune to be born looking shifty. "And you've no idea where I can find Mr Harris?" I asked.

He shook his head and said, "Absolutely not. No idea whatsoever."

"I'm a bit surprised," I said. "I'd have thought that his address would have appeared on the contracts."

Cheetham's fingers drummed that neat little riff from the "1812 Overture" on the bundle of papers. "Of course, of course, how stupid of me, I didn't even think of that," he gabbled. Again, he flicked through his papers. I waited patiently, saying nothing. "I'm sorry, this shocking business has really unsettled me. Here we are. How foolish of me. T. R. Harris, 134 Bolton High Road, Ramsbottom."

I wrote it down, then got to my feet. I didn't feel like someone who's had a full and frank exchange of views, but I could see I wasn't going to get any further with Cheetham unless I had specific questions. And at least I could go for Harris and his solicitor now.

I took a short cut down the back stairs, a rickety wooden flight that always makes me feel like I've stepped into a timewarp. My spirits descended as I did. I still had some conservatories to check out south-west of the city, and I was about as keen on that idea as I was on fronting up T. R. Harris's brief. But at least I was getting paid for that. The thought lifted my spirits slightly, but not as much as the hunk I clapped eyes on as I yanked open the street door. He was jumping out of a Transit van that he'd abandoned on the double yellows, and he was gorgeous. He wore tight jeans and a white T-shirt—on a freezing October day, for God's sake!—stained with plaster and brick dust. He had that solid, muscular build that gives me ideas that nice feminists aren't supposed to even know about, never mind entertain. His hair was light brown and wavy, like Richard Gere's used to be before he found Buddha. His eyes were dark and glittery, his nose straight, his mouth firm. He looked slightly dangerous, as if he didn't give a shit.

He sure as hell didn't give a shit about me, for he looked straight through me as he slammed the van door shut and headed past me into the Corn Exchange. Probably going to terrify someone daft enough not to have paid his bill. He had that determined air of a man in pursuit of what's owed to him. Ah well, you lose some and you lose some. I checked out the van and made a mental note. Renew-Vations, with a Stockport phone number. You never know when you're going to need a wall built. Say across a conservatory . . .

6

I stopped by the house to pick up my sports bag. I figured if I was on that side of town anyway, I might as well stop in at the Thai boxing gym and see if there was anyone around to share a quick work-out. It would be better for me than lunch, and besides, after the breakfast I'd had, I needed to do something that would make me feel good about my body. Alexis was long gone, and Richard appeared to have returned to his own home. There was a message on the answering machine from Shelley, so I called in. Sometimes she really winds me up. I mean, I was going to check in anyway, but she'd managed to get her message in first and make me feel like some schoolkid dogging it.

"Mortensen and Brannigan, how may I help you?" she greeted me in the worst mid-Atlantic style. That wasn't my idea, I swear. I don't think it was Bill's either.

"Brannigan, how may I help you?" I said.

"Hi, Kate. Where are you?"

"I'm passing through my living room between tasks," I replied. "What's the problem?"

"Brian Chalmers of PharmAce called. He says he needs to talk to you. Asap, not lad." M & B code for "As soon as possible, not life and death."

"Right. I have to go over to Urmston anyway, so I'll come back via Trafford Park and see him. Can you fix up for me to see him around two? I'll call in for an exact time."

"Fine. And Ted Barlow rang to ask if you'd made any progress."

"Tell him I'm pursuing preliminary inquiries and I'll get back to him when I have something solid to report. And are you?"

"Am I what?" Shelley sounded genuinely baffled. That must have been a novel experience for her.

"Making any progress."

"As I'm always having to remind my two children," heavy emphasis on the "children," "there's nothing clever about rudeness."

"I'll consider my legs well and truly smacked. But are you?"

"That's for me to know and for you to find out. Goodbye, Kate." I didn't even have time for the goodbye before the line went dead.

It was just before twelve when I managed to find someone who could give me any useful information about my missing conservatories. But when I did, it was worth the wait. Diane Shipley was every private investigator's dream. She lived at the head of Sutcliffe Court, her bungalow commanding a view of the whole close. With a corner of my brain, I had noted the raised flower beds and the ramp leading up to the front door, but it still didn't stop me having my eyes at the wrong level when the door opened. I made the adjustment and found myself staring down into a face like a hawk; short, salt and pepper hair, dark beady eyes, deep set and hooded, narrow nose the shape of a puffin's beak, and, incongruously, a wide and humorous mouth. The woman was in a wheelchair, and it didn't seem to bother her in the slightest.

I delivered my usual spiel about the house next door's conservatory, and her face relaxed into a smile. "You mean Rachel Brown's conservatory?" she inquired.

I checked my list. "I've got Rowena and Derek Brown," I said.

"Ah," said the woman. "Dirty work at the crossroads. You'd better come in. My name's Diane Shipley, by the way."

I introduced myself as I followed her down the hall. We turned left into an unusual room. It ran the whole depth of the house, with windows on three walls, giving a sensation of light and air. It was painted white, with cork-tiled flooring. The walls were decorated with beautifully detailed drawings of flowers and plants. Across one corner was a draughtsman's table, set at the perfect height for her chair. "I illustrate children's books for a living," she said. "The other stuff I do for fun," she added, gesturing at the walls. "In case you were wondering, I had a riding accident eight years ago. Dead from the waist down."

I swallowed. "Right. Em, sorry about that."

She grinned. "That's not why I told you. I find that if I don't, people only concentrate on half of what I'm saying because they're so busy wondering about my disability. I prefer a hundred per cent attention. Now, how can I help you?"

I trotted out the old familiar questions. But this time, I got some proper answers. "When I'm working, I tend to do a fair bit of staring out of the window. And when I see people in the court, I must confess I watch them. I look at the way their bodies move, the shapes they make. It helps when I'm drawing action. So, yes, I noticed quite a lot about Rachel."

"Can you describe her?"

Diane wheeled herself across to a set of map drawers. "I can do better than that," she said, opening one and taking out an A4 file. She shuffled through the sheets of paper inside, extracted a couple and held them out to me. Curious, I took them from her. They were a series of drawings of a head, some quite detailed, others little more than a quick cartoon of a few lines. They captured a woman with small, neat features, sharp chin, face wider across the eyes. Her hair was shoulder-length, wavy. "It was streaked," Diane said, following my eyes. "I wondered a couple of times if it might be a wig. It always looked the same. Never looked like she'd just been to the hairdresser. If it was a wig, though, it was a good one. You couldn't tell, not even face to face."

"How well did you know her?" I asked.

"At first, not at all. She didn't spend that much time here. It was May when she moved in, and really, she was only here perhaps three or four nights a week, Monday to Friday. She was never here at weekends. Then, one evening in June, she came over. It was about half past nine, I'd guess. She said she had a gas leak and she was waiting for the emergency engineers. She told me she was nervous of staying in, especially since they had told her not to turn any lights on. So I invited her in and gave her a drink. White wine. I had a bottle open already."

I loved it. A witness who could tell me what she'd had to drink four months before. "And did she tell you anything about herself?"

"Yes and no. She told me her name, and I remarked on the coincidence. She said yes, she had noticed when she exchanged contracts to buy the house that she had the same name as the vendors, but she'd got used to that kind of coincidence with a name like Brown. I was a little surprised, because I had no idea that Rowena and Derek had actually sold the house."

I had that feeling you get when you walk into a theatre halfway through the first act of a new play. What she was saying made perfect sense, but it was meaningless unless you'd seen the first twenty minutes. "I'm sorry, you're going to have to run that past me a little more slowly. I mean, surely you realized they'd sold the house when they stopped living there and a new person moved in?"

It was her turn to give me the baffled look. "But Derek and Ro haven't lived in the house for four years. Derek is an engineer in the oil industry, and he was away two weeks in four, so Ro and I got to be really good friends. Then, four years ago, Derek was offered a five-year contract in Mexico with a company house thrown in. So they decided to rent out their house over here on a series of short-term lets. When Rachel moved in, I thought she was just another tenant till she told me otherwise."

"But surely you must have realized the house was up for sale? I mean, even if there wasn't an estate agent's board up, you can't have missed them showing people round," I remarked.

"Funny you should say that. It's exactly what I thought. But Rachel told me that she'd seen it advertised in the *Evening Chronicle*, and that she'd viewed it the next day. Perhaps I was out shopping, or she came after dark one evening when I wasn't working. Anyway, I saw no reason to doubt what she was telling me. Why lie about it, for heaven's sake? It's not as if renting a house is shameful!" A laugh bubbled up in Diane's throat.

"Was she on her own, or was she living with someone?" I asked.

"She had a boyfriend. But he was never there unless she was. And he wasn't always there even if she was. I tended to see him leave, rather than arrive, but a couple of times, I saw him pay off a taxi around eleven o'clock at night."

"Did he leave with Rachel in the mornings?" I couldn't see how this all fitted together, but I was determined to make the most of a co-operative witness.

Diane didn't even pause for thought. "They left together. That's why I don't have any drawings of him. She was always between me and him, and he always got in the passenger side of the car, so I never really got a clear view of him. He was stylish, though. Even at a distance I could see he dressed well. He even wore a Panama hat on sunny mornings. Can you believe it, a Panama hat in Urmston?"

Like cordon bleu in a motorway service station, it was a hard one to get my head round. "So tell me about the conservatory."

This time she did take a moment to think. "It must have been towards the end of July," she said slowly but without hesitation. "I was away on holiday from the first to the fifteenth of August. The conservatory went up a couple of days before I left. Then, when I came back from Italy, they'd all gone. The conservatory, Rachel Brown and her boyfriend. Six weeks ago, a new batch of tenants arrived. But I still don't know if Rachel has let the house, or indeed if Rachel ever bought it in the first place. All I know is that the chaps in there now rented it through the same agency that Derek and Ro used, DKL Estates. They've got an office in Stretford, but I think their head office is in Warrington."

I was impressed. "You're very well informed," I said.

"It's my legs that don't work, not my brain. I like to make sure it stays that way. Some people call me nosy. I prefer to think of it as a healthy curiosity. What are you, anyway? Some kind of bailiff? And don't give me that stuff about being a representative of the conservatory company. You're far too smart for that. Besides, there's obviously been something very odd going on there. You're not just following up who you've sold conservatories to."

I could have carried on bluffing, but I couldn't see the point. Diane deserved some kind of quid pro quo. "I'm a private investigator," I said. "My partner and I investigate white-collar crime."

"And this is the case of the missing conservatories, eh? Wonderful! You have made my week, Kate Brannigan."

As I drove off towards Trafford Park, I began to suspect that Diane Shipley might just have made mine.

Brian Chalmers of PharmAce was less than thrilled when I told him the results of my work both inside and outside his factory and warehouse. He was furious with himself for employing a senior lab technician whose loyalty lay to his bank account rather than his boss. Unfortunately, because of my cock-up with the surveillance film, he didn't have any evidence other than my word, which wasn't enough for him to drag the guy into his office and fire him on the spot. So, since he had to take his

anger out on someone, I got the lab technician's kicking. And
because the client is always right (at least while he's actually in
the room) I had to bite the bullet and stand on for the bollocking.

I let him rant for a good ten minutes, then offered to repeat
the surveillance exercise over the weekend at a reduced rate. That
took the wind out of his sails, as it was meant to. Unfortunately,
as I left Chalmers' office, I passed one of the technicians I had
dealt with during my short spell working undercover at Pharm-
mAce but, although he looked at me as if he ought to know me,
he passed by without greeting me. Looked like I'd been lucky.
The phenomenon of not recognizing people out of context had
worked in my favour. After all, what would a temporary stock
clerk be doing in the managing director's office, all suited up?

It was just before three when I pulled up outside the Thai
boxing gym. My head felt like it was full of cogs and wheels all
spinning out of sync, trying to assimilate everything that Diane
Shipley had told me and make it fit what I'd been told at the other
houses. None of it really made any sense so far. I know from
bitter experience that when my mind is churning and fizzing,
there's nothing better than some hard physical exercise. Which
for me these days means Thai kick-boxing.

It started off as purely utilitarian. My friend Dennis the
burglar pointed out to me that I needed self-defence skills. He
wasn't so much thinking about the job I do as the neighbourhood
where I live. He persuaded me to come along to the club where
his adored teenage daughter is the junior champion. When I saw
the outside of the building, a horrible, breeze-block construction
like an overgrown Scout hut, I was deeply unimpressed. But
inside, it's clean, warm and well-lit. And the women's coach,
Karen, is a former world champion who gave up serious competition to have a family. One of the wildest sights in our club is
watching her three-year-old toddling round the ring throwing
kicks at people twice his size, and causing them a lot of grief.

I was in luck, for Karen was in the tiny cubicle she calls an
office, desperate for an excuse to avoid doing the paperwork. She

was in luck too, for I was so bagged off at the verbal beating I'd had from Brian Chalmers that I gave her the most challenging work-out I'd ever managed.

Left to their own devices, the tumblers in my brain started to slot into place. By the time we'd finished trading blows, I knew where I had to look next on the trail of the missing conservatories.

7

Since the Land Registry keeps office hours rather than supermarket ones, I couldn't have done anything more that afternoon, even supposing they didn't insist that you make a prior appointment to look at the registers. The real blow was that Ted had inconsiderately sold his conservatories to properties that were covered by two separate offices; the Warrington ones came under Birkenhead, the Stockport ones under Lytham St Annes, an arrangement about as logical as having London covered by Southampton. Just to confuse things even more, the Lytham registry is in Birkenhead House . . . Ever get the impression they really don't want you to exercise your rights to examine their dusty tomes? However, I did manage to get an appointment in Birkenhead for the Monday morning. When I read over the list of addresses, the woman I spoke to sounded positively gleeful. It's a joy to deal with people who love their work. After sorting that out, I felt I could pursue Alexis's dodgy builder with a clear conscience.

I went home to change into something a little less threatening than a business suit. While I was there, I tried to ring T. R. Harris's solicitor, Mr Graves. The number rang out without response. The idleness of some of the legal profession never ceases to amaze me. Twenty past four and everyone had knocked off for the day. Maybe Thursday was early closing day in Ramsbottom.

I couldn't find T. R. Harris in the phone book, which was annoying but not too surprising, given the habits of builders.

My hair was still damp from my shower at the gym, so I gave it a quick blast with the hair dryer. I decided a couple of months ago to let it grow. Now it's reached my shoulders, but instead of growing longer, it just seems to get wilder. And I've noticed a couple of grey hairs in among the auburn. Some hair colours go grey gracefully, but auburn ain't one of them. So far, there are few enough to pull out, but I suspect it won't be long before I have to hit the henna, like my mother before me. Muttering under my breath, I chose a pair of russet trousers, a cream poloneck angora and lambswool jumper and a tweedy jacket. Now the nights were drawing in, it was time for my favourite winter footwear, my dark tan cowboy boots that might have seen better days but fit like a pair of gloves. Just the thing for a trip to the horrid, nasty, windy, wet, dark countryside. If you have to abandon the city, you might at least be dressed for it. Remembering the lack of street lights out there, I slipped a small torch in my bag.

As I drove across town towards the motorway, I decided that I needed to track down the farmer who had sold the land to T. R. Harris in the first place. But on the way, I decided to check out Harris's premises. I wanted to know where I could lay hands on him once I had my ammunition.

134 Bolton High Road wasn't the builder's yard I'd been expecting. It was a corner shop, still open for the sale of bread, chocolate, cigarettes and anything else the forgetful had omitted to lay in for the evening's viewing. An old-fashioned bell on a coiled spring jangled as I opened the door. The teenage lad behind the counter looked up from his motor-bike magazine and gave me the once-over reserved for anyone who hadn't been crossing the threshold on a regular basis for the last fifteen years.

"I'm looking for a builder," I said.

"Sorry, love, we don't sell them. There's no demand, you see." He struggled to keep a straight face, but failed.

"I'm demanding," I said. I waited for him to think of the reply.

He only took a few seconds. "I bet you are, love. Can I help?"

"A builder called Harris. T. R. Harris. This is the address I've got for him. Do you act as an accommodation address for people?"

He shook his head. "Me mam won't stand on for it. She says people who won't use their own address must be up to no good. Tom Harris, the guy you're looking for, he rented one of the offices upstairs for a couple of months. Paid cash, an' all."

"So you don't live over the shop, then?"

"No." He closed his magazine and leaned back against the cigarette shelves, happy to have a break in routine. "Me mam told me dad it was dead common, made him buy the house next door. He turned the upstairs here into offices. Brian Burley, the insurance broker, he's got two offices and a share of the bathroom and kitchenette. He's been here five years, ever since me dad did them up. But the other office, that's had loads of people through it. I'm not surprised. You couldn't swing a rat in there, never mind a cat."

"So, Tom Harris isn't here any longer?" I asked.

"Nah. He was paid up to the end of last week, and we ain't seen him since. He said he just needed an office while he sorted out a couple of deals over here. He said he was from down south, but he didn't sound it. Didn't sound local neither. Anyway, what're you after him for? He stood you up, or something?" He couldn't help himself, and he was cute enough to get away with it. Give him a few years and he'd be lethal. God help the women of Ramsbottom.

"I need to talk to him, that's all. Any chance of a look round upstairs? See if he left anything that might give me an idea where he moved on to?" I gave him my sultriest smile.

"You'll not find so much as a fingerprint up there," the lad told me, disappointed. "Me mam bottomed it on Sunday. And when she cleans, she cleans."

I could imagine. There didn't seem a lot of point in pushing it, and if Harris had paid in cash, there wasn't likely to be any other clue as to his whereabouts. "Did you know him at all," I asked.

"I saw him going in and out, but he didn't have no time for the likes of me. Fancied himself, know what I mean? Thought he was hard."

"What did he look like?" I asked.

"A builder. Nowt special. Brown hair, big muscles, quite tall. He drove a white Transit, it said 'T. R. Harris Builders' along the side. Here, you're not the cops, are you?" he asked, a sudden note of apprehension mixing with excitement.

I shook my head. "Just trying to track him down for a friend he promised to do some work for. D'you know if he hung out in any of the local pubs?"

The lad shrugged. "Dunno. Sorry." He looked as if he meant it, too. I bought a pound of Cox's Orange Pippins to stave off the hunger pains and hit the road.

Some days things get clearer as time wears on. Other days, it just gets more and more murky. This one looked like a goldfish bowl that hasn't been cleaned since Christmas. The address I'd carefully copied down from Graves' letterhead that Martin Cheetham had showed me wasn't the office of a solicitor. It wasn't any kind of office at all, to be precise. It was the Farmer's Arms. The pub was about a quarter of a mile from the nearest house, the last building on a narrow road up to the moors where Alexis and Chris had hoped to build their dream home. In spite of its relative isolation, the pub seemed to be doing good business. The car park was more than half full, and the stonework had been recently cleaned.

Inside, it had been refurbished in the "country pub" style of the big breweries. Exposed stone and beams, stained-glass panels in the interior doors, wooden chairs with floral chintz cushions, quarry-tiled floor and an unrivalled choice of fizzy keg beers that all taste the same. There must have been getting

on for sixty people in, but the room was big enough for there
still to be a sense of space. Two middle-aged women and a man
in his late twenties were working the bar efficiently.

I perched on a stool at the bar and didn't have long to wait
for my St Clement's. I watched the clientele for ten minutes or
so. They sounded relatively local, and were mostly in their twenties and thirties. Beside me at the bar was the kind of group I
imagined T. R. Harris would feel one of the lads with. But first
I had to solve the problem of the moody address for his solicitor.

I waited for a lull, then signalled one of the barmaids.
"Same again, love?" she asked.

I nodded, and as she poured, I said, "I'm a bit confused. Is
this 493 Moor Lane?"

It took a bit of consultation with bar staff and customers,
but eventually, consensus was reached. 493 it was. "I've been
given this as the address for a bloke called Graves," I told them.
For some reason, the men at the bar convulsed with laughter.

The barmaid pursed her lips and said, "You've got to excuse
them. They're not right in the head. The reason they're laughing
is, the pub car park backs on to the churchyard. We're always
having a to-do with the vicar, because idiots that know no better
go and sit on the gravestones with their pints in the summer."

I was beginning to feel really pissed off with T. R. Harris
and his merry dance. Wearily, I said, "So there's no one here
by the name of Graves? And you don't let rooms, or have any
offices upstairs?"

The barmaid shook her head. "Sorry, love. Somebody's
been having you on."

I forced a smile. "No problem. I don't suppose any of you
know a builder called Tom Harris? Bought some land up the
road from here?"

There were smiles and nods of recognition all around me.
"That's the fella that bought Harry Cartwright's twelve-acre
field," one said. "The man from nowhere," another added.

"Why do you say that?" I asked.

"Why are you asking?" he countered.

"I'm trying to get hold of him in connection with the land that he bought."

"He doesn't own it any more. He sold it last week," the barmaid said. "And we haven't seen him since."

"How long has he been coming in here?" I asked.

"Since he first started negotiating with Harry about the land. Must be about three months ago, I'd guess," one of the men said. "Good company. Had some wild stories to tell."

"What kind of wild stories?" I asked.

They all laughed uproariously again. Maybe I should audition for the Comedy Store. "Not the kind you tell when there are ladies present," one of them wheezed through his laughter.

I couldn't believe I was putting myself through this out of friendship. Alexis was going to owe me a lifetime of favours after this. I took a deep breath and said, "I don't suppose any of you knows where his yard is? Or where he lives?"

They muttered among themselves and shook their heads dubiously. "He never said," one of them told me. "He rented an office above the corner shop on Bolton High Road, maybe they'd know."

"I've tried there. No joy, I'm afraid. You lads are my last hope." I batted my eyelashes, God help me. The appeal to chivalry often works with the kind of assholes who sit around in pubs telling each other mucky stories to compensate for the lack of anything remotely exciting in their own squalid little lives.

Depressingly, it worked. Again, they went into a muttering huddle. "You want to talk to Gary," the spokesman eventually announced confidently.

Not if he's anything like you lot, I thought. I smiled sweetly and said, "Gary?"

"Gary Adams," he said in that irritated tone that men reserve for women they think are slow or stupid. "Gary cleared the land for Tom Harris. When he bought it, half of it was copse, all overgrown with brambles and gorse between the trees.

Gary's got all the equipment, see? He does all that kind of work round here."

I kept the smile nailed on. "And where will I find Gary?" I said, almost without moving my lips.

Watches were studied, frowns were exchanged. Exasperated, the barmaid said, "He lives at 31 Montrose Bank. That's through the centre of the village, up the hill and third left. You'll probably find him in his garage, rebuilding that daft big American car of his." I thanked her and left, managing to keep the smile in place for as long as the lads could see me. My face muscles felt like they'd just done a Jane Fonda work-out.

As predicted, Gary was in the garage tacked on to a neat stone cottage. The up-and-over door was open, revealing a drop-head vintage Cadillac. The bonnet was up, and the man I took to be Gary Adams was leaning into the engine. As I approached, I could see him doing something terribly brutal-looking with a wrench the size of a wrestler's forearm. I cleared my throat and instructed the muscles to do the smile again. Reluctantly, they obeyed. Gary glanced up, surprised. He was in his mid-thirties, with a haircut that looked like it came right out of National Service.

"Gary?" I said.

He straightened up, placed the wrench lovingly on the engine block, and frowned. "That's right. Who wants to know?"

Time for another fairy story. "My name's Brannigan. Kate Brannigan. I'm an architect. A friend of mine bought some land from Tom Harris, and she needs to get in touch with him about another deal. The lads at the Farmer's Arms reckoned you might know where I can find him."

Gary gave a knowing smile as he wiped his hands on his oily overalls. "Owes you money, does he?"

"Not exactly," I said. "But I need to speak to him. Why? Does he owe you?"

Gary shook his head. "I made sure of that. His kind, they're ten a penny. Ask you to do a job, you do it, you tell them what they owe, they ignore you. So, I made him pay up in cash. Half before, half after. Glad I did, an' all, looking at the way he's sunk without trace since he sold them plots on."

"What made you think he was dodgy?"

Gary shrugged. "I didn't know him, that's all. He wasn't from round here. And he obviously wasn't stopping, neither."

This was like drawing teeth. Sometimes I think I might have been better suited to a career in psychotherapy. The punters might not want to talk to you either, but at least you get to sit in a warm, comfy office while you're doing it. "What makes you say that?" I asked.

"When you're in business and you're planning to stop somewhere, you get a local bank account, don't you? Stands to reason," he said triumphantly.

"And Tom Harris didn't?"

"I saw his chequebook. He was going to give me a cheque for the advance on the work, but I said no way, I wanted cash. But I got a good enough look at it to see that it wasn't a local bank that he had his account with."

I tried to hide the deep breath. "Which bank was it?" I inquired, resisting the temptation to kick-box him to within an inch of his life.

"Northshires Bank, in Buxton. That isn't even in *Lancashire*. And the account wasn't in his name, either. It was some business or other." I opened my mouth and a smile twitched at the corner of Gary's mouth as he anticipated me. "I didn't pay attention to the name. I just noticed that it wasn't Tom Harris."

"Thanks, Gary," I said. "You've been a big help. I don't suppose you'd know anybody else who might know where I can get hold of Tom Harris?"

"It's really important, is it?" he asked. I nodded. "Harry Cartwright's the farmer who sold him the land. He might know."

"Where's his farm?" I asked.

Gary shook his head with the half-smile of a man who's dealing with a crazy lady. "How good are you with Dobermans?

And if you get past them, he'll have his shotgun ready and waiting. He's not an easy man, Harry." I must have looked like I was
going to burst into tears. I imagine he thought they were tears
of despair; they were really tears of frustration. "Tell you what,"
he said. "I'll come with you. Give me a minute to get out of
my overalls, and phone the old bugger to let him know we're
coming. He's known me long enough to talk before he shoots."

I walked back to the car and turned the heater up full. I
hate the country.

8

Within ten minutes of leaving Gary's, we were driving up an unmetalled track. I stopped at a five-barred gate festooned with barbed wire, and Gary jumped out to open it. When he closed it behind me, he sprinted for the car. He'd barely slammed the door behind him when a pair of huge Dobermans hurled themselves at the passenger side of the car, barking and slavering hysterically. Gary grinned, which convinced me he wasn't the full shilling. "Bet you're glad you brought me along," he said.

I slammed the car into gear and continued up the track. Half a mile on, my headlights picked out a low stone building in the gathering rural gloom. The roof appeared to sag in the middle, and the window frames looked so rotten that I couldn't help thinking the first winter gales would have the glass halfway across the farmyard. I could tell it was a farmyard by the smell of manure. I drove as close as I could to the door, but before I could cut the engine, an elderly man appeared in the doorway. As confidently predicted by Gary, he was brandishing an over-and-under double-barrelled shotgun. Just then, the dogs arrived and started a cacophony of barking that made my fillings hurt. I *really* love the country.

"What now?" I demanded of Gary.

The old man approached. He wore a greasy cardigan over a collarless shirt that might have started its life the colour of an oily rag, but I doubted it. He walked right up to the car and stared through the window, the gun barrels pointing ominously through the glass. My opinion of T. R. Harris's bottle had just gone up a hundred per cent. Having satisfied himself that my passenger really was Gary, Cartwright stepped back a few feet and whistled to the dogs. They dropped at his feet like logs. Gary said, "It's OK, you can get out." He opened his door and climbed out. Warily, I followed.

I moved close enough to get a whiff of the old man. It was enough to make me pray we could conduct our business out in the farmyard. Cartwright said, "Gary says you're after Tom Harris. What I did with him was all legal, all above board."

"I know that, Mr Cartwright. I just need to speak to Tom, and no one seems to know where I can find him. I hoped maybe you would know."

He tucked his gun under one arm and fumbled in the deep pocket of his grimy corduroy trousers and produced a document which he waved under my nose. "That's all I know," he said.

I reached for it, but he snatched it back. "You can look but you mustn't touch," he said, just like a five-year-old. I held my breath and moved close enough to read it. It was an agreement between Henry George Cartwright of Stubbleystall Farm and Thomas Richard Harris of 134 Bolton High Road, Ramsbottom. I didn't have to read any further. I had more bells ringing in my head than Oxford on May morning. I smiled politely, thanked Harry Cartwright and got back in my car. Looking bewildered, Gary folded himself in beside me and we shot back down the track again.

Thomas Richard Harris. Tom, Dick and Harry. If Thomas Richard Harris was a straight name, I was Marie of Romania.

By eleven on Friday morning, I was stir crazy. Shelley was thrilled that I was stymied on our two paying jobs, the conservatories and the pharmaceuticals, and she wasn't about to let me bunk off and follow the clues to Alexis's con man. I was trapped in an office with a woman who wanted me to do paperwork, and I had no excuse to get away. By ten, all my files were up to date. By eleven, my case notes were not only written but polished to the point where I could have joined a writers' group and read them out. At five past eleven, I rebelled. Clutching the Ted Barlow file, I sailed through the outer office, telling Shelley I was following a new lead. It led me all the way to the Cornerhouse coffee shop, where I browsed through the file as I sipped a cappuccino. As I ploughed through my interview notes yet again, it hit me. There was something I could do while I was waiting for my Monday morning appointment at the Land Registry.

DKL Estates, the estate agents Diane Shipley had mentioned, was a shopfront opposite Chorlton Baths. DKL looked reasonably prosperous, but I realized almost immediately that there was a good reason for that. They specialized in renting, and in selling the kind of first-time-buyer properties that shift even at the bottom of a recession. There are always people desperate to climb on to the property ladder, not to mention the poor sods trading down. It looked to me as if they'd also got a significant number of ex-council houses on their books, which took a bit of courage. Their gamble seemed to have paid off in terms of customers, though. One woman walked in just ahead of me, but there were already a couple of other serious browsers. I joined them in their study of properties for sale.

The woman I had followed in selected a couple of sets of details, then approached the young man behind the desk that sat at an angle to the room. He looked as if he should be in a classroom swotting for his GCSEs. I know they say you should worry when the policemen start looking younger, but estate agents? She asked in a low, cultivated voice if she might arrange to view both properties. I was surprised; she was wearing a knitted Italian suit that couldn't have cost less than three hundred pounds, her shoes looked like they'd come from Bally or Ravel,

the handbag was a Tula, and I'd have put money on the mac
being a four hundred pound Aquascutum. Put it another way, she
didn't look like a terraced house in Whalley Range was her idea
of a des. res. Maybe she was looking for a nice little investment.

As I studied her, the lad behind the desk was phoning to
fix her up with viewing appointments. I took in the grooming:
the polished nails, the immaculately styled dark brown hair, the
expert make-up that accentuated her dark eyes. I had to admire
her style, even though it's one I've no desire to aspire to.

I'd stared too long, however. The woman must have felt
my eyes on her, for she turned her head sharply and caught my
gaze. Her eyes seemed to open wider and her eyebrows climbed.
Abruptly, she turned on her heel and walked quickly out of the
agency. I was gobsmacked. I didn't know her from a hole in the
ground, but she clearly knew me. Or maybe I should say, she
clearly knew who I was.

The lad looked up from his pad and realized his customer
was halfway out of the door. "Madam," he wailed. "Madam,
if you'll just give me a minute . . ." She ignored him and kept
walking without a backward glance.

"How bizarre," I said, approaching the desk. "Do you
always have that effect on women?"

"It takes all sorts," he said with a cynical resignation that
would have been depressing in a man ten years his senior. "At
least she took the details with her. If she wants to view, she can
always phone. Maybe she remembered an appointment."

I agreed. Privately, I was dredging my memory of recent
cases, trying to see if I could place the elegant brunette. I gave
up after a few seconds when the lad asked if he could help me.
"I'd like to talk to whoever's in charge," I said.

He smiled. "Can you tell me what it's in connection with?
I might be able to help."

I took a business card out of my wallet, the one that says
Mortensen and Brannigan: Security Consultants. "I don't mean
to appear rude, but it's a confidential matter," I told him.

He looked slightly disconcerted, which made me wonder what little scam DKL were up to. He pushed his chair back and said, "If you'd care to wait a moment?" as he reversed across the room and through a door in the far corner. He emerged less than a minute later, looking slightly shaken. "If you'd care to go through, Mrs Lieberman will see you now."

I flashed him a quick, reassuring smile, then opened the door. As I entered the back office, a woman I put in her late forties rose from a typist's chair behind an L-shaped desk. On one leg of the desk, an Apple Mac stood, its monitor showing a full page mock-up of some house details. Mrs Lieberman extended a well-manicured hand displaying a few grands' worth of gold, sapphires and diamonds. "Miss Brannigan? I'm Rachel Lieberman. Do sit down. How may I help you?" I instantly realized who had taught the young man in the front office his style.

I gave her the quick once-over as I settled into a comfortable chair. Linen suit over a soft sueded silk blouse. Her brown hair, with the odd thread of silver, was swept up into a cottage loaf above a sharp-featured face that was just beginning to blur around the jawline. Her brown eyes looked shrewd, emphasized by the slight wrinkles that appeared as she studied me right back. "It's to do with a matter I'm looking into on behalf of a client. I'm sorry to arrive without an appointment, but I was in the area, so I thought I'd drop by on the off-chance of catching you," I started. She looked as if she didn't believe a word of it, a smile twitching at one corner of her mouth. "I wonder if you can clear something up for me. I realize that your main office is in Warrington, but are you actually the owner of DKL, or do you manage this branch?"

"I own the company, Miss Brannigan." Her voice had had most of the northern accent polished off. "I have done since my husband died three years ago. Daniel Kohn Lieberman, hence the name of the company. What, if anything, does that have to do with your client?"

"Nothing, Mrs Lieberman, except that I shouldn't imagine a manager would have the authority to release the information

I'm after. Mind you, a mere employee probably wouldn't grasp the importance of it, either." I tried that on for size. I hoped she was a woman who'd respond to flattery. If not, that left me with nothing but threats, and I hate to threaten anyone in daylight hours. It takes so much more energy.

"And what exactly is this information?" she asked, leaning forward in her chair and fiddling with a gold pen.

"I'd like to level with you, if I may. My company specializes in white-collar crime, and I'm investigating a serious fraud. We're looking at a six-figure rip-off here, probably more like a million. I suspect that the perpetrators may be using properties on a short-term lease for their particular scheme." Mrs Lieberman was listening, her head cocked on one side. So far, no reaction was making it through to the surface. I soldiered on.

"One of the addresses I'm looking at was rented through your agency. What I'm trying to do here is to find a common factor. The thing is, I'm beginning to think the renting of the houses is a key factor in the way the fraud is organized, and I hoped that if I gave you the addresses of the other houses I suspect have been involved, then you could check for me and see if they are on your books." I paused. I wanted some feedback. I'd never have made a politician.

Mrs Lieberman straightened up in her chair and drew her lower lip under her teeth. "And that's all you want to know? Whether or not they're on my books?"

"Not quite all, I'm afraid. Whether they are now or have ever been on your books is the first step. Once we've established that, I want to ask you the names of the owners."

She shook her head. "Out of the question. I'm sure you'll appreciate that. We're looking at very confidential matters here. There are only a few agencies that specialize in rental properties in this area, and we are by far the biggest. I act as agent for almost three hundred rental properties, the bulk of them on short-term leases. So you can imagine how important it is that my clients know they can trust me. I can't possibly start giving you their names. And I can't believe you really expected me to. I'm sure you don't release information like that about your clients."

"*Touché.* But surely you can tell me if a particular property is on your books? Then when you call up the details on your screen, you might notice a pattern emerging."

"What sort of a pattern did you have in mind, Miss Brannigan?"

I sighed. "That's what I don't know, Mrs Lieberman. So far, all I have to go on is that I think most of the addresses involved in this scam have been rented. In one case that I'm sure about, I know that the couple who rented the house shared the surname of the couple who actually owned it."

Rachel Lieberman leaned back in her chair and gave me the once-over again. I felt like a newly discovered species of plant—strange, exotic and possibly poisonous. After what seemed to me to be a very long time, she nodded to herself, as if satisfied.

"I'll tell you what I'll do, Miss Brannigan. If you give me the addresses you're interested in, I'll look through my records and see what I can come up with. Frankly, I have to say, I think it'll be a waste of time, but then I wasn't doing anything this evening anyway. I'll call you and let you know. Will Monday morning do, or would you prefer me to ring you at home over the weekend?"

I grinned. Deep down, Mrs Lieberman was a woman after my own heart.

I spent the afternoon with Ted Barlow, doing the boring stuff of checking back through all his records, making notes of ex-salesmen who'd been sacked, and learning exactly how a conservatory is installed. I glanced at the dashboard clock as I got back behind the wheel of my Nova. Just after seven. I figured I'd be quicker picking up the motorway than going home by the more direct crosstown route. A few minutes later, I was doing eighty in the middle lane, the Pet Shop Boys blasting out of all four speakers. The huge arc of Barton Bridge glittered against the sky, sweeping the motorway over the dark ribbon of the Manchester Ship Canal. As the bridge approached, I moved over to the inside lane, positioning myself to change motorways at the exit on the far side. I was singing "Where the streets have no name" at full belt when I automatically registered a white Ford Transit coming up outside me in the middle lane.

I paid no attention to the van as it drew level then slightly ahead. Then, suddenly, his nose was turning in front of me. My brain tripped into slow motion. Everything seemed to last forever. All I could see out of the side of my car was the white side of the van, closing in on me fast. I could see the bottom edge of some logo or sign, but not enough to identify any of the letters. I could hear screaming, then I realized it was my own voice.

The nightmare was happening. The van swiped into me, crushing the door of my car against my right side. At the same time, the car skidded sideways into the crash barrier. I could hear the scream of metal on metal, I could feel the rise in temperature from the friction heat, I could see the barrier buckle, I could hear myself sobbing, "Don't break, bastard thing, don't break!"

The front of my car seemed to be sandwiched between the struts of the crash barrier. I was tilted forward at a crazy angle. Below me, I could see the lights twinkling on the black water of the Ship Canal. The cassette player was silent. So was the engine. All I could hear was the creaking of the stressed metal of the crash barrier. I tried to open the driver's door, but my right arm was clamped in place by the crushed door. I tried to wriggle round to open it with my left arm, but it was no use. I was trapped. I was hanging in space, a hundred feet above the empty depths of the canal. And the Ford Transit was long gone.

9

I came to a very important decision sitting in a cubicle in the casualty department of Manchester Royal Infirmary. Time for a yuppie phone. I mean, have you been in a casualty department lately? Because I was a road traffic accident, I was whizzed straight through the waiting area on a trolley and deposited in a cubicle. Not that that meant I was going to be attended to any more quickly, oh no. I realized pretty soon I was supposed to regard this as my very own personal waiting room. And me not even a private patient!

I stuck my head out of the curtains after about ten minutes and asked a passing nurse where I could find a phone. She barked back at me, "Stay where you are, Doctor will be with you as soon as she can." I sometimes wonder if the words that people hear are the same ones that come out of my mouth.

I tried again a few minutes later. Different nurse. "Excuse me, I was supposed to be meeting someone before I had this accident, and he'll be worried." Not bloody likely, I thought. Not while we're in the same calendar month. "I really need to phone him," I pleaded. I didn't want sympathy, nor to allay his non-existent worries. I simply didn't feel up to walking the half-mile home or coping with a taxi. Yes, all right, I admit it, I was shaken up. To hell with the tough guy private eye image. I was trembling, my body felt like a 5' 3" bruise, and I just wanted to pull the covers over my head.

The second nurse had clearly graduated from the same charm school. "Doctor is very busy. She doesn't have time to wait for you to come back from the phone."

"But Doctor isn't here," I said. "I'm not convinced that doctor is even in this hospital."

"Please wait in the cubicle," she ordered as she swept off. That was when I realized that my resistance to a mobile phone was a classic case of cutting off my nose to spite my face. Never mind that they always ring at the least convenient moment. Never mind that even the lightest ones are heavy enough to turn your handbag into an offensive weapon or wreck the line of your jacket. At least they can summon knights in shining armour. I'll rephrase that. At least they can summon rock journalists with customized hot pink Volkswagen Beetle convertibles.

They let me at a phone about an hour and a half later, when they'd finally got round to examining me, X-raying me and prodding all the most painful bits. The doctor informed me that I had deep bruising to my spine, ribs, right arm, and right leg, and some superficial cuts to my right hand, where the starburst from the driver's window had landed. Oh, and shock, of course. They gave me some pain killers and told me I'd be fine in a few days.

I went through to the waiting room, hoping Richard wouldn't be long. A uniformed constable walked over and sat down beside me. "Miss Brannigan?" he said.

"That's right." I was beyond surprise. The pain killers had started to work.

"It's about the accident. A few questions, I'm afraid."

I closed my eyes and took a deep breath. That was my first mistake. My ribs had decided to go off duty for the night and I ended up doubled over in a gasping cough. Of course, that was precisely the moment Richard chose to arrive. The first I knew of it was the yell. "Oi, you, leave her alone! Jesus, don't you think she's been through enough tonight?" Then he was crouched in front of me, gazing up into my eyes, genuine fear and concern in his face. "Brannigan," he murmured. "You're not fit to be let out on your own, you know that?"

If I hadn't feared it would kill me, I'd have laughed. This, from the man who gets to the corner shop and forgets what he went out for? All of a sudden, I felt very emotional. Must have been the combination of the shock and the drugs. I felt a hot tear trickle down my nose. "Thanks for coming," I said in a shaky voice.

Richard patted my shoulder softly, then straightened up. "Can't you see she's in a state?" he demanded. I twisted my head round to look at the constable, a young lad who was scarlet with embarrassment. The rest of the waiting room were avidly following the drama, momentarily forgetting their own pain.

"I'm sorry, sir," the cop mumbled. "But I need to get some details of the accident from Miss Brannigan. So we can take appropriate action."

Richard appeared to relax slightly. Uh-oh, I thought. "And you can't wait till morning? You have to harass an innocent woman? What's your problem, pal? Got no real criminals out there in the naked city tonight?"

The constable looked hunted. His eyes flickered round the room, desperately seeking a Tardis. I took pity. "Richard, leave it. Just take me home, please. If the constable needs some details, he can follow us there."

Richard shrugged. "OK, Brannigan. Let's roll."

We were halfway to the door when the cop caught up with us. "Em, excuse me, I don't actually have your address."

Richard said "Four," I said "Two" then we chorused "Coverley Close." The copper looked completely bemused.

"Em, can I ask you to take me with you, sir? I'm afraid I haven't any transport here." The poor lad looked mortified. He looked even more mortified folded into the back seat of Richard's Beetle, helmet on his knees.

By the time I had dragged my weary body up the path, I was seriously considering a jacuzzi as well as a mobile phone. I certainly wasn't in the mood for a police interview. But I wanted to get it over with.

We got name, address, date of birth and occupation (security consultant) out of the way while Richard brewed up. The constable looked utterly bewildered when Richard dumped the tray on my coffee table, announced that I was out of milk and wandered off into the conservatory. As Richard came back clutching half a bottle of milk, I put the young copper out of his misery.

The conservatory runs across the back of both houses," I explained. "That way, we don't get under each other's feet."

"She means she gets out of washing my dishes and my socks," Richard said, settling down on the couch beside me. I winced as he leaned into me, and he pulled away quickly. "Sorry, Brannigan," he added, stroking my good arm.

I outlined what had happened on Barton Bridge. I have to admit it was satisfying to see both Richard and the copper turn pale as I gave them the details. "And then the fire brigade arrived and cut me free. Just about the time I should have been eating my first crispy prawn wonton," I added, for Richard's benefit.

The constable cleared his throat. "Did you see the driver of the van at all, miss?"

"No. I wasn't paying attention till it was too late. Far as I was concerned, it was just a van overtaking me."

"And did the van have any identification?"

"There was something, but I couldn't see what. It was higher than the top of my window. I could just catch the bottom couple of inches. And I didn't get his number, either. I was too occupied with the thought of plunging into the Ship Canal. I mean, have you seen the state of the water in there?"

The constable looked even greener. He took a deep breath. "And was it your impression that this was a deliberate attempt to run you off the road?"

The $64,000 question. I tried to look innocent. It wasn't that I felt like being a hero and sorting it all out myself. I just couldn't cope with a long interrogation right then. Besides, that would mean giving them the kind of confidential client information that we're supposed to guard with our lives, and I couldn't do that without consulting Bill. "Officer, I can't imagine why anyone would want to do that," I said. "I mean, this is Manchester, not LA. I suppose I was in the guy's blind spot. If he was tired, or he'd had a few too many on the way home from work, he probably didn't even register I was there. Then when he hit me, he panicked, especially if he'd had a drink. I don't think it's anything more sinister than that."

He fell for it. "Right." He closed his notebook and got to his feet, replacing his helmet. "I'm really sorry to have bothered you when you weren't feeling too good. But we want to catch this joker, and we had to see what you could tell us that might help."

"That's all right, officer. We all have our jobs to do," I said sweetly. Richard looked as if he was going to puke. "See the nice officer out, Richard, would you?"

Richard returned. "We all have our jobs to do," he mimicked. "Dear God, Brannigan, where do you dig that shit up from? OK, you fooled the sheriff, but you can't fool the Lone Ranger. What really went down there tonight?"

"Wonderful," I muttered. "The feds aren't allowed to interrogate Tonto, oh God no. But you get to ask all the questions you want, huh?"

He smiled and shrugged. "I love you. I'm entitled."

"If you really loved me, you'd run me a bath," I told him. "Then I'll tell you all about it."

Ten minutes later, I was soaking in the luxuriant bubbles of Van Cleef & Arpel's First. When I say luxuriant, I mean it. Richard has a heavy hand with the bubble bath. I reckoned there was at least a fiver's worth of foam bath surrounding me. I was decent enough to have starred in a forties Hollywood extravaganza.

Richard sat on the closed toilet lid, smoking a joint that smelled heavily loaded to me. His glasses had steamed up, so he'd shoved them up on his head like flying goggles. His hazel eyes peered short-sightedly at me. "So, Brannigan. What really happened out there tonight?" he asked the mirror above my head.

"Somebody was either trying to frighten me off or see me off." There wasn't any point in dressing it up.

"Shit," Richard breathed. "Do you know who?"

"I couldn't swear it in a court of law, but I've got a good idea. I've just turned over a fraud at a pharmaceutical company running into a hundred grand or so. They use white Ford Transits with a logo quite high up on the side. I think that probably covers it, don't you?" I stretched gingerly, then wished I hadn't. The next few days were not going to be fun.

"So what are you going to do about it?" Richard asked. I'll say this for him: he doesn't come on like macho man where my work is concerned. He doesn't like the fact that I have to take risks, but he generally keeps his mouth shut on the subject.

"Tomorrow I'm going to get one of our leg men to go over there and take a look at their rolling stock. And I'm going to get him to keep the place under surveillance until we get the pics we need. And you, my sweet darling, are going to take me for a day out in Buxton."

"Buxton? What's in Buxton?"

"Lots of lovely things. You'll like it. But right now, what I'm going to do is lie in this bath till the hot water runs out, then I'm going to crawl into bed."

"Fair enough. D'you want supper in bed? If you do, I'll nip out for a Chinese."

The words were poetry to my ears. I wasn't convinced that I could handle anything as complicated as chopsticks, but there was only Richard to see. And if he ever threatened to tell, I was

sure I could find something to blackmail him into silence with.
After all, I know he's got a Barry Manilow CD.

I woke in the same position I'd gone to sleep in. When I tried
to move, I understood why. Inch by agonizing inch, I got myself
out of bed and on to my feet. Making it to the bathroom was
hell on legs. I'd just made it back to the hall when Richard
appeared at the other end, hair awry, duvet trailing behind him.
He rubbed the sleep out of his eyes, muttered, "You OK?" and
reached for his glasses. When he'd put them on and looked at me,
he couldn't stifle a snort of laughter. "I'm sorry," he gasped. "I
really am. But you look like Half Man, Half Biscuit. One side's
flesh coloured, the other side's all brown and purple. Wild!"

I looked down. He was right. At least he'd found it funny
rather than repulsive. "You really know how to make a woman
feel special," I muttered. It was kind of him to have slept on
my sofa rather than going back to his own house. I was about
to thank him when I saw the havoc he'd managed to wreak in
my kitchen with one Chinese takeaway. It looked like the entire
People's Army had marched through on their stomachs. I didn't
have the energy or the mobility to do anything about it, so I
tried to blank it while I poured a cup of coffee from yesterday's
jug and waited for the microwave to do its magic.

By the time I'd got my first cup down, Richard was back,
showered and shaved. I was just beginning to realize how much
my accident had frightened and upset him. He knows how much
I hate fuss, so he was trying desperately to disguise the fact that
he was running round like a mother hen. I know it's disaster for
the image, but I was touched, I have to admit it.

"What's the plan for today, then?" he asked. "You still
want to go to Buxton?"

"How are you fixed?" I asked.

"I can be free. Couple of calls to make, is all."

"Can you drive me round to the Turkish? And pick me up an hour later?"

The Turkish is bliss. It's part of the Hathersage Road Public Baths, a magnificent Victorian edifice about ten minutes' walk from my flat. If walking's your thing. Because it's owned by the city council, there's never been any money to gut it and refurbish it, so it's still filled with the glories of its Victorian heyday. The original green, yellow and blue tiles adorn the walls. They still have the old-fashioned wrap-round showers: as well as water coming at you from above, hot water hits you from the pipes that surround you on three sides as well. The only concession to the last decade of the twentieth century is the plastic loungers that complement the original marble benches in the steam room. Like I say, it's always bliss. But that particular Saturday morning was more blissful than most.

I came out an hour later feeling almost human. Richard was only five minutes late in collecting me, which approaches an all-time record. Back home, I called the garage who had towed the remains of my Nova away, and my insurance company. Next, I left a message on the office answering machine asking Shelley to sort out the best possible deal on a mobile phone for me first thing Monday morning.

Finally, I rang Brian Chalmers of PharmAce. "Sorry to bother you at home, Brian, but have any of your vans been in an accident over the last twenty-four hours?"

"I don't think so. Why do you ask?"

"I thought I saw one in a crash on the motorway last night. I reckoned you might need a witness. Can you check for me?"

He obviously wondered why on earth I was so interested, but I'd just plugged a leak that was costing him a fortune, so he decided to humour me.

He got back to me ten minutes later. "None of our vans has reported any accidents last night," he said. "However, one of our Transits was stolen from the depot on Thursday night. So I suppose it's possible that was the van you saw."

Thursday night. Just after I'd talked to Chalmers at Pharm-Ace's office. The only thing I needed now was proof. Perhaps after we'd fronted up the errant lab technician, we could persuade him to confess. By then, maybe I'd be fit enough to make his kidneys feel the way mine felt.

We were just about to leave when the phone rang again. "Leave it," Richard shouted from halfway down the hall. But I can't help myself. I waited till the answering machine clicked in.

"This is Rachel Lieberman calling Kate Brannigan on Saturday . . ." was broadcast before I got to the phone.

"Mrs Lieberman?" I gasped. "Sorry, I was just walking through the door. Did you manage to go through those details?"

"There is a pattern, Miss Brannigan. All but one of those properties are now or have been on our books. They are all rented out on short-term leases of between three and six months. And in every case, the tenants have shared the surname of the real owners."

I nearly took a deep breath to calm my nerves before I remembered that wasn't part of my current repertoire. Thank you very much, Mrs Lieberman," I said. "You have no idea how much I appreciate it."

"You're welcome. I enjoy a challenge now and again," she replied, a warmth in her voice I hadn't heard before. "It may not mean much, however. These are common names—Smith, Johnson, Brown; it's not such a big coincidence. By the way, I don't know if you're interested, but after I'd worked through these details I checked out recent rentals. There are three other properties where the same pattern seems to be repeated. One was rented three months ago, the other two months ago and the third three weeks ago."

I closed my eyes and sent up a prayer of thanks. "I'm interested, Mrs Lieberman. I don't suppose . . ."

She cut me off. "Miss Brannigan, I like to think I've got good judgement. I faxed the addresses to your office overnight. I'm not happy with the idea that my business is being used, however innocently, in any kind of fraud. Keep me posted, won't you?"

Keep her posted? I could find myself sending Chanukah cards this year!

10

I didn't get much chance to mull over what Rachel Lieberman had told me. I find I have some difficulty in concentrating when Edward the Second and the Red Hot Polkas are being played at a volume that makes my fillings vibrate. I know this is a measure of my personal inadequacy, but we all have to live with our little weaknesses. And it was keeping the chauffeur happy. I decided to put my new information in the section of my brain marked "pending." Besides, until I'd been to the Land Registry, and collated all the information from there, from Ted's records and the material Josh's Julia had faxed to the office the previous afternoon, I didn't want to fall in love with any theories that might distort my judgement.

We made it to Buxton before lunch with only a couple of wrong turnings. I'm not quite sure what I expected, but it wasn't what I got. There's a grandiose little opera house with a conservatory that some spiritual ancestor of Ted Barlow's had installed. I'd have loved to have heard the salesman's pitch. "Now, Mr and Mrs Councillor, if I could show you a way to enhance the touristic value of your opera house for less than the product of a penny rate, I take it that would be something you would be pleased to go along with?" There's also a magnificent Georgian crescent that ought to blow your socks off, but it's been allowed to run to seed, rather like an alcoholic duchess who's been at the cooking sherry. Frankly, I couldn't see what all the fuss was about. If this was the jewel in the crown of the Peak District, I wasn't keen on seeing the armpit. I guess growing up in Oxford spoiled me for any architecture in the grand style that isn't kept in tip-top condition.

Like Oxford, Buxton is a victim of its own publicity. Everyone knows Oxford because of the university; what they don't realize is that it's really much more like Detroit. It's the motor car that puts money in the pockets of Oxford's shopkeepers, not the privileged inhabitants of the colleges. Walking round Buxton, it didn't take me long to figure out that it isn't culture or the spa that keeps the wheels of commerce turning there. It's limestone.

Richard was as enamoured of the place as I was. Before we'd walked the length of the rather dismal main street, he'd already started grumbling. "I don't know why the hell you had to drag me here," he muttered. "I mean, look at it. What a dump. And it's raining."

"I think you'll find the rain isn't just falling on Buxton," I said.

"I wouldn't bank on it," he replied gloomily. "It's a damn sight colder than it was in Manchester. I don't see why it shouldn't be a damn sight wetter too." He stopped and stared with hostility at the steamed-up window of a chip shop. "What the hell are we doing here, Brannigan?"

"I'm just doing what you told me," I said sweetly.

"What *I* told you? How d'you figure that one out? I never said let's go and find the most horrible tourist attraction in the North West and spend the day wandering round it in the rain." He does a good line in outrage, does Richard. Before he got into his stride and started ranting for England, I relented.

I slipped my arm through his; more for support than to show solidarity. "The guy who ripped off Alexis and Chris has some connection with Buxton," I explained. "He used a hooky name to pull off the scam, and the only clue I've got on him is that his bank account is in Buxton." Richard's mouth opened, but I carried on relentlessly. "And before you remind me that your bank account is still in Fulham, let me point out that this guy is supposedly a builder and the account in question appears to be a business account."

"So what do we do? Wander round Buxton asking people if they know any iffy builders who might have ripped off our friends? Oh, and here's the big clue. We know which bank he keeps his overdraft in! I mean, do we even know what this guy looks like?"

"Alexis says he's in his late twenties, early thirties. Wavy brown hair, medium height, regular features. According to another witness, brown hair, big muscles, fancies himself, drives a white Transit," I said.

"A white Transit?" Richard interrupted. "Jesus! You don't think it was him that tried to run you off the road last night?"

"Behave," I told him. "Half the tradesmen in the world drive Transits, and half of them are white. You can't go round suspecting every plumber, joiner or glazier in Greater Manchester. Whoever this guy is, he hasn't got the remotest notion that I'm even interested in him, never mind that I'm after him for fraud."

"Sorry," Richard said. "So what do we do, then?"

"The first thing we do is we buy a local paper and then we find a nice place to have lunch, and while you're stuffing your greedy little face, I will study the paper and see who the local builders are. Then, after lunch, we will behave like tourists and do a tour of Buxton. Only, instead of taking in the sights, we'll be taking in the builders' yards."

"But there won't be anyone there on a Saturday afternoon," Richard objected.

"I know that," I said through tight lips. "But there will be neighbours. You know. The sort of net-twitchers who can tell you what people drive, what they look like and whether vans marked 'T. R. Harris, Builders' ever find their way into the yard."

Richard groaned. "And I'm missing Man United and Arsenal for this."

"I'll buy lunch," I promised. He pulled a doubtful face. "And dinner." He brightened up.

We ended up in a pub near the opera house that looked like it had been single-handedly responsible for Laura Ashley's profits last year. The chairs were upholstered in a fabric that matched the wallpaper, and the mahogany-stained wood of the furniture was a perfect match for the big free-standing oval bar in the centre of the big room. In spite of the décor, however, they were still clearly not catering for anything other than a local clientele. Richard complained bitterly because their idea of designer beer was a bottle of brown ale. He ended up nursing a pint of lager, then insisted on sitting in a side bar with a view of the door so if anyone he knew came in he could swap his drink for my vodka and grapefruit juice. Humouring him, I settled for a view of the rest of the room. Luckily, the food was good. Wonderful sandwiches, stunning chips. Proper chips, big fat brown ones like my Granny Brannigan used to make in a chip pan so old and well-used that it was black. And the campaign to keep Richard happy got a boost when he discovered Sticky Toffee Pudding on the sweet menu.

After his second helping, we were ready to make a move. I staggered upstairs to the ladies while Richard attempted to scrape the pattern off the plate. Coming back down the wide staircase, I got the kind of surprise that makes people miss their footing and end up looking like human pretzels in hallways. It also has the unfortunate side effect of attracting an enormous amount of attention. Luckily, because of my brush with permanent disability the night before, I was clutching the banister tightly.

I moved gingerly down the last few stairs and slipped round the back of the oval bar where I could study my prey rather less obviously. Halfway down the stairs may well be a nice place to sit, but it sure as hell is an appalling place to do a stake-out. I edged round the bar, getting a couple of strange looks from the barman, till I could see them in the mirror without them being able to get a clear view of me.

Over at a small table in the bay window, Martin Cheetham was deep in earnest conversation with someone I'd seen before. The hunk with the van who'd looked straight through me outside the Corn Exchange after I'd interviewed Cheetham. Today, they were both out of their working clothes. Cheetham wore a pair of cords and an Aran sweater, while his companion looked even hunkier than before in a blue rugby shirt tucked into a pair of Levi's. There was a black leather blouson slung over the arm of his chair. Whatever they were talking about, Cheetham wasn't happy. He kept leaning forward, clutching his glass of beer tightly. His body was like a textbook illustration of tension.

By contrast, his companion looked as relaxed as a man on his holidays. He leaned back in his seat, casually smoking a slim cigar. He kept flashing smiles at Cheetham which didn't reassure him one little bit. They'd have reassured me if I'd been on the receiving end, no messing. He was seriously sexy.

Unfortunately, it was beginning to look as if he might just be seriously villainous too. Here was Martin Cheetham, the man who had offered the land deal to Alexis and Chris, sitting drinking and talking with a guy in Buxton that I had pegged as a builder. And Alexis and Chris had been cheated out of their money on a deal arranged by the same Martin Cheetham with T. R. Harris, a builder with Buxton connections. I tried to remember the name on the van the hunk had parked outside the Corn Exchange, but the brain cell that had been taking care of the information appeared to be one of the ones that perished on Barton Bridge.

I realized that watching the pair of them wasn't really getting me anywhere. I needed to be able to hear their conversation. I gave the layout of the room some attention. Obviously, I didn't want Cheetham to see me. Of course, if he was innocent of any shady dealing, he'd have no problem with my presence. But I was beginning to have serious suspicions about his role in the business, so I wasn't about to take the chance.

I figured that if I cut across the room behind Cheetham, I could slide along an empty banquette till I was just behind him. From there, I should be able to hear something of their conversation. It wouldn't require much in the way of stealth, which was just as well, given the condition of my body. I made it across the room, but as I was edging towards the end of the banquette the hunk caught sight of me. He was instantly alert, sitting up and leaning forward to say something to Cheetham. The solicitor immediately swivelled round in his chair. I was well and truly blown.

Bowing to the inevitable (not a position that comes naturally to me), I got up and walked towards them. Cheetham's face registered momentary panic, and he cast a look over his shoulder to his companion, who flicked an alert look at me and said something inaudible to Cheetham. Cheetham ran a nervous hand through his dark hair then took a step towards me. "Miss Brannigan, what a surprise, let me buy you a drink," he said without drawing breath. He stepped to his left, blocking the way past him.

In total frustration, I watched his companion turn on his heel and practically run out of the bar. I gave Cheetham the hard stare. There was a sheen of sweat on his forehead, and the colour had vanished from under his tan, leaving him looking like he'd suddenly developed cirrhosis. "I was hoping you'd introduce me to your friend," I said, making the best of a bad job.

His smile barely made it to his lips, never mind his dark eyes. "Er, no, sorry, he had to rush." He picked up his glass and took a swift sip. "Do let me buy you a drink, Miss Brannigan," he pleaded.

"No thanks. I was just leaving myself. Do you have a lot of friends in the building trade, Mr Cheetham?"

He looked as if he wanted to burst into tears. "The building trade? I'm sorry, I'm not at all sure that I understand you."

"Your friend. The one who just left? He's a builder, isn't he?"

He gave a nervous laugh. It sounded like a spaniel chok-
ing on a duck feather. From the look on his face, he realized it
hadn't really worked either. He shifted gear and tried for the
throwaway approach. "You must be mistaken. John's a lorry
driver. He works for one of the quarry companies."

"You're sure about that, are you?" I asked.

"Well," he said, recovering his poise, "I've known him
and his family for years, and if he's not a lorry driver, he's done
a good job of fooling the lot of us. I was at university with his
sister." It was a great performance.

I had no evidence. All I had were a lot of suspicions and
one or two coincidences. It wasn't nearly enough to harass a
member of the Law Society. "I'll be seeing you around," I said,
trying to make it sound like a threat rather than a promise. I
stalked off, the effect rather spoiled by the limp.

I found Richard waiting crossly on the pavement outside
the pub. "At last!" he sighed. "Do you need to go to a chemist
for some laxatives, or were you just enjoying the *Buxton Advertiser*
so much you didn't notice the time? I've been standing here like
patience on a flaming monument."

"Did you happen to notice a guy tearing out of the pub
a few minutes ago? Black leather jacket, brown hair, moody
looking?" I asked, ignoring his complaints.

"Hasn't realized he's too old for the James Dean impersonation? That the one?"

"That's right. I don't suppose you noticed where he went?"

"He took off across the park," Richard said, waving a hand
in the vague direction of the Pavilion Gardens. "Why? Did he
do a runner without paying for his butty or something?"

"I think that was our man. T. R. Harris himself. Shit! If I
could only remember the name on his van!" I snarled.

Richard looked blank. "But he wasn't driving a van."

"He was the last time I saw him. It was some dreadful pun
of a name," I muttered, opening the paper again and scanning
the ads.

"Bricks and Motor? Mean and Roofless?" Richard wittered on as I continued my fruitless scrutiny.

Then an advert caught my eye. "Doing up your house? Don't touch a thing till you've called us. Cliff Scott & Sons." Then, in bold capitals, "Renovations our speciality." I let out a sigh of satisfaction. "Renew-Vations," I announced triumphantly.

"Yeah, right," Richard said, giving me the kind of uneasy look we normally reserve for those in the later stages of dementia.

The look didn't go away as I marched back into the pub and asked for their phone book. While I was waiting, I noticed Cheetham had been joined by a stylish and attractive brunette with a clutch of carrier bags. Judging by the logos, she hadn't been to Safeway for a frozen chicken. She was stroking Cheetham's thigh proprietorially while he appeared to be conducting an inquisition about the carrier bags. Then the phone book arrived and I had to drag my attention away from them. Surprise, surprise. Renew-Vations didn't have a listing. Back to Plan A.

Amazingly enough, Richard was still standing on the pavement when I emerged from the pub for a second time. He had the look of a man who has decided that happiness lies along the line of least resistance. "What now, my love," he sang in a bad imitation of Shirley Bassey as he attempted to sweep me into his arms. I dodged, wincing, and he instantly stopped. "Sorry, Brannigan, I keep forgetting you're one of the walking wounded."

I didn't need reminding. I was beginning to feel tired and a bit shaky. To be honest, I was glad of the chance to sit in the car while Richard drove me round the builders' yards I'd marked. Again, we drew a blank. There was no sign of a van marked Renew-Vations. Or, come to that, T. R. Harris. Questioning local residents established that six out of nine builders drove white Transits. Four of them answered the general description of Tom Harris. When I asked where they banked, I got some very strange looks and not a lot of help.

By four o'clock, I was worn out. But I wasn't ready to give up, in spite of Richard's heavy hints about it being time to go home.

"I've got an idea," I said as we drove back towards the town centre. "Why don't we find ourselves a nice little hotel and book in for the night? That way, you won't have to drive me back here tomorrow."

"You what?" he exploded. "Spend a *night* in this dump? You have got to be kidding, Brannigan. I'd rather go to a Richard Clayderman concert."

"That could be arranged," I muttered. "Look, I've got a gut feeling about this guy. I need to find out his name and where he lives. I'm not going to be able to do that in Manchester."

"So wait for a weekday when there are some builders around in their yards and the builders' merchants are open," Richard said reasonably.

"The only problem is that I'm doing this job as a favour for Alexis. Bill's back from the Channel Islands on Monday morning, and he's not going to be thrilled if I'm off doing a freebie instead of the jobs I'm paid for. I'd really like to try and get this cleared up tomorrow. Besides, I've got to go to the Land Registry on Monday," I added, laying on the pathos.

Richard scowled. "OK, Brannigan, you win."

Had he ever doubted I would?

11

It was a whole new adventure in pain, finding a hotel room in Buxton acceptable to Richard. For a start, it had to have a colour television and a phone in the bedroom. It had to have a proper bar, not a poxy built-in cocktail bar like darts and snooker players have in one corner of the lounge. It also had to feel like part of the twentieth century, which ruled most of them out. His final insistence was that it had a lift, on account of I was injured, couldn't they see that? After he'd ranted at the woman in the Tourist Information Office about the plight of the disabled, we finally ended up in an extremely pleasant establishment overlooking the park. At least, they were pleasant as we booked in. I had this horrible feeling that by the time we left, relations would be a lot more strained. When Richard gets one on him, the staff at Buckingham Palace would be hard pressed to meet his demands.

I headed straight for the bath to ease my aching limbs, while Richard turned on the TV and collapsed on the bed, complaining about the lack of a) a remote control and b) satellite television. I have to confess I wasn't sorry. My head was splitting, and I didn't think I could put up with his usual channel hopping or MTV at full volume without giving way to the urge to commit GBH. I closed the bathroom door so I didn't have to listen to his comments on the football match reports, and subsided thankfully into the hot water while I attempted to order my thoughts.

First, the conservatories. Thanks to Rachel Lieberman, I now knew that the houses where the conservatories had disappeared had all been rented. It seemed that the people who had rented them shared their surname with the real owners. Was there any significance in the fact that they'd all been rented through DKL? Or was it simply that DKL was one of the few agencies around who specialized in rental property? What I didn't understand was where the conservatories had gone, or how the con with the second mortgages had been worked. After all, these days, financial institutions are a little bit fussier than they used to be about who they lend money to. The other problem was that I didn't have the first idea of who was pulling the scam. Maybe there was something I wasn't understanding, but the more I found out, the more it seemed to me that there wasn't necessarily any connection between Ted Barlow and the criminals. But until I figured out how it worked, I couldn't see a way of finding out who was behind it. It was enormously frustrating. Perhaps it would all become clearer after I'd been to the Land Registry and studied the stuff Julia had dug up.

Next, PharmAce. I felt reasonably certain that Paul Kingsley, the freelance operative I'd laid on for tonight, would come up with the necessary photographs. But after the previous night's run-in on the bridge, I felt a more personal interest in the case. If it had been a PharmAce van that had tried to cut short my promising career, then I wanted to know who had done it so someone could make him feel as shaky if not as sore as I was feeling.

And finally, the case of the bent builder. I had a gut feeling about "John." There were too many coincidences piling up. Besides, there was a matter of professional pride at stake here. I reckoned I'd always managed to impress Alexis with my skills, largely because she only ever saw the end result. I didn't want her to start seeing the feet of clay.

However, I still didn't have any bright ideas about how to find the elusive "John," alias "T. R. Harris," and the bath was starting to cool off. Gingerly, I pushed myself up till I was perched on the end of the bath, then I swung my legs over the edge and on to the floor. I wrapped myself in a generous bath sheet and joined my beloved, who was now pouring scorn on a mindless game show.

I snuggled up to him and he paused in his stream of invective long enough to say, "Have they got a Chinese in Buxton?"

"Try looking in the paper. Or the phone book. Or ring reception."

The last suggestion obviously required the least effort. While he made the receptionist's day, I staggered back to the bathroom and struggled into my clothes, wishing I'd thought to bring an overnight bag. Luckily, my handbag always contains a tiny bottle of foundation and a functional compact with eyeshadows, blusher, mascara and lipstick, so I managed to hide the black shadows under my eyes and the bruise on my jaw.

By the time I'd finished, Richard was raring to go. I couldn't help feeling it was a little early for dinner and said so. "I'm hungry," Richard said. I raised my eyebrows. He smiled sheepishly. "The receptionist said there's a pub that does live music on a Saturday night. Local bands, that sort of thing. I thought you'd probably want an early night, and I thought I might drop by later and see if there was anything worth listening to."

Which translated as, "This trip looks like a wash-out. If one of us can get something out of it, it won't have been a complete waste of time." One of the ways rock journos like Richard get their stories is to maintain good relations with the record company A & R men. They're the ones who sign up new acts and build them into the next U2. So Richard's always on the look-out for U3 so he can tip the wink to one of his mates.

"No problem," I sighed. "Let's go and eat." It was easier to give in, especially since I didn't think waiting till later would improve my appetite. The reaction to the accident seemed to have set in, and I was secretly grateful at the thought of an early night without having to worry about entertaining Richard.

The Chinese restaurant was in the main street, above a travel agency. Considering it was half past six on a Saturday night, the place was surprisingly busy. At least a dozen tables were occupied. We both took that as an indication that the food must be reasonable. I should have known better. All the other signs said the opposite. The fish tank was filled with goldfish rather than koi carp, the tables were already set with spoon and fork, there wasn't a Chinese character in sight on the menu, which was heavy on the sweet and sour and the chop suey. I've never fancied chop suey, not since someone told me with malice aforethought that it's Chinese for "mixed bits." Besides, it's not even a proper Chinese dish, just something they invented to keep the Yanks happy.

Richard grunted in outrage as he read the menu. As the waiter returned with our two halves of lager, Richard opened his wallet and pulled out a heavily creased piece of paper which he unfolded and waved under the waiter's nose. The waiter studied the Chinese characters gravely. At least he seemed to recognize Richard's favourite half-dozen Dim Sum dishes. A while ago, he persuaded the manager of his regular restaurant in town to write them down for him in case of emergency. This was clearly an emergency. The waiter cleared his throat, carefully folded up the paper and handed it back to Richard.

"No Dim Sum," he said.

"Why not? I've shown you what I want," Richard protested.

"No Dim Sum. Bamboo not hygienic," the waiter retorted. He walked off before Richard could find his voice.

"Bamboo not hygienic?" Richard finally echoed, incredulity personified. "I have now heard everything. Dear God, Brannigan, what have you got me into this time?"

I managed to pacify him long enough to order, which was my next mistake. They didn't do salt and pepper ribs, but

barbecue ribs were on the menu. They were orange. I don't
mean glossy reddish brown. I mean orange, as in Jaffa. The taste
defied description. Even Richard was stunned into silence. He
took a swig of tea to get rid of it, and nearly gagged. After a
cautious sip, I understood why. Clearly unaccustomed to people
wanting Chinese tea, they'd served us a pot of very weak yet
stewed tea bag.

I thought it couldn't get worse, but it did. When the
main courses arrived, I thought Richard was going to burst a
blood vessel. The sweet and sour pork consisted of a mound of
perfectly spherical balls topped with a lurid red sauce that I'd
bet contained enough E numbers to render half the population of Buxton hyperactive. The chicken in black bean sauce
looked as if it had been knitted, and the fillet steak Cantonese
appeared to have escaped from the Mister Minit heel bar. The
waiter refused to understand that we wanted chopsticks and
bowls. The final indignity came when I took the lid off the
fried rice. It was pink. I swear to God, it was pink. Richard
just sat staring at it all, as if it was a bad joke and the real food
would arrive in a minute.

I took a deep breath and said, "Just try to think of it as one
of those things we do for love."

"Does that mean if I threw it at the waiter, you'd think I
didn't love you any more?" Richard growled.

"Not exactly. But I don't think it's going to get any better
and I don't feel strong enough to cope with you shredding the
waiter just as an act of revenge. Let's just eat what we can and
go." Normally, I'd have been the first to complain, but I didn't
have the energy. Besides, I couldn't face the thought of trailing
round Buxton trying to find somewhere half-decent to eat.

I think Richard saw the exhaustion in my face, since he
caved in without a performance for once. We both picked at
the food for a few minutes, then demanded the bill frostily. The
waiter appeared oblivious to our dissatisfaction until Richard
subtracted the ten per cent service charge from the bill. This

was clearly a novel experience, and one that the waiter wasn't standing on for.

I couldn't handle the aggravation, so I walked downstairs to the street, while Richard was explaining in words of several syllables to the waiter why he had no intention of paying a shilling for service. I was leaning against the door jamb, wondering how long I'd have to wait to see another human being, when the patron saint of gumshoes looked down on me and decided it was time I got something approaching an even break.

A white Transit van came down a side street facing me and turned on to the main street. Following my current obsession, I made a mental note of the name on the panels bolted on to the side of the van. "B. Lomax, Builder," I read. His was one of the yards I'd visited that afternoon. The van drew up, and I heard the driver's door open and close, though I couldn't see anything since the van was between us. I guessed that the driver was heading for the pizzeria I'd noticed on the opposite side of the street.

Just then, Richard emerged, a grim smile on his face. "Crack it?" I asked.

"I got him to knock a couple of quid off as well, on account of the ribs had triggered off an allergy and given you an asthma attack."

I don't have asthma. As far as I am aware, I'm allergic to nothing except bullshit. I pointed this out to Richard as we walked back to the car. "So?" he replied. "They don't know that, do they? And besides . . ."

"Shut up!" I interrupted, guessing what was coming next. "I do *not* need to be told that I look shitty enough to be suffering from an asthma attack."

"Please yourself," he said.

I eased myself into the car, then screeched in excitement. "It's him, Richard, it's him!" I shouted, digging Richard in the ribs more savagely than I intended.

"Who?" he yelped.

"The guy I'm looking for," I yelled, unable to take my eyes off the man who had come out carrying three pizzas which he was carefully placing on the passenger seat of the white Transit. It was the man I'd seen with Cheetham, the same man I'd seen in the Renew-Vations van, the man I strongly suspected was also T. R. Harris.

"That's the guy that came horsing out of the pub at lunchtime," Richard said, on the ball as ever.

"I know. I think he's the guy who ripped off Alexis and Chris," I told him.

"So let's see where he goes," Richard said. He waited till our man climbed back into the driver's seat before starting the distinctive Beetle engine. A hot pink VW convertible wasn't the car I'd have chosen to tail someone in, but then I didn't have a choice.

"Keep as far back as you can," I cautioned him.

We stayed where we were as the van pulled out and drove slowly towards a mini-roundabout, where the driver paused momentarily. As he turned right, Richard released the clutch and shot off in pursuit. When we turned, we could just see the tail lights of the van rounding the bend ahead. Moments later, we came round the bend to see the van turning at the traffic lights. "Go for it," I shouted at Richard as the lights changed to amber.

He stamped on the accelerator and hauled on the steering wheel, cornering with a shriek of rubber. Thank God for low profile tyres and customized Beetles. The van was still in sight, and we followed it sedately through another set of lights and up a hill. Then it pulled into a drive. I let my breath out in a sigh of relief. It's harder than most people think to tail another vehicle. A good thirty per cent of the time you lose them completely.

"Well done. But don't slow down," I told Richard. "Just pull up round the next corner."

He drew up a few seconds later and I was out of the car before he'd switched off the engine. The aches and pains I'd forgotten in the excitement of the chase suddenly reasserted themselves. I winced as I straightened up and tottered back down the street, which gave Richard the chance to catch up with me.

"What d'you think you're doing?" he demanded. "You should be in bed, not tearing round the back streets of Buxton."

"I just want to check the house out."

"You've done enough for one night," Richard replied. "Come on, Kate, don't be silly. You're supposed to be taking it easy. Alexis wouldn't expect any more."

I shook off his restraining hand. "I've got to make sure I know which house it is," I said. "I'm not about to do anything more adventurous than that." Which was nothing less than the truth. At least for the time being.

Forty minutes later, I was striding openly up the drive of "Hazledene." That's a tip I learned very early on in this game. Never skulk, creep or sidle when you can boldly go. There's nothing less suspicious than someone who looks as if they know where they're going and have a perfect right to be there. Luckily, the drive was tarmacked, so there was no chance of anyone in the house hearing me crunch gravel underfoot.

Richard had delivered me back to the hotel after we'd strolled past the residence of B. Lomax, Builder. I'd told him I was going to settle down with the TV then have an early night. I hadn't specified when, or that that was all on my agenda. However, he'd trotted off happily to check out the local bands, kindly leaving his car keys behind in anticipation of finding something he might enjoy drinking. I gave him fifteen minutes to get clear, then I drove back to the side street near Lomax's.

The house was solid, four-square and looked as if it would still be standing after the nuclear holocaust. I suppose it needed to be like that to survive Buxton winters. I'll say this for the Victorians; they really knew how to build things to last. I bet designers get down on their hands and knees every morning and give thanks for the death of that particular tradition. The drive was lined on one side with a solid privet hedge and tall trees that looked as if they'd been there as long as the grey stones of the house. As I neared the house, I moved closer to the hedge, letting myself be absorbed into its shadow.

A black BMW 3-series sat on the curve of drive that swept round the front of the house. The van was parked round the side, blocking the doors of a large detached wooden garage. There were no lights showing at the front of the house, except for a stained-glass lantern above the sturdy front door. I moved as cautiously as my stiffness would allow, keeping the van between me and the house. When I reached the end of the van's cabin, I could see a couple of patches of light spilling out on to the lawn at the back of the house.

It was almost spookily silent. The hum of traffic was so distant I had to make a conscious effort to hear it. I slipped back to the side of the van and carefully took my mini flashlight out of my bag and shone it on the side of the van. It was impossible to tell what was behind the bolt-on plywood panel. However, I was a Girl Guide. I'd also taken the precaution of raiding the tool box in Richard's boot. The small wrench I'd selected was perfect for the job.

Unfortunately, I wasn't. The top set of bolts were just too high for me. And there was nothing immediately obvious to stand on. So I made the best of a bad job and undid the four bolts along the bottom edge of the panel. They came off smoothly. The fact that they weren't rusted on seemed suspicious to me.

I pushed a screwdriver under the edge of the panel and levered it away an inch or so. By twisting my head round and angling the torch under the panel, I could just make out the "Renew-Vations" logo along the side of the van. Bingo! I made a note of the phone number, then screwed the bolts back in place. Even that small effort was enough to have me breaking out in a sweat. I really felt like going back to the hotel and crawling into bed, but I didn't want to waste the opportunity of having a good nose around while my man was otherwise engaged with a pizza and a couple of guests.

I slipped back down to the front of the van and studied the garage. The van was parked about two feet away from the double doors. They were held shut by a heavy bolt with a padlock. I've never been very good at picking locks, in spite of the expert tuition of my friend Dennis the burglar, and I didn't really feel up to it. Then I realized that if I stood on the bumper of the van, I might just be able to see through the grimy windows at the top of the doors. That would at least tell me whether or not it was worth going into my master cracksman routine.

I eased myself up and leaned forward against the doors, which gave a creak that nearly gave me a coronary. I held my breath, but nothing stirred. I gritted my teeth and raised the torch above my head, so it was shining through the glass and into the garage.

My hunch about the garage had been right. But I didn't have to indulge in any breaking and entering to see all the proof I needed.

12

I waited till Richard was halfway through his second cup of coffee before I gave him the good news. "You can go back to Manchester if you like," I said, nonchalantly buttering a slice of toast.

"Do what?" he spluttered.

"You can go back to Manchester if you like." I glanced at my watch. "In fact, if you shoot off in the next half-hour, you'll probably be back in time for your football match," I added, smiling sweetly. I've never understood why Richard feels the need to run around a muddy field with a bunch of his fellow overgrown schoolboys every Sunday morning. I keep telling him he doesn't need an excuse to go to the pub at Sunday lunchtime, but he's adamant that this ritual is a vital part of his life. He'd been grumbling about missing his game ever since I'd pitched him into staying over in Buxton.

"But what about this guy? Lomax, or Harris, or whatever he's called. I thought you had it all to do?"

"I decided that since it's Alexis's business, she can come over and help me with the legwork. And I didn't think spending a Sunday in Buxton with Alexis was your idea of a good time," I said solicitously.

The waitress arrived with his full English breakfast and my scrambled eggs just then, so we had a pause while he scoffed one of his fried eggs before it congealed. "So what exactly is Alexis going to do that I can't?" he asked suspiciously. "I'm not sure I trust the pair of you let loose together. I mean, if this is the guy that ripped off Alexis, isn't she going to go apeshit when she sees him? And you're in no fit state to take anybody on right now."

I was touched. It was worrying. A year before, I'd have bitten the head off any man who suggested I might not be up to looking after myself. Now, I was touched. Definitely worrying. "It'll be fine," I said. "After we had that lucky break last night, I realized there wasn't anything more I could do till Alexis had positively ID'd the guy." I hadn't told Richard about my little excursion. Judging by his concern for my health, it was probably just as well.

He looked doubtful. "I don't know," he said through a mouthful of sausage. "You drag me over to this Godforsaken hole, you make me eat the worst Chinese I've ever had in my life, with the possible exception of the one in Saltcoats where there was a prawn in the banana fritter, you send me off to endure the most derivative and listless music I've heard since Billy Joel's last album, then you tell me you're replacing me with an evening paper hackette! What's a man to think?"

"Just be grateful I'm not making you stay here for Sunday lunch, pal," I replied with a grin. "Look, I'll be fine. I promise not to take any risks." That was a promise I could make with hand on heart. After all, I'd already taken all the risks I needed to take where T. R. Harris was concerned.

"All right," he said. "As long as you promise me one other thing?" I raised my eyebrows in a question. "Promise me you'll force Alexis to take several risks. Preferably of the potentially fatal kind." I told you he pretends they hate each other.

"Pig," I said mildly. "If Alexis heard you say that, she'd be cut to the quick."

"Heard him say what?" Alexis boomed threateningly as she pulled out a chair and threw herself into it, waving at the waitress. "Good morning, children," she greeted us. "Full English," she added to the waitress.

"Kate's in no state for anything strenuous—"

"Lucky Kate!" Alexis interrupted Richard, ducking her head in a louche wink.

"So I said if anyone's got to take any physical risks, it had better be you," he concluded, on his dignity.

"Well, of course, it stands to reason," Alexis replied. "First sign of danger, you're off over the nearest distant horizon, leaving us women to deal with the physical risks."

I thought he was going to choke. "You'd better get a move on if you're going to make it back in time for the match," I said, treading on Alexis's toe under the table.

Richard glanced at his watch, said, "Shit!" and shovelled the rest of his breakfast down in record time. Then he pushed back his chair, got to his feet, downed a cup of tea in a oner and planted a greasy kiss somewhere in the region of my mouth. "See you tonight, Brannigan," he said, then headed for the door.

"Typical male," Alexis called after him. "When the going gets tough, the tough get going."

"The only reason it's safe to leave things in your hands is that all the real work's been done already," Richard shouted back.

By now, we had more viewers than BSkyB TV. The rest of the breakfasters were agog. "Shut up," I muttered through clenched teeth at Alexis. I waved goodbye to Richard, and he left, giving me a smile and a wink. "Honestly," I complained. "What are you like? And don't tell me he started it, because you're each as bad as the other. Thank God we're not trying to do some quiet, unobtrusive undercover!"

"Sorry," Alexis said unrepentantly. "Anyway, now the Gary Lineker of the Press corps has departed, tell me all about it! You only gave me the bare bones over the phone." She lit a cigarette and squinted at me through the smoke.

I started to tell her how I'd tracked down T. R. Harris, but she interrupted me impatiently. "Not my stuff," she said. "You!

Tell me how you are? I mean, I don't want to make you feel even worse, but you don't look like a woman who should be chasing the guys in the black hats all over Derbyshire. God, Kate, you shouldn't have been running around after Harris yesterday! You should have been in bed, recovering."

I shook my head. "With Richard ministering to my every need? Have you any idea what my kitchen would look like after he'd had a free rein in there for twenty-four hours?" I shuddered. "No thanks. Besides, I was quite glad to have something to take my mind off what happened. Knowing there's someone out there who either wants to kill you or wants to warn you off so badly they're prepared to risk killing you isn't very relaxing."

"Any idea who's behind it?" Alexis asked. She couldn't help herself. Once she'd established she was a caring friend, she just had to go into journo mode.

"I think it might have a connection to a job I'm working on. I should have a better idea in a day or two. Don't worry, you'll be the first to know when there's anything fit to print," I reassured her.

"That's not why I was asking," Alexis scolded. "Aren't you worried that they'll have another go?"

"I suppose they might. But no one followed us yesterday. I've put a new face on the job in question, and I should be able to get it cleared up tomorrow. I feel like I've done everything I can to minimize the risk."

The waitress arrived and dumped a steaming plateful in front of Alexis. It was the second time that morning I'd had to look at enough fried food to feed a Romanian orphanage for a week, and I began to feel faintly queasy. "So, tell me about T. R. Harris," Alexis prompted as she ground out her cigarette.

I filled her in on my search for the missing builder. "And when I shone my torch in the garage window, there it was," I ended up.

"The other panel?" Alexis asked.

"The same. The one that says 'T. R. Harris, Builder'. Of course, I still need you to ID the guy, but I reckon that's just a formality."

"So Cheetham set the whole thing up?" Alexis demanded. "I'll kill the little shit when I get my hands on him."

"I'm still not sure exactly what his role in the whole thing was," I said. "He's obviously in it up to the eyeballs, but I'm not sure who's been pushing who."

"Does it matter? The pair of them are crooks! Let me tell you, they're both going to regret the day they crossed me and Chris!" Alexis fumed. She ran a hand through her hair angrily then lit a cigarette, sucking the smoke deep into her lungs.

"We'll cross that bridge when we come to it," I soothed. "First things first. We've got to make sure we've got the right guy, that there's not some innocent explanation for what I've seen."

"Oh yes? Like what?" Alexis scoffed. "Like Cheetham is secretly working undercover for the Fraud Squad?"

"No, like B. Lomax, Builder, is renting out his garage to T. R. Harris, Builder. Like B. Lomax, Builder, is an old friend of Martin Cheetham's who introduced them to each other, and Cheetham, like you, is an innocent dupe." That shut her up long enough for me to explain I was going to check out of my room.

Back upstairs, I dialled Paul Kingsley's home number. It was a call that could comfortably have waited till later in the day, but I was desperate to know if the surveillance had worked out. Paul answered on the third ring. Luckily, he didn't sound like a man who's just been roused from sleep. "How did it go?" I asked after we'd got the pleasantries out of the way.

"Just as you predicted it would," he said, unable to keep the disappointment from showing. They can't help themselves, can they? "Our man turned up about nine o'clock, loaded up his hatchback with boxes and took off into the night."

"Did he seem at all suspicious?" I asked.

"He drove all round the car park before he parked up by the loading bay. Then he did the circuit on foot," Paul said.

"I take it he didn't spot you?" It was a safe bet. Paul's a good operator. He's a commercial photographer who thinks it's great fun to do the odd job for us. I think it makes him feel like James Bond, and he's probably got more professional pride in his work than those of us who do it for a full-time living.

Paul chuckled. "Nah. They've got these industrial-sized rubbish bins. I was inside one." See what I mean? There's no way I'd have spent an evening communing with maggots in the line of duty. Apart, of course, from the occasional journalistic piss-up Richard drags me along to.

"And you got pics?"

"I did. I popped back to my darkroom to dev and print them later. I've got great shots of him prowling round, loading up, then transferring the gear to an unmarked Renault van at Knutsford motorway services," Paul said proudly.

"You managed to follow him?" I was impressed. It was more than I'd achieved.

"I got lucky," he admitted. "I had to wait till he was out of sight before I could get out of the bin, and I'd left my car round the back of the warehouse next door. But he was headed the same direction as I was going, and I was obviously luckier with the lights. I pulled up at a junction in Stretford, and there he was, right in front of me. So I stayed with him, and snapped the handover. And I got the van's number, so you can find out who's handling the stuff at the other end."

"Great job," I said, meaning it. "Can you do me a favour? Can you drop the prints in tomorrow at the office and tell Shelley what they're about? I won't be in first thing, but I'll get to it later in the day."

"No problem. Oh, and Kate?"

"Mmm?"

"Thanks for thinking of me," he said, sounding sincere. I'll never understand men. Stand them in a dustbin for hours and you've made their Saturday night.

Alexis was pacing up and down the hall, doing that agitated flicking of the filter when there's no loose ash that smokers do when they're feeling twitchier than nicotine can soothe. When she saw me, she stopped pacing and started rattling her car keys, unnerving the poor receptionist who was trying to do my bill.

Reluctantly, I climbed into Alexis's car. Journalists seem to need to take the office with them in all its horror wherever they go. Alexis's Peugeot contained more old newspapers than the average chip shop could use in a week. The ashtray had been full since a month after she bought the car last year. The parcel shelf was home to a clutch of old notebooks that slid back and forwards every time she cornered, and there was a portable computer terminal that lived under the passenger seat and bruised the passenger's heels every time Alexis braked. I'd be ashamed to let anyone in my car if it was like that, but journalists always seem strangely proud of their mobile rubbish dumps.

First, we went to the local cop shop and checked out the electoral roll. There were two residents at that address, Brian and Eleanor Lomax. His wife, I presumed. Next, we slowly drove past the house. The black BMW had gone, but the van was still parked outside. I told Alexis to park up, and she turned the car round in the side street and drove back towards Lomax's house. She stopped about one hundred yards away from the house. We could see the front door and the drive, though we couldn't actually see the van.

Alexis, as much a veteran of the stake-out as me, pulled a paperback out of her handbag and settled back in her seat to read, secure in the knowledge that any movement round the house would instantly register in her peripheral vision. Me, I sucked peppermints and listened to the radio.

It was a couple of hours before there was any sign of life. We both spotted him at the same moment. Alexis sat up in her seat and chucked her book into the back seat. Brian Lomax had appeared round the side of the house and was walking down the drive. He wore the familiar black leather blouson and jeans, this time with a cream polo-neck sweater. At the end of the drive, he turned right, down the hill and towards the traffic lights.

"That him?" I asked. Nothing like the obvious question.

Alexis nodded grimly. "T. R. Harris. I'd know the bastard anywhere." She turned the ignition key and the Peugeot coughed into life.

"Wait a minute!" I said sharply. "Where are you going?"

"I'm going to follow him," Alexis said sharply. "And then I'm going to front him up." She shoved the car into gear.

I pulled it out again. "No you're not," I told her.

"I bloody am!" Alexis exploded. "That bastard is walking around with five grand of our money, and I want it back."

"Look, cool it," I commanded. Alexis obviously recognized I meant it, for she subsided, showing her feelings by revving the engine at irregular intervals. "Now you know his name and where he lives, you can lay your hands on him any time you want to. And so can the cops."

Alexis shook her head. "No cops. I want our money back, and if the guy's in custody, he's not earning. All I want is to front him up and get our money back."

"Fronting him up isn't going to get your money back. He'll just laugh at you. And even if you go round with some of your less pleasant associates, I'm not convinced he's the kind of guy who'd be scared into handing the money over."

"So what do you suggest? I just lie down and die?"

"No. I know it's a bit radical, but why don't you sue him? As long as you don't use Cheetham, that is," I added, trying to get her to lighten up a bit.

"Because it'll take forever," Alexis wailed.

"It doesn't have to. You get your solicitor to write a letter demanding payment, and if he doesn't cough up, you get her or him to issue a Statutory Demand, which means Lomax has to pay up within a certain time or you petition for bankruptcy. And since what he's done is illegal, he's not likely to quibble about repaying your money as soon as you start making legal noises," I explained.

Alexis sighed. "OK, you win. But on one condition."

"What's that?"

"That you keep tabs on him for a day or two. I want to know, his haunts, where he works out of, who he works with, just in case he decides to go to ground. I'll pay you, of course. Put it on an official footing."

It was my turn to sigh. "You've picked the worst possible week. I'm up to my eyeballs with vanishing conservatories and hooky drugs."

"I won't institute proceedings till I know where we can lay hands on him if he's not home," Alexis said obstinately.

My exertions of the previous day and a half had finally caught up with me. I didn't have the energy left to argue, so I caved in. "OK. Put the car in gear. I'll get to it as soon as I can."

13

The Birkenhead Land Registry's address is Old Market House, Hamilton Square. Sounds almost romantic, doesn't it? I pictured a mellow stone building, Georgian, with perhaps a portico. Wood panelling, maybe, with grey stooped figures shuffling past in a Dickensian hush. Fat chance. Negotiating the one-way system brought me to a modern dark red brick building, seven storeys tall with plenty of windows overlooking breathtaking views of the entrance to the Mersey tunnel.

I found a space in the car park for the Fiesta I'd hired to replace my wrecked Nova and tagged on to a group of women heading for the building. They were having the Monday morning chatter to each other about the weekend, obviously familiar with each other's routines. The leading pair stopped at the entrance to the building and keyed a number into a security lock. The women swept on into the building. One of them held the door open for me. That was when I noticed the sign informing me that the public entrance was at the front of the building. One of the great truisms of our business is that the more security a building has, the easier it is to penetrate. I caught the door and stood uncertainly for a moment. It was tempting to waltz in the back door and have a good wander round, just for the hell of it. But prudence won over my sense of adventure and I reluctantly let the door swing closed. I was too busy to spend a day down the police station explaining why I'd hacked into the Land Registry computer network.

I walked round to the front of the building, distinguishable from the back only by the double doors. I entered a cheerless foyer with a security booth and banks of stainless-steel lift doors. The Scouse security officers were as efficient as if they'd been privatized. Name and purpose of visit, who visiting, where car parked, car registration number. Then they note your arrival time and issue a security pass. If I were a dedicated hacker, I could see half a dozen ways to get my hands on one of their terminals.

Again, I restrained my more piratical instincts and went across the hall to Inquiries. It was like a dentist's waiting room, complete with year-old magazines sitting on a low table. The chairs were the cloth-upholstered sort two grades up from those hideous orange plastic ones you get down the Social Security. Everything was a bit scuffed, as if it was last redecorated before Thatcher came to power. I walked over to a high counter in the corner of the room. It was empty except for a cash register and a computer monitor and keyboard. I craned my neck round to read "Welcome to the Land Registry Computer System" in amber letters on the black screen.

The sign on the desk said, "Please ring for attention." They obviously brought the sign with them from the old building, since it's probably the only thing in the whole place made of wood. It's certainly the only thing made of wood with gilt lettering on it. I rang the bell and waited for a desiccated old man in a frock coat to shuffle through the door.

That'll teach me to make my mind up in advance of the facts. It took less than a minute for a young woman to appear who, frankly, wasn't my idea of a civil servant. For a start, she wouldn't have looked out of place at one of Richard's gigs in her fashionably baggy Aran sweater and jeans. For another, she looked like she enjoyed her work. And she didn't behave as if having to deal with members of the public was a major pain for her. All very novel.

"I wonder if you can help me," I said. "My name's Brannigan, Kate Brannigan. I rang last week with a list of addresses that I needed copies of the register for."

The woman smiled. "That's right. It was me you spoke to. I've got the copies ready, if you don't mind waiting a minute?"

"Fine," I said. As she disappeared back through the door, I allowed myself a grim smile of satisfaction. No doubt this was where the wait began. I helped myself to one of the elderly magazines and sat down. I was only one paragraph into the fascinating tale of a soap star's brush with death on the motorway when she returned with a thick bundle of documents.

"Here you are," she announced. "Seven sets of copies of the register. It's not often we get asked for so many, except by conveyancing experts. And in so many different locations," she added, obviously fishing.

I dumped the magazine and went back to the counter. "I suppose it made life a lot more complicated for you when they changed the rules to allow anyone to examine any entry in the register," I parried.

"I don't know about complicated," she said. "But it's made it a lot more interesting. I only ever used to talk to solicitors and their secretaries, and occasionally people who wanted copies of their own entries. Now we get all sorts coming in. Often, they want to check the register on their neighbours' properties because they think they might be in breach of some covenant or other, like no caravans, or no garden bonfires. A right lot of Percy Sugdens, some of them are," she added with a giggle.

She turned to the cash register. I'd taken the precaution of hitting the hole in the wall with the company cashpoint card, so I wasn't flummoxed by her demand any more than she was by my request for a VAT receipt. I made a mental note to ask Shelley to keep a running total of Ted Barlow's account and to bill him as soon as it went five hundred pounds over the retainer he'd given us. I didn't want us to end up working for nothing if I couldn't clear up the scam fast enough to keep his business afloat.

I picked up my copies of the register entries and squeezed them into the back pocket of my handbag. Then, a thought occurred to me. "I wonder if you could clear something up for me?" I said.

"If I can, I'd be happy to," the young woman said, giving me a bright smile that appeared to be completely natural. She obviously wasn't destined to last long in the Civil Service.

"What's the actual process here? And how long does it take between details being sent to you and them being entered into the register? I was thinking particularly of land that's being registered for the first time and has then been split into parcels." If anyone could help me work out Martin Cheetham's role in the double-sale scam, it had to be the Land Registry.

"Right," she said, dragging the word out into three distinct Scouse syllables. "What happens is this. Every morning, a Day Listing gets put on the computer. That lists all the title numbers that are the subject of alteration, inquiry, registration or anything else. Once a title number has appeared on the Day Listing, it stays listed until it has been entered into the full register. At any one time there are about 140,000 properties on the Listing, so it takes a little time to get round to them all."

Suddenly, I began to understand how the Land Registry got its reputation for being as slow as a tortoise on valium. Before they started their computerization, it must have been a nightmare. "So what sort of time scale are we looking at?" I asked.

"It depends," she said. "We've got about half a million records on computer, which has speeded things up a bit, except when the system crashes."

"So, allowing for that, how long does it take for changes to make their way on to the register?"

"For a change of ownership, we've got it down to about four weeks. A first registration takes about eleven weeks, and for a transfer of part, it's about fifteen weeks," she said.

Light was beginning to glimmer, very faintly. "So if someone was registering a piece of land for the first time, then almost immediately registering the division of that land into plots and the sale of those plots, the whole thing could take six months?"

"In theory, yes," she admitted, looking slightly uncomfortable.

"So if someone tried to sell the same plot twice, they might be able to get away with it?"

She shook her head vehemently. "Absolutely not. Don't forget, it would be on the Day Listing. As soon as the second purchaser's solicitor instigated a search, they would be told that the file was already active, which would ring alarm bells and put any transaction on hold."

"I see," I said, smiling my thanks. "You've been very helpful."

"No problem. Any time." She returned the smile.

I walked back to the car in thoughtful mood. I was pretty convinced now that I knew how Alexis and Chris had been ripped off. The root of the scam lay in the difference between registered and unregistered land. I dredged my memory for all I'd ever learned about land, which wasn't that much, since land comes in the final year of a law-degree course. I suspect that might have been one of the factors in my decision to duck out after my second year. But sometimes, like now, that last year would have come in handy.

The ownership of about a third of the land in the North West of England has never been registered. If you think about it, it's only in relatively recent times that there was any need for registration, when we all became economically and socially mobile, as the academics put it. In the olden days before the Second World War, if you were buying a property or a piece of land, you usually knew the person who was selling it. Probably, they'd been your employer, or had sat in the front pew of the local church all your life. Some form of independent registration only became an issue when you were buying from a stranger and you had no proof of their reputation; they just might not actually *own* London Bridge, after all. Since the Land Registry really got going in the thirties, most transactions have been registered in what was supposed to be a slow but sure process. Ho, ho.

In practice, before compulsory registration was introduced in the late sixties and seventies, a lot of properties still changed ownership on a handshake and the exchange of a fistful of title deeds for a fistful of readies. And, since those properties haven't changed hands again since then, they're still not registered. This doesn't just apply to farmland that's been in families for generations; there are whole chunks of rented terraced housing in Manchester where ownership has remained the same for thirty or forty years. In terms of the Registry, it just doesn't exist. Frankly, I think it'd be an enormous improvement if it didn't exist in reality either.

Anyway, when someone like Brian Lomax pitches a farmer like Harry Cartwright into selling him a chunk of land, all the paperwork goes off to the Land Registry. And I'm not talking pristine forms and word processor-generated contracts. I'm talking dirty bits of paper covered in spidery writing and sealing wax. When it got to the Land Registry, I now knew, it would go on the Day Listing and be given a provisional title number. When Lomax then split the land into plots and sold them, the buyers' solicitors would carry out searches with the Land Registry to see if Lomax really owned it, and the individual plots would be given a number. So far, all very straight.

What happened next was what had done the damage. Lomax had obviously sold the land twice over in short order. But for the scheme to work, there had to be a crooked solicitor handling the second, moody purchase of the land, a solicitor who wouldn't consult the Land Registry's Day Listing, a solicitor who would lie to his clients about the title to the land. And that solicitor was Martin Cheetham.

The problem, as I saw it, was that it was a lot of risk to take for so small a profit. When the people who had been ripped off realized what had happened, they'd be on to the Law Society with their complaints faster than a speeding bullet. Which might well mean the end of Martin Cheetham's career as a solicitor, and all for a half-share of fifty grand. Unless . . . I had a horrible thought. What if they hadn't just sold the land twice, but had sold it three or four times over? What if there was a queue of punters who didn't even know yet that they'd been conned? After all, it was only by coincidence that Chris had happened upon the surveyors. If they hadn't been there, Chris, Alexis and all their self-build cronies probably would have handed over the rest of the cash. The mind boggled! I began to wonder if getting Alexis's money back was going to be quite so easy after all. If Lomax and Cheetham had any sense, they'd be planning to do a runner any day now before it all came on top.

And there was very little I could do about it. Apart from anything else, I had to sort out Ted Barlow's problem before he went bankrupt. I pulled into a Happy Eater and ordered a brunch of hash browns, omelette and beans while I studied the register entries for the seven properties which had lost their conservatories. I'd also taken the precaution of dropping by the office to pick up the stuff from Josh and from Rachel Lieberman. Taken together, an interesting picture began to emerge. Unfortunately, it was more like a Jackson Pollock than a David Hockney.

Firstly, all the houses in question had been rented from DKL. All the tenants in question shared their surname with the owners of the house. All the title deeds showed that there was a charge against the property. Unfortunately they didn't tell me how much, although the dates of these existing charges corresponded roughly to the dates the conservatories had been bought, and in all cases the charge was held by the finance company that was a subsidiary of Ted Barlow's bank. Surprise, surprise. Interestingly, Josh's searches had revealed that all the owners had good to excellent credit ratings, which explained why Ted's bank's finance company had been so ready to grant them the remortgages. What it didn't explain was how those remortgages came to be granted to someone other than the owner.

Somehow, the remortgages held the key. What I needed to find out fast was how big they were. If those charges were anything like you'd expect from a one hundred per cent remortgage, then things would begin to fall into place. Bearing in mind that each of the houses had been owned by its present owners for at least four years, then the houses had been bought for significantly less than they were now worth. Given that the mortgages had presumably been paid for at least four years, the amount now outstanding should be considerably less than the current value of the house. I wandered across to the phone-booth and dialled Josh. Luckily I got straight through.

"Just a quickie," I said. "How do I find out the amount outstanding on a mortgage?"

"You can't," he said.

I was overcome with the desire to kick someone.

"Oh shit," I moaned.

"But I probably can," he added smugly.

Then I knew I wanted to kick someone, only he wasn't within range.

"As a finance broker I can ring up the charge holder and tell them I have a client who's looking to make a second loan against his property, can they tell me how much their outstanding charge is so that I can check whether there's enough equity left in the property. Is this to do with your conservatory scam?"

"Yes. It's slowly beginning to make sense," I told him.

"I'll ask Julia to do it this afternoon," he said.

I decided not to kick him after all. "She's already got the names and addresses, hasn't she?"

I arranged to call back in the afternoon. I was still cross and frustrated because I didn't fully understand how the con was working. But I did have one thing going for me. Rachel Lieberman had given me the addresses of three other properties that fitted the bill. Looking at the dates on the previous sales that had turned into missing conservatories, the scammers seemed to work a production-line system. They were getting the loans through at the rate of about one a month, so, given that it can take up to three months for the money to come through from finance companies, they must have been working three properties at any given time, each at various stages of the operation. Dear God! They really were serious about this!

It was three weeks since the last one had gone down, so by my reckoning, we were due for another any day now. I had a good idea where, a rough idea when. And I had an excellent idea how to discover exactly what was going on. All it should take was a phone call.

14

I sat in the back of a bright yellow van, headphones clamped to my ears. My friend Dennis sat next to me, looking for inspiration in the pages of an Elmore Leonard. To anyone wandering along this Stockport cul-de-sac, it looked like a British Telecom van. The inside would have completely confounded them. Instead of racks of tools, spare parts and cable, there were a couple of leather car seats, the kind you get in top-of-the-range Volvos or Mercs, and a table, all bolted to the floor. There was a portable colour TV and a video fixed to the top of a fridge. There was also a hatch in the floor. The van belongs to Sammy, one of Dennis's mates. I don't want to know what he uses it for on a regular basis. I know for sure it isn't anything to do with telecommunications.

Dennis O'Brien and I have been friends now for years. I know he's a criminal, and he knows I put criminals out of business. But in spite of, or maybe because of, that we've each got a lot of respect for the other. I respect him because in his own way he's a highly skilled craftsman who sticks rigidly to his own rules and values. They might not be the same as mine, but who's to say mine are any better? After all, this society that puts burglars behind bars is the same society that helps the really big bandits like Robert Maxwell thrive.

I owe Dennis a lot. My martial arts skills, my knowledge of lock-picking, and the part of Mortensen and Brannigan's income that depends on being able to think like a burglar so you can construct a security system that will defeat the real thing. He likes having me around because he thinks I'm a good role model for his teenage daughter. There's no accounting for tastes.

After I got back from the Land Registry, I'd rung Dennis on his mobile phone. It's a fascinating thing, the mobile phone. In London, when one starts ringing in a pub, chances are it's someone in the City on the receiving end. In Manchester, it's a bob to a gold clock it's a villain. It's a mystery to me how they get past the creditworthiness checks that the airtime companies run. Now I think about it, they've probably got their very own airtime company, Criminal Communications, or Funny Phones, just for bad lads. With absolutely no directory enquiries service.

Anyway, I caught Dennis at a good time, so I invited him to find Sammy and help me out. I didn't even have to mention money before he agreed. He's nice like that, is Dennis. Unlike me, he doesn't think a friend in need is a pain in the arse. Which is why I was sitting in a fake Telecom van while Sammy was planting Mortensen and Brannigan's bugs in the three-bedroomed semi that Brian and Mary Wright were renting through DKL Estates.

Normally, when we use surveillance equipment, we place it ourselves. It's seldom a problem, since more often than not we're being paid by the person who is in charge of the place we're bugging. It usually arises because a boss suspects one of their subordinates of a) flogging information to a competitor; b) embezzling money or goods from the firm; or c) just a bit of good, old-fashioned internecine warfare against the boss. In those cases, we just wander in after closing time and drape the place in all the electronic surveillance a body could want. Sometimes, however, we have to be a little more discreet. While Bill and I have an agreement that we won't do things that are outrageously illegal, we occasionally find ourselves technically a

little bit on the wrong side of the law when acquiring information. In situations like that, one of us insinuates ourself into the
building in question by some subterfuge or other. Personally, I
always find the most effective one is to claim to be the woman
who's come to refill the tampon dispensers. Not a lot of security
guards want to look too closely inside your boxes.

However, in this case, none of the usual ploys would work.
And I didn't really want either Brian or Mary Wright to see
me, since I'd be the person hanging round the street checking
out the surveillance tapes. Hence Sammy's van. I'd given him
a quick crash course in how to take apart the phone sockets and
install the simple bug I'd decided to use. It consisted of a phone
tap and a tiny voice-activated mike that would pick up the
conversation in the room itself. The bug had a range of about
one hundred and fifty metres, though reception in the metal-
walled van wasn't as good as it would be once I'd transferred
my receiver into the unobtrusive rented Fiesta where I could
leave it sitting on the parcel shelf.

Sammy had marched up the path in his Telecom overalls
ten minutes ago, and the woman who answered the door had let
him in without even asking to see the carefully forged ID card he
always carries. Perhaps she'd tried to dial out in the five minutes
since I'd fiddled with her phone at the junction box round the
corner. The reason I know about all these exotic things is that I
once had a fling with a Telecom engineer. He came to install a
second line in my bungalow for my computer modem and fax
machine and stayed for a month. He had wonderfully dexterous
fingers, and, as a bonus, he taught me everything I'd ever need to
know about the British telephone system. Unfortunately, he felt
the need to tell me it five times over. When he started telling me
for the sixth time about new developments in fibre optic technology, I knew he'd have to go or I'd be risking a murder charge.

What I was waiting for now was the sound of Sammy's
voice over my headphones. As soon as I was receiving him loud
and clear, I'd nip back to the junction box, restore the telephone

to full working order, and leave the receiver in my car wired up to a very clever tape recorder that a sound engineer friend of Richard's built for me. It links the mechanisms of six Walkmans to a signal-activated mike/receiver. When the bug's signal comes in, the first tape starts running. When the counter mechanism hits a certain number, it sets tape two running and switches off tape one. And so on. So, it gives a minimum of six hours' recording time when you're not actually there listening in.

Five minutes later, I heard, "Two sugars, love," booming in my ears. Thanks to Sammy, I was all wired up and ready to roll. Half an hour later, I was back in the office, ready to debrief Bill. He was, of course, horrified about my brush with death on Barton Bridge. Together we went through Paul's photos and the report from his surveillance of PharmAce, Bill muttering into his thick blond beard about the temerity of anyone who would mess with his partner.

"Paul's done a good job there. You did absolutely the right thing, laying him on like that," he rumbled, shuffling the pics together into a neat pile. "I'll go and see them this afternoon." He got to his feet, shouting, "Shelley? Get Brian Chalmers at PharmAce and tell him I'm on my way to see him."

"Wait a minute," I protested, angry at what felt like Bill pulling rank. "I'd planned to take those pictures over myself."

"I'm sure you did," he said. "And I don't have a problem with the way you've handled things. But I want someone with Chalmers when he fronts up the lab technician. And I'd rather it was me if only to show this creep that he's up against more than a one-woman show. If it was him that ran you off the road, he's got to be made to realize that there's no point in trying to write you off because it's not just you who knows what he's up to. Besides, we need a lot more information about this stolen van, and you've got enough on your plate right now with your missing conservatories."

I couldn't find any good reason for arguing with Bill. Personally, if I had his six foot plus towering over me, I'd admit to just about anything to get him to back off. So I left him to it. On my way out the door, I picked up the hand-held computer scanner which had been his monthly contribution to the office gadget mountain back in June. At last, I had found a use for it. As I crossed the outer office, Shelley said, "Ted Barlow's been on. That's the second time today. He's really starting to get desperate. He says he can pay his staff this week's wages, but he's not sure about next week. He wants to know if he should warn them or whether you think you'll have sorted it out by then."

I sighed. "I'm doing my best, Shelley," I said.

"Can't you do it a bit faster, Kate? Ted's scared he's going to lose his business."

"Shelley, I'm dancing as fast as I can, OK," I snapped, and stomped into my office. I'm ashamed to admit that I slammed the door. Unfortunately, I used the muscles that were still solid as a rock from the accident, so I lost out on comfort as well as dignity. Just to put the tin lid on it, the vibration of the door caused the last three leaves on the rubber plant to fall off. I threw the plant in the bin and made a note to stop by the florist in the morning. I'd had nine weeks out of that rubber plant, which was approaching a record for me and the chlorophyll kingdom.

I picked up the phone, dialled Josh's number and asked for Julia. I've never actually met her but her voice conjures up this image of a bright-eyed blonde with her hair in a neat bun, a Country Casuals suit and the hips of a girl raised on the Pony Club. The nearest I ever got to that was reading *Bunty.*

"Hello, Kate," she enthused down the phone at me. "Fabulous little challenge, darling!" I swear she really does say "Darling."

"Any joy?" I asked gruffly. For some reason Julia always brings out the peasant in me.

"I only tried three of them," she said. "With the charges all being held by the same finance company, I had to be a little bit cautious. However, the interesting thing is that, in each case, what we're looking at is a hundred per cent remortgage. The people I spoke to all said the same thing. 'There's not a shilling of equity left for your client.' So there you have it, Kate."

I could have kissed her. But she'd probably have misunderstood and taken my name off her database. I thanked her prettily, just like my mother always told me to, put down the phone and yelled, "Yo!" in satisfaction. The way things were heading, I was going to make Shelley a very happy woman.

I booted up my computer and entered my notes. Then I used the scanner on the Land Registry documents and saved them all to disc. It wasn't as easy as it was supposed to be, since the scanner had the unhelpful tendency to turn things into gobbledygook unless I kept my hand steady as a rock. I felt virtuous enough after all that to ring Richard and suggest a movie that evening. "Sorry, Brannigan," he said. "I'm going to a rave."

Richard may be four years older than me, but at times he makes me feel like my Granny Brannigan. Except that my Irish Granny B would probably love the idea of an all-night party where you can dance as much as you want. She'd even feel at home with the smell of the Vick's Vapor Rub that the ravers massage each other with in their bizarre search to improve the high of the designer drug cocktails they swallow. "Why?" I asked.

I could picture the shrug. "I need to keep in touch. Besides, they've got this new DJ. He's only thirteen and I want to take a look." Thirteen. Dear God, the Little Jimmy Osmond of Acid House. "You can come if you want," he added.

"I think I'll pass, Richard. Nothing personal, but frankly I'd rather go on a stake-out." At least I could choose the music. At least I'd be able to recognize what I was hearing as music.

I left the office just after four, picked up a pizza from the local trattoria and headed back out to Stockport in the Little Rascal. I parked round the corner from the target house, strolled round to the Fiesta and checked out the tape machine. The third was rolling, and I had a quick listen on the headphones. Blue Peter, by the sound of it. That's the trouble with Elint (electronic intelligence, or bugs to you). It has as much discrimination as a hooker on smack. I restrained myself from listening in to the rest of the Blue Peter tape, helped myself to the two I'd made earlier, and locked up the Fiesta.

Back in the van, I munched my pizza and listened to the tapes. The first one featured ten minutes of small talk with Sammy, a phone call to the hairdresser, a phone call to a friend who whined for twenty minutes about her business, her ex and her garage bill. Then the TV had gone on, its tinny sound an interesting contrast to the live voices I'd been hearing. An Australian soap, then a pre-teen comedy drama, then cartoons. I whizzed through the programmes on double speed, ear cocked for any more real conversations amongst the Mickey Mouse squeaks. Nothing.

Bored, I went back to the Fiesta and listened in again. By now, we were on to *Granada Reports*. Why couldn't my target have been one of these quiet, refined people who don't feel the need of some kind of audio wallpaper? I reset the recording machine with fresh tapes and decided to give my eavesdropping another hour before heading home. I reminded myself that I had a right to some free time of my own. Besides, I was feeling cold and stiff and I was longing to get to grips with my latest computer game purchase. *Civilization* promised to be the most enthralling strategy game I'd played for a long time, taking the player from the dawn of man to the space age. So far, I hadn't been able to get much further than settlements of tent dwellers who'd just discovered the wheel before the barbarians came along and clobbered us.

I was trying to work out an approach that would be more fruitful when everything changed. The noise in my ears suddenly stopped altogether. For a few heart-stopping seconds I thought she'd discovered the bug. Then I heard a dialling tone and the click of numbers being keyed in. Maybe I'd be able to identify the number when I had the chance to analyse the tape at more length. The phone at the other end rang three times before it was picked up. An answering machine clicked and a man's voice

said, "I'm sorry, I'm not taking calls right now. Leave your message after the bleep, and we'll talk soon." The voice was cool,
with a suggestive edge that made me smile rather than squirm.

After the tone, the woman said, "Hi, it's me. It's just before
seven. I'm going round to my mother's, then I'll be at Colin and
Sandra's. See you there. Love you. Bye." There was a click as
she put the phone down. I scrambled out of the car and hurried
down the street towards the van. The last thing I wanted was
for her to become suspicious of the Fiesta.

I had just shut myself into an atmosphere of stale pizza
when a square of light from the front door spilt over the drive
of my target's house. The light disappeared as she shut the door
and opened the garage. I concentrated on the features. The
hair might change, the clothes might change, the height might
change with the shoes, but the face wasn't going to, especially
the profile. I registered small, neat features, sharp chin, face
wider across the eyes. Just like Diane Shipley's sketch. A couple
of minutes later, a white Metro emerged and drove past me,
heading south towards Hazel Grove. I'd gambled when I parked
that if she was going to drive off anywhere, she'd be heading
north into Manchester. Wrong again. I did as quick a three-
point turn as I could manage, which wasn't fast enough. By the
time I reached the end of the road, she was gone. There was just
enough traffic around to make it impossible to guess which set
of distant tail lights were hers.

There was nothing else for it. I'd just have to go home and
bring my own unique blend of civilization to some unsuspecting
barbarian tribe. Maybe this time I should develop map-making
ahead of ceremonial burial . . . ?

When I got home, my answering machine was flashing. I
pressed the playback button. "Kate, Bill here. I've just got back
from PharmAce. We need to talk. This is the number where
you can reach me this evening after seven."

He rattled off a Didsbury number, which I failed to recognize. Hardly surprising. Bill changes his girlfriends as often as

Rod Stewart in his bachelor days. When I dialled the number, true to form, a woman's voice answered. While I waited for her to fetch Bill, I conjured up the image her voice generated.

"Twenty-five, Home Counties, graduate, blonde, smokes," I said when Bill answered.

"Well done, Sherlock. You're two years too generous, though," he said.

"You said we need to talk. Will the phone do, or shall I come over and meet you for a drink?" I asked maliciously.

"The phone will do nicely," he said. "First, the good news. Brian Chalmers is delighted, and has sacked the senior technician on the spot, with no reference. And tomorrow I'm meeting someone from Knutsford CID to see if they'd like to pursue the company receiving the stolen goods."

"Fine," I said. "And the bad news?"

"It wasn't a PharmAce van that ran you off the road. They had a call today from the police in Devon. The van that was stolen from PharmAce was written off in some village on Dartmoor on Friday morning after being used in a supermarket robbery down there. So it couldn't have rammed you on Friday night. Kate, whoever had a go at you on Barton Bridge is still out there."

15

I could get used to being waited on hand and foot at breakfast. What I couldn't handle is the early rising that seems to go hand in hand with business briefings over the bacon butties. The following morning, I was back in the dining room of the Portland at Josh's invitation. "I've got someone I want you to meet," he'd said mysteriously on the phone, refusing to be drawn further.

I approached with caution, since I could see Josh's companion was a woman. I hoped he hadn't dragged me out of bed to tell me he was getting married. That was news I couldn't handle on an empty stomach. I saw Josh spot me and say something to his companion, who glanced over her shoulder at me. She didn't look Josh's type. For a start, she looked in her middle thirties, which made her at least ten years too old. The most striking thing about her was her hair, the colour of polished conkers, hanging down her back in a thick plait.

When I reached the table, Josh half-stood and said, "Kate! I'm glad you could make it. Della, this is Kate Brannigan, the private investigator I told you about."

A potential client, then, I thought. I smiled. Josh continued, "Kate, this is Detective Chief Inspector Della Prentice. She's just been transferred to the Regional Crime Squad. We were at Cambridge together, and I thought the pair of you ought to meet."

I tried not to look as gobsmacked as I felt. There aren't a lot of women who make it to the rank of DCI, especially not at the sharp end of crime. Della Prentice smiled and extended her hand. "Pleased to meet you, Kate," she said. "At the risk of making your heart sink, Josh has told me a lot about you."

"I wish I could say the same about you," I replied, shaking a dry, firm hand. I sat down with a bit of a bump. I didn't expect to be dragged out of bed at sparrowfart to meet a copper. Especially not a ranking woman officer. I gave her the quick once-over. Deep-set greenish eyes, good skin, the kind of strong bones that look lumpy in teenagers but become more attractive with every year that passes after the age of thirty.

"He tries to keep me under wraps because I know where the bodies are buried," she said, as she gave me the same scrutiny. "I could tell you a tale . . ."

Josh cleared his throat and said hastily, "Della's something of an expert in the kind of fraud you seem to be dealing with in your conservatory case," he said. "I rather thought she might be of some help to you."

"I've just done eighteen months with the West Yorkshire Fraud Squad," Della said. "Now I've been transferred to the RCS to be the operational head of a fraud task force."

"How are you finding it?" I asked.

"It's always a bit of an uphill struggle, learning to work with a new team." Of course. She wouldn't have climbed that far up the ladder if she hadn't been something of a diplomat.

"Made five times worse because you're a woman?" I asked.

"Something like that."

"I can imagine. Plenty of that dumb insolence, literal interpretation of orders and no respect till they decide you've earned it."

Della's twisted smile said it all. "What we're doing is working with banks and other financial institutions on the kind of small-scale fraud that doesn't warrant the attentions of the Serious Fraud Office. Usually, it involves forgery or the kind of deception where people assume someone else's identity for the purposes of obtaining goods or cash."

"At the risk of sounding like the punters I meet at parties, that must be fascinating," I said.

She smiled. "It can be very satisfying to put together the pieces of the jigsaw."

"Yes, you get a better class of villain in your line of work than your colleagues who get lumbered with the ram raiders and the drug dealers," I said. "For me, it's a little out of the usual run of things. I'm more accustomed to poking about in computers' memories than fronting people up."

Della leaned back in her chair. "Now, that really *must* be fascinating. No, I mean it. I'd love to have the time to learn more about computers. Mind if I smoke?" I shook my head. She took out a pack of Silk Cut and a Zippo lighter. As she lit up she said, "Josh tells me you've got a problem with defaulting mortgagees. Maybe we could do each other a bit of good here. I might be able to shed some light for you and, frankly, if you can stand it up, I could really use the collar."

I liked Della Prentice's candour. And she came vouched for by Josh, which in my book was the seal of professionalism. So I took a deep breath and said, "This is off the record. Agreed?" I had no authority from Ted to involve the police. Added to which, as yet, I had no real evidence that a crime had been committed, only a lot of circumstantial coincidences.

A waitress appeared and we ordered our breakfasts before Della could reply. When she'd gone, she said, "Off the record."

I gave Della the bare bones. To her credit, she heard me out in silence. Most of the questions she asked afterwards were sensible and to the point, just as I'd expected. "The banks have got their own investigators, you know," she said at last. "I'm surprised they haven't been digging around in this one themselves."

"I don't know that they haven't been," I said. "But if they have, they've been going at it from a different angle. They're probably trying to prove Ted Barlow is bent, whereas I'm trying to establish the exact opposite."

She nodded. "I don't mean to sound like I'm teaching you to suck eggs, but I suppose you have considered that your client might be at it?"

"It was the first thing I thought of. But people who know him say he lacks the imagination or the inclination to be that bent. Besides, he's telling the truth about the missing conservatories. Even I can see they were installed originally, and if he was behind it himself, he wouldn't have to bother with that," I explained.

Della considered while she lit another cigarette. Then she said, "He might have been doing that to cover his own back when it all came on top. And who better than him to find a new home for the conservatories? After all, he could just recycle them. And he could simply be employing you to make it look good to the bank—and to us, if we're called in eventually by the bank's security crew."

I shook my head. "It's not Ted. I know it's possible to find an explanation that points the finger at him. But the clincher for me is that he just doesn't match the descriptions I've got of the man who spends the night at these houses."

"It's an unusual one, Kate," she said. "Very unusual. But if it really is a scam that's being pulled by one or two people rather than a string of coincidences, then they must have cleared a lot of cash by now."

"Over half a million after expenses, by my estimates," I said calmly. "They probably can't believe their luck. If I was them, I'd be planning to pull out before the shit hit the fan."

"How do you know they haven't?" Della asked.

"I don't. I'm banking on the fact that they haven't. That way, the next time they pull one, I can get on their tail while the trail's still warm." Much as I liked Della, I wasn't about to tell her that I thought I'd spotted the next target. I was perfectly happy for her to think I was playing a waiting game. It would keep the Regional Crime Squad off my back. Besides, I didn't want to get into a discussion on the subject of illegal phone taps. I hate the sound of people in glass houses throwing stones.

I scooped the last mouthful of scrambled egg on to a triangle of toast and managed to savour it, Della being between cigarettes. "Let me know how you get on. I'm really fascinated by the sound of this one. I'm sure we could help." She took a card out of the jacket of her charcoal grey suit. "And if they do seem to have done a runner, get in touch anyway. You never know, we might be able to put something together with what you've got."

"I appreciate that. Soon as I've something concrete, I'll call you. Josh, thanks for introducing us. It's the first time I've met someone you actually shut up for," I said.

"You don't deserve me, Kate," he said sadly.

"Thank God for that. Now, if you'll both excuse me, I've got to run," I said. I stood up and shook Della Prentice's hand. "I'll be in touch. Oh, and Josh? Thank Julia for that information she dug out for me." I gave him a peck on the cheek.

My guilty conscience over talking to DCI Della Prentice about Ted's problem gave me a severe prick when I walked into the office to find the conservatory builder and the lovestruck secretary with their heads together. Ted Barlow was perched on the edge of Shelley's desk, while she ignored her computer screen and stared instead into his eyes. Before I'd even got my duffel coat off, Ted was apologizing for bothering me and Shelley was twittering about interim reports and mobile phones. I invited Ted into my office and brought him as up to date as I dared. I didn't trust him entirely with full knowledge of my current surveillance. He may have been footing the bill, but he was far too transparent for me to feel comfortable with him knowing my every move. Besides, he was so obviously one of life's honest guys that he might be uncomfortable at the thought of me bending the law on his behalf.

So I told him that I was making progress, and that I was close to working out how it all came together. He seemed satisfied with that. Maybe all he was looking for was some reassurance. When I emerged from my office a couple of minutes after he'd left me, he was still hanging round Shelley's desk looking nervous. I couldn't stand it, so I grabbed my coat and the mobile phone that had arrived that morning and headed for the door.

First stop was the hired Fiesta with the receiving equipment. At first, when I checked the cassettes, my heart sank. Nothing seemed to have been recorded at all since I'd left it the previous evening. When I reset it, I must have made a mistake, I decided. Then I noticed that the first tape wasn't quite empty.

I pulled it out of the machine and smacked it in the car cassette. There was the unmistakable sound of a door slamming, then a phone ringing, unanswered. I breathed a sigh of relief. Neither I nor the machine was faulty. It seemed the woman just hadn't come home. In case she or one of her neighbours was the noticing kind, I drove the Fiesta round the block and reparked it in an obviously different position. I didn't want to be in the embarrassing position of having the bomb squad called because some civic-minded nosy-parker thought the receiver on the parcel shelf was an IRA car bomb. It happened to Bill last year. Luckily for him, the receiver was switched off at the time. Luckily, because the offence is using the equipment, not possessing it, which is the kind of logic the law specializes in.

I reckoned it still wasn't safe to go back to the office, so I decided to poke a stick into the hornet's nest of Alexis's little problem and see what flew out. It was late morning when I reached Cheetham's office. His obliging secretary told me he was in a meeting, but if I cared to wait . . .

I took the computer magazine I usually carry out of my handbag and settled down with an article about RAM expansion kits. If I decided we needed something similar, the technique is to leave the magazine lying around the office, open at the appropriate page, and wait for Mortensen the gadget king to fall upon it and embrace it as if it were his own idea. Never fails.

Before I could reach a firm decision, the door to the inner office opened and Cheetham ushered out the woman I'd seen with him in Buxton. He had his arm round her in that familiar, casual way that people use with the kind of partners you sleep with rather than work with. When he saw me, he twitched and dropped his arm as if he'd been jabbed with a cattle prod. "Miss Brannigan," he said nervously.

Hearing my name, the woman, who until then had been focused on Cheetham, switched her attention to me. She sized me up in an instant, from the top of my wavy auburn hair to the tips of my brown boots. She probably misjudged me, too. She wasn't to know that the reason I was wearing enough make-up to read the six o'clock news was that the bruises on my jaw and cheekbone had gone a fascinating shade of green.

She looked like serious business, groomed to within an inch of artificiality. I hated her. Our mutual scrutiny was interrupted by Cheetham stammering, "If you'd like to come through, Miss Brannigan?"

I acknowledged them both with a nod and walked past them to his office. I didn't hear what the woman murmured in his ear after I passed, but I heard him say, "It's all right, Nell. Look, I'll see you this afternoon, OK?"

"It had better be," I thought I caught as she swept off without so much as a smile for the secretary. You can tell a lot about people by the way they treat other people's office staff.

I waited for Cheetham to return to his chair. I could see the effort it was taking for him to sit still. "How can I help you?" he asked.

"I just thought I'd drop by and give you a progress report," I said. "Our builder friend, T. R. Harris, seems not to exist. And neither does the solicitor whom you appear to have corresponded with." I knew this for certain, since I'd checked out the list of qualified briefs in the Solicitors' Diary.

Cheetham just sat and stared at me, those liquid dark eyes slightly narrowed. "I don't understand," he said, rather too late.

"Well, it seems as if Harris used a false name, and made up a non-existent solicitor for the purpose of conning your clients out of their money. It was lucky that Miss Appleby happened to discover the land had already been sold, otherwise they'd all have lost a lot more money," I tried. If he was straight, he'd be at great pains to point out to me that they couldn't have lost another shilling, since he, their diligent solicitor, would have discovered from the Land Registry that the land in question had already been sold, or was at least the subject of other inquiries.

He said none of that. What he did say was how sorry he was that it had happened, but now I seemed to have cleared it all up, it was obvious that he had been taken for a ride as much as his clients.

"Except that, unlike you, they're all out of pocket to the tune of five thousand pounds each," I observed mildly. He didn't even blush.

Cheetham got to his feet and said, "I appreciate you letting me know all this."

"They might even have to take the matter to the Law Society. They have indemnity insurance to cover this sort of negligence and malpractice, don't they?"

"But I haven't been negligent," he protested weakly. "I told you before, the searches came back clear. And the letters from Harris's solicitor assured me that although he'd had other inquiries, no one else was in a position to pursue a possible purchase at that point in time. How was I to know the letters were fakes?"

"It's a pity you solicitors always have to put everything in writing," said. "Just one phone call to the so-called Mr Graves' office would have stopped this business stone dead."

"What do you mean?" he asked hesitantly.

"The number on the letterhead is the number of a pay phone in a pub in Ramsbottom. But I suppose you didn't know that either," I said.

He sat down again in a hurry. "Of course I didn't," he said. He was as convincing as a cabinet minister.

"There was one other thing," I said. I'd rattled his cage. Now it was time for a bluff. "When I was here the other day, I saw a guy come into your office after me. I had some other business in the building, and when I left, I saw him getting into his van. Some company called Renovations, or something like that? Looked a bit like your friend from Buxton, which, of course, is why I thought *he* was a builder."

Cheetham's eyes widened, though he kept the rest of his face under control. Clearly, he was one of those people whose eyes really are the windows of the soul. "What about him?" he asked nervously.

"Well, my boyfriend and I have just bought an old house out in Heaton Chapel, and it needs a lot of work doing, and I noticed the van had a Stockport number on the side. I wondered if they specialized in that kind of job and, if they did, maybe you could give me their number? I tried Yellow Pages, but I couldn't find them," I said.

Cheetham's mouth opened and closed. "I . . . er . . . I don't think they'd be what you're looking for," he gabbled. "No, not for your problem at all. Old barns, that's what they do. Conversions, that sort of thing. Sorry, I . . . er . . . Sorry."

Satisfied that I'd put the cat among the pigeons, as well as establishing Cheetham's guilt firmly in my own mind, I gave him a regretful smile and said, "Oh well, when we do buy ourselves an old barn, I'll know where to come. Thanks for your time, Mr Cheetham."

An hour later, I was lurking behind a fruit and veg stall in the indoor market at Stockport. The bright autumn sunlight poured in through the high windows of this recently restored cathedral to commerce. It illuminated a fascinating scene. Across the crowded aisles of the market, in a little café, Martin Cheetham was in earnest conversation with none other than Brian Lomax, alias T. R. Harris.

Now I knew all I needed to know. All that remained was some proof.

16

I bought a couple of Russet apples and half a pound of grapes from the fruit and veg stall to keep my mouth occupied while I watched Cheetham and Lomax talk. Cheetham appeared to be both worried and angry, while Lomax seemed not so much tense as impatient. Cheetham was doing most of the talking, with Lomax nodding or shaking his head in response as he munched his way through a couple of barm cakes and a bowl of chips. Eventually, Lomax wiped his mouth with the back of his hand, leaned across the table and spoke earnestly to Cheetham.

There are times when I wish I'd learned to lip read. Or to predict the future. That way, I'd have been able to plant a radio mike under the table in advance. As it was, I was stuck in my less than blissful ignorance. All I could do was keep on Martin Cheetham's tail as he left the café and pushed his way through the shopping crowds back to the supermarket car park where he'd left his black BMW. A black BMW which I'd last seen parked outside Brian Lomax's house on Saturday night.

It wasn't hard to keep tabs on him. He drove back to Manchester like a man who's preoccupied with something other than the road and traffic conditions. Expecting him to go straight back to his office, I hung back a little as we neared the city centre, and that's when I almost lost him. At the bottom of Fennel Street, instead of turning left towards the Blackfriars car park where he'd been parked that morning, he turned right. I was three cars behind him, and I barely made it to the junction in time to see him turn left by the railway arches, heading for the East Lancs road. "Oh, shit," I groaned, stamping on the accelerator and skidding across four lanes of traffic in his wake. The Little Rascal really wasn't my vehicle of choice for a car chase. I only hoped the cacophony of horns wouldn't penetrate Cheetham's apparent reverie.

He wasn't in sight when I got to the next set of lights. I had to gamble that he'd gone straight on, out past Salford Cathedral and the university, past the museum with its matchstick men Lowrys, as reproduced on a thousand middle-class walls. I stayed in the middle lane, on the alert for a glimpse of his gleaming black bodywork. I was beginning to sweat by the time I passed the grimy monolith of Salford Tech. It looked like I'd lost him. But I stuck with it, and two miles down the East Lancs I spotted him up ahead, turning left at the next lights.

By the time I hit the lights, they'd just turned red, something I chose to ignore, to the horror of the woman whose Volvo I cut across as I swept round the corner. I gave her a cheery wave, then put my foot down. I picked Cheetham up a quarter of a mile down the road. He turned right, then second left into Tamarind Grove, a quiet street of between-the-wars semis, not unlike Alexis and Chris's. The BMW swung into the drive of a trim example of the type about halfway down on the left.

I drew up sharply in the little red van, keeping my engine running in case he was merely dropping something off or picking someone up. Cheetham got out of the car, locking it carefully behind him and setting the alarm, then let himself in the front door with a key. I drove slowly past the house and parked. I stationed myself by the rear door, keeping watch through the one-way glass of the window. I wasn't even sure why I was doing it. This had started off as a search for hard evidence of what Cheetham and Lomax had done to my friends. But I couldn't help feeling there was a lot more going on. What was Renew-Vations up to that sent Cheetham running down the road like a scalded cat to front up his partner in crime? And what was happening now? I have the kind of natural curiosity that hates to give in till the last stone is turned over and the last creepy-crawly firmly ground into the dirt. I kept coming back to the thought that whatever was going down here, Cheetham was the key. He knew I was poking my nose into his business. And Cheetham's partner in crime drove a white Transit van. Admittedly, the van in his drive at the weekend had been unscathed, but I figured it was a strong possibility that his business ran to more than one van.

If there's a more boring job than staking out someone who's enjoying the comforts of their own home, I've yet to discover it. To relieve the monotony, I used my new toy to call the Central Reference Library and asked them to check the electoral roll for this address. Cheetham was the only person listed. Then I rang Richard to tell him my new number. This week, his answering machine featured him rapping over a hectic backing track, "Hi, it's Richard here, sorry, but I'm out, leave your name and number and I'll give you a shout." At least it was an improvement on the throaty, sensuous one he'd had running the month before. I mean, you don't expect to find yourself in the middle of a dirty phone call when it's you who's done the dialling, do you?

Then I settled down to listen to the play on Radio 4. Inevitably, five minutes before the denouement, things started happening. A white convertible Golf GTi pulled up outside Cheetham's house. A brown court shoe appeared round the driver's door, followed by an elegant leg. The woman Cheetham had called Nell emerged, wearing a Burberry. Her choice of car came as no surprise, though I've never understood the fascination the Golf convertible holds for supposedly classy women. It looks like a pram to me, especially with the top down.

Nell followed Cheetham's path to the door, and also let herself in with a key. Then, about twenty minutes later, a white

Transit van turned into the street and parked a couple of doors away from Cheetham's house. Lomax got out, wearing a set of overalls like a garage mechanic, a knitted cap covering his wavy brown hair. He didn't give my van a second glance as he marched straight up to Cheetham's front door and pressed the bell. He only had moments to wait before the door opened to admit him. From where I was parked, I couldn't actually see who opened the door, but I assumed it was Cheetham.

I thought about sneaking round the back of the house to see if there was any way of hearing or seeing what was going on, but it was way too risky to be anything other than one of those tantalizing fantasies. So I waited. The plot was thickening, and I was powerless to do anything about it.

I phoned the office, on the off-chance that Bill would have some emergency that required me to abandon my boring vigil. No such luck. So I baited Shelley about Ted Barlow. "Has he asked you out, then?"

"I don't know what you mean," she said huffily. "He's just a client. Why should he ask me out?"

"You'll never make a detective if you're that unobservant," I teased. "So are you seeing him again? Apart from in reception?"

"He's coming round about a conservatory," she admitted.

"Wow!" I exclaimed. "Terrific! You be careful now, Shelley. This could be the most expensive date you've ever had. I mean, they don't come cheap, these conservatories. You could just ask him to Sunday dinner, you know, you don't actually have to let him sell you enough glass to double glaze the town hall."

"Do you realize your feeble attempts to wind me up are costing the firm 25p a minute? Get off the phone, Kate, unless you've got something useful to say," Shelley said firmly. "Oh, and by the way, the garage rang to say your Nova is definitely a write-off. I've phoned the insurance company and the assessor's coming to look at it tomorrow."

For some reason, the thought of a new car didn't excite me as much as it should have done. I thanked Shelley, pressed the end button on the phone and settled down gloomily to watch Cheetham's house. About an hour after he arrived, Lomax appeared on the doorstep, struggling with a large cardboard box which appeared to be full of document wallets and loose papers. He loaded them into his van, then drove off. I decided it was more important, or at least more interesting, to follow Lomax and the papers than to continue watching the outside of a house.

I waited till he rounded the corner before I set off in pursuit. The height of his van made it easy for me to keep him in sight as he threaded his way through the afternoon traffic. We headed down through Swinton and cut across to Eccles. Lomax turned into a street of down-at-heel terraced houses and stopped in front of one whose ground floor windows were boarded up. Lomax unlocked the door, then returned for the bulky box. He slammed the door behind him and left me sitting watching the outside of a different house.

I gave it half an hour then decided I wasn't getting anywhere. I decided to swing round via Cheetham's house to see if anything was happening, then head back to my other stake-out to see if the tapes were running with anything interesting. As I turned into the street that Cheetham's road led off, I nearly collided with a Peugeot in too much of a hurry. To my astonishment, I realized as I passed that it was Alexis. Unaccustomed to seeing me driving the van instead of my usual car, she obviously hadn't noticed the driver she'd nearly hit was me. I hoped she hadn't been round at Cheetham's house, giving him a piece of her mind. That was the last thing I needed right now.

More likely, she was hot on the trail of some tale to titillate her readers. There was nothing unusual in her driving as though she were the only person on the road. Like most journos, she operates on the principle that the hideous road accidents they've all reported only ever happen to other people.

The Golf had gone from outside the house in Tamarind Grove. Cheetham's BMW was still sitting outside the garage, but there were no lights on in the house, though it was dark enough outside for the street lights to be glowing orange. Chances were Cheetham had been driven off somewhere by the lovely Nell. Which meant there was probably no one home.

To make doubly sure, I got his number from Directory Enquiries. The phone rang four times, then the answering machine cut in. "I'm sorry, I can't take your call right now . . ." And all the rest. It wasn't proof positive that the house was unoccupied, but I figured Cheetham was too stressed out just now to ignore his phone.

I couldn't resist it. Within minutes, I'd changed from my business clothes into a jogging suit and Reeboks from the holdall I'd removed from my wrecked Nova. I added a thin pair of latex gloves, just in case. Out of my handbag, I took my Swiss Army knife, my powerful pocket torch, an out-of-date credit card, a set of jeweller's tools that double as lock-picks, and a miniature camera. All the things a girl should never be without. Checking the street was empty, I slipped out of the van and down the flagged path that ran by the side of Martin Cheetham's house. Fortunately, although the bell box on the front of the house indicated he had a burglar alarm, he hadn't invested in infra-red activated security lights, as recommended by Mortensen and Brannigan.

The back garden was enclosed by a seven-foot fence, and the gloom was compounded by thick shrubs that cast strange shadows across a paved area which featured the inevitable brick-built barbecue. There was no sign of light through the pair of patio doors that led into the garden so I cautiously turned on my torch. I peered in at a dining room with a strangely old-fashioned air.

I switched the torch off and moved cautiously across the patio to the kitchen door. It was the solid, heavy door of someone who takes their security precautions seriously. So I was rather surprised to see the top section of the kitchen window ajar. I carried on past the door and glanced up at the window. It was open a couple of notches, and although it was too small to allow anyone to enter, it offered possibilities.

I shone my torch through the window, revealing an unadventurous pine kitchen, cluttered with appliances, a bowl of fruit, a rack of vegetables, a draining board full of dry dishes, a shelf of cookery books, a knife block and an assortment of jars and bottles. It looked more like a table at a car boot sale than a kitchen.

The door leading from the kitchen to the hall was ajar, and I shifted slightly to let the beam from my torch play across the room. Caught between the beam of my torch and the gleam of the street light out front, I could see the body of a woman twisting slowly round and round, round and round.

17

Next thing I knew, I was crouched down on the patio, my back pressed against the wall so hard I could feel the texture of the brickwork against my scalp. I didn't know how I'd got there. My torch was turned off, but the sight of the dangling corpse still filled my vision. I squeezed my eyes closed, but the image of the body hanging in mid-air was still vividly there. It sounds callous, but I felt outraged. I don't do bodies. I do industrial espionage, fraud and white-collar theft. The desire to curl up in a tight little ball was almost overwhelming. I knew I ought to get the hell out of there and call the police, but I couldn't get my limbs to move.

It looked like an open and shut case. The woman called Nell had arrived earlier in the afternoon; now there was a woman's corpse in the house, and her car was missing. What it meant to me was that Cheetham would be facing a murder charge rather than one of fraud. Either way, he wouldn't be practising as a solicitor again in a hurry. But Lomax, on the other hand, would almost certainly live to defraud another day. All he had to do was deny everything and blame it all on Cheetham.

I struggled to my feet. I wished Richard was with me. Not because he'd be any practical use, but because he'd be talking me out of what I was about to do. I knew it was crazy, knew I was taking the kind of stupid chance that Bill would seriously fall out with me over. But I'd come this far, and I couldn't stop now. If there was any proof of what had been going on, I wanted to have a good look at it before the police sequestrated it. As Richard has pointed out on several occasions, I subscribe to the irregular verb theory of language: I am a trained investigator, you have a healthy curiosity, she/he is a nosy-parker.

I took a deep breath and studied the kitchen window, carefully averting my eyes from the doorway leading into the hall. If I could get up to it, I thought I might be able to reach through the open window and slip open the catch on the side section, which would be big enough to let me climb in. Unfortunately, the sill wasn't wide enough to stand on, and there was no conveniently placed ladder. The only things that were remotely portable were the carefully arranged bricks of the circular barbecue. They weren't mortared together, merely assembled like a child's building bricks.

With a sigh, I started shifting the bricks to build a platform beneath the window. I was grateful for the latex gloves; without them, my hands would have been in shreds. It didn't take long to construct a makeshift set of steps that brought me high enough to slide my arm inside the unfastened window. My fingertips could barely brush the top of the window catch. I withdrew and opened the blade of my Swiss Army knife that looks as if its only purpose is to remove Boy Scouts from horses' hoofs. It has a sort of hooked bit on the end and almost certainly has some quaint name like "cordwangler's grommet disengager."

With the blade extended, I was able to flick the catch upwards. I pushed the window towards me and it swung open. I stepped into the kitchen sink and closed both windows behind me. I searched the draining board for a cloth then carefully wiped the sill and the sink to remove any obvious traces of my entry. The last thing I wanted was to be lifted for murder. What I was really doing was putting off the moment when I'd have to confront Nell's dangling body. She must be suspended from the banister, I realized as I braced myself to go through the doorway.

I emerged into the hall, gritted my teeth and switched on my torch. The body was still twisting languorously in some faint draught. Steeling myself, I started at the floor and worked upwards. A brown court shoe like the one I'd seen emerging from the Golf a couple of hours ago lay on its side on the plain oatmeal Berber carpet, as if it had been idly kicked off. Its partner was on the left foot of the body. The ankles were lashed together with an incongruous Liberty silk scarf. The scarf was tied in a slip knot that had tightened to cut into the flesh above the ankle bones. She wore sheer dark-tan stockings. They looked like silk to me. I caught a glimpse of suspenders under the full, swirling skirt. I couldn't see the underwear. The smell made me glad of that. My eyes travelled upwards, over a silk tunic cinched in at the waist by a woven leather belt with gilt studs, like a stylized leather queen's. The shapely legs were bent at the knees, held in place by another scarf that was tied to the belt.

The wrists were tied together in front of the body with another scarf, clasped like an innocent Doris Day in a nineteen-fifties film. Again, a slip knot had been used. It looked like a bizarre sexual fantasy, the stuff of snuff movies. I tried not to look too closely at the ligature, but it was obvious that the woman had been hanged by a rope of silk scarves. I closed my eyes, swallowed hard and made myself look at the face.

It wasn't Nell.

Not by any stretch of the imagination was that swollen, engorged face the same one I'd seen in Buxton and later in Cheetham's office. From below, it was hard to say more than that, but the hair looked strangely asymmetrical. The one ear I could see was an ominous bluish purple, and the skin of the face was an odd colour. Horrified but oddly fascinated, I skirted the body to climb the stairs for a better vantage point. Five steps from the top of the flight, I was almost level with the staring eyes. Dots of blood peppered the whites of the eyes. I tried not to think of this as a human being, but simply as a piece of evidence. Close to, it was clear that the brown hair was a wig. What was also clear, in spite of the hideous distortion of the features and the heavy make-up, was the identity of the corpse. That was when I lost it.

I splashed cold water over my face, drawing my breath in sharply as it hit. I dried myself on toilet paper, then flushed it down the loo. Then I flushed the loo again, the sixth time since I'd lost my lunch. Just because you're paranoid doesn't mean the forensic scientists aren't out to get you. I gave the toilet bowl a last wipe down, then flushed again, praying the U-bend was now free from any traces of my reaction to discovering Martin Cheetham hanging from a banister dressed in women's clothing.

I closed the toilet lid and sat down on it. It was only my second corpse ever, and the discovery seemed to be taking a bit of getting used to. The voice of wisdom and self-preservation was telling me to get out of there as fast as possible and wait till I was in another county before calling the police. The bloody-minded voice from the other side of my brain reminded me that I'd never get another chance like this to get to the bottom of whatever had brought matters to this pass. I couldn't believe Cheetham had killed himself because he thought I'd uncovered his dishonesty in the land sale. There had to be more.

I forced myself out of the bathroom and back on to the landing. "It's not a person," I kept saying out loud to myself, as if that could convince me. I stood on the landing, above the banister where Cheetham's body was suspended by the rope of silk scarves. From here, it didn't look quite so terrible, though at this angle I could see what had been obscured from below, that he had an erection. I forced myself to reach down and touch the skin of the face. There was no perceptible difference in temperature between my hand and the corpse. I didn't know enough about forensic medicine to understand the significance of that.

I turned my back on the body and started my search. The first room I entered was obviously the spare room. It was lit dimly by the glow of the street lamps. The room was clean and neat, but again, curiously old fashioned, like a room in my parents' house. The wardrobe was empty except for a white tuxedo, dress trousers and a couple of frilly evening shirts. The chest of drawers was empty except for towels in the bottom drawer. On the off-chance, I lifted an insipid watercolour of the Lake District away from the wall. I couldn't think of any reason for keeping it except to obscure a safe. No such luck.

The next bedroom appeared more promising. It overlooked the garden, so I took the risk of drawing the heavy, floor-length chintz drapes and switching on the light. Mirrored wardrobes the length of the far wall doubled the apparent size of the room. A king-size bed dominated the other wall. The plain green duvet cover looked rumpled, as if someone had been lying on it. On the floor by the bed, a magazine lay open. I crouched down and studied it, gingerly turning the pages. It was sadomasoch-istic pornography of the kind that makes me feel like joining Mary Whitehouse and the Moral Majority. The key pages came just before the one that lay open on the floor. They featured an illustrated story about a man who got his satisfaction from pretending to hang himself.

As I crouched there, feeling soiled just looking at the porn, by a strange contrast I noticed the bed linen still smelled fresh and clean. I looked carefully at the pillows, then moved round the bed to the undisturbed side, where I lifted the duvet: no stray hairs, no wrinkles in the sheet, no depression in the pil-lows. I may not have had much experience of suicides, but I couldn't see someone changing the bedding before they topped themselves. On a hunch, I walked across the room to the wicker linen basket. It contained two shirts, two pairs of socks, two pairs of boxer shorts and a bath towel. But no sheets, pillow cases or duvet cover. Curiouser and curiouser.

I started on the wardrobes. The first revealed half a dozen business suits and a couple of dozen shirts, all from Marks & Spencer. A shoe rack along the bottom held a mixture of formal and casual footwear. A tie rack was fixed to the inside of the door, revealing a taste in ties as exotic as an undertaker's. The next section contained leisure wear—polo shirts, rugby shirts, jeans, all carefully pressed and hung. The next unit disguised a tower of drawers. T-shirts, underwear, socks, sweaters, jogging pants, all neatly folded in piles.

The last two sections appeared to be a double wardrobe, and it was locked. The lock was different from the flimsy ones on the other doors and their keys didn't fit. I wondered where Cheetham's key ring was, and doubled back to the drawer in the bedside table. It held a wallet and a bunch of keys, but not the key to the wardrobe. Oh joy, oh rapture. There was nothing else for it. I'd have to try picking the lock, and be careful not to leave it looking like someone had had a go at it.

I took out the slender tools and gently began to probe the inside of the lock with a narrow, flexible strip of metal. Just the thought of picking the lock had my hands sweating inside the thin gloves. I started to poke about in what I hoped was a reasonable approximation of what my friend Dennis had taught me. After a few minutes that felt like hours, my probe met the kind of resistance that shows a bit of give. Praying the strip I was using was strong enough, I twisted it. There was a click, and the doors slowly opened out towards me.

I could see why Martin Cheetham didn't want any casual snoopers to open them. It was the last thing you'd expect to find in a conveyancing specialist's wardrobe. There were a dozen chic outfits on hangers, each covered with a transparent plastic sheath. They ranged from a cocktail dress with a froth of multicoloured tulle and sequins to an elegant business suit with pencil skirt. There was also a mac and a camel wraparound coat. On a rack on the door was an exotic collection of silk scarves ranging from Hermès to hippie-style Indian. A chest of drawers occupied the lower section of half the wardrobe. The top drawer was filled with an astonishing and luxurious collection of ladies' underwear in both silk and leather. Believe me, I mean "ladies." The second drawer contained an assortment of foam and silica gel prostheses, which I managed to sort into three categories: breasts, hips and buttocks. It also held more make-up than I've ever possessed, even as an experimenting teenager, and a selection of false nails.

The lower drawers were filled with a bizarre assortment of straps, clamps and unidentifiable bits of leather with buckles and studs. I didn't even want to start imagining how they all fitted into the strange world of Martin Cheetham's sexual life. There were also a couple of vibrators, one so large it made my eyes water just to look at it. There were, however, no more magazines like the one by the bed. I slammed the drawers shut and concentrated on the less threatening contents of the wardrobe. Along the bottom was a shelf of shoes and matching handbags. They alone must have cost the best part of a couple of grand.

I picked up the first handbag, a soft black Italian leather satchel that Alexis would have killed for. The stray thought brought me up with a jolt. Alexis! I'd completely forgotten our close encounter at the end of the road! She couldn't have anything to do with all this. I knew she couldn't, yet the little traitor voice in my head kept saying, "You don't know that. She might just have tipped him over the edge." I shook my head vigorously, like a dog emerging from a river, and carried on with my search.

The third bedroom, little more than a boxroom, had been fitted out as an office, with a battered old filing cabinet, a tatty wooden desk and a very basic PC, compatible with the one in his office so he could presumably bring stuff home. A quick search revealed where Lomax had got his documents from. Three of the four drawers in the filing cabinet were empty. The fourth held only a couple of box files filled with what appeared to be personal receipts, credit card bills and the sort of miscellaneous garbage that every householder accumulates. I riffled quickly through the pair of boxes, finding nothing of interest.

The desk had even less to offer. The drawers contained only paper, envelopes and the bizarre mixture of odds and ends that always inhabits at least one drawer in every work space. The interesting thing was what wasn't there. There wasn't a single floppy disc in the place, a serious omission given that the computer in Cheetham's home office had no hard disc drive. In other words, the computer itself had no permanent memory. Every time it was switched on, it was like a blank sheet of paper. If Lomax had cleared the discs out, I suspected it had been done without Cheetham's permission or co-operation, for if he'd been trying to get rid of incriminating material, there was no reason on earth why he'd also feel the need to dump the software programs that were necessary to make the computer work.

Musing on this, I finished my search of the office and moved downstairs, trying to avoid looking at the body. As I entered the living room, I checked my watch. I'd been in the house just under an hour. I really couldn't afford to hang around much longer. All it needed was for Nell or Lomax to come back and find me here.

As it happened, it didn't take long for me to complete my search, ending up in the kitchen, where, incidentally, neither the washing machine nor the tumble dryer contained bedding. The most useful thing I'd found was a spare set of keys in the cutlery drawer. As I let myself out of the back door, I felt an enormous sense of anticlimax. The tension that had been holding me together suddenly dissipated and I felt weak at the knees. Somehow, I found the strength to replace the bricks in something approximating the right barbecue arrangement, then I sneaked back round the house to the street, checking there was no one in sight before returning to the van. I could only hope that when the neighbours heard about Cheetham's death, none of them would remember any details about the strange van parked a few doors away from his house.

I drove home at a law-abiding speed for once. It was the traffic that was my downfall. I had to pass the Corn Exchange on my way home, and as I drove up Cateaton Street, everything ground to a complete halt. The lights at the bottom of Shude Hill had died, and the resulting rush-hour chaos brought the city centre to a standstill. It seemed like a sign from the gods, so I pulled off the main drag on to Hanging Ditch and parked the van.

Five minutes later, I was inside Martin Cheetham's office.

18

Kate Brannigan's Burglary Tip No. 3: Always burgle offices in daylight hours. People notice lights in offices at night. And people who notice lights in offices that shouldn't be lit up have a nasty habit of being security staff. However, rules are made to be broken, and besides, I wasn't the first unauthorized visitor to Martin Cheetham's office.

That much was obvious from the safe. The reproduction of Monet's *Water Lilies* that had covered it on my previous visit lay on the floor, while the door of the safe stood ajar. With a frustrated sigh, I took a look inside. I found exactly what I expected. Nothing.

I looked round the room in something approaching despair. There was enough paper in here to keep the least popular detective constable on the force busy for a month. Besides, I wasn't convinced that I would find anything enlightening. I was still pinning my hopes on Cheetham's computer files, particularly since he had the kind of scanner that would have allowed him to import a copy of any document straight into his computer. A quick check of the desk revealed the same absence of discs that I'd noted back at the house. But there was one difference here. The PC sitting on the desk had a hard disc. In other words, the chances were that the master copy of the material on the discs that had been stolen was permanently stored in the machine in front of me.

It was last resort time, so I did the obvious. I switched on the machine. It automatically loaded the system files. Then a prompt appeared, demanding input. I asked the machine to show me the headings under which it was storing stuff. In the following list, I spotted a couple of familiar software names—a word-processing package, a spreadsheet and an accounts program. The rest of the list were probably data files. First, I loaded the word-processing package which would allow me to read the data files, then I tried a directory called WORK.C. It seemed to be all the correspondence plus details of deeds on the properties currently being handled. The files were subdivided according to whether Cheetham was acting for vendor or buyer, and what stage he was up to. It was incredibly boring.

The next directory I tried was called WORK.L. When I attempted to access it, nothing happened. I tried again and nothing happened. I tried one or two other ways of getting into the directory, but there was clearly some kind of access block on it. Desperately, I searched Cheetham's drawers again, looking for a single word scribbled somewhere that might be a password for the directory, but without success. I knew that, given time, Bill or I could hack our way into the hidden files of the locked directory, but time was the one thing I wasn't sure I had.

What the hell? I'd taken so many chances already, what was one more? Closing the door on the latch behind me, I left Cheetham's office and returned to the van. I unlocked the security box welded to the floor and took out our office laptop PC. It's a portable machine, more compatible with its desktop equivalents than any married couple I know. It can store the equivalent of sixty novels. I walked back into the Corn Exchange with the fat briefcase, trying hard to look nonchalant, and returned undetected to Cheetham's office by some miracle.

Amongst the resident software on our portable's hard disc was a program that could have been designed for situations like this. It's a special file transfer kit that is used to move data at high speed between portables and desktop machines. I uncoiled the lead that would form the physical link between the two machines and plugged it in at both ends. I switched on my machine and booted up the software.

The program sends over a highly sophisticated communications program, which is then used to "steal" the files from the target machine. The big advantage of using these kits is that you leave no trace on the machine you've raided. The very process itself also often bypasses any security package that the target PC's operator has installed. The final advantage is that it's extremely fast. Ten minutes after returning to Cheetham's office, I was ready to walk out of the door with the contents of WORK.C and WORK.L firmly ensconced on my own hard disc.

There were just a couple of things I had to do first. I picked up the phone and dialled my favourite Chinese restaurant for a takeaway. Then I called Greater Manchester Police's switchboard. I calmly told the operator who answered that there was a dead body at 27 Tamarind Grove, and hung up.

The traffic had begun to clear, and I picked up my Chinese fifteen minutes later. I'd just parked the van on the drive of my bungalow when I remembered I hadn't checked the tapes from the surveillance. I had two choices. Either I could go indoors and eat my Chinese, preferably with Richard, then, once I'd got all comfy and relaxed, I could schlep all the way over to Stockport and do the business. Or I could go now, and hope that there was nothing that would require my presence there all night. Being what Richard would describe as a boring old fart, I decided to finish the day's work before I settled down. Besides, my bruises were aching, and I knew that if I sank into the comfort of my own sofa, I might never get up again unless it was to crawl into a hot bath.

The drive to Stockport was the Chinese aroma torture. There's nothing worse than the smell of hot and sour soup and salt and pepper ribs when nothing's stayed in your stomach since breakfast and you can't have them. What made it even more frustrating was that there was no one home in my nice little staked-out semi. And, according to my bug, no one had been home either. The phone had rung another couple of times, and that was the sum total of my illegal surveillance.

When I finally got home, the offer of a share in my Chinese distracted Richard from a pirate radio bhangra station he'd been listening to in the course of duty. Sometimes I think his job's even worse than mine. I brought him up to date with my adventures, which added a spice to dinner that even the Chinese had never thought of.

"So he topped himself, then? Or was it one of those sleazy deaths by sexual misadventure?" he asked, doing his impersonation of a tabloid journo as he poked through the *char siu* pork to get at the bean sprouts below.

"It looks like it. But I don't think he did," I said.

"Why's that, Supersleuth?"

"A collection of little things that individually are insignificant, but taken together make me feel very uneasy," I replied.

"Want to run it past me? See if it's just your imagination?" Richard offered. I knew he really meant: because you're too well brought up to talk with your mouth full, that means there will be more for me. I gave in gracefully, because he was quite right, I did want to check that my suspicions had some genuine foundation.

"OK," I said. "Point one. I take Nell to be Martin Cheetham's girlfriend, judging by the body language on the two occasions I saw them together. She was in the house for about twenty minutes, thirty max, before Lomax arrived. Now if she and Cheetham were getting it on together, that might explain why he was in his drag. But if they were busy having a little loving, what was going down with Lomax and the files?"

"Maybe he just sneaked in and helped himself," Richard suggested.

"No, he didn't have a key. Someone let him in, but I couldn't see who. I'm convinced Lomax cleared the files out, without Cheetham's co-operation."

"Why?" Richard asked.

"Because if Cheetham had simply been trying to get incriminating evidence off the premises, he'd only have dumped discs with data on. He wouldn't have ditched the discs with the software programs, because he'd have known enough to realize that a computer with no discs at all is a hell of a lot more suspicious than one with only software and no data," I explained. Richard nodded in agreement.

"Also, the bedding was clean. It had been changed since the last time the bed had been slept in or bonked on. And there was no bedding in the linen basket or the washing machine or the tumble dryer either. So where are the dirty sheets? Now if Cheetham and Nell had been having a cuddle, or whatever it is that transvestite sadomasochists do in bed, there would be forensic traces of her on the bedding. These days, every television viewer knows about things like that. So if she and Lomax had actually killed Cheetham and wanted to make it look like an accidental death during some bizarre sexual fantasy, they'd have to make it look like he'd been alone with his dirty magazine. And that's the only explanation I can find."

"Maybe he's got a cleaner who comes in and takes his washing home with her," Richard suggested, sharing his own fantasy.

"Maybe, but I don't think so. The linen basket in the bedroom had dirty clothes in it. Then there's another point about the computers. Whoever cleared out the office safe and took the discs from there, it wasn't Cheetham himself."

"What makes you say that?" Richard asked. "I mean, if he was starting to get a bit unnerved by you poking around, wouldn't he try to get rid of anything incriminating?"

"You'd think so. But it was his computer. Whoever did the clearing up of evidence, it was someone who didn't understand that the discs were just the back-up copies of whatever was on the hard disc. They didn't understand about the hard disc, because they left the data on it."

Richard shook his head. "I don't know, Brannigan. It's all a bit thin. I mean, ever since you solved Moira's murder back in the spring, you keep seeing suspicious deaths everywhere. Look at the way you got all wound up about that client who died after he changed his will, and it turned out he'd had a heart condition for years, nothing iffy about it."

"But this is suspicious, even you've got to admit that," I protested.

"I could give you an explanation that would cover the facts," Richard said, helping himself to the last of the prawn wontons.

"Go on then," I challenged, convinced I could unravel any theory his twisted mind could come up with.

Richard swallowed his mouthful, leaned back in his seat and polished his glasses in a parody of the learned academics who pontificate on TV. "OK. He's had this showdown with you then he's rushed off to meet Lomax. As a result of all this, he's really wound up, but he thinks he's handled it beautifully and he deserves a treat. So he arranges that what's-her-name, the girlfriend, is going to come around for a bit of afternoon delight. Now, from what you've told me about his little treasure trove, who knows what that pair get up to when they're getting their rocks off? Just supposing he's staged this tableau to get her going—he's all done up in his drag and tied up and pretending to hang himself when she arrives. Only it gets out of hand and he snuffs it. OK so far?"

I nodded, reluctantly. Certainly, Cheetham had had enough time alone in the house for that scenario to be feasible. "OK," I sighed.

"So what would your reaction be if you arrived at your boyfriend's house to find him hanging dead from the banisters in a frock? Especially if you knew he was into some hooky business that was going to come on top now he's popped his clogs?

Remember, for all you know, the lovely lady could be right up to her eyeballs in his little schemes. You'd want to cover your back, wouldn't you?" He gave me that smile of his, the one that got me in this mess in the first place.

"You would indeed," I conceded.

"So Lomax turns up like a bat out of hell and the pair of them clear out everything that might be remotely connected to Cheetham's little rackets. Lomax takes off with all the incriminating documents and what's-her-name . . . ?" He gave me an inquiring look.

"Nell," I prompted him.

"Yeah, Little Nell, how could I forget?"

"This is no time for obscene rugby songs," I said.

"Wrong sport, Brannigan. *You'll Never Walk Alone* is more my speed than *The Ball of Kirriemuir*. Anyway, as you so correctly pointed out, any fool knows these days that forensic science could place Little Nell not just at the scene of the crime but in the bed if they'd bonked in it since the last time the sheets were changed. She does nothing more than take off the dirty linen so she can wash it in private. Meanwhile, Lomax goes down Cheetham's office and clears out the safe and has it away on his toes with the computer discs in the office. Pick the holes in that," he ended triumphantly.

I thought about it for a moment, then I jumped to my feet. "Hold everything," I said on my way through to my spare room, which doubles as study and computer room. I pulled out a book on forensic medicine written for the popular market that Richard had bought me for my birthday as a kind of joke. I ran my finger down the index and turned to the section on body temperature. "Got it!" I shouted. Richard appeared in the doorway, looking crestfallen. I pointed to the relevant sentence, "'The rule of thumb applied by pathologists is that a clothed body will cool in air at between two and five degrees Fahrenheit per hour', it says here," I said. "And, when I touched him, he was the same temperature as I was, near as dammit. No way was he between four and ten degrees colder than me, which he should have been if he'd died when you suggested."

Richard took the book from me and read the relevant section. As usual, the journalist in him took over and he found all sorts of fascinating things he simply had to read about. Leaving him to it, I started to clear up the debris of dinner. I'd just dumped the tinfoil containers in the bin when he reappeared, brandishing the book with a look of of pure triumph.

"You should have kept reading," he said sanctimoniously. "That way, you wouldn't have given me half a tale. Look," he added, pointing to a paragraph on the following page.

"'Typically, death by asphyxiation raises the body temperature. This must be taken into account in estimates of the time of death, and is known to have caused confusion in some historical cases'." I read. "Bollocks," I said. "OK, you win," I sighed. "I'm letting my imagination run away with me."

"So you accept my theory?" Richard asked, a look of total disbelief on his face.

"I guess so," I admitted.

"There's one good thing about it," he said. "I mean, I know I've just deprived you of all the excitement of chasing a murderer, but look on the bright side. It puts Alexis in the clear."

"I never thought for a moment she wasn't in the clear," I lied frostily.

"Course you didn't," Richard said, with a broad wink. "Anyway, now I've saved you all the work of a murder hunt, do I get a reward?"

I checked my body out for bruises and stiffness. I was beginning to heal, no doubt about it. I leaned into Richard's warmth and murmured, "Your place or mine?"

19

The bulging eyes stared fixedly at me, the blue lips twitching some message I could neither hear nor read. I moved back, but the face kept following me. I shouted at it, and the sound of my voice woke me up with the kind of staring-eyed shock that sets the adrenalin racing through the veins. The clock said six, Richard was lying on his stomach, breathing not quite heavily enough to be called snoring, and I was wide awake with Martin Cheetham's face accusing me.

Even if he hadn't been murdered, Nell and Lomax had behaved unforgivably, always supposing there was anyone still around to forgive them. Nell's actions in particular sickened me. I know I couldn't behave like that if someone I'd been lovers with was hanging dead in the hall. There must have been a lot at stake for Nell and Lomax to have had the nerve to carry off their cover-up and, although the voice of reason said it was none of my business, I wanted to get to the bottom of it.

Since I was awake anyway, I decided to do something useful. I slipped out of Richard's bed and cut through the conservatory to my house. A steaming shower banished the morning stiffness that still lingered in my muscles, and a strong cup of coffee kick-started my brain. I chose a pair of bottle green trousers and a matching sweater to go under the russet padded silk blouson that I'd picked up for a song on Strangeways market.

It was a quarter to seven when I parked outside Alexis's house. As I'd expected, her car was still in the drive. I knew her routine of old. Up at six, in the bath with a pot of coffee, the phone and her notebook at five past. Morning calls to the cops, then out of the bath at half past. Then toast and the tabloids. I estimated she'd be finishing her second slice of toast about now. Unfortunately, she wouldn't be in the office at seven *this* morning.

I looked through the kitchen window as I knocked on the door. Alexis dropped her toast at the sound of the knock. I waved and grinned at her. With a look of resignation, she opened the door.

"I have a question for you," I announced.

"Come in, why don't you?" Alexis said as I walked across the kitchen and switched the kettle on.

"When you left Tamarind Grove yesterday afternoon, did you already know that Martin Cheetham was dead?" I asked conversationally, spooning coffee into a mug.

Alexis's face froze momentarily. Always pale, she seemed to go sheet white. "How the hell did you know about that?" she asked intensely. If she used that tone of voice professionally, she'd get all sorts of confessions she wasn't looking for.

"I don't suppose you remember a red Little Rascal van that you nearly drove into, but that was me. I remember it particularly because for a brief moment, I wondered what Bill would say if I wrote off a second company vehicle inside a week," I said, trying to lighten the atmosphere a bit.

"I might have known," Alexis sighed. "If you're brewing up, I'll have another cup."

I made the coffees and said, "I'm listening."

Alexis lit a cigarette and took a couple of deep drags before she spoke. I sometimes think it must be lovely to have an instant trank permanently to hand. Then I think about my lungs.

"I'd had a couple of drinks at lunchtime. I wasn't pissed, just a bit belligerent. So I bought a can of spray paint. I was going to spray some rude graffiti on Cheetham's house," she said, looking as embarrassed as she must have felt. "Anyway, I got there and there was his car in the drive. I thought about spraying 'You dirty rat' on the bonnet, then I realized if he was home I might as well give him a piece of my mind. So I rang the doorbell. There was no reply, so I looked through the letter box. And I saw these feet, legs, just dangling there."

"Tell me about it," I said with feeling, remembering my own experience.

"So I took off like a bat out of hell," Alexis said, dropping her head so that her haystack of unruly black hair hid her face.

"You didn't phone the cops?" I asked.

"How could I? I didn't have any legit reason for being there. I didn't even know who the body was. And I couldn't have done it anonymously, could I? Half the cops in Manchester know who it is on the phone the minute I open my gob." She was right. Anyone who'd ever spoken to Alexis would remember that smoky Liverpudlian voice.

"I'm sorry," I said. "I should have rung you about it last night. I was just too wiped out. So, when did you realize it was Cheetham?"

"When I did my calls this morning. They told me about it as a routine non-suspicious death. If he hadn't been a solicitor, I doubt they'd even have mentioned it. It made my stomach turn over, I can tell you."

"Any details?" I asked.

"Not a lot. Unattributed, I got that he was wearing women's clothing and playing bondage games. According to the DI at the scene, he had a proper little torture chamber in his wardrobe. They reckon he died some time yesterday afternoon. He didn't have any form for sexual offences. Not so much as a caution. He's not even on their list of people they know get up to naughties in their spare time. They don't think there was anyone else involved, and they're not treating it as a suspicious death. They don't even think it was suicide, just an accident. All I can say is thank God he didn't have nosy neighbours, or else the lads might be asking me what exactly I was doing kicking his door in yesterday afternoon." Alexis managed a faint smile. "Especially if they knew I had a private eye working on how to recover the five grand he helped to con me out of."

"You weren't the only person who was there yesterday," I said, and went on to fill her in on the events of the afternoon. "I was convinced they'd killed him," I added. "But Richard persuaded me that I was just seeing dragons in the flames."

"So what happens now?" Alexis asked.

"Well, theoretically, we could just ignore the whole thing, and I could still follow Lomax like you asked me to and try to get some money back from him. The problem is that now Cheetham's dead, I'm afraid Lomax might try to deny any criminal involvement in the whole thing and blame it all on Cheetham."

"You don't really think he'd get away with that, do you?" Alexis demanded, lighting up another cigarette.

"I don't honestly know," I admitted. "Personally, I think there's been a lot more going down between Lomax and Cheetham than we know about. And if there's any proof of a connection other than the fact that I know I've seen them together, it could be buried in the other stuff. So I want to keep digging."

Alexis nodded. "So how can I help?"

There are parts of Greater Manchester where it wouldn't be too big a shock to encounter a shop catering for the needs of transsexuals and transvestites. A back street in Oldham isn't one of them. I find it hard to imagine anyone in Oldham doing anything more sexually radical than the missionary position, which only goes to show what a limited imagination I have. The locals clearly didn't have a problem with Trances, since there was nothing discreet about the shopfront, sandwiched rather unfortunately as it was between a butcher's and a junk shop.

On the way over, Alexis had told me about the shop and its owner. Cassandra Cliff had endured a brief spell of notoriety in the gutter press a few years previously when some muck-raking journo had discovered that the actress who was one of the regulars in the country's favourite soap opera was in fact a male-to-female transsexual. In the flurry of "Sex Swap Soap Star" stories that followed, it emerged that Cassandra, previously Kevin, had been living as a woman for a dozen years, and that no one among cast or production team had a clue that she wasn't biologically of the same gender as the gossipy chip-shop owner she played. Of course, the production company of *Northerners* denied that the uncovering of Cassandra's secret would make any difference whatsoever to their attitude to her.

Two months later, Cassandra's character perished in a tragic accident when the extension her husband was building to their terraced house collapsed on her. The production company blandly denied they had dumped her because of her sex change, but that didn't much help Cassandra, on the scrap heap at thirty-seven. "She didn't let them get away with it," Alexis said. "She sold her own inside story to one of the Sunday tabloids, dishing the dirt on all the nation's idols. Then with the money she set up Trances, and a monthly magazine for transvestites and transsexuals. She's got so much bottle, Kate. You can't help respecting Cassie."

Alexis skirted the one-way system and cut round the back of the magistrates' court. Modern concrete boxes and grimy red brick terraced shops were mixed higgledy-piggledy along almost every street, a seemingly random and grotesque assortment that filled me with the desire to construct a cage in the middle of it and make the town planners live there for a week among the chip papers blowing in the wind and the empty soft-drink cans rattling along the gutters. I tried to ignore the depressing townscape and asked, "So how come you know her so well? What's she got to do with the crime beat?"

"I interviewed her a couple of times for features when she was still playing Margie Grimshaw in *Northerners*. We got on really well. Then after the dust settled and she set up Trances, I gave her a call and asked if we could do a piece about the shop. She wasn't keen, but I let her have copy approval, and she liked what I wrote. Now, we do lunch about once a month. She's got such a different grapevine from any of my other contacts. It's amazing what she picks up," Alexis said, parking in a quiet side street of terraced houses. It could have been the set for *Northerners*.

"And she passes stuff on to you, does she?" I asked.

"I suspect she's highly selective. I know that after what happened to her, she's desperately protective of other people in the same boat. But if she can help, she will."

I followed Alexis round the corner into one of those streets that isn't quite part of the town centre, but would like to think it is. I glanced in the window as we entered. The only clue that Trances was any different from a hundred other boutiques was the prominent sign that said, "We specialize in large sizes. Shoes up to size 12." The door itself provided the warning for the uninitiated. "Specialists in supplies for transvestites and trans-sexuals" was painted on the glass in neat red letters at the eye level of the average woman.

I followed Alexis in. The shop was large, and had an indefinable air of seediness. The décor was cream and pink, the pink tending slightly too far to the candy floss end of the spectrum. The dresses and suits that were suspended from racks that ran the full length of the shop had the cumulative effect of being over the top, both in style and colour. I suspect that the seediness came from the glass cases that lined the wall behind the counter. They contained the kind of prostheses and lingerie I remembered only too well from Martin Cheetham's secret collection. In one corner, there was a rack of magazines. Without examining them too closely, the ones that weren't copies of Cassandra's magazine *Trances* had that combination of garishness and coyness on the cover that marks soft porn.

The person behind the counter was also clearly a client. The size of the hands and the Adam's apple were the giveaways. Apart from that, it would have been hard to tell. The make-up was a little on the heavy side, but I could think of plenty of pubs in the area where that wouldn't even earn a second glance. "Is Cassie in?" Alexis asked.

The assistant gave a slight frown, sizing us up and clearly wondering if we were tourists. "Are you a friend of Miss Cliff, madam?" she asked.

"Would you tell her Alexis would like a word, if she's got a few minutes?" Alexis said, responding in the same slightly camp vein. I hoped the conversation with Cassie wasn't going to run along those lines. I can do pompous, I can do threatening, I can even do "OK, yah," but the one style I can't keep up without exploding into giggles is high camp.

The assistant picked up a phone and pressed an intercom button. "Cassandra? I have a lady with me called Alexis who would like a moment of your time, if it's convenient," she said. Then she nodded. "I'll tell her. Bye for now," she added. She replaced the handset and said decorously, "Miss Cliff will see you now. If you'd care to take the door at the back of the shop and follow the stairs . . ."

"It's all right, I know the way," Alexis said, heading past the clothes racks. "Thanks for your help."

Cassandra Cliff's office looked like something out of *Interiors*. It could have been a blueprint for the career woman who wants to remind people that as well as being successful she is still feminine. The office furniture—a row of filing cabinets, a low coffee table and two desks, one complete with Apple Mac—was limed ash, stained grey. A pair of grey leather two-seater sofas occupied one corner. The carpet was a dusty pink, a colour echoed in the Austrian blinds that softened the lines of the room. The walls were decorated with black and white stills of the set and stars of *Northerners*. A tall vase of burgundy carnations provided a vivid splash of colour. The overall effect was stylish and relaxed, the two adjectives that sprang into my mind when I first met Cassandra Cliff.

She wore a linen suit with a straight skirt and no lapels. It was the colour of an egg yolk. Her mandarin-collared blouse was a bright, clear sapphire blue. I know it sounds hideous, but on her it was glorious. Her ash blonde hair was cut short but full on top, shaped, gelled and lacquered till it resembled something out of the Museum of Modern Art. The make-up was the kind of discreet job that looks completely natural.

As Alexis introduced us, Cassie caught me studying her and the corners of her mouth twitched in a knowing smile. I could feel my ears going red, and I returned her smile sheepishly. "I know," she said. "You can't help it. You have to ask yourself, 'If I didn't know, would I have guessed?' Everyone does it, Kate, don't feel embarrassed about it."

Completely disarmed, I allowed myself to be settled on one of the sofas with Alexis while Cassie ordered coffee then sat down opposite us, crossing a pair of elegant legs that certain women of my acquaintance would cheerfully have killed for. "So," Cassie said. "A private investigator and a crime reporter. It can't be me you're after. The jackals that Alexis hangs out with left me not so much as a vertebra in my cupboard, never mind a skeleton. So, I ask myself, who?"

"Does the name Martin Cheetham mean anything to you?" Alexis asked.

Cassie uncrossed her legs then recrossed them in the opposite direction. "In what context?" she said.

"In a business context. Your business, not his."

Cassie shrugged elegantly. "Not everyone who uses our services likes to be known by their real name. You could say that their real name is what they're trying to escape from."

"He died yesterday," Alexis said bluntly.

Before Cassie could respond, a teenage girl came in with coffee. At least, I'm pretty certain it was a girl. The process of pouring our coffee gave Cassie plenty of time to recover from the news. "How did he die?" she asked. In spite of her conversational tone, for the first time since we'd arrived she looked wary.

"He was wearing women's clothing and hanging from the banister in his home. The police think it was an accident," Alexis said. I was content to sit back. Cassie was her contact, and she knew how to play her.

"Do I take it that you don't agree with them?" Cassie asked, moving her glance from one to the other of us.

"Oh, I think they're probably right. It's just that he ripped me off to the tune of five grand a few weeks ago, and I'm trying to get it back. Which means trying to untangle what he was up to, and who with," Alexis said determinedly.

"Five thousand pounds? My God, Alexis, no wonder you're working with Kate." Cassie smiled, then sighed. "Yes, I knew Martin Cheetham. He bought a lot of stuff from Trances, and he was a regular at our monthly Readers' Socials. Martina, he called himself. Not terribly original. And before you ask, I don't think he had any particular friends among the group. Certainly, I don't know of anyone he saw socially between meetings. He wasn't someone who appeared to find it easy to open up. A lot of men really blossom when they're cross-dressing, as if they've suddenly become themselves. Martina wasn't like that. It was almost as if it was an obsession that he had to indulge rather than a release. Does that make any sense to you?"

I nodded. "It fits the picture I have in my mind, certainly. Tell me, was he a particularly effective woman? I mean, without wishing to be offensive, some men are never going to look like anything other than a man in women's clothes. On the other hand, it's hard to imagine that you were ever anything other than a woman. Where on the spectrum did Cheetham fall?"

"Thank you," Cassie said. "Martina was actually superb. He had a lot of natural advantages—he wasn't particularly tall, he had small hands and feet, quite fine bones and good skin. But the real clincher was his clothes. He could get into a standard size sixteen, and he didn't seem to care how much he spent on clothes. In fact . . ." Cassie got up and went over to one of the filing cabinets. She returned a moment later with a photograph album.

She started flicking through the pages. "I'm sure he's on a couple of these. I took a couple of rolls of film at the Christmas Social." She stopped at a photograph of a couple of women leaning against a bar, laughing. "There, on the left. That's Martina."

I studied the picture and realized where I'd seen Martina Cheetham before.

20

I sat in the Ford Fiesta listening to *Coronation Street* on head-phones. Mary Wright had returned to the house I was bugging, her appetite for soap opera unabated. The mysterious Brian was still nowhere to be seen or heard, however. Perhaps he didn't exist. At least his absence freed me from having to listen to domestic chitchat, which meant I could concentrate on trying to crack the password that would let me into Martin Cheetham's secret directory.

Alexis had been as puzzled as me when I revealed where I'd seen Martin Cheetham in his drag before. The photograph had jogged my memory as the distorted face of the corpse could never have done. But there was no mistaking it. The elegant woman who'd been looking at cheap terraced houses in DKL Estates was Martin Cheetham. No wonder he'd taken off like a bat out of hell at the sight of me. Whatever their little game was, he must have thought I was on to him, which also explained why he'd gone into panic mode when I paid my second visit to his office. If I'd needed proof that Cheetham and Lomax were up to something a lot more significant than the land fiddle, I had it now. The only question was, what?

As the familiar theme music from *Coronation Street* died away, a Vauxhall Cavalier drove slowly past me and pulled up outside my target. When I saw Ted's favourite salesman was driving it, I couldn't help myself. I punched the air and shouted, "Yo!" just like some zitty adolescent watching the American football on Channel 4. Luckily, Jack McCafferty wasn't interested in anything other than the house where he intended to sell a state-of-the-art Colonial Conservatory. I'd been right! The pattern was working out, just as I'd anticipated.

What I hadn't expected was Jack's passenger. Unfolding himself from the passenger seat came a sight to quicken Shelley's pulse. Ted Barlow stretched himself to his full height, then held a quick conference with his ace salesman. Tonight, Jack McCafferty's designer suit looked almost black under the street lights, his flamboyant silk tie like a flag of success. His brown curls had the glossy sheen of a well-groomed setter. Beside him, Ted looked more like the assistant than the boss. He wore the only suit I'd ever seen him in, and the tight knot of his striped tie was askew. Shelley would never have let one of her kids out of the door looking like that. I didn't need to be Gipsy Rose Lee to predict big changes for Ted Barlow in the months to come.

The two men marched up the path. As Jack's hand reached out for the bell, I experienced the strange sensation of hearing it ring in my ears. The television was abruptly turned off, just as I was getting interested in the latest episode in the steamy series of instant coffee adverts. Unfortunately, because there was a wall between the bug and the door, all I could hear of the doorstep exchange was the murmur of voices, but it became clear as the three of them entered the living room.

"What a delightful room!" I heard Jack exclaim.

"Isn't it?" Ted echoed, with as much conviction as a famous actress endorsing the rejuvenating powers of a brand of soap.

"We like it," the woman's voice said.

"Well, Mrs Wright, if I might introduce ourselves to you, my name is Jack McCafferty and I'm the chief sales executive of Colonial Conservatories, which is why your telephone inquiry about our range was passed on to me. And you are very privileged tonight to have with you my colleague Ted Barlow, who is the managing director of our company. Ted likes to take a personal interest in selected customers, so he can keep his finger on the pulse of what you, the public, actually want from a conservatory, so that Colonial Conservatories can maintain its position as a market leader in the field." It flowed virtually without a pause. In spite of myself, I was impressed. I could picture Ted standing there, awkwardly shifting from foot to foot, failing dismally in his attempt to look like a Colossus of Commerce.

"I see," said Mary Wright. "Won't you sit down, gentlemen?"

As soon as his backside hit the chair, Jack was off and running, his pitch fluent and flawless as he sucked Mary Wright into the purchase of a conservatory she didn't need at a price she couldn't afford for a house that wasn't hers. Every now and again, he sought a response from her, and she chimed in as obediently as the triangle player in the orchestra counting the bars till the next tinkling note. They established that her husband was working abroad, what kind of conservatory she favoured, her monthly incomings and outgoings. Jack conducted the whole exposition as if it were a symphony.

Eventually, Ted was despatched out the back with a tape measure and notebook. That was when it really got interesting. "Slight problem," Jack said in a low voice. "Ted's having aggravation with the bank."

"You mean, because of us?" Mary Wright asked.

"Probably. Anyway, bottom line is, I can't get a finance deal through the usual channels. We're going to have to arrange the finance ourselves, but that shouldn't be too hard. I've got the names of a couple of brokerages where they don't ask too many questions. The only thing we'll lose out on is the finance company kick back to me, but we'll just have to live with that. I'm only warning you, because the close will be a bit different. OK?" he said, as laid back as if he was asking for a second cup of tea.

"Sure, I'll busk it. But listen, Jack, if the bank's being difficult, maybe we should pack it in before it starts getting dangerous," the woman said.

"Look, Liz, there's no way they could trace it back to us. We've covered our tracks perfectly. I agree, we should quit while we're ahead. But we've already got the next two up and running. Let's see them through, then we'll take a break, OK? Go off to the sun and spend some of the loot?" Jack said reassuringly. If I'd have been her, I'd probably have fallen for it too. He had the real salesman's voice, all honey and reassurance. If he'd become a surgeon, he'd have had sacks of mail every Christmas from adoring patients.

"OK. Are you coming back here tonight?" she asked.

"How could I stay away?" he parried.

"Then we'll talk about it later." Whatever else she was going to say was cut off by the return of Ted.

"If you'll just give me a minute with the old pocket calculator, I'll give you a price on the unit you'd decided on," Ted said. The presumptive close.

The price Ted quoted made my eyes cross. Of course, Liz/Mary didn't turn a hair. "I see," she said.

"Normally, we could offer you our own financial package, sponsored by one of the major clearing banks," Jack said. "Unfortunately, we at Colonial Conservatories are the victims of our own success, and we have surpassed our target figures for this quarter. As a result, the finance company aren't in a position to supply any more cash to our customers, because of course they have limits themselves and, unlike us, they have people looking over their shoulders to make sure they don't exceed those limits. But what I would suggest is that you consult a mortgage broker and arrange to remortgage for an amount that will cover the installation of your conservatory," he added persuasively. "It's the most effective way of utilizing the equity you have tied up in your home."

"What about a second mortgage? Wouldn't that do just as well?" Liz/Mary asked.

Ted cleared his throat. "I think you'll find, Mrs Wright, that most lenders prefer a remortgage, especially bearing in mind that our house prices up here in the North West have started dropping a tad. You see, if there were to be any problems in

the future and the house had to be sold, sometimes it happens
that there isn't enough money left in the pot for the lender of
the second mortgage after the first lender has been paid off, if
you see what I mean. And then the holder of the second charge
doesn't have any way of getting his money back, if you follow
me. And lenders are very keen on knowing they could get their
cash back if push comes to shove, so they mostly prefer you to get
a remortgage that pays off the first mortgage and leaves you with
a few bob left over." I couldn't see Ted getting a job presenting
The Money Programme, but he'd put it clearly enough. What a pity
he'd wasted it on a pair of crooks who'd forgotten more than
he ever knew about property loans and how to exploit them.

"So what happens now?" the woman asked.

"Well, you have to talk to a mortgage broker and arrange
this remortgage. And of course, if you need any advice filling in
the forms, don't hesitate to call me. I could fill these things in in
my sleep. Then, as soon as you get confirmation of the remortgage, let us know and we'll have your conservatory installed
within the week," Jack said confidently.

"As quickly as that? Oh, that's wonderful! It'll be in when my
husband comes home for Christmas," she exclaimed. Shame, really.
She could have been earning an honest living treading the boards.

"No problem," Jack said.

Ten minutes later, Jack and Ted were walking back to
the car, slapping each other on the back. Poor sod, I thought. I
wasn't relishing the revelation that the person responsible for the
wrecking of his business was his good buddy Jack. The whole
thing had taken just over an hour. I reckoned that in a dozen
of those hours spread over the last year, Liz and Jack must have
cleared the best part of half a million quid. It was gobsmacking.
The most gobsmacking thing about it was how simple it all was.
I still had a few loose ends to tie up, but I had a pretty clear
picture now of how they had scammed their way to a fortune.

Since Jack had promised he'd be back later, I decided to stay
put. It was a freezing cold night, frost forming on the roofs of the

parked cars, and my feet were like ice. I knew I couldn't endure a couple more hours of that, so I nipped back to the van, swapped my thin-soled court shoes for a pair of thick sports socks and my Reeboks. The feeling returned to my feet almost as soon as I tied my laces. Wonderful invention, trainers. The only problem comes when you go striding into an important business meeting, done up to the nines in your best suit, then you look down and realize that instead of your chic Italian shoes, you're still wearing the Reeboks you drove there in. I know, I was that soldier.

Left to her own devices, Liz was clearly lost without the box. We caught the tail-end of the nine o'clock news, the weather (the usual tidings of comfort and joy; freezing fog in the Midlands, ground frost in the north, rain tomorrow), then a dire American mini-series started. I wished I could change channels. Instead, I turned the receiver volume down low enough to tune out anything other than phone calls or conversations and opened up the laptop.

I'd tried all the obvious ones. Martin, Martina, Cheetham, Tamarind, Lomax, Nell, Harris, scam, land, deeds, titles, secret, locked, private, drag, Dietrich, Bassey, Garland, Marilyn, password. No joy. I was running out of inspiration when my phone rang. "Hello?" I said.

"Kate? Alexis." As if she needed to tell me. "Listen, I had a brainwave."

My heart sank. "What?" I asked.

"I remembered that the *Sunday Star*'s got a reporter called Gerry Carter who lives in Buxton. Now, I've never actually met the guy, on account of the Sundays don't usually hang out with the pack, but I dug his number out of a mate of his and gave him a call, hack to hack."

I was interested now I realized her brainwave didn't involve me in anything illegal or life-threatening. "And did he have anything useful to say?"

"He knows Brian Lomax. In fact, he lives about five houses down from Lomax." Alexis paused to let that sink in.

"And?" I asked.

"I think I know who the mystery woman is."

"Alexis, you already have one hundred per cent of my attention. Stop tantalizing me as if I was a bloody-minded news editor. Cough it!" I demanded, frustrated.

"Right. You remember we saw two names on the electoral roll? And we assumed the other one was his wife? Well, it's not. According to Gerry, Lomax's wife left him a couple of years ago. In his words, 'Once she'd installed flounced Austrian blinds at every window and redecorated the place from top to bottom, there was nothing else for her to do. So she shagged Lomax's brickie and ran off to some Greek island with him.' Unquote." Alexis chuckled. "Where presumably she is complaining about the shortage of windows to clothe in frilly chintz, always assuming Laura Ashley's opened a branch on Lesbos. Anyway, once the pair of them had done their disappearing act, Lomax's sister moved in with him, on account of it's a bloody big house for one bloke on his own, and she'd just sold her own house to raise the capital to start her own business." I could hear the sound of Alexis dragging smoke into her long-suffering respiratory tract.

"Carry on, I'm fascinated," I said.

"D'you remember the second name on the electoral roll?"

"Not off the top of my head," I confessed. Embarrassing, isn't it? The short-term memory's going already, and me only twenty-seven.

"Eleanor. And what's Nell short for?"

"Lomax's *sister,*" I breathed. "Of course. Which would explain how they met in the first place. It would even explain why Martin Cheetham needed more money. She's an expensive-looking woman; I can't see her settling for suburbia with a fortnight on the Costa Brava once a year. This business of hers—did your mate say what it was?"

"He did. She owns one of those small, select boutiques where the assistants sneer at you if you're more than a size eight and you've got less than five hundred pounds to spend. It's in the main shopping arcade, apparently. Called Enchantments, would you believe?"

"I would. Great work, Alexis. If they ever get round to firing you, I'm sure Mortensen and Brannigan could put the odd day's work your way," I said.

"So what now?" she demanded.

I sighed. "Can you leave it with me? I know that doesn't sound very helpful, but something I've been working on for a week now is about to come on top. With a bit of luck, I'll have it all wrapped up by tomorrow afternoon, and I promise that as soon as I'm clear I'll follow this up. How's that?"

"I suppose it'll have to do," Alexis said. "It's OK, Kate, I knew you were tight for time when I asked you to take this on. I can't start complaining now. You get to it when you can, and I'll try to be patient."

That I really wanted to see. We chatted for a few minutes about the stories Alexis was currently working on, then she signed off for the night. I turned my attention back to the computer. At least Alexis had given me a couple of fresh ideas. I typed in ELEANOR, and the screen filled magically with a list of file names. Some days you eat the bear.

I'd only just started working through the files when the Cavalier returned. Jack drove straight into the garage, and closed the door behind him. I turned up the volume control, and a couple of minutes later he and Liz were doing the kind of kissing, fondling and greeting that brings a blush to the cheeks of even the most hard-nosed private eye. Unless, of course, you're the kind who gets off on aural sex.

However, it soon became clear that Jack and Liz had different things on their minds. While he seemed intent on making the earth move, she was more concerned about where the next fifty grand was coming from. "Jack, cut it out, wait a minute, I want to talk to you," she said. And all the rest. Eventually, it sounded like she broke free from the clinch, judging by the fact that her voice was noticeably fainter than his. "Listen, we need to talk about this finance problem. What's gone wrong?"

"I don't know, exactly. All I know is that when I came into work tonight, Ted told me to stop writing finance proposals. He said the finance company were having problems processing applications, and that there was a temporary block on new business. But he was about as convincing as the Labour Party manifesto. I think what's really happened is that they've had enough of defaulting remortgages," he said, his tone so casual I had to remind myself he was the man behind the problem. The man who faced at least a couple of years behind the picket fence of an open prison if he was ever nailed.

Liz wasn't anything like as cool. "We're going to have to stop this, Jack. The bank won't just leave it at that. They'll call the Fraud Squad in, we'll go to prison!" she whined.

"No we won't. Look, when we started this, we knew it couldn't last forever. We always knew that one day, the finance company would notice that too many of Ted Barlow's conservatory customers were defaulting on their mortgages, and we'd have to pull out," he said reasonably. "I just didn't think they'd go straight to the bank before they warned Ted."

"I always said we should spread the risk and go to outside lenders," she whinged. "I said it was crazy to use a finance company that's a subsidiary of Ted's bank."

"We went through that at the time," Jack said patiently. "And the reasons for doing it my way haven't changed. For one, we're not involving anybody else. It's just you, me and a form that goes to a finance company who knew Colonial were a sound firm. For two, it's faster, because we never had to trail round mortgage brokers and building societies trying to find a lender, and run the risk of being spotted by somebody that knows me. And for three, I've been raking in commissions on the kick backs from the finance company, which has earned us a fair few quid on top of what the scam has made us. And doing it my way is why we're still safe, even though Ted's bank's put the shaft into him. There's no obvious pattern, that's the thing. Don't forget, we're in the middle of a recession. There'll be real mortgage defaulters in there as well as the ones we've pulled," he said reassuringly. It was really frustrating not being able to see their faces and body language.

"Except that they'll still have conservatories attached to their houses. They won't have been up all night once a month dismantling a conservatory and loading it into a van so that Jack McCafferty can spirit it away and sell it on to some unsuspecting punter who thinks they're getting a real bargain! I'm telling you, Jack, it's time to pull out!"

"Calm down," he urged her. "There's no hurry. It'll take them months to sort this mess out. Look, this one's in the home stretch. We can go and see a mortgage broker tomorrow and blag our way into a remortgage on this place, no bother. Where are we up to with the other two?"

"Just let me check. You know I don't trust myself to keep it all in my head," she said accusingly. I heard the sound of briefcase locks snapping open and the rustle of paper. "10 Cherry Tree Way, Warrington. You've done the credit check, I've got the new bank account set up, I've taken off the mail redirect, and I've got the mortgage account details. 31 Lark Rise, Davenport. All we've got on that is the credit check. I cancelled the mail redirect yesterday." I really had got a result tonight. The two addresses Liz had just read out were identical with the ones Rachel Lieberman had already given me.

"So can we speed them up? Bring them in ahead of schedule?" Jack asked.

"We can try to speed things up at our end. But if we're going to have to find outside mortgagers to finance the remortgages, that's almost certainly going to slow the process down," Liz said. I could hear the worry in her voice, in spite of the tinny quality of the bug's relay.

"Don't worry," Jack soothed. "It's all going to be OK."

Not if I had anything to do with it, it wasn't.

21

Bank managers or traffic wardens. It's got to be a close-run thing which we hate the most. I mean, if you got the chance to embarrass someone on prime-time TV, would you choose the bank manager who refused your overdraft or the traffic warden who ticketed your car while you nipped into Marks & Spencer for a butty? I only had to talk to the guy in charge of Ted Barlow's finances to know that he deserved the worst that Jeremy Beadle could do.

To begin with, he wouldn't even talk to me, not even to arrange an appointment. "Client confidentiality," he explained superciliously. I told him through clenched teeth that I probably knew more about his client's current problems than he did, since I was employed by said client. I restrained myself from mentioning that Mortensen and Brannigan had standards of confidentiality and service that were a damn sight higher than his. We don't sell our customer list to junk mail financial services outfits; we don't indulge ourselves on the old boys' network to blackball people whose faces don't fit; and, strangely enough, we actually work the hours that suit our clients rather than ourselves.

But Mr Leonard Prudhoe wasn't having any. Finally, I had to give up. There was only one way I was going to get to see this guy. I rang Ted and asked him to set the meeting up.

"Have you sorted it all out?" he asked. "Do you know what's been going on?"

"Pretty much," I said. "But whatever you do, don't so much as hint to anyone, and I mean anyone, that anything's changed." I explained that he'd have to set up a meeting with Prudhoe so we could get the whole thing sorted out. "Then, if you come to the office beforehand, I'll fill you in first."

"Can't you tell me now? I'm on pins," he said.

"I've got a couple of loose ends to tie up, Ted. But if you can fix up to see Prudhoe this afternoon, I should be able to give you chapter and verse then. OK?"

The relief in his voice was heartwarming. "I can't tell you how pleased I am, Miss Brannigan. You've no idea what it's been like, wondering if I was going to lose everything I've worked for. You've just got no idea," he burbled on.

I might not have, but I had a shrewd idea who did. When I managed to disentangle myself from his effusive thanks, I wandered through to the outer office. Shelley's fingers were flying over the keyboard as she worked her way through the proposals Bill had put together for our Channel Islands clients. "Ted's little problem," I said. "I'm just nipping out for a couple of hours to tie up the last loose ends. He should be ringing back to let me know when we're seeing his bank manager. Give me a bell on the mobile when you know."

She gave me one of her looks. The ones I suspect she reserves for her kids when she thinks they're trying to dodge out without finishing their homework. "You mean it?" she asked.

"Brownie's honour," I said. "Would I lie to you about something so close to your heart? Are you familiar with the works of Rudyard Kipling?"

She looked at me as if I was out to lunch and not coming back for a long time. "Wasn't he the one who went on about the white man's burden?" she said suspiciously.

The same. Knew all about keeping the yellow and brown chappies in their places. However, he was not entirely a waste of oxygen. He also wrote the private eye's charter:

> *I keep six honest serving men*
> *(They taught me all I knew)*
> *Their names are What and Why and When*
> *And How and Where and Who.*

"Well, as far as Ted's case is concerned, I know the what, the why, the when, the where and the who. I know most of the how, and after I've paid a little visit to one of my contacts, I expect to know the lot." I smiled sweetly as I shrugged into my coat and headed for the door. "Bye, Shelley."

"You worry me, Brannigan, you really do," floated after me as I ran downstairs. The day had not been wasted.

Rachel Lieberman was doing front of house at DKL Estates when I walked through the door. The suit she was wearing looked as if it was worth about the same as the deposit on any one of her first-time-buyer properties. I pretended to study the houses for sale while she made appointments for a potential buyer to view a couple. Five minutes later, the grateful house-hunter went on his merry way with a handful of particulars, leaving Rachel and me facing each other across the desk. "Lost your young man?" I asked.

"His mother says he's got a bug. I think it may have more to do with the fact that United won last night," she said.

"You just can't get the help these days," I commiserated.

"You can say that again. Anyway, what can I do for you? Still hunting for your mysterious con artists?"

I'd already decided that whoever was supplying Jack McCafferty and Liz with the information they needed, it wasn't Rachel Lieberman. I hadn't made that decision purely on women's intuition. I reckoned she'd have found a way politely to show me the door if she'd been involved. So I smiled and said, "Nearly at the end of the road. I was hoping you could help me out with a couple of loose ends."

"Fire away," she said. "You've got me quite intrigued. My son was enthralled when I told him I was helping a private eye with her inquiries. So I owe you some co-operation. It's not easy for a mother to impress a ten-year-old, you know."

"Do you store all the details of your rented properties on your computer?"

"It all goes in there, whether it's for rental or for sale," she said.

"So how does the Warrington office get your data, and vice versa?"

"I don't mean to be rude, but how well do you understand computers?" she asked.

I grinned. "If you left me alone with yours for half an hour, I could probably figure it out for myself," I said. I was almost certainly exaggerating, but she wasn't to know. Now, if I had Bill with me, he'd definitely be in there before I'd had time to brew a pot of coffee.

"I'll save you the bother," she replied. "Twice a day, at one and again at five, I access the Warrington office computer via a modem. The software identifies any new files, or files that have been modified since the machines last conversed. Then it exports those files from my machine and imports the ones from the Warrington computer. The system also warns me in the unusual event of the same file having been modified by both offices."

"Sounds like a nifty bit of programming," I said.

"Our software was written by my brother-in-law, so he had to make sure it does what it's supposed to, or I'd make his life hell," Rachel said. I could imagine. One of the things I learned in law school was, never cross a Jewish princess.

"Now for the hard question," I said.

"I can guess. Who has access to the computers?" she asked. I nodded. "Is this really necessary?" I nodded again. "And I suppose you won't be satisfied if I tell you that they're only accessible to members of my staff?" I began to feel like I was following the bouncing ball.

"You want names, do you?" she said.

"Photographs would be even better," I said.

Her eyebrows arched, then she snorted with laughter. "Have you ever considered a career in estate agency? With cheek like yours, you could stand in the middle of a decaying slum with rising damp, dry rot and subsidence and persuade the clients that the property has unique potential that only they are capable of exploiting."

"Kind of you, but I prefer catching crooks to becoming one," I said.

"It's flattery that's supposed to get results, not insults," she retorted. "All the same, would you mind terribly keeping an eye on the shop while I attempt to meet your demands?"

I even went so far as to sit behind the desk while Rachel disappeared into the back office. I suppose she could have been phoning the baddies to tip them off, but I didn't think so. Luckily, no one came in during the few minutes she was gone. Thursday morning obviously isn't the busy time for estate agents. Rachel returned with an envelope of photographs. "Here we are," she said. "We had a staff Christmas dinner last year. The only person who's new since then is Jason, and you've already met him."

Rachel handed me the bundle of snaps. They'd celebrated in one of the Greek tavernas, and the pictures had obviously been put back in reverse order, for the first few showed one of those organized riots that the Greeks, like the Scots, call dancing. There was no one that I recognized. I carried on. Then, on the seventh photograph, shot from the opposite end of the table, there she was. Small, neat features, sharp chin, face wider across the red eyes. Just like Diane Shipley's sketch, except that her natural hair was dark blonde, cut short in a feathered, elfin style. I pointed to the woman. "Who's that?"

Rachel's face seemed to close down on me. "Why? What makes you ask?"

"I don't think you want me to answer that," I said gently. "Who is she?"

"Her name is Liz Lawrence. She works two afternoons a week in our Warrington office. She has done for nearly three years. I think you must be making a mistake, Miss Brannigan. She's . . . she's a nice woman. She works hard," Rachel insisted.

I sighed. Sometimes this job makes me feel like the bad fairy who tells children there's no Santa Claus. The worst of it was that I had another sackload of disillusion to dump on someone before the day was over.

Ted's suit was having yet another outing. When I got back to the office, he was perched on the edge of Shelley's desk, looking as cheerful as a bloodhound whose quarry has just disappeared into the river. "And you know what garages are," I heard him say as I came in. "They don't know when they'll have either van back on the road."

"More problems?" I asked.

"You're not kidding. Two of my three vans are off the road. Which means my installations have slowed right down. It's a disaster," Ted said mournfully.

"Are you sure it's just a coincidence?" Shelley demanded. "On top of everything else, it's beginning to sound as if somebody's got it in for you!"

Ted managed to look both wounded and baffled. "I don't think so, Shelley, love," he said. "It's just been bad luck. I mean, the first one was parked up when it happened. Somebody'd obviously smacked into it in the pub car park while Jack was busy inside."

"Jack McCafferty? What was he doing with one of the vans? Surely he's got nothing to do with installations?" I asked, too sharply. They both gave me odd looks.

"He borrows it now and again. He runs a little disco business with his brother-in-law, and sometimes they're double booked so he borrows one of my vans overnight to run the disco gear around in," Ted said. The final piece slotted into place.

Then I remembered what kind of vans Colonial Conservatories use. My stomach felt like I'd eaten too much ice-cream too fast. "What night was it that he had the accident, Ted?" I asked.

Ted frowned and cast his eyes upwards. "Let me see . . . It must have been Monday night. Yes, Monday. Because we were running round like lunatics Tuesday trying to fit everything in, and that's why Pete was going too fast to stop at the roundabout. And now we're two vans down, and no sign of either of them back till next week at the very earliest." Out of the corner of my eye, I noticed a flicker of movement as Shelley's hand sneaked out to pat Ted's.

Oh well, at least it hadn't been Ted's white Transit van that had tried to push me off Barton Bridge. "I wish I had some good news for you, Ted," I said, "but I'm afraid it's a bit mixed. We're not due at the bank for another half-hour yet. D'you want to come into my office and I'll run it past you before we go and see Prudhoe?"

I thought I wasn't going to be able to get Ted to the bank. When I unfolded the tale of Jack's treachery, he went white round the mouth and headed for the door. Luckily, the sight of Shelley's astonished face slowed him down long enough for me to grab his arm and steer him into a seat. Shelley got a medicinal brandy into him and he recovered the power of speech. "I'll kill the bastard," he ground out between clenched jaws. "I swear to God, I'll kill him."

"Don't be silly," Shelley said briskly. "Kate will have him put in prison and that's much more satisfying," she added. Taking me to one side while Ted stared into the bottom of his empty glass, she muttered, "Which bastard are we talking about here?"

I gave her the last five seconds of the tale, which was enough to get her crouching beside Ted, murmuring the kind of comfort that it's embarrassing to witness. Of course, that was when Detective Chief Inspector Della Prentice chose to put in an appearance. I immediately steered her towards the door and said, "Ted, I'll see you downstairs in five minutes."

I'd rung Della as soon as Shelley gave me a time for the meeting with Prudhoe. I figured it would save me a bit of time if I outlined the case to her at the same time as I told the bank. I knew that the bank might be less than thrilled, but frankly, they were just going to have to lump it. I still had to find enough proof to nail Brian Lomax, and I simply didn't have the time to go into a ritual dance with Ted Barlow's bank manager about ethics.

Leonard Prudhoe was just as I'd expected. Smooth, super-cilious, but above all, grey. From his silver hair to his shiny grey loafers, he was a symphony in the key of John Major. The only splash of colour was the angry purple zit on his neck. God knows how it had the temerity to sit there. Also, as I'd expected, he treated us like a pair of naughty children who've been reported to the head so they can learn how the grown-ups behave. "Now, Miss Brannigan, I believe you think you might have some information pertinent to Mr Barlow's current problems. But what I really can't understand is why you feel it necessary to have Chief Inspector Prentice present, charming as it is to make her acquaintance. I'm sure she's not in the least concerned with our little difficulties . . ."

I cut across the patronizing bullshit. "As far as I'm concerned, a crime has been committed and that's more important than your sensibilities, I'm afraid. How much do you know about fraud, Mr Prudhoe? Am I going to lose you three sentences in? Because if you're not well versed in major fraud inquiries, I suggest we get someone in here who is. I'm a very busy woman, and I haven't the time to go through this twice, which is why DCI Prentice is here," I said briskly. He couldn't have looked more shocked if I'd jumped on the desk and gone into a kis-sagram routine.

"Young woman," he stuttered, "I'll have you know that I am an expert in financial defalcations of all sorts."

"Fine. Pin your ears back and take notes, then," I retorted. There's something about pomposity that brings out the toe-rag in me. It must be the Irish quarter of my ancestry.

Prudhoe looked affronted, but out of the corner of my eye, I noticed Ted looked a fraction less miserable. Della Prentice seemed to have developed a nasty cough.

"There's really no need to take this attitude," Prudhoe said frostily.

"Listen, Mr Prudhoe," Ted interrupted. "You people tried to take my business away from me. Kate's been trying to sort it out and, as far as I'm concerned, that entitles her to take any attitude she damn well pleases."

The turning worm shut Prudhoe up long enough for me to get started. "On the surface, it looks as if what has happened to Ted is a sequence of unfortunate coincidences, culminating in you cutting off his line of credit. But the truth is, Ted is the victim of a very clever fraud. And if the perpetrators hadn't got so greedy that they decided to go for a second bite of the cherry no one would ever have cottoned on, because the frauds would have looked all of a piece with genuine mortgage defaulters." In spite of himself, I could see Prudhoe's interest quicken. Perhaps, under his patronizing pomposity there was a brain after all.

I outlined the reasons why Ted had come to us in the first place. Della Prentice had her notebook out and was scribbling furiously. When I got to the missing conservatories, Prudhoe actually sat forward in his seat. "This is how it works," I said, thoroughly into my stride.

"You need a bent salesman and you need an insider in the office of an estate agency that specializes in decent-quality rental property. In this case, they used a firm called DKL Estates, who are as innocent of any criminal involvement as Ted is. The insider, let's call her Liz, picks houses that are to let where the owners have fairly common names and, preferably, where they are abroad, either working or in the services. Ideally, they want a couple who have been paying the mortgage for a fair few years, so that there's a substantial chunk of equity in the house. Liz then tells the office computer that she has found someone who wants to rent the place and whose references check out.

"The surname of the couple renting the house is identical with that of the real owners, but because they've chosen common names, if anyone in the office other than Liz notices the coincidence, they can all stand around going, 'Well, stone me, isn't that incredible, what a small world, etc.' Of course, because Liz has access to all the original paperwork from the owners, they've got copies of the signatures, and possibly info on bank accounts, mortgage accounts, service contracts and everything else. With me so far?"

"Fascinating," Prudhoe said. "Do go on, Miss Brannigan."

"The salesman, who has access to credit-checking agencies via your financial services company, runs a check to see what other information about the owners it throws up. Then Liz opens a false bank account in the renter's name at that address, and stops any Post Office redirect on mail for the real owners. She spends a minimal amount of time in the house and pays rent for a while. Incidentally, they have three operations in the planning stage at any one time, so she never spends long enough in any of the houses for the neighbours to get close. They all think she works away, or works nights, or has a boyfriend she stays with a lot. She also changed her appearance with wigs, glasses and make-up to cover their tracks.

"Next, Jack McCafferty, Ted's top salesman, says he's had a call from her asking for an estimate for a conservatory. The following day, he comes in with an order, financed by a remortgage with this bank. And if it was one of those periodic nights where Ted goes out on the call with him, then Jack and Liz would just pretend they'd never met before and he'd pitch her just like any other punter. After all, remortgaging would be a perfectly legitimate way of doing it, and wouldn't ring any alarm bells with Ted or anyone else since everybody who can't sell their house right now is desperately trying to liberate some capital. I tracked all this down via the Land Registry's records, but I'm sure you can verify the remortgage details with your own records. I suspect they used your finance people all the time because they'd also earn the finance company's commission that way too," I added.

"But wouldn't there be a problem with the original mortgage?" Della asked. "Surely, once that had been paid off, either the building society would be alerted because payments were still continuing from the real owners, or else the real owners would notice that their mortgage was no longer being taken out of their bank account."

I hadn't thought of that. But then I remembered an experience Alexis and Chris had had when they first sold their separate homes to move in together. Alexis, being a fiscal incompetent, had carried on blithely paying her old mortgage for six months before she'd noticed. I shook my head. "It would have taken ages for the building society to spot what was happening. And then they'd send a letter, and the letter would drop into a black hole because of the mail redirect being cancelled. It could drift on for ages before anyone at the building society got seriously exercised enough to do anything about it."

Della nodded, satisfied. "Thanks. Sorry, do carry on. This is fascinating."

"Right. So, when the bank checks the remortgage application, because the names are the same, all the information they get relates to the real owners, so there's never any problem. And the money is handed over. Think of the figures involved. Imagine a property bought ten years ago for twenty-five thousand pounds, which is now worth ninety thousand. The outstanding mortgage is only about seventeen thousand. They remortgage for the full ninety thousand, pay off the existing mortgage all above board to prevent any suspicion, then do a runner. Our friends Jack and Liz have netted approximately seventy thousand pounds after expenses.

"I reckon they've pulled the same scam at least a dozen times. And the only reason I was able to catch on is that they got so greedy they decided to dismantle the conservatories after they'd been installed and sell them on to another punter with an identical house at a rock-bottom price of a couple of grand." I turned to Ted. "That's what Jack was doing with the van when you thought he was playing at DJs."

I didn't get the chance to enjoy their reactions. Now I remember why I resisted a mobile phone for so long. They always interrupt the best bits.

22

They say the Victorian era was the age of the gifted amateur. All I've got to say is that I'm glad I wasn't a private investigator then. I mean, if there's one thing worse than amateurs who insist on offering you the kind of help that completely screws up an investigation, it's the ones who are more on the ball than you. The way Alexis was operating in this case, I was soon going to have to start paying her, rather than the other way round.

What I'd heard when I went into a huddle with my telephone in Prudhoe's office wasn't the kind of news to gladden the heart. "He's going to skip the country," Alexis started the conversation.

"Mr Harris, you mean?" I said cautiously. I was trying to keep my end as short and uninformative as I could. After all, I'd suddenly become the rather embarrassing centre of attention. I wasn't bothered about Ted or Prudhoe, but the presence of police officers induces a paranoia in private eyes that makes Woody Allen look well-balanced by comparison.

"Of course, Harris, Lomax, whatever! Who else? He's going to do a runner."

"How do we know this?"

There was a momentary pause while Alexis decided how to play it. "After you'd explained how busy you were today, I managed to swap my days off. I thought if I kept an eye on him, at least we wouldn't have missed anything. And I was right," she added defiantly.

I felt a guilt trip coming on. Somehow, I just knew that I wasn't going to be spending my evening as Emperor Brannigan of the Zulus, civilizing the known universe. "What's happened?" I asked.

"He's got a passport application form," Alexis announced triumphantly. "I followed him to the Post Office. He's obviously planning to leave the country."

It was a reasonable deduction. What it didn't tell us was whether he planned to take off to the Costa del Crime with his ill-gotten gains as soon as air traffic control would let him or whether he was simply planning ahead for his winter skiing holiday. "Where are you?" I said.

"In the phone box just down the road from his yard. I can see the entrance from here. He hasn't moved since he came back from the Post Office."

I gave in. "I'll be there as soon as I can," I said. After all, I'd given Ted and Prudhoe enough to keep them gossiping for hours. I ended the call and smiled sweetly at my fascinated audience. "I'm very sorry about this, but something rather urgent has come up. No doubt the three of you have a lot to discuss, so if you'll forgive me, I'll leave you to it. Ted, I'll let you have a full written report as soon as possible, but certainly by Monday at the latest." I got to my feet. "I'd just like to say it's been a pleasure, Mr Prudhoe," I added, reaching over his desk and seizing his hand in a firm grip. Poor sod, he still looked like he'd been hit by a half-brick. I seem to have this effect on men. Worrying, isn't it?

Della Prentice followed me into the corridor. "Hell of a tale, Kate. You've done a great job. We'll need a formal statement, of course," she said. "When can we do the business?"

I glanced at my watch. It was getting on for three. "I don't know, Della, I can't see me being able to sit down with you until the weekend, at the very earliest. Surely you've got enough to get a search warrant on the addresses they're using for the scam?" I opened my bag and took out my notebook, and copied down the addresses as I spoke. "Look, talk to Rachel Lieberman at DKL Estates. The woman you're after is called Liz Lawrence and she works part-time in their Warrington office. And Ted can tell you all he knows about Jack McCafferty. I don't mean to be difficult, but I'm really up against it."

"OK. I can see you've got problems. Let me know when you've got the time to sit down and put it all together. And give me your mobile number so I can reach you if I need some background," she said. I added my number to the sheet of paper and thrust it at her as I rushed off. I know that technically there was no desperate hurry for me to link up with Alexis, but if I hadn't got my adrenalin going, I might never have managed to drag myself back down the traffic-choked A6 and across that switchback road over the hills to Buxton. The locals must have amazing wrists.

I was back behind the wheel of the Fiesta. I'd got a taxi to drop me off there that morning, since there was no need to keep up my surveillance now. I swung round via the office to pick up the laptop with Cheetham's files, and a couple of my legal textbooks. I still hadn't had the chance to plough through the files, so I had no idea what twisted little schemes the dead lawyer had been up to. But I had a shrewd suspicion that they might need a bit more knowledge of the ins and outs of conveyancing than I had in my head. Better to have it at my fingertips instead.

It was nearly five by the time I overtook the last quarry wagon and dropped down the hill into Buxton. I cruised past Lomax's yard and clocked Alexis in her car. I had to admit I couldn't have picked a better spot myself. She was tucked in between two parked cars, with an uninterrupted view through the windows of the car in front to Lomax's yard. I parked round the corner and walked back.

I climbed into the Peugeot, shoving a pile of newspapers and sandwich wrappers on to the floor. "Better be careful the bin men don't come round and claim you," I said. "Any action?"

Alexis shook her head. "There are two vans. The one that Lomax drives and an identical one. The other one's been in and out a couple of times, but he hasn't shifted."

"Unless of course he's lying in the back of the other van disguised as a bag of cement," I pointed out. Alexis looked crestfallen. Oh great, now I felt even more guilty. "Don't worry, it's not likely. He doesn't know anyone's watching him. Cheetham's death has been written off as an accident. As far as he knows, he's perfectly safe. Now, you can sod off home and let me earn a living instead of taking the bread out of my mouth," I added.

"Don't you want me to hang on? In case he makes a run for it?" she asked, almost wistfully.

"Go home, have a cuddle with Chris. If he was planning to disappear over a distant horizon tonight, he wouldn't be sitting around in his yard. He'd be twitching in the queue at the passport office," I said sensibly. Judging by the scowl on Alexis's face, she likes sensible about as much as I do.

She sighed, one of those straight-from-the-heart jobs. "OK," she said. "But I don't want this guy to get away."

I opened the car door. "Don't forget, there's the small matter of proof," I said. "Now Cheetham's dead, Lomax can claim he did nothing dishonest. T. R. Harris is a business name, no more, no less. He just showed prospective buyers the land. He had no idea who bought it or when. Now, you and I know different, but I'd like to be in a position to prove it."

Alexis groaned. "All I want is a lever to get our money back, Kate. I don't care if he comes out of it all smelling of roses."

"I hear and obey, oh lord," I said, getting out of the car. "Now shift this wheelie bin and let the dog see the rabbit."

She waved as she drove away and I slipped the Fiesta into the space she'd left. I flipped open the laptop and accessed the WORK.L directory. The files were sorted into two directories.

One was called DUPLICAT, the other RV. The files in RV each related to a house purchase. In some cases, the house had been sold about five months later, always at a substantial profit. I was about to check out the addresses in my *A-Z* when a white Transit van appeared in the gateway of Lomax's yard. My target was at the wheel. Fast as I could, I closed the laptop and dumped it on the passenger seat.

Don't let anyone tell you being a private eye is a glamorous way to earn a living. I followed Lomax from his yard to his house. Then I sat in the car for two hours, plodding wearily through Martin Cheetham's files. The houses in RV were all in the seedier areas south and east of Manchester city centre— Gorton, Longsight, Levenshulme. The kind of terraced streets where you can buy run-down property cheap, tart it up and make a modest killing. Or at least, you could do until the bottom started to drop out of the North West property market a few months ago. Looking at these files, it seemed that Lomax and Cheetham had been doing this on a pretty substantial scale. I did a quick mental calculation and reckoned they'd turned over getting on for two million quid in the previous year. Since my mental arithmetic is on a par with my quantum mechanics, I decided I'd got it wrong and scribbled the sums out in my notebook. I got the same answer.

Suddenly we were in a whole new ball game. I wasn't looking at a pair of small-time operators chiselling a few grand on a dodgy land deal. I was looking at big money. They could have cleared as much as three-quarters of a million in the last year. But they must have had a substantial pot to buy the houses in the first place. Where the hell had the seed money come from to generate that kind of business?

While I'd been doing my sums, the last of the light had faded. I began to feel pretty exposed, which in turn made me feel deeply uncomfortable. I couldn't help remembering that less than a week ago someone had wanted to warn me off something so badly they'd taken the risk of killing me. If they were still around, I made a hell of a target, sitting all by myself in a car.

The answer to my fear was just behind me. I was parked on the opposite side of the street to Brian Lomax's house, about thirty yards further up the hill, outside a substantial Victorian pile with a Bed and Breakfast sign swinging slightly in the chilly wind. I collected a small overnight holdall from the boot, stuffed the law books into it and walked up the short drive.

I'd have taken the landlady on as an investigator any day. By the time I'd paid for a night in advance and she'd left me alone in my spotless little room, I felt like I'd had a bright light shining in my eyes for days. Never mind grace under pressure; there should be a private investigators' Oscar for lies under pressure. At least I was in a suit, which made it easier to be convincing about my imaginary role as a commercial solicitor acting for a local client who was interested in buying property in Manchester to expand his business. She'd gone for the lie, agog at my close-lipped refusal to breach client confidentiality. I was half-convinced that, come the morning, she'd be tailing me just for the hell of picking up some juicy local gossip.

My room was, as requested, at the front of the house, and on the second floor, Which gave me a better view of Brian Lomax's house than I'd had from the car. Glad to get out of tights and heels, I changed into the leggings, sweatshirt and Reeboks that had been relegated to the emergency overnight kit and settled down in the dark to keep watch. I passed the time dictating my client reports for PharmAce and Ted Barlow. That would take Shelley's mind off romance for a couple of hours.

Nell arrived home about half past six, parking her GTi in the garage. It was gone nine before I saw some more action. Lomax appeared round the side of the house, walking along his drive. He turned right and started towards town. I was out of the room and down the stairs a hell of a lot more quickly than I'd have been able to manage just a couple of days before. If Mortensen and Brannigan ever take on an assistant, I think we're going to have to stipulate "Must be quick healer" on the job description.

He was still in sight as I ran out of the guest house, trying to look like a jogger nipping out for her evening run. At the traffic lights, he turned left, walking up the hill towards the market place. I reached the corner in time to see him entering a pub. Wonderful. I didn't even have a jacket on, and I couldn't follow him into the pub because he knew only too well who I was. Furious, I walked right up to the pub and peered through the stained-glass door. Through a blue haze, I saw Lomax at the bar, talking and laughing with a group of other men, all around the same age. By the looks of it, he was having his regular Thursday night down his local with the lads, rather than meeting a business contact. That much was a relief. I stepped back and had a look round. Across the street, on the opposite corner, there was a fish and chip shop that advertised an upstairs dining room. I had nothing left to lose.

It's amazing how long I can take to work my way through steak pudding, chips, mushy peas, gravy, a pot of tea and a plate of bread and butter. Oddly enough, I actually enjoyed it, especially since I'd missed lunch. Best of all was the spotted dick and custard that tasted better than anything my mother used to make. I managed to make the whole lot string out until half past ten, then it was back out into the cold. Of course, it started to rain as soon as I emerged from the chippy. I crossed to the pub and had another look through the glass. The scene hadn't changed much, except that the pub had got busier. Lomax was still standing at the bar with his cronies, a pint pot in his fist. I couldn't see any point in getting soaked while he got pissed, so I jogged back to the guest house, my dinner sitting in my stomach like a concrete block.

He came back, alone, just on half past eleven. Five minutes later, a light went on in an upstairs room and he appeared at the window to close the curtains. Ten minutes after that, another light went on and Nell did the same thing in her room. I didn't bother waiting for their lights to go out. I bet I was asleep before they were.

I bet I was up before them too. I'd set my alarm for six, and I was out of the shower by quarter past. Lomax's curtains opened at a quarter to seven, and my heart sank. My landlady didn't start serving breakfast till eight, and it looked like he'd be out of the house by then. I consoled myself with the individually wrapped digestive biscuits supplied with the tea- and coffee-making facilities. (Fine if you like sterilized milk, tea bags filled with house dust and powdered instant coffee that tastes like I imagine strychnine does.)

Wearily, I packed my bag and returned to the car. I was beginning to wonder if there was any point to this surveillance. I sometimes think my boredom threshold's too low for this job. Twenty minutes later, the nose of a white E-type appeared in his gateway. I'd seen the Jag sitting next to Nell's GTi in the garage the night I'd spotted the T. R. Harris signboard. The classic car's long bonnet emerged cautiously, until I could see Lomax himself was at the wheel. He drove past me without so much as a glance. I watched him round the bend in my rearview mirror, then quickly reversed out of the guest house drive and sped after him.

I'd thought the road from Manchester had been bad enough. The one we took out of Buxton was that nightmare you wake up from in a clammy sweat. The road corkscrewed up through a series of tight bends with sheer drops on the other side, just like in the Alps. Then it became a narrow bucking switchback that made me grateful for missing breakfast. The visibility was appalling. I couldn't decide if it was fog or cloud I was driving through, but either way I was glad there weren't too many side turnings for the E-type to disappear into. What left me gasping with disbelief was the amount of traffic on this track from hell. Lorries, vans, cars by the dozen, all bucketing along as if they were in the fast lane of the M6.

Eventually, we left the grey-green moors behind and dropped into the red brick of Macclesfield. I felt like an explorer emerging from the jungle after a close encounter with the cannibals. These were proper roads, with traffic lights, roundabouts, and white lines up the middle. Through Macclesfield, we emerged into the country again, but this was more my idea of what countryside should be. None of those dreadful moors, heather stretching to infinity, dilapidated dry-stone walls with holes in where someone failed to make the bend, grim pubs stranded in the middle of nowhere and trees that grow at an angle of forty-five degrees to the prevailing wind. No, this was much more like it. Neat fields, pretty farmhouses, Little Chefs and garden centres, notices nailed to trees announcing craft fairs and car boot sales. The kind of country you might just be tempted to take a little run out to in the car.

We roared down the slip road of the M6 at 8:14, according to my dashboard clock. I began to feel excited. Whatever Lomax was up to, it was more interesting than repairing guttering. As the speedo hit ninety, I really began to miss my Nova. It may not have looked much, but it was a car that only really ever seemed to get into its stride over eighty. Unlike the Fiesta, which had an interesting shake in the steering wheel between eighty-two and eighty-eight. As we changed lanes to head west down the M62, I remembered the phone call from Alexis that had started this latest phase of the operation. A passport application form.

To obtain a full British passport, you have to fill in a complicated form, have your photographic identity attested by a supposedly reputable member of the community who's known you for at least two years, and send it off to the passport office. Then you sit back and wait for a few weeks while the wheels of bureaucracy grind exceedingly slow. If you're in a hurry, you take yourself off to one of the five passport offices on the UK mainland—London, Liverpool, Newport, Peterborough or Glasgow. I remember the performance well. Richard and I booked a fortnight's holiday in July driving round California in a Winnebago. Two days before we were due to leave, he materialized in my office mid-morning to announce his passport was out of date. Of course, he was too busy to sort it out himself, could I possibly . . . ?

If you get there on the stroke of nine, they deign to take your paperwork off you and tell you to come back in four hours' time. If you're late, you have to wait in the queue and pray they get round to you before closing time. If that was where Brian Lomax was headed, he was clearly determined to avoid queuing all day.

He headed straight for the centre of Liverpool, and parked his car in the multi-storey nearest the passport office at ten to nine. I stayed in my car and watched him through the door of India Buildings. He might well have been headed for any of the offices on any floor except the fifth, but I doubted it. He was out within twenty minutes but, instead of going straight back to his car, he headed off towards the city centre. I swore steadily under my breath as I tried to keep him in sight. As long as he didn't turn into a pedestrian precinct, I might just be OK.

I was and I wasn't. About a mile from the passport office, Brian Lomax marched purposefully into a travel agency.

23

I burst through the door, fighting back the tears, rushed up to the assistant and wailed, "Where's he taking her? Tell me! I've got a right to know where he's going with the bitch!" Then I burst into tears and collapsed into the chair that Brian Lomax had just vacated.

"I know it's stupid, but I still love him," I sobbed. "Whatever he might have done with that cow, he's still my husband." Through the tears I could see the travel agent looking completely stricken. Her mouth was opening and closing.

"For God's sake, put me out of my misery! Let me know the worst. You're a woman, you should understand," I added, accusingly.

Another woman pushed the younger assistant out of the way. "What is it, queen?" she said soothingly.

"My h-husband," I hiccuped. "He's got a girlfriend, I just know it. So I've been following him. When he came in here, I thought, he's taking her away, never mind that me and the kids haven't had a holiday for two years. And something just snapped. You've got to tell me," I added, on a rising note. Then I gulped noisily.

"Sharon," the older woman said. "The gentleman who was just in."

"Lomax," I said. "That's his name. Brian Lomax."

"Mr Lomax," the woman echoed. "What was he after, Sharon?"

"I thought we weren't supposed to discuss clients?" the younger girl muttered.

"Have you got no heart, girl? That could be you one day. Us girls have got to stick together," the woman said. Then to me she said, "Men. They're all the same, eh, girl?" Thank God for the legendary hearts of gold of Liverpudlians.

I nodded and made a great show of trying to get myself under control while Sharon nervously jabbed the keys of her computer with nails that would have had Cruella de Vil looking to her laurels. "There, Dot," she said, pointing at the screen.

The older woman nodded sagely and swung the screen round so I could see it for myself. "Whatever he might be up to, he's not going off with her," she said. "Look. He's only booked for one person. Fly/drive to Florida. Flight, car hire and accommodation vouchers, including single person supplement." As she spoke, I was taking it all in. Airline, flight number, price. Flying out of Manchester on Monday night. "He paid in cash an' all," Dot added. "Now that's something we don't see a lot of in here these days."

"What about his tickets?" I demanded. "I bet he's not having them sent to the house."

"No," Dot said. "With him going on Monday, he'll get them off the ticket agent at the airport."

"Selfish bastard," I spat.

"You're not kiddin', girl," Dot said. "Still, look on the bright side. At least he's not got the cow with him, has he?"

I got to my feet. "By the time I've finished with him, he won't be fathering any more kids in a hurry," I said.

"Attagirl!" Dot called after me as I stormed out of the travel agency.

By the time I rounded the corner and climbed into the Fiesta, which had miraculously escaped a parking ticket, the reaction to my performance had set in. My legs felt like jelly and my hands were shaking. Thank God for the solidarity of women whose men done them wrong.

So Alexis had been right, I thought as I drove back more sedately along the M62. Brian Lomax was about to do a runner. And the only thing that could stop him was me finding out what exactly he'd been up to. I decided to spend the rest of the day ignoring all distractions and getting to the bottom of Martin Cheetham's files. But before I did that, I reckoned I deserved the breakfast I'd missed out on earlier. On the horizon, I could see the Burtonwood motorway services building, a dead ringer for the Roman Catholic cathedral in Liverpool. If I tell you that the locals call the house of God "The concrete wigwam," maybe you'll get the picture.

I pulled off the road and cruised into the car park. And there it was. Smack bang in the middle of the car park: Brian Lomax's E-type. I parked the car then cautiously explored the service area. He wasn't in the shop, or playing the video arcade machines. I finally spotted him in the cafeteria, alone except for a huge fry-up. Goodbye breakfast. With a sigh, I returned to my car and headed for the service road that led back to the motorway. When I reached the petrol pumps, I pulled off and parked. I nipped in to the shop and bought a bottle of mineral water and a bacon and egg sandwich, the nearest I was going to get to a proper breakfast that day. Back at the car, I let the engine idle while I ate my butty and waited for Lomax. I couldn't help myself; since the gods had handed him back to me on a plate, I just had to see what he was up to.

Quarter of an hour later, we were heading back towards Manchester. The traffic was heavy by now, but the E-type was so distinctive it was easy to tail. On the outskirts, he took the M63 towards Stockport. He turned off at the cheaper end of Cheadle, where you don't have to be able to play bridge or golf to be allowed to buy a house, and cut across to the terraced streets that huddle round Stockport County's football ground. Tailing him through the tight grid of narrow streets was a lot trickier, but luckily I didn't have to do it for long. And Lomax acted like the idea of being followed hadn't even crossed his mind.

He pulled up outside a house where a couple of workmen seemed to be removing the windows, and a youth up a ladder was clearing moss out of the guttering. A sign on the ladder had the familiar "Renew-Vations" logo, as did the scruffy van parked with two wheels on the kerb. Lomax had a few words with the workmen, then went inside. Ten minutes later, he re-emerged, gave them the thumbs-up sign then drove off.

We went through the same routine a couple more times, in Reddish then in Levenshulme. All the houses were elderly terraced properties in streets that looked as if they were struggling upwards rather than plunging further downhill. On the third house, it clicked. These were some of the most recent purchases in the RV directory. I was actually looking at the houses Cheetham and Lomax had bought cheap to do up and sell dear.

The last stop was on the fringes of Burnage, but this time it was a between-the-wars semi that looked completely dilapidated. There was grass growing through the gravel, the gate was hanging from one hinge. So much paint had peeled off the door and window frames it was a miracle they hadn't dropped to bits. Two men were working on the roof, replacing broken slates and pointing the chimney stack. Lomax got out of the Jag and shouted something to the men. Then he took a pair of overalls out of the boot, put them on over his jeans and sweatshirt and walked into the house. A few minutes later, I heard the high whine of a power drill. I decided I could use my time more fruitfully back in the office with the computer files.

Shelley was on the phone making "new client" noises when I walked in, but judging by the speed with which the coffee appeared on my desk, she'd already had the rundown on my success with Ted's conservatories. "Good news travels fast, huh?" I said.

"I don't know what you mean," she said haughtily. "Have you done the client reports for PharmAce and Ted Barlow yet?"

I took the cassettes out of my handbag. "*Voilà!*" I said, handing them over with a flourish. "God forbid we should keep Ted waiting. How is he, by the way? Happy as a sandboy?"

"As if it isn't bad enough spending my days with someone who thinks she's a genius, I now have to listen to Ted Barlow telling me you're a genius. The bank's agreed to restore his loan and his access to their financial services division, and he's got an advert in Monday's *Evening Chronicle* for a new sales person. The police raided the three houses last night and got enough evidence to arrest Jack McCafferty and Liz Lawrence. They should both be charged later today, and Ted's completely in the clear," Shelley said, unable to keep the smile out of her eyes.

"Great news. Tell me, Shelley, how come you know all this?"

"Because it's my job to answer the phone, Kate," she replied sweetly. "Also, I've had calls from a DCI Prentice, a woman called Rachel Lieberman, Alexis Lee and four calls from Richard who says he doesn't want to trouble you but have you charged the battery on your mobile because it's not responding."

I knew there had to be a reason why I'd had peace all morning. I'd remembered to charge the phone up overnight. I'd just omitted to make sure it was switched on this morning. Feeling like a fool, I smiled sweetly at Shelley. "I must have been in one of those black holes when he tried me," I said.

Shelley gave me the look my mother used to when I swore blind I'd not eaten the last biscuit. "If you're having that much of a problem, maybe we should just send it back," she said.

I bared my teeth. "I'll manage, thanks. So now he's got that load off his mind, how's Ted? Able to devote one hundred per cent of his attention to helping you achieve the full potential of your house?"

"Have I ever told you what a blessing it is for me to work with you, Kate? You're the only person I know who makes me realize just how mature my two kids really are." She turned and headed for the door. I poked my tongue out at her retreating back. "I saw that," she said without turning her head. At the door, she looked back at me. "Joking apart, it's OK." Then she was gone, leaving me alone with the laptop and my phone messages, which I chose to ignore.

Now I'd worked out what the RV directory was all about and I'd actually seen some of the properties in question, I had to unravel the contents of DUPLICAT. At first sight, they seemed to be completely innocuous. They were files relating to the purchase of various properties by assorted individuals and the mortgages that had been arranged for them. The material seemed exactly the same sort of stuff that was in the unprotected WORK.C directory. The only difference was that in DUPLICAT every single mortgage lender was different. In the few instances where the same building society had been used more than once, Cheetham's clients had chosen different branches.

It was only when I'd worked my way through to the most recent of the files that something finally caught my eye. Even then, I had to look twice and cross-check with another file to make sure it wasn't just boredom and tiredness that were tricking me. But my first reaction was right. The property in the file was a detached house on an exclusive development in Whitefield. But another couple had arranged a mortgage on the same property and their address was none other than the dilapidated semi I'd left Brian Lomax working on.

I could feel a dull ache starting at the base of my skull. The combination of staring into my laptop and trying to work out what was going on was getting to me. I stood up and stretched, then moved around the office doing some of the warm-up exercises I'd learned down the Thai boxing gym. I swear the routine sends my brain into an altered state. As my body found its rhythm, the tension flowed out of me, and my mind went into free fall.

Then all the assorted bits and pieces of information that had been swilling round in confusion inside my head came together in a pattern. Abruptly, I stopped leaping around the room like Winnie the Pooh's imitation of Mikhail Baryshnikov and dropped into my chair. I didn't have a split screen facility on the laptop, so I hastily scribbled down half a dozen of the addresses of the houses that had been mortgaged according to DUPLICAT, along with the names of their buyers. Then I called up the files from WORK.C, the directory of Cheetham's straight conveyancing business.

It didn't take me long to discover that for every file in DUPLICAT there was another file in WORK.C that corresponded to it. In each case, the house was the same but the buyers and the mortgage lenders were different. Now I understood exactly what Brian Lomax and Martin Cheetham had been up to. They'd exploited the system's weaknesses in a scam that would have given them a tidy profit almost indefinitely. The pair of them were committing the classic victimless crime. But someone had grown greedy, and that greed had led to Martin Cheetham's death.

I glanced at my watch. It was just on four. I still had no proof that Brian Lomax had been an active conspirator rather than a mug that Martin Cheetham and, possibly, Nell Lomax had exploited for their own ends. But I was convinced that whatever had gone wrong with Cheetham's carefully worked out scheme could be traced straight back to Lomax. There was something about his body language, a kind of swagger in the way he carried himself. Brian Lomax was no more one of life's victims than Warren Beatty. And I had to get him in the frame before a jumbo jet took off into the sunset on Monday night.

I closed the laptop and took it through to Bill's office. He was staring at an A4 pad, gnawing the end of a pencil. "Bad time?" I asked.

"I'm trying to write a memory resident program that will automatically check for any date-activated programs hiding in the computer's memory," he said. He dropped the pencil with a deep sigh and started chewing his beard instead. I'm often tempted to ring his mother and ask what experience he had in his infancy that's made him so oral.

"Virus protection?" I asked.

"Yup. I've been meaning to get to it since the débâcle on Yom Kippur, but this is the first chance I've had." He pulled a face. Bill was still smarting from the computer virus that had attacked one of our clients at the beginning of October. The virus had been set to activate itself on the Jewish Day of Atonement. Our clients, a firm of accountants called Goldberg and Senior, had taken it very personally when all of their records had been turned into gobbledygook. They didn't find it a consolation when Bill told them it was a one-off that wouldn't recur in other years, unlike the really vicious Friday the Thirteenth and Michelangelo viruses that attack again and again till they're cleansed for good.

"I'm putting the laptop in the safe. It's got the data from Martin Cheetham's hard disc on it, and I think it's probably the only evidence left of what he and Brian Lomax were up to," I said.

"You've cracked it, then?" Bill looked eager and stopped chewing.

"I think so. The only problem is that it's hard to prove Lomax was actively involved with the criminal aspect of it. So I've got a little experiment in mind to sort it out one way or the other." I crossed the office and pushed the frame of the print of Escher's *Belvedere*. The spring-loaded catch released itself and the picture swung back on its hinges to reveal the office safe.

"You want to enlighten me?" Bill asked as I keyed in the combination. The door clicked open and I cleared a space on the bottom shelf for the laptop.

"I'd love to, but I haven't got the time right now. I need to be in Buxton before six if this is going to work. Besides, this is not a tale you want to try and digest on a Friday teatime. The twists and turns in this make Yom Kippur look as simple as Space Invaders." I closed the safe, then unlocked the cupboard that contains all our Elint equipment.

"I don't want you to think I'm being chauvinist about this, but you're not going to do anything dangerous, are you?" Bill asked anxiously.

"I wasn't planning to, no. Just a simple bit of bugging in the hope of picking up something incriminating." I chose a directional bug with a magnetic base, and added the screen that indicates where the bug is relative to the receiver. I also helped myself to a couple of tiny radio mikes with integral batteries, each about the size of the top joint of my thumb, and the receiver that goes with them. The tape recorder was still in the Fiesta, so I'd be able to record anything I overheard. I screwed each mike into a plastic pen-housing that also contained a U-shaped length of wire which acted as an aerial.

Bill sighed. "As long as you're careful. We don't want a repeat performance of last Friday night." From anyone else, it would have sounded patronizing. But I recognized the genuine concern that lay behind Bill's words.

"I know, I know, the firm can't afford the insurance premiums to get any higher," I said. "Look, there's been no sign of anyone having another go. Maybe it was the real thing, a genuine accident. You know, someone a bit pissed or tired? Stranger things have happened."

"Maybe," Bill agreed reluctantly. "Anyhow, take care. I haven't got the time to train a replacement." He grinned.

"I promise. Like I said, just a simple bit of bugging, that's all." I didn't want to upset him. That's why I chose not to tell him I was going out to find me a murderer.

24

Enchantments didn't. Enchant me, that is. There was something about their stock of expensive clothes that screamed "girlie." I'd only ever have shopped there if I'd been deliberately looking for something that made me look like a middle-class bimbo. It wasn't so much mutton dressed as lamb, as "little baby lambikins." It was obviously what the locals wanted, since it certainly wasn't a style that came naturally to the fiercely elegant Nell Lomax. Today, her wavy brown hair tumbled round the shoulders of what looked to me like a classic Jaeger suit and blouse. She looked like an advert for one of those richly spicy perfumes that we career girls are supposed to love.

I'd drifted past the shop to check she was there, then I'd slipped out the rear entrance of the modern glass and concrete shopping arcade where the boutique sat uneasily between a butcher's and a shoe shop. A quick prowl round the car park revealed there was only one white convertible Golf there. On the pretext of tying my lace, I slipped the directional bug inside the wheel arch. Now I could keep tabs on Nell without sitting tightly on her tail.

Nell was sitting on a high stool behind the counter reading *Elle*. She glanced up when I walked in, but clearly didn't think a woman who would be seen out of doors in jogging pants, sweatshirt and ski jacket was the sort of person worth lavishing her personal attention on. I'd pulled my hair back and tied it in a pony tail, and now my bruising had gone down, I was back to my usual light application of cosmetics, so it's not really surprising she didn't recognize me as the smartly dressed, over-made-up private eye she'd come face to face with a few days before. Besides, a lot had happened since then to take her mind off my face.

As she read on, I browsed among the racks of overpriced merchandise, trying to imagine anyone I respected wearing any of these clothes. I did find one skirt my mother would probably have liked, but she'd have wanted to pay about a third of the price for it, and I can't say I'd have blamed her. Keeping half an eye on Nell, I worked my way round the shop.

Eventually, I approached the counter from the side, so I was close to her coat, which was slung over a chair, and to her handbag, on the floor at her feet. "We need to talk, Ms Lomax," I said, dropping on to the chair with the coat and letting my bag slide on to the floor next to hers.

She looked startled, as she was meant to. "I'm sorry, I don't think I . . . ?" she said.

"We haven't been introduced," I said, leaning forward to open my bag. I took out a business card and handed it to her. While she was frowning at it, under the pretext of closing my bag, I slipped one of the radio mikes into her handbag.

"I still have no idea who you are, Miss Brannigan," she said uneasily. Not a good actress; I could see the nervous flicker of her eyes as she lied.

"We met in Martin Cheetham's office. The day he died," I said. I leaned back and casually draped my arm over the back of the chair. I managed to slip the second mike into one of the deep pockets of her Burberry without taking my eyes off her face.

"I don't know what you're talking about," she replied with a nervous shake of the head.

I sighed and ran my hand over my hair. "Ms Lomax, we can do this the hard way or the easy way. Martin Cheetham was your boyfriend. He did business with your brother. Very dodgy business, some of it. You were both at his house on the afternoon he died, something which I don't believe you've seen fit to discuss with the police. Now, I know about the double dealing with the land, I know about the mortgage frauds and I know how the money's been laundered. And I know why Martin Cheetham had to die."

Nell Lomax's chic façade crumbled, leaving a frightened woman whose eyes couldn't keep still. "You're talking rubbish," she gabbled. "I don't know what you're on about. How dare you— coming in here and talking about Martin and my brother like that." Her attempt at defiance didn't even convince her, never mind me.

"Oh, you know all about it, Nell," I said. "What you don't know is that your lovely brother is planning to skip the country and leave you holding the sticky end."

"You're mad," she said. "I'm going to call the police."

"Be my guest. I'd be happy to tell them what I know, and to show them the proof. It's in a very safe place, by the way, so there's no point in trying to get rid of me like you got rid of Martin Cheetham," I added.

"I think you'd better leave," she said, unconsciously backing away from me.

"I came to deliver a message. Your brother and your lover conned my client out of five thousand pounds. They did the same to another eleven people in the same scam. I want that sixty thousand back before he leaves the country on Monday, otherwise the police will be waiting at the airport for him." I indicated my card, which she was still clutching tight. "You've got my number. When he's got the money together, tell him to ring me and we'll arrange a hand over."

I picked up my bag and stood up. "I'm deadly serious about this, Nell. You're in the frame too, don't forget. That should be a hell of an incentive to convince your brother to refund my clients." I walked briskly across the shop. At the door, I contemplated kicking over a rail of clothes, but I decided the air of low-key menace was probably more effective than going over the top. I marched out, not looking back.

I gambled on Nell shutting up shop and going off to find brother Brian. Since it was just after half past five, I thought there was a good chance that she'd head straight for home, so I checked back in to my cheap and cheerful guest house. The landlady nearly burst with curiosity at my return, especially when she spotted the electronic equipment. I closed the door firmly behind me and settled down at the window, the directional receiver on a low coffee table beside me. I plugged an earphone from the micro-phone receiver into my ear and waited. So far, nothing. Either Nell was too far away for me to pick anything up or she'd found the bugs and flushed them down the toilet. Given the state she'd been working up to when I left the shop, I frankly didn't think she'd have noticed if they'd jumped out of the bag and bitten her.

Then the screen started to flash. The bug itself has a radius of about five miles, and it transmits back to the receiver. The screen shows the direction of the bug relative to the receiver, and there's a display of figures along the bottom of the screen which gives the distance in metres between the bug and the receiver. At first, the numbers started climbing, which got me twitching. Had I guessed wrong? Was she heading for some building site where her brother would be working late? Just as I reached the point of panic, the direction changed and the numbers started to plummet. When it showed 157, I could actually see the white Golf racing up the hill towards the house. Then the earphone came alive and I could hear engine noise.

She was driving like a woman who'd lost control. It was a miracle she didn't leave her front bumper on the gatepost as she shot into the drive. As it was, I heard a harsh scraping as she pulled off the road. She didn't even bother garaging the car, simply abandon-ing it on the Tarmac in front of the house. I watched and listened as she jumped out of the car, slammed the door and let herself in.

"Brian," she shouted. I could hear her footsteps, the rustle of her clothes and her quick breathing as she hurried through the house calling his name. But there was no reply. Then it sounded like she'd taken her coat off and thrown it down somewhere.

I heard the electronic chirruping of a phone as she keyed in a number. I could faintly hear the distinctive ringing tone of a mobile phone. Someone answered, but even I could hear the static on the line. "Brian?" she said. "Is that you? Brian, I've got to talk to you. Brian, it's that Brannigan woman. Hello? Hello? You're breaking up, Brian!" He wasn't the only one. Nell sounded like she was in pieces.

"Brian? Where are you?" she yelled. There was a pause, and I couldn't hear what was coming down the phone at all. "You'd better get here soon, Brian. This is real trouble."

It was working. I waited patiently while Nell poured herself a drink. Luckily she was one of those women who are attached to their handbags by an umbilical cord. More often than not, they're smokers, I've noticed. I heard the unmistakable click of a lighter. She was on her third cigarette by the time Lomax turned into the drive. Seemingly unperturbed by his sister's panicky phone call, he calmly garaged the E-type and strolled unhurriedly round to the back of the house.

A moment later, I heard Nell shout, "Brian?"

"What the hell's the matter with you?" I heard, the voice muffled at first but growing clearer as he approached her.

A chair scraped on a hard floor, then Nell said, "That Brannigan woman. The private eye, the one who was sniffing round Martin? She came into the shop this afternoon. Brian, she says she knows everything that's been going on!" She sounded as though she were on the verge of hysterics. It was like listening to a radio play, trying to conjure up the picture that matched what I was hearing. I checked that the tape was running, then concentrated on what I could hear.

"And you fell for that bullshit? Christ, Nell, I told you, no one can pin a thing on us. We're in the clear now. What did she say anyway? She could only have been bluffing." He sounded angry rather than edgy, as if he wanted someone to blame and Nell was handy.

"She said she knew all about the land deals, and the mortgage scam, and about using the old houses to launder the money," Nell reported, surprisingly faithfully.

"Jesus, that really is bullshit. She must have been guessing. And even if she did guess right, there's not a shred of proof." Another chair scraped on the floor and a different lighter clicked.

"She said she had proof," Nell said.

"She can't have. I got rid of everything after Martin. Every bit of paper, every computer disc. There isn't any proof. For Christ's sake, Nell, get a grip."

"What if she does have evidence? What if there was something you don't know about? I'm telling you, Brian, she *knows*. And she knows Martin's death wasn't an accident."

"Now you're really on Fantasy Island," Lomax snapped. "Look, the cops think it was an accident. The inquest is going to say it was an accident. You and me are the only ones who know any different. How the fuck could this private eye know anything? She wasn't there, was she? Or did I miss her? Was she there giving us a hand to drop your precious boyfriend over the banister? Did that somehow escape my notice?" he demanded. "Listen, there's no way she could know anything about that gutless little shit."

"Don't talk about him like that," Nell said.

"Well, he was. Saying he wasn't going to have anything to do with violence," Lomax mimicked in a namby-pamby voice. "Saying he was going to the police if I didn't lay off the nosy bitch. As if it wasn't his stupid fault in the first place that something had to be done about her. If I'd done the fucking job properly to begin with, we wouldn't be getting any fucking aggro off this Brannigan cow. She'd be on the bottom of the bloody Ship Canal where she fucking belongs."

In spite of myself, I shivered. There's something very stomach-churning about listening to someone who's tried to kill you whingeing because they didn't succeed. A bit like reading your own obituary.

"Well, you didn't do it properly, did you? And now she says she knows. And she wants sixty thousand from you or she'll go to the cops," Nell said. Her voice sounded shaky, as if she was forcing herself to stand up to her brother.

"Sixty grand? She's trying to blackmail us?" Lomax's voice rose, incredulous.

"Not blackmail. She says you ripped off her client for five thou, and there's another eleven in the same boat. She wants their money back."

"She wants their money back," Lomax echoed, a snort of laughter in his voice.

"And she wants it back before you catch the plane on Monday night. What plane is that, Brian?" Nell's voice cracked. Even at my remove, I could sense the tension between these two.

"I told you, she's a bullshit merchant. She's just trying to drive a wedge between us, to make you crack and tell her all the stuff she doesn't know but wants you to think she does," he said. He was as likely to win an Oscar as his sister.

"You're running out on me, aren't you?" Nell said. "You're going off somewhere with all the money, leaving me to clear up the mess."

"There isn't going to be any mess, I keep telling you. And I am not doing a runner," Lomax shouted.

Confusion reigned in my right ear. It sounded like a chair scraping back, a scuffle then a slap. "Oh no?" Nell almost screamed. "So why have you got a bloody passport in your pocket?"

"Give me that," he yelled.

"You thought you could just clear off and leave me? You bastard, Brian! You said we were in this together. I've put up with all the worry while you and Martin were playing your silly games. I was even stupid enough to listen to you when you said Martin was too much of a risk. And now you think you can just write me off and sod off with the money that's mine by rights?" She was ranting hysterically now.

"Fucking shut up," Lomax exploded. I heard the sound of another slap. "You silly bitch. All you ever wanted was the money. You didn't give a shit about Martin. You were willing to fuck your brains out to keep him quiet just so long as the money kept coming in. So don't give me all that stuff."

There was sudden silence. Then Nell Lomax said softly, "But nobody would ever believe that, would they? They'll believe me, though, when I break down and tell the police that I've discovered my brother killed my fiancé and now he's planning to skip the country with all the money they embezzled."

"You wouldn't have the bottle," Lomax said contemptuously.

"Wouldn't I," Nell said bitterly. "You're not leaving me without a shilling while you live it up on my money."

There was a crash. "You just went too far, little sister," Lomax hissed.

The sounds of struggle intensified. Suddenly afraid, I whipped the earphone out and hit the floor running. I tore down the stairs, out of the front door and across the street, willing my stiff muscles to drive me forward. Up the drive, round the side of the house, the blood pounding in my ears, Lomax's voice echoing in my head.

As I rounded the corner of the house, I saw a long conservatory. Beyond it, I could see the kitchen. In an instant I took in the scene. Nell, bent forwards over the kitchen table, her hands scrabbling uselessly frantic behind her. Masking her body with his, Lomax leaned forward, bearing down on her with his superior weight, his hands round her throat.

I tried the door, but it was locked. Urgently, I scanned the UPVC door frame, estimating the weak point. Then I positioned myself and aimed a kick with my full weight behind it. The force of the blow cracked the frame, and had the added benefit of stopping Brian Lomax. I took a deep breath, trying to block out the pain that had jarred every bone in my body, and concentrated all of my body's energies into my leg and foot. The second kick jerked the door out of the frame, leaving it swinging inwards.

My momentum carried me forward into the conservatory. Lomax had abandoned Nell and was coming for me. He was bigger, heavier, stronger and fitter. I knew I'd only get one chance. I balanced myself and twisted round so I was side on to him. I feinted on one foot, then as he dived towards me, I brought the other foot round in a fast, short arc. The crack of bone as his femur snapped was sickeningly loud. He crashed to the floor like a felled tree. His scream of pain made the hairs on the back of my neck stand on end.

"Hanging in space over Barton Bridge wasn't a whole lot of fun either," I said as I stepped over him towards Nell.

"Bitch," he gasped.

I could hardly bring myself to talk to him, but, mindful that the tape was still running, I said, "You brought it on yourself. You got greedy. You didn't have to kill Martin Cheetham."

"What's it to you? He was a no-mark. I should have killed you when I had the chance," I heard him say as I stooped over the slumped body of his sister.

I felt her neck for a pulse. There was a faint fluttering beneath my fingers. Gently, I raised her body and eased her to the floor. I loosened her blouse, then put my ear to her mouth. Her breathing was weak and ragged, but it was still coming. "You'll be pleased to hear she's still alive," I said.

"Bitch," he repeated.

I stood up and moved to the phone. I was beginning to feel shaky, my muscles protesting at such a heavy work-out after no activity for a week. I picked up the phone and dialled 999. "Emergency operator. Which service do you require?" The words were music to my ears. I looked round at the shambles I'd helped to create. This kitchen sure wasn't going to make this month's *Homes and Gardens*.

"You'd better make it the police," I said. "And throw in a couple of ambulances for good measure."

25

I pulled up in a side street in Bolton. "What are we doing here, Brannigan?" Richard asked.

I got out of the car, and he followed. "After that Chinese in Buxton, I thought we deserved something a bit special," I said, turning the corner and pulling one of the double doors open. Richard followed me down a flight of stairs and into a marble foyer with a fountain filled with koi carp. "They do a ten-course Imperial Banquet," I told him as we walked into the restaurant proper.

His face lit up. His eyes even twinkled. I doubt I'd have got that strong a response if I'd jumped on one of the tables and stripped off. I gave the waiter my name and we followed obediently to a table shut off from the main body of diners by tall lacquered screens. By the table, as ordered, was an ice bucket filled with Chinese beer and a bottle of Apollinaris mineral water for me.

"Times like this, I'm tempted to make you an offer you couldn't refuse," Richard said as the waiter opened a beer.

"I don't do 'married'," I reminded him. "Married is for mugs, masochists and mothers. None of which I am."

"Yet," he said.

I scowled. "Do you want to eat this meal or wear it?"

Richard held his hands up, palms towards me. "Sorry!"

The dim sum arrived, and we both observed the requisite awed appreciation. Five seconds later, we attacked.

Through a mouthful of *char siu bau*, Richard said, "So fill me in on the details. All I know is that these days, the best place to find you Friday nights is talking to a copper."

The poor sod had finally reached me on my mobile some time after ten. I'd been sitting in an interview room at Buxton police station, going over the whole story with the local inspector plus Della Prentice, whom I'd asked them to ring because of the fraud stuff. Just for once, I fancied having someone on my side during a police interrogation. Neither of them had been particularly amused when I broke off to answer my phone.

I'd finally got home in the small hours, posted the "Do Not Disturb on Pain of Castration" notice on my bedroom door and slept till mid-afternoon. By then, of course, Richard was at the match. Sometimes it's like being married anyway.

"Cutting a long and boring story short," I said, "when I put all the computer files together, the picture emerged. You have to remember that Martin Cheetham was an expert in arranging the sale and purchase of houses. What happened was that when he acted for the buyers of a property, he just omitted to forward all the paperwork to the Land Registry."

"Sweetheart, you might as well be talking Mandarin," Richard said. "Let's have it from the top. Mortgage fraud for beginners."

I sighed. "This is how to get two mortgages on one property. Mr and Mrs X buy a house. They go to Martin Cheetham, solicitor. The mortgage is arranged and granted. Then Cheetham should send the paperwork to the Land Registry, who issue what's called a charge certificate, which shows that there is a mortgage outstanding on the property, and who carries the mortgage.

"But Cheetham used to delay a few weeks before he sent the documentation off to the Land Registry. He would then apply for a second repayment mortgage with another lender, as if it had never been bought by Mr and Mrs X. According to Nell, who couldn't stop talking once her throat started working again, she used to front up with Cheetham at the mortgage interviews and pretend to be his wife. As the first charge certificate hasn't been issued yet, there is therefore no official record of it when the lender checks it out with the Land Registry, so there's no problem and the mortgage is granted. You with me so far?"

Richard nodded. "I think so."

I scoffed a couple of prawn wontons and some tiny spring rolls before all the dim sum disappeared down Richard's throat. A more suspicious soul than me might wonder why it is I always seem to end up explaining the intricacies of my cases when there's food on the table.

"That second lot of paperwork never goes anywhere," I said. "It sits in a safe in Cheetham's office. It would take the building society at least a year even to notice that they hadn't received the appropriate charge certificate, never mind do anything about it. Cheetham and Lomax have meanwhile got a (say) £100,000 cheque, because the building society paid the money to Cheetham on behalf of the second, fictitious buyers. As long as the mortgage instalments were made each month, there'd be no problem. No one would be any the wiser for at least a year. Multiply that by ten and a completely un-creditworthy person has a million."

"Shit," Richard breathed.

"Now, you can go for a short-term fraud and do a runner with the money, in which case you have the police looking for you. Or you can do what Cheetham and Lomax had been doing very successfully until a few months ago. What they did with the money was buy up derelict property. Lomax would send in his labourers and do it up, and then they'd sell at a huge profit, thus laundering the money as well. They could have carried on with this indefinitely if the bottom hadn't dropped out of the housing market, since they were paying off the bent mortgages within a year of taking them out."

"You mean, before the lender noticed they hadn't got this charge certificate for the loan, Cheetham paid all the money back?" Richard asked.

"Correct. And in the meantime, he and Lomax had made about fifty per cent profit with the capital. It's a victimless crime. The lenders lose nothing; they don't even know anything dodgy's happened."

Richard laughed. "That's brilliant! And hey, they even did their own conveyancing, so they didn't have to fork out those exorbitant lawyer's fees. So why did it all come on top?"

"Like I said, the bottom dropped out of the market. Property stopped moving. They were lumbered with houses they couldn't sell. That's why they tried that hooky land scheme that caught Alexis and Chris. They were getting desperate for cash flow. So Lomax persuaded Cheetham to get a dozen new mortgages to keep them afloat. He'd no intention of ever paying a shilling on those mortgages. According to Nell, he reckoned that if they did that, they could have a million in capital. The three of them could flee the country to somewhere like Spain. Then when the market picked up, they could offload the rest of the houses and cash in on them too. We're talking twenty-seven houses, with an average value of thirty-seven thousand pounds, by the way. Which is another cool million."

"Shit," Richard said again. "That is serious money, Brannigan. Why didn't you finish your law degree?"

I ignored him and concentrated on the aromatic crispy duck that had just arrived, piling shredded duck and spring onion on to a pancake covered in plum sauce. Some things are too important to be distracted from.

"So why did they kill Cheetham? I mean, everything seems to have been going OK. Why get rid of the only guy who knew how to work the scam?"

I fiddled with my food. "According to Nell, that was my fault."

"How'd she work that one out, then? Doesn't sound like she's got a degree in logic," Richard said.

"Cheetham panicked when I started sniffing around," I explained. "Then when he was tarted up in his drag in DKL Estates and I turned up, he was convinced I was on to their major scam. So he told Lomax to warn me off. Apparently, he meant just that. Lomax or one of his labourers was supposed to threaten me in a dark alley. Instead, Lomax must have picked me up outside DKL, then followed me over to Ted's factory, and then, on the way home, he got a bit carried away, and tried to run me off Barton Bridge. He must have completely freaked out when I turned up the very next day on his home turf. Especially since he was actually with Cheetham."

"So why kill Cheetham? Why not just finish the job they'd started on you?" he asked.

"Thank you, Richard. You don't have to sound quite so eager. The reason I'm still here is that they didn't know how much I knew, or how many people knew what I knew. But the Lomaxes figured Cheetham was the weak link in the chain, the one who'd crack under pressure. They also figured that with him out of the way they could destroy the evidence and leave themselves in the clear. So Nell arranged to meet Cheetham for one of their little games sessions. Then, when she'd got him all tied up, Brian arrived and smothered him. The pair of them tipped him over the balcony, so it looked like a nasty sex game that had gone horribly wrong."

"And I thought my ex-wife was a bitch. Jesus. What kind of a woman does that to her lover?"

"One who's more in love with money than she is with him, I guess," I said. "They thought they'd got rid of all the evidence. But neither of them knew anything about computers. They thought all the data was on the floppies."

"And will Alexis get her money back?"

"She'll probably have to take Brian Lomax to court. But at least she knows where he's going to be for the foreseeable future. She won't have any trouble filing the papers. Her money should be safe as houses."